DEAD
CALM

**Books by Annelise Ryan
(who also writes as Allyson K. Abbott):**

A Mattie Winston Mystery:

Working Stiff
Scared Stiff
Frozen Stiff
Lucky Stiff
Board Stiff
Stiff Penalty
Stiff Competition
Dead in the Water
Dead Calm

**Books by Allyson K. Abbott
(who also writes as Annelise Ryan):**

A Mack's Bar Mystery:

Murder on the Rocks
Murder with a Twist
In the Drink
Shots in the Dark
A Toast to Murder

DEAD CALM

Annelise
Ryan

KENSINGTON BOOKS
http://www.kensingtonbooks.com

KENSINGTON BOOKS are published by

Kensington Publishing Corp.
119 West 40th Street
New York, NY 10018

All Kensington titles, imprints and distributed lines are available at special quantity discounts for bulk purchases for sales promotion, premiums, fund-raising, educational or institutional use. Special book excerpts or customized printings can also be created to fit specific needs. For details, write or phone the office of the Kensington Special Sales Manager: Kensington Publishing Corp., 119 West 40th Street, New York, NY 10018. Attn. Special Sales Department. Phone: 1-800-221-2647.

Library of Congress Card Catalogue Number: 2017951259

ISBN-13: 978-1-4967-0668-3
ISBN-10: 1-4967-0668-4
First Kensington Mass Market Edition: March 2018

eISBN-13: 978-1-4967-0670-6
eISBN-10: 1-4967-0670-6
First Kensington Electronic Edition: March 2018

10 9 8 7 6 5 4 3 2 1

Printed in the United States of America

For Adam

DEAD
CALM

CHAPTER 1

The chiming ringtone of a phone awakens me from a deep sleep, and out of habit, I roll over and grab my cell in an effort to silence it as fast as I can. My bleary eyes try to focus on the screen, but sleep's hold is too great; the whole thing is a blur. I blink hard, glance at the clock on my bedside table, and see that it's just after three in the morning. The ringing stops, and for a moment, I think the caller must have hung up because I haven't hit the answer icon yet. Then I hear a voice behind me say, "Hurley," and realize it wasn't my phone ringing.

Just as I'm thinking that my husband and I need to personalize our ringtones so we can distinguish whose phone is getting called, the chiming sound starts up again. This time I know it's my phone because I feel it vibrating in my hand. I finally see the answer icon and swipe at it, silencing the ring. I realize as I do so that if both my husband's phone and mine are going off in the middle of the night, it means someone is dead.

My name is Mattie Winston, and I'm a medicolegal death investigator for the medical examiner's office in Sorenson, Wisconsin. My husband, Steve Hurley, is a homicide detective here in town. There are no regular hours to either of our jobs, though we try to maintain a façade of normalcy by getting up every weekday morning and heading into our offices. But people don't die on a Monday-through-Friday, nine-to-five schedule, and that means there are plenty of times when we put in a lot of long, extra hours.

"This is Mattie," I say into my phone. I sit up straighter in bed and look over at Hurley as I hear the voice of my boss, Izzy, emanate from my phone. I used to work at the local hospital; my original career was in nursing, and I spent six years in the ER and seven in the OR, good prep for the slicing and dicing I have to do in my current job. Now I'm an assistant to Dr. Izthak "Izzy" Rybarceski, the medical examiner in Sorenson, though for the past three weeks Izzy has been out on sick leave following a heart attack. I've been working with Izzy for almost three years now, and we work well together, in large part because we were friends—and, at one point, neighbors—before I started my current job.

"Mattie, we have a call," Izzy says. His voice sounds energized and excited, and that does my heart good because it means his heart is good. "It's a two-fer, so we should both go."

"A two-fer?" I echo, looking at Hurley with eyebrows raised. He nods, confirming that he has received the same info.

"The cops say it looks like a murder-suicide," Izzy says.

"Okay," I say, flinging back the covers. "Where?"

"It's out at the Grizzly Motel."

This gives me pause. "That's quite a way outside the city limits. Who's investigating?"

"The county guys pulled it, but they're terribly short-handed. They've got two men out on sick leave, another one out for paternity leave, and there are two accident scenes they're investigating right now in other areas of the county. And if the tentative IDs are correct, the victims are both

Sorenson residents, so Hurley's probably going to get a call to assist."

"Yeah, I'm pretty sure he just did. Give us ten minutes to get going, and we'll meet you out there."

I disconnect my call and get out of bed, heading for the bathroom. Hurley is still on his phone, but he isn't saying anything at the moment; he's just listening. Our dog, Hoover, a yellow Lab mix—and, judging from the way he eats, I'm convinced there's a bit of vacuum cleaner in those genes—opens his eyes and watches me, his big head resting on his paws.

By the time I emerge from the bathroom with my bladder emptied, teeth brushed, and my hair partially tamed into a cowlicky mess of blond mayhem, Hurley is already dressed. We pass one another just outside the bathroom door.

"The Grizzly Motel?" I say.

"Yep. Murder-suicide?" he counters.

"Yep." I head for the dresser and grab a pair of jeans, a bra, and a T-shirt. "I'll go wake Emily," I say as I pull on my jeans beneath my nightgown. Then I peel the nightgown off, put on the bra and shirt, and shuffle my way down the hall to Emily's room, stepping over Hoover. Along the way I stop at our son Matthew's room and poke my head in.

He is sound asleep, and I utter a silent prayer of thanks that the ringing phones didn't wake him. His thick, dark hair—the color just like his father's—is sticking out on top of his head like a rooster's comb, the style surprisingly similar to mine even if the color is at the opposite end of the spectrum. He has his left thumb firmly planted in his mouth, but he is still, not sucking, not moving, no muscles twitching. A persistent internal alarm clamors, one I've had to quell hundreds of times in the twenty-two months of Matthew's existence, and I focus my gaze on his chest until I detect a slow rise and fall. Reassured, I resist an urge to tiptoe into the room and kiss him, knowing there's a good chance the action will wake him. And at this age, a just wakened Matthew is like the Tasmanian Devil cartoon character, a whirlwind of seemingly endless and frenzied energy with a penchant for creating crayon artwork on the walls and an apparent belief that any remotely wet form of food he eats is also a hair product.

I sense Hurley behind me—I can feel the heat of his body along my back—and his face appears over my right shoulder. We stand there that way for several seconds, both of us drinking in this most precious sight.

Finally, Hurley whispers in my ear. "I'll go nuke us a couple of cups of coffee. I think there's enough left in the pot."

I nod, and as he turns and heads downstairs, I make my way to the door of Emily's room and open it. The room is a mess, its normal state. Clothes are strewn about on the desk, the chair, the floor, and the bed, and two of the drawers in the dresser are open, with items hanging over the edges. The top of the desk is a chaotic riot of papers, as if a tornado had spun above it. There is half of a sandwich, the edges dry, brittle, and curling, on the bedside table. Out of habit, I head for the sandwich, intending to take it downstairs with me, but I change my mind. My seventeen-year-old stepdaughter and I reached a peace treaty some time back about the state of her room. We agreed that it is her space to do with as she wants, and that I won't nag her about the state it's in, nor will I venture into it and try to clean it up. Treaty or not, the mess still bothers me, but as long as there aren't any bugs in the room or mold growing on the walls, I'm determined to abide by our terms.

Emily is sound asleep in the bed amidst all this squalor, and I feel a twinge of guilt at having to wake her. But it's late July and summer vacation for her—no school to worry about, and she has no job other than the frequent babysitting she does for us—so I know she'll manage.

"Em?" I say in a low voice, giving her shoulder a gentle shake. This first effort does nothing, so I try a second time, speaking a little louder and shaking a little harder. I'm rewarded for my efforts with a grunt.

"A call?" she mumbles, not opening her eyes.

"Yes," I say. "Can you watch Matthew until we get back? I'm not sure how long we'll be gone, but I can get Desi to come and pick him up later this morning if need be."

She sits up and rubs her eyes. "I'm good for the day," she says. She drops her hands into her lap, glances at the alarm clock beside her bed, and smiles at me. "Of course, given the hour and the short notice, this job should probably be paid at triple time."

I smile back at her. "You got it." The girl excels at extortion, and her babysitting money goes into a fund she calls her funny money, money she is saving up to buy herself a car. Hurley and I have argued over this because I feel we should buy her a car, and frankly it would be nice to get rid of the chauffeuring duties I'm constantly having to do. But he is insistent that she earn the money and buy the car herself. So for now, I'm speeding up the process by caving in—willingly and happily—to Emily's attempts to pad her fund.

Emily's smile broadens at my capitulation. "I might get that car before school starts at this rate," she says.

"Indeed, you might," I say, giving her a kiss on the forehead. "Now go back to sleep."

She plops back down, fluffing her pillow beneath her head. I go downstairs, where I find Hurley nuking coffee that was left in the pot from earlier in the day. It won't be gourmet, by any means, but at this hour, just about any coffee will do.

Wordlessly, we fix our coffees in travel mugs and head out, slipping on shoes that are kept by the door. Hurley's car is parked in the driveway. Mine, a midnight-blue hearse, is parked in the street. Without any discussion, we both head for Hurley's car. While seeing a hearse at a death scene shouldn't be too shocking—in fact, it's ironically apropos—the car at times tends to attract attention that I can do without.

As soon as we're settled and underway, I say, "We probably should have iced these coffees instead of nuking them. It's still in the eighties out here."

Our weather for the past week or so has been a blast of furnace-quality heat and dripping humidity. The temps have been well into the nineties, and the humidity has been hovering in the 80th-percentile range. Though some people love this hot weather, it's not my favorite. I come with plenty of natural insulation, and my tolerance of heat is about as good as my tolerance of the tongue-in-cheek Wisconsin state bird: the mosquito. They've been out in force this past week, too, and I have the bites to prove it.

It's a Wednesday night—though technically it's now Thursday morning—and I spent the better part of the past weekend traveling to the land Hurley and I bought right before we tied the knot a few weeks ago, giving up our independence on Independence Day. The land is out in the country; the mosquitos were apparently having some sort of convention out there all weekend, and I was on the menu for every meal. As a result, I now look like I have the measles. It's a small price to pay, however, for moving along our building project. I'm desperate to get into our new home. The house we're living in now is Hurley's, one he bought and lived in for two years before I moved in. Now, with the two of us, two kids, two cats, and a dog in it, it's feeling kind of tight. It also feels like Hurley's house, and I'm eager to have a place to live that is not only roomier, but ours, with no prior history.

Emily and I have tried to fem up the place some, but our efforts have done little to eliminate the overall bachelor pad feel of the place. Apparently, it takes more than some curtains, throw rugs, and a box of tampons in every bathroom to lend a house a feminine air.

The only thing that truly felt like home to me before moving in with Hurley was a small cottage that Izzy had built behind his house. Back when I was married to a local surgeon named David Winston, Izzy was my neighbor. He built a cottage behind his house for his then-ailing mother, Sylvie, but Sylvie rallied after a year and then opted to move out and into senior housing. This happened right around the time my marriage to David went south, along with most of the local geese, after I caught him canoodling with an OR nurse at the local hospital where we both worked at the time. So I moved into Izzy's cottage until I could sort things out, a process complicated by my starting a whole new career, meeting Hurley, getting pregnant, and dealing with the discovery of Hurley's daughter, Emily, who he didn't know existed until two years ago. Her arrival, along with that of her mother, an ex that Hurley discovered wasn't really an ex because she never filed the divorce papers, coincided with me discovering I was pregnant.

For the better part of a year and a half, Izzy's cottage was my home. It was my fortress of solitude, the place where I acquired my fur family of one dog and two cats, the place where I launched my new career, the place where I learned how to be on my own again, the place where I gave birth to my son—literally, since it happened in the bathtub—and raised him on my own for most of his first year. It was small—what Realtors euphemistically refer to as cozy—and I'm not, since I stand six feet tall and typically weigh in somewhere between one-seventy and none of your damned business. Considering that I moved into the cottage after living in a McMansion with David, one might think I found it to be a humbling, if not humiliating step down in life. But I never saw it that way. I grew to love the place, and it was one of the few things at that time that I could call my own. The facts that it was next to my old house—offering me ample spying opportunities—and only steps away from my two favorite therapists—Izzy and his life partner, Dom—were bonuses. To be totally honest, my favorite therapists are Ben & Jerry, but Izzy and Dom are a close second and kinder to my hips.

The house David and I once shared burned to the ground not long after I moved out—a whole other story in itself—though it has since been rebuilt. The new house is even bigger, and David still lives there, along with his new wife, Patty Volker, who at one time was our mutual insurance agent. Though the destruction of the house saddened me at first, it seemed fitting after a while. That fire gave me closure. It also gave me a decent little divorce settlement when the insurance check came.

Unfortunately, Sylvie's good health didn't last, requiring her to move back into the cottage. It was a move she didn't accept gracefully, given that it meant not only giving up some of her independence, but living in close proximity to Izzy and Dom. Sylvie doesn't approve of her son's sexual orientation, and having evidence of it in her face every day is something she hasn't taken to very well. She spent the first two months there without bathing, a curious quirk that almost led to Izzy putting her in a home. Then we learned that Sylvie knew I'd delivered Matthew in the bathtub, and in her mind that area was now like sacred ground. She wouldn't stand in it, sit in it, or run water in it. Izzy had to find a local priest to come in and do a special ceremony—one I suspect he made up—in which he "captured" the sacred essence Sylvie thought was in the tub and put it in a mason jar. Sylvie insisted on giving me the jar afterward, and I thought about tossing it out. But some superstitious vestigial corner of my brain wouldn't let me—that and a fear of what Sylvie would do if she ever asked to see it and discovered I no longer had it.

Since I had to vacate the cottage for Sylvie, moving in with Hurley was the logical option. But it wasn't an easy decision for three reasons. For starters, my relationship with Emily was iffy at the time, iffy being a euphemism for a barrel of

TNT connected to a short, lit fuse. Her mother died not long after the two of them showed up on Hurley's doorstep unannounced, and while I understood Emily's emotional turmoil—losing the only family she had known for more than fourteen years, discovering she had a father she'd always thought was dead, and then learning that he was starting a new family with me—her behavior at one point bordered on frightening. We eventually worked it out with the help of time, patience, a lot of counseling, and a near-death experience for Emily. I have grown to love Emily as if she were my own daughter, but for a while there it was touch and go.

Another thing that made moving in with Hurley an iffy prospect was the state of our relationship. He'd asked me to marry him—several times—and I wanted to. But I couldn't shake the feeling that the only reason he was asking was because I was pregnant and he felt it was the right and proper thing to do.

The final complication in our decision to cohabitate was the four-legged baggage I brought with me. Hoover, who I found hungry, skinny, and dirty, trying to eat out of a garbage bin behind a local grocery store, wasn't really an issue. Hurley adores Hoover, and the feeling is mutual. But I also managed to rescue two cats: a gray-and-white kitten I found abandoned in a Dumpster outside of a convenience store and decided to name Rubbish, and a black-and-white cat named Tux that had belonged to a murder victim on a case we investigated two years ago. And Hurley really, really doesn't like cats. In fact, he's afraid of them, not that he'd admit to it. If I ever had any doubts about whether or not Hurley really loves me, they were eliminated when he agreed to let me move into his house with my cats. It hasn't been an easy adjustment for him, but over time we've managed to achieve a peaceful state of tolerance. This has been challenged of late, however, because Rubbish has started stalking and pouncing on all kinds of things: dust bunnies, shoes,

Matthew and his toys, Hoover, Tux, and yes, Hurley. When Rubbish leapt at Hurley's feet from beneath Matthew's bed the other day, I heard my husband scream like a girl one second and swear like a salty sailor the next.

I'm not sure how I became a pet magnet, because I never had any pets before these. My mother is a germaphobe and hypochondriac of the highest order who considers animals of all kinds to be dirty, vermin-ridden sources of contagion. And David was allergic to pet hair, or so he claimed, though I came to doubt this as time went by.

While Hurley and I have managed to work through most of our issues over time, the housing arrangement remains uncomfortable. The solution we came up with was to buy a piece of land just outside of town and build a house on it that will be uniquely, and jointly, ours.

We drive past our new property on our way to the motel, and I gaze out the window longingly at it, imagining how nice the house will be. The property includes a slope of land that runs back from the road for several hundred feet, topping out on a rocky bluff with a forty-foot face. From the top of the bluff, one has a spectacular view of the surrounding countryside, and that's where we plan to build, taking advantage of that view as much as we can. If all goes according to plan, we hope to have it built and be in it in time for the holidays. But if there is one consistency in my life of late, it's that almost nothing goes according to plan.

CHAPTER 2

It takes us just over half an hour to drive to the Grizzly Motel, an isolated, somewhat seedy joint located on a country highway bearing the ironic name of Morals Road, though it was named after a person rather than a tribute to ethics. The motel is easy to spot thanks to a giant green-and-pink neon bear out front, and a sign boasting of seventy-five cable channels. It's a long, sprawling structure with two wings branching off either side of a central office area and rooms on both the front and back of each wing. A thick copse of woods borders it in the back behind the rear parking area.

I've been here before, back when I was investigating the death of the woman my ex had his affair with, so I know that the rooms in the left wing are typically used for overnight customers, whereas the right wing tends to do a brisk trade in hourly rentals. It's hard not to make political jokes about this setup, but I'm too tired to be funny at the moment.

Even at this hour, there is a maid's cart parked outside one of the rooms in the right wing. There are lots of people milling about in the front parking lot—most of them huddling in groups of two: gay couples, straight couples, and a couple of couples I'm not sure of.

We see Izzy and a county cop standing inside the office talking to the woman behind the desk, so we park, get out of the car, and head inside as all the lookie-loos stare after us, whispering and muttering among themselves. A bell jangles over the door to announce our arrival, and the county cop turns around and gives us a relieved look.

"Thank goodness," he says, walking over and extending a hand to Hurley. They shake, and since the county guy, whose name tag says J MATHERS, is ignoring me, I head over to the desk and Izzy.

"The bodies are in a room in this wing around on the back side," Izzy informs me. "I haven't been there yet."

I nod and look at the woman behind the desk. She is a solid mass of flesh with a thick neck, broad shoulders, heavy arms, and a nearly square-shaped torso. Her hair is cropped short, and she is dressed in a plain white T-shirt with the sleeves rolled up and jeans.

"You're Cinder, right?" I say.

She nods.

"I met you a couple of years ago when I was investigating another case."

She shrugs. I can't tell if she remembers me or not, or if she even cares. It was a very memorable visit for me, however. I was unfamiliar with the Grizzly Motel back then, and it was an eye-opener for me when I realized they rented rooms by the hour, had VCR players in each unit (modern technology hadn't yet made it to the Grizzly), and had a special collection of rentable movies that were rated like the spot to dig on a treasure map, movies that sported titles like *Assablanca*, *Womb Raider*, and *Twin Cheeks*—riffs on other, gentler movies.

"I introduced you to Joey Dewhurst," I try.

With that revelation, Cinder's face lights up. "Oh, yeah. Joey."

"I thought the two of you might hit it off."

She shrugs again. "We're good friends," she says. "He's a nice guy, but a little slow." She taps the side of her head. "He's dating someone else now, someone his own . . . speed."

I get what she's saying. Joey is mentally challenged and has an IQ approximately equivalent to that of a ten-year-old. But he also has an amazing savant ability with computers: hardware, software, and writing code. He considers himself a superhero of sorts—HackerMan—and he often wears a red bodysuit under his regular clothes that has a big, yellow *H* on the chest and a cape that hangs off the back.

Mathers is apparently ready to take us to the bodies because Hurley is beckoning to us. I tell Cinder it was nice to see her again, and then Izzy and I follow Hurley and Mathers out of the office and around the right end of the building to the back. Yellow police tape has been strung up from the back corner of the building to a county cop car parked near the bordering woods, and we duck beneath it. I can see similar tape strung up halfway down the building, effectively cordoning off the rear area of this wing.

"I've chatted with all the people who were in rooms back here inside the taped area," Mathers says. "They're all out front, and I've asked them not to leave." He shrugs. "Though I didn't have the manpower to make sure they stayed. I have names, however, assuming they're legit names."

With a place like this, the odds of that are small, I think.

"Who called it in?" Hurley asks.

"That behemoth of a woman in the office," Mathers says with a roll of his eyes. "I sure wouldn't want to piss her off," he adds with an arch of a brow. "She said the people in the room to the right of our victim's heard gunshots and called her at the front desk. She locked the office and came around back to check. Knocked three times, and when no one answered, she unlocked the door and went in. She swears she didn't go very far into the room or touch anything. She could tell they were both dead from the door, so she shut it, letting it lock, and went back to her office to call 911."

Hurley looks up and scans the roofline of the building. "No security cameras?"

Mathers shakes his head, looking irritated. "Apparently the clientele who frequent this place aren't too keen on such things."

"Did the people in the adjacent rooms see anyone?" Hurley asks next.

Again, Mathers shakes his head. "The ones who called the office said they heard a man's and a woman's voice through the wall earlier, but they were muffled, and they couldn't tell what they were saying. The voices weren't raised like they were arguing or anything. Then they heard the shots, two of them, fairly close together. They were, um, otherwise disposed at the time, and it took them a minute or so to get out of bed, put on some clothes, and peek through first the peephole and then the window."

We have arrived at the door to the room in question, and Mathers uses a key card to unlock it. When he pushes it open, the distinct, acrid smell of blood wafts out into the hot, humid, night air, and my coffee gurgles and lurches in my gut. Hurley, Izzy, and I all don gloves and paper booties from the scene kit I've brought along. As Hurley and Izzy head inside, I swallow hard, hoping to keep my peristalsis moving in the right direction, and follow them.

There are two of our local cops in the room: Patrick Devonshire and Brenda Joiner. Also in the room is Jonas Kriedeman, the police department's evidence technician. The bodies are on the queen-sized bed: a man and a woman, both lying on their backs. The woman is closest to us, her head to our right, and she has what appears to be a bullet hole in her chest, right where her heart is. Her death was most likely instantaneous. The man beside her has an entry wound on the right side of his head, with a corresponding exit wound on the left side. Judging from the brain matter I can see splattered on the pillow and on the woman's face, his death was also instantaneous, not to mention messy. His right arm is hanging off the bed, and there is a gun on the floor beneath his hand.

"It's a grim one," Devonshire says with a grimace, staring at the mess on the man's pillow. He looks a little pale. Devonshire isn't known for having a strong stomach, and I'm worried he's going to barf on our crime scene.

Hurley must be thinking something similar because he says, "Patrick, why don't you go stand by the door to the room to make sure none of those rubberneckers try to get in here."

Patrick obliges, looking relieved.

We are standing in front of a credenza located at the foot of the bed, and Mathers turns to point to something next to the bolted-down TV. "They left a note," he says. "Or rather our male vic did."

I look at the note. It's computer-printed on plain paper, the type you can find in most any house, and it's written in all capital letters.

I'M SORRY, MEREDITH. THIS ISN'T HOW IT WAS SUPPOSED TO END, BUT NOW WE ARE TOGETHER FOREVER. TO WHOEVER READS THIS NOTE, PLEASE TELL MY WIFE, PAMELA, I DIDN'T MEAN TO CAUSE HER ANY PAIN.

At the bottom of the page is a big, handwritten letter C, presumably scribbled with the pen lying next to the paper. Given that there is no computer or printer in the room, it seems obvious that the note was brought along to the motel. The pen is a generic ballpoint that could have originated in the room—though Cinder doesn't strike me as the type to provide perks that can easily be taken—or it might have been left behind by a previous guest or brought along by one of our victims. I try to imagine the man asking the woman for a pen so he could sign the note with a one-letter closing before giving it to her and then killing her. It feels wrong in a hundred different ways. And yet the note is written as if it was intended to be read by the female victim, presuming that the dead woman is the Meredith mentioned in the note.

I look at Mathers. "I'm assuming you have IDs on them? We heard they're from Sorenson."

Mathers nods. "We found a purse over there," he says, pointing to a chair. "Wallet inside belongs to a woman named Meredith Lansing, and the driver's license picture matches that of our female vic. The guy left his wallet on the bedside table. It belongs to a Craig Knowlton. And again, the license picture matches."

So the Meredith in the note and the dead woman are likely one and the same, and the name Craig fits with the letter C at the bottom of the suicide note. All neat and tidy . . . too much so for my tastes.

"This note seems wrong to me," I say to no one in particular. "It doesn't make sense to type out a note for the girlfriend and bring it along for her to read before killing her. And then leave it here for . . . for who? For us? A note that says something along the lines of *Good-bye, cruel world, I couldn't live without her* would make more sense."

"You're trying to make sense of illogical, crazy thought patterns," Hurley says. "Anyone crazy enough to kill the woman they love because they can't have her couldn't have been firing on all cylinders."

"Maybe," I say, still bothered by the note. I take out my camera and start shooting pictures, beginning with the note. Then I look over at Jonas. "Be sure and bag this pen and dust it for prints."

He nods, grabs an evidence bag, and moves in on the pen.

"Know anything else about our victims?" Hurley asks. He is staring at the bodies, so his question isn't directed at anyone.

Brenda Joiner provides the first answers. "A little. Meredith Lansing had an ID card in her purse indicating she works at the hospital in Sorenson. Craig had some business cards in his wallet that state he's a financial adviser for a company called Carrier Investments, also in Sorenson."

Mathers jumps in. "I had our dispatcher run down what she could find on the two of them. They're both married—to other people," he adds with a wry arch of his brow. "Meredith's husband is John Lansing; Craig's wife is Pamela Knowlton. A Google search revealed that Pamela also works at Carrier Investments. In fact, she and Craig own the company. It's some type of investment company franchise."

"Have you sent anyone to notify the relatives yet?" Hurley asks.

Mathers shakes his head, giving us an apologetic look. "We're so short on manpower at the moment that I didn't have anyone to send. That's one of the reasons we're pulling you guys in on the case. In fact, my boss says you can have the whole thing if you want since the victims are both from Sorenson. We're stretched pretty thin right now, and we'll assist you with what we can, but . . ." He shrugs.

"No problem," Hurley says. "Happy to help." He looks over at Izzy. "Are you comfortable making IDs based on the license pictures? If you are, I'll go and notify the families."

Izzy frowns at this. "It's not what I prefer, but under the circumstances . . ." He trails off and moves over to look at the licenses, both of which are at the end of the credenza. Meredith's license photo shows her smiling, with dark hair framing her face. Craig's picture is more serious; both his short dark hair and his expression look very businesslike. Izzy picks the licenses up and carries them over to the bed.

One at a time, he holds the licenses out and compares the pictures to the faces of the victims.

When he's done he looks at Hurley. "I suppose I'm okay with it."

Jonas, who has been standing by in his biohazard gear, says, "We've got that tablet app for fingerprints. Can't we scan them in here and see if we get a match?"

"Great idea," Izzy says.

Jonas digs the tablet out of his scene kit and fires it up. A minute later, he has the app launched, and he reaches over Craig Knowlton's body for his left hand; the right hand, the one that had held the gun, will need to be tested for gunshot residue. It only takes Jonas a few minutes to place each of the fingers on the screen and scan them in. When he's done, he says, "One hand ought to be enough if they're in AFIS. And I suspect Craig here will be. A lot of financial advisers have to have their fingerprints on file in order to be licensed." He taps the screen a couple of times, says, "That one is searching," and then heads to the other side of the bed and Meredith's left hand, which is closest. When he's done scanning her prints in, he tells us so. "It may take an hour or so to get a hit," he says. And then to prove how wrong he is, a little chime sounds from the tablet. "Or not," he says with a smile, looking at the tablet. "As I suspected, Craig Knowlton is in the system, and we have a positive ID."

Izzy nods and looks at Hurley. "I'm comfortable with the woman's ID if you want to do the notifications." Hurley nods, and then Izzy looks at me. "Why don't you go with him, and I'll stay here with Jonas and help him process the scene."

Brenda pipes up and says, "Patrick and I can stay. We called in some extra help to cover the town while we're out here, so we're yours for the duration."

"That's great," Izzy says.

I've been busy with my camera the entire time, and I've

taken dozens of pictures—general shots of the room and the tiny attached bathroom, followed by close-ups of the bodies, the gun, the blood spatter, the note, the pen, the purse, and the wallet—basically everything in the small room.

I say to Izzy, "I think I've got a picture of everything in here, and I thought I'd get some exterior shots on the way out. Do you need my camera for anything?"

"No, I've got mine in my kit if I need it," Izzy says. He starts assigning tasks to the others in the room. Jonas is going around the room, dusting various surfaces for fingerprints, while Brenda Joiner does a quick test for gunshot residue on Craig Knowlton's right hand. To no one's surprise, the GSR test comes up positive. With that done, she sets about securing the hands of both victims in paper bags to protect any other evidence that might be on them. In the meantime, Hurley picks up the gun with his gloved hand, examines it closely, and then writes down its serial number in his notebook before bagging and tagging it as evidence.

Hurley turns and stares at the bodies again, his eyes narrowed in thought. Then he looks at Mathers. "What did the woman in the motel office have to say about them?"

Mathers consults his little notebook, a required piece of equipment in police work. "She said the gentleman checked them in around midnight as John and Jane Smith." He punctuates this with a roll of his eyes. "Apparently she doesn't require ID for check-ins. They booked the room for," he pauses and makes air quotes with his fingers, "the four-hour-or-less rate, and they paid in cash."

"Vehicle?" Hurley asks. "They had to get here somehow."

Mathers shifts nervously and clears his throat. "Haven't had a chance to check into that yet," he says, looking apologetic. "I do know that the four cars parked out back here inside the tape belong to other, um, guests. But I haven't had time yet to look for the victims' car or cars."

Hurley turns to Patrick, who is standing by the door, and raises his eyebrows. "Can you look into it, please?"

"On it," Patrick says, looking eager and stepping outside. I imagine he's more than happy to be released from duty anywhere near the mess in the room.

Hurley turns back to Mathers. "You said you talked to the people who were in the neighboring rooms?"

Mathers nods. He refers to his notebook and gives Hurley the names, contact information, and room locations of these guests. When he's done with that, he gives us a brief summary of what each of these potential witnesses had to say. It isn't much. The people who were in the room to the left of our victims—a middle-aged man and a woman who appeared to be a decade or so younger—claimed they heard nothing, though it's hard to imagine they didn't hear the sound of the gunshots. I suspect they did hear them but don't want to get involved in any way, particularly if they are here at the motel for the same reason many of the right-wing guests are: for an illicit liaison of some sort.

The couple in the room on the right were also a man and a woman, both in their mid-thirties. They were the ones Mathers had mentioned earlier, the couple who called the front desk. The remaining guests consisted of two all-male couples, two more heterosexual couples, and one female trio.

Hurley turns to me and says, "I need to make a couple of phone calls to verify some things, and then you and I can go talk to the people outside. Now would be a good time to take your outdoor pictures, if you want."

I nod and step outside into the humid night air. After making some adjustments to my camera for the nighttime setting, I snap pictures of the motel room door, the adjacent room doors, the parking lot and the vehicles in it, including the license plates, and the woods. The trees behind the motel are a heavy mix of oaks, maples, and pines. I imagine on many a night the branches would be swaying in the wind, the leaves rustling and whispering. But tonight the air is heavy and utterly still; the trees are unmoving. The woods extend along the back of the motel and beyond, curving around on one end to border a field of corn, and ending at a side road on the other end, about a hundred feet from the opposite end of the motel.

I venture a little closer to the edge, squinting into the darkness. I see there is a path of sorts, a narrow, trampled trail of ground extending into the woods, and I wonder where it leads. If it was light out, I might venture in there purely out of curiosity, but for the moment I can't see a reason to do so. I'm even less inclined when I hear a rustling sound from deep inside the woods, a sound like small scampering feet scurrying over the ground. Clinching my decision is Hurley's voice hailing me from the motel room doorway. I turn my back on the woods, though not without one last paranoid glance over my shoulder, and hurry back to the motel room door.

As we head around to the front side of the motel, Hurley says, "This one looks cut-and-dried as far as the manners of death, but I still want to talk to some of the witnesses out front."

"Maybe," I say, still bothered by that note. I stop walking, and it takes Hurley a few steps to realize it. He turns and looks at me with a confused expression before walking back to me.

"What?" he asks, his voice an odd mixture of impatience and curiosity.

"I'm a little confused as to the motive behind it all. If we assume Craig and Meredith were having an affair, what made Craig take such a drastic step?"

"Meredith wanted to end things," Hurley says in a tone that makes it sound as if he's explaining the obvious to a simpleton.

I give him an annoyed look. "If that's the case, then why did she come out here with him tonight? If she was going to cut him loose, I'd think she'd do it somewhere a little less . . . erotic."

Hurley scratches his head and shrugs. "Maybe she wanted one last roll in the sack for old time's sake," he says. I can hear the tired irritability in his voice.

"Maybe," I say again, unconvinced.

"Let's not build this into something it isn't," he says. "Sometimes I think you hang around Arnie too much, because lately it seems like you expect to find a conspiracy in every nook and cranny."

He's referring to Arnie Toffer, our lab tech and resident conspiracy theorist, a man who thinks space satellites were launched to give the government a way to monitor our every conversation and action, that every tap on our computer keyboards is monitored by some highly classified, black-ops government employee, and that some of the homeless people out there on the streets are really government spies in disguise. Sometimes I think Arnie has cornered the market on paranoia, but then again . . .

"Just because you're paranoid . . . ," I say to Hurley, letting him finish the cliché in his head. He simply rolls his eyes at me, turns, and once again heads toward the front of the motel.

CHAPTER 3

The crowd out front has diminished some, but there are still several people milling about. I see Patrick downstream in the parking lot, standing between some cars, his cell phone to his ear.

When the crowd sees us emerge from beneath the police tape, the questions start firing.

"What happened in there?"

"Who is it?"

"Is someone dead?"

"It sounded like gunshots. Was someone shot?"

"Can we leave now?"

Hurley zooms in on the man who asked about leaving, and we head toward him and the woman standing next to him. Both of them look awkward, guilty, and embarrassed. I'd bet money the two of them are having an affair.

Hurley says, "Would you two please come with me?"

They turn and glance at one another with sheepish, worried expressions before looking back at Hurley, who walks toward the taped-off area at the back of the motel. The couple doesn't move at first, so I stay where I am, staring at them expectantly. The woman lets out an exasperated sigh, glares at her partner, and finally turns to follow Hurley. The man looks at me and scowls.

"After you," I say with a forced smile, waving a hand in Hurley's direction.

With an exaggerated *harrumph* of annoyance, he follows the woman, while I bring up the rear. Hurley herds them to a corner of the taped-off area by the woods. He takes out his notebook, squinting as he tries to read what he has scribbled there. There are a few portable light stands set up in the taped-off area, but none of them are pointed in this direction.

After half a minute of silent squinting at his notebook, a gesture I'm pretty sure Hurley is doing simply to make our guests even more uncomfortable, Hurley looks up and introduces himself, flashing his badge. "I understand the two of you were in one of the rooms next to our victims," Hurley says without introducing me.

The man and the woman both nod.

Hurley then shifts his attention to the woman. "Can you tell me your name?"

She chews her lip and looks off to the side for a second before saying, "Lisa. Lisa Martin."

"Not the name you used here," I say. "Your real name. If you lie to us, you can be arrested for interfering with a murder investigation." I have no idea if this is true, but it doesn't matter. The police are allowed to lie when interviewing or interrogating witnesses and suspects, and I figure that courtesy extends to me as well, since I'm assisting them at the moment.

The woman shoots me an annoyed look, trying to appear offended by my suggestion that she has lied. But she can't quite pull it off. There are too many nerves firing away beneath her skin.

I see Hurley giving me a curious, questioning look. "I saw that name in the registration book on Cinder's desk," I tell him with a shrug. "She signed in with that name. Nobody who's renting a motel room by the hour signs in with their real name."

"Damn it, Tom," the woman snaps, slapping her male companion on the arm. "I told you we'd get in trouble if we lied to the cops."

The man scowls and mutters something under his breath. He shifts nervously from one foot to the other and rakes his teeth over his lower lip. "Look," he says, "we don't want it known that we were here. We . . . I . . . she . . ."

"The two of you are having an affair," Hurley says with bored nonchalance. "We get it. Even if your nervousness and the fact that you rented a room here didn't clue us in, your mismatched wedding rings are a dead giveaway."

I glance at their rings and see what Hurley is referring to. Tom is wearing a wide gold band with a thin black stripe around the middle, whereas his female companion is wearing a thin silver band. I feel a moment of pride in our collective abilities to read people and situations. Hurley and I make a great team, both on and off the job.

"We don't care about why you're here," Hurley goes on. "All we care about is what you might have seen or heard from the room next to yours."

"So you won't tell anyone we were here?"

"Not unless you give me a reason to," Hurley says.

They both look visibly relieved.

"So tell me your real names, and then tell me what happened," Hurley says, addressing this question to no one in particular. I'm curious to see which one of them will speak first.

"My name is Susan Richter," the woman says.

"And I'm Tom Collins," the man says. Hurley arches a skeptical eyebrow at this. "I swear, that's my real name," the man insists. He digs in his pocket and pulls out a wallet, flipping it open to his driver's license, which he shows to Hurley. "Believe me, I've spent my entire life hearing jokes about my name."

Satisfied, Hurley jots down the name and then asks them both for contact information. When they are done providing it, he looks at Tom Collins and says, "Okay, now tell me what happened."

Susan looks at Tom, chewing on the side of her thumb. Tom says, "We were in our room . . . in bed." He shrugs and seems a little embarrassed. "You know."

Hurley nods impatiently.

"Things were getting kind of loud in our room," Tom says, making Susan squeeze her eyes closed and look away, a grimace on her face. "And I heard a loud bang. At first, I wasn't sure what it was, and I didn't pay it too much attention because I didn't want to . . . well, things were . . . you know."

Hurley nods again, letting out a get-on-with-it sigh.

"And then I heard a second bang, and I was pretty sure it was a gunshot. I froze, and Susan asked me what was wrong."

Hurley looks over at Susan. "You didn't hear the shots?"

Her face flushes red. "Not exactly," she says. "I kind of had the pillow wrapped around my ears. I heard them, but I didn't pick up on them as being anything worrisome."

"She was rather distracted at the time," Tom says with a salacious wink. "Anyway, I told Susan that I thought I'd heard gunshots outside our room, and I stopped what I was doing and got out of bed. I pulled on my pants and told Susan to get dressed. We pulled on some clothes and then we went over to the door and looked out the peephole."

"Did you see anything?" Hurley asks.

Tom shakes his head. "When we didn't see anyone out there, we went over and peeked out the window, moving the curtain aside. But we still didn't see anything. So we decided to call the front desk. A few minutes later we heard the woman from the office knocking on the door to the room next door. After a couple of knocks, she opened it, and then she just closed it again and disappeared."

"What did you do after that?" Hurley asks.

"We sat and waited. I didn't think it would be smart to go outside since we didn't know what was going on. Then we heard a siren, and the cops showed up. We stayed put until an officer came knocking on our door."

Hurley scrunches his face in thought for a second. Then he says, "I'd like you both to think back to when all this happened and tell me if you heard any other noises before, between, or after the shots."

They both look down at the ground, staring at their feet. Then Susan perks up. "There was a noise right after the shots."

"After?" Hurley says, sounding skeptical.

"Yeah, it was a thud, you know, like someone hitting the wall or something. In fact, the wall that adjoins that room shook a little." She looks over at Tom. "Remember?"

Tom gives a slow nod, his eyes narrowed in thought. "Yeah, you're right," he says. "I do remember the wall shaking a little."

Hurley's brow furrows. I imagine mine is doing the same, trying to determine what could have made the sound they're describing. Presumably, both people in the other room were dead by then.

"How much time was there in between the two shots?" Hurley asks.

"Not much," Tom says. "Maybe ten seconds?"

Hurley has apparently filed this information away and moved on. "What time did the two of you check into your room?" he asks.

"Around twelve-thirty," Tom answers.

"Did you hear anyone or anything from the other room before the shots? Voices or anything like that?"

Both of them shake their heads.

"Okay," Hurley says. "That's all I need from you for now. You're free to leave if you want."

Both Susan and Tom sag with relief. Then Tom says, "My car is that one over there." He points to a Ford SUV parked inside the taped-off area.

Hurley looks over at it, then at the tape. "I'll remove the tape so you can leave," he tells them. Then he does so as both Tom and Susan hurry to the car. A minute later they are gone, and Hurley puts the tape back up.

We head out front to the remaining crowd, who are now looking less interested in finding out what's going on and more interested in running away. Hurley motions at Patrick, who is walking toward us, and we reconnoiter just outside the main office area.

Hurley says, "What have you got for me?"

Patrick flips back some pages in his notebook and starts talking. "That Lexus over there belongs to Craig Knowlton," he begins, pointing toward a black vehicle at the very end of the front parking lot. "Mathers had already verified the owners of the cars inside our crime tape out back, and that's who's waiting here." He nods toward the remnants of the crowd. "I've run plates on all the other cars here, and none of them belong to Meredith Lansing or anyone else named Lansing."

Hurley nods and says, "Good work, Devonshire. Go back to the motel room and see if anyone has come up with a set of keys so we can get into that Lexus. Once you get them, just stand by the car until I can join you. In the meantime, we're going to talk to the rest of these people."

Patrick nods and takes off at a lope toward the back of the building. Hurley moves in on the remaining crowd, which is now down to seven people. I notice as I follow that no one wants to make direct eye contact with him.

Based on the descriptions Mathers gave us, it's not hard to

guess who is who. We approach the couple with the age disparity—the man looks to be in his forties, the girl in her early thirties, if that—and question them. Despite being in the room on the other side of our crime scene, they swear they heard nothing. They provide us with honest IDs and appear to have nothing to hide, stating that they are from out of town, traveling to Minnesota, and stopped here for a few hours of sleep, facts Hurley is able to verify by phone. Hurley lets them go, and I volunteer to take down the tape so they can leave.

When I return, Hurley is questioning the trio of women who were staying in a room two doors down from the crime scene. All three of them reek of booze, and they are clearly drunk, judging from their giddy behaviors and tittering laughter. They offer nothing of use, and when Hurley releases them, they head back to their motel room.

The final twosome are two men who are both restless and pacing, staying a personal space of distance away from one another. When Hurley approaches them, they both look at him with wide, anxious eyes.

"Sorry to keep you waiting," Hurley says. "Can I ask you for your names?"

"I'm Jim Peters," the guy on the left says quickly. He is tall, slender, balding, and has a prominent Adam's apple that is sliding up and down his throat like the puck on the strongman game at a carnival. I half expect to hear a bell ring when he swallows and the lump leaps up his throat.

"I'm Sal Mastroianni," the second man says. He is shorter, with a full head of dark hair and an olive complexion.

Hurley eyes the two of them for a few seconds, then looks at his notes. "The two of you were in room 15, two doors down from our investigation."

Before he can say anything else, Sal pipes up. "Look, I heard someone was killed in that room. But we don't know anything about it. We didn't hear anything or see anything.

In fact, we didn't know anything had happened until the cops showed up."

Jim Peters nods vigorously, like a just-flicked bobblehead doll.

"What time did the two of you check in?" Hurley asks.

"Around eleven, I think it was," Sal says. He looks to Peters for confirmation, and the other man's head bobs some more. "We were asleep with the TV on when the cops knocked on our door."

"And you didn't see or hear anything?" Hurley asks.

Both men shake their heads. Then Sal says, "We had the TV on kind of loud."

"And you slept through that racket?" Hurley asks, sounding skeptical.

Both men nod; Sal shrugs and smiles.

Hurley scratches his head, thinking. Then he asks them for contact information.

"Why do you need that?" Peters asks, his puck going up and down, up and down. I notice both men are wearing wedding rings that, like the earlier couple's, are nothing alike.

"In case I have any other questions for you."

"But we didn't hear or see anything," Peters insists.

"Be that as it may," Hurley says with irritation, "there might be something else I need to ask you." The men exchange looks. "I promise to be discreet if that happens," Hurley adds.

With this, the two men acquiesce, though they still look frightened. If we were anywhere else, I might think they had seen or heard something and had been threatened to keep their silence. But given our current circumstances and location, I feel certain their wariness is about their liaison being discovered.

As soon as the two men are done providing their information, which Hurley verifies with the dispatcher over his phone, we let them go, releasing the last two cars inside the tape.

With that done, we head for the front of the motel, where Patrick Devonshire is waiting patiently next to Craig Knowlton's Lexus. He hands Hurley a fob. "There was a key ring with a fob and several other keys on it," Patrick explains. "But this car doesn't have a key, just a fob. Jonas removed the ring and the keys and bagged them for evidence. And he dusted this fob for prints, so we're free to use it. Apparently, it not only unlocks the car, you have to have it in the car in order to start the engine. And you don't need to push the unlock button on the fob if you have it on you. You can simply open the door, even when it's locked, as long as you're carrying the fob."

Hurley frowns at this. "Modern technology," he grumbles, shaking his head. "What the hell is wrong with a simple old key?" He looks at me and does a *gimme* gesture with one of his hands. "I need some more gloves," he says. I set down the scene kit I've been carrying with me, open it, and take out a pair of gloves for him. He dons them, opens the driver's door, and looks inside. The car is neat and clean, almost obsessively so. The only stray item I can see is a coffee mug on the passenger side of the cup holder in the middle console.

"I need an evidence bag," Hurley says. I retrieve one from my kit and hand it to him. Then, with his gloved hand, he removes a four-inch-long, blond hair from the headrest and drops it into the bag.

"Not sure how important it is," he says. "But both of our victims have dark hair. It will be interesting to see what color hair Mrs. Knowlton has." He seals the bag, and when I hand him a marker, he labels, dates, and times it before handing it to me. Then he locks and shuts the door, and turns back to Patrick. "Have it towed in to the police garage," he says. "It doesn't look like there's much here, but maybe we can verify that Meredith Lansing was in the car."

Patrick drops the fob into an evidence baggie, but he doesn't seal it. For a moment, the three of us stand there in silence, taking in our surroundings. I hear birdsong emanating from the back of the motel—presumably from the woods—and glance at my watch. It's almost five, and the sun will be up soon. Already the skyline in the east is lightening.

Hurley finally turns to Patrick and says, "Mattie and I are going to head into town to do the notifications. You might as well go help the others in the motel room. Call me if anything significant crops up."

Patrick gives a quick nod of assent and then shuffles back to the room, looking like he's going off to his execution.

CHAPTER 4

"I hate doing these notification things," Hurley says, once we're on the road. "And this one is particularly nasty."

"I wonder if either of the spouses knew about the affair."

"Hard to say. I'm rather hoping they didn't."

"Why?"

"Because it eliminates any possibility of this being something other than what it appears to be. Hopefully this will be a straightforward case, a quick and easy one for us that we can put to bed fast." He yawns, and adds, "Which is where I'd like to be right about now."

Quick and easy sounds good to me, too. But first we have the dreaded notifications to make.

After a couple of miles go by, I broach a topic that has been high in my thoughts for the past few weeks. "Have you made any progress on the Jeremy Prince case?"

Jeremy Prince is an ex-military man who killed three, possibly four people in the area a few weeks back. A young student nurse named Carolyn Abernathy was one victim, and my coworker, Hal Dawson, and his fiancée, Tina Carson, were the others that we're sure of. There is good reason to think he might have also killed Marla Weber, the girl whose headless body was found in some woods near Pardeeville. Evidence we found at that scene—a prescription for insulin—led us to the home of a man named Tomas Wyzinski, a diabetic who lived in a house in the country with his mentally challenged brother, Lech. When Bob Richmond—another Sorenson detective—and I arrived at the Wyzinski house, we looked through the window in a back door and saw Tomas Wyzinski collapsed on the floor of his kitchen. In an effort to help him, we entered the house, whereupon I quickly determined he was in insulin shock and in need of some form of sugar. I went to his refrigerator to look for some orange juice, but what I found instead was Marla Weber's missing head.

I had to testify in the Tomas Wyzinski trial, a nerve-wracking experience since it was my first time in a courtroom as anything other than a spectator. Izzy has been prepping me for testifying for the past two years, but until the Wyzinski case, I never had to do it.

It seemed like an open-and-shut case. I mean, let's face it, the woman's head was in the man's refrigerator; evidence doesn't get much more damning than that. But after giving my testimony, questions began to arise about the case, questions related to our other homicides. I discovered that both Hal and his fiancée, Tina, had been in touch with Tomas's brother, Lech, and had been looking into the case. Initially, Hurley and I thought maybe it was because Tina, who was a local librarian, was working on writing some mystery novels of her own, and she had thought the case would be good research material. But when I went out to the Wyzinski house and talked to Tomas's brother, Lech, more doubts arose. Lech showed me a notebook his brother had kept with extremely detailed information about everything that Tomas ate, what his blood sugars were, and how much insulin he took. Tomas Wyzinski was a very well controlled diabetic who took his illness seriously and managed it with admirable oversight. So how had someone that anal about his food and medication managed to take too much insulin? Had it been a suicide attempt? An accident? Or had someone tried to kill Tomas, too, framing him for Marla Weber's murder in the process?

When I learned that Tomas Wyzinski had taken and passed a lie detector test, it added to my growing doubts about the case. The prosecuting attorney dismissed the test, stating that sociopaths and a few others could pass them even when they were lying. And it wasn't admissible as evidence anyway.

In addition, Lech had mentioned something to me about a "bad man" who had visited the Wyzinski house, and he described the car the man came in as "blue" and "topless." Jeremy Prince had driven a blue convertible.

"I get the feeling you're holding out on me, Hurley," I say. "We can't just let this case slip away."

"I know that," he says irritably. "But this case is dangerous. Meddling in it is like playing with fire. And I think you're too involved. It's become too personal for you."

His use of the word "meddling" irks me. "Of course it's personal," I shoot back at him. "My friend and coworker was murdered, as were other people. And my testimony might have helped convict a possibly innocent man."

There is a moment of silence before Hurley addresses the elephant in the room. "And then there's your father."

Ah, yes. My father.

In the process of investigating Hal's and Tina's deaths, we learned that a man had been sighted lurking around both of their houses on the day they were killed. We eventually figured out that this man was none other than my father, Cedric Novak, a man who left my mother and me when I was four years old, never to be heard from again until recently.

Our inquiries rang a bell at the U.S. Marshal's Office in Chicago at one point, and after a visit there, we learned the real reason my father had left thirty years ago. He'd gotten into trouble with some very bad and powerful people who were involved with the pharmaceutical industry. As a result, he ended up in the Witness Protection Program for a number of years. He eventually left it, but he stayed off the grid as much as possible, maintaining a low profile and a philosophy of no contact with my mother and me.

Unfortunately, after leaving the Witness Protection Program, he managed to get himself into trouble again, albeit unwittingly, when he took a job in a Chicago mail store run by a corrupt man named Quinton Dilles, who was using it to smuggle drugs and launder money. An undercover cop named Roy Gilligan, who at one time was Hurley's partner, was investigating the place and ended up murdered. My father was the primary suspect—and in some circles, he probably still is—though I now know he didn't do it. He was in the company of the U.S. Marshals when the killing happened—an unimpeachable alibi, but one no one was eager to share.

These matters complicated my burgeoning relationship with Hurley. The point in time when I learned that my father was a suspected cop killer was also the point in time when I discovered I was pregnant. Hurley started proposing to me soon after, and I kept declining, both because I had the secret knowledge that my father was a suspected cop killer, and because I feared Hurley was offering to marry me simply because of the pregnancy.

I spent nearly a year believing my father was a cop killer. Then his past met our present when we tied Hal's and Tina's murders to that of Carolyn Abernathy. We learned that Carolyn was subsidizing her nurse's training by working in the medical records and billing department in the clinic attached to the local hospital in Sorenson. We also discovered that Hal had a sister who had died the year before under questionable circumstances after taking a new weight-loss drug—a death Hal had been investigating at the time of his murder—and it steered us down a path that tied our current case to the one that had led to my father's disappearance into the Witness Protection Program thirty years before.

Then we learned that Tomas Wyzinski had a degree in chemistry and had worked for a pharmaceutical company up until a few years ago. That's when we realized our modern-day case and the one my father was involved in were inexplicably entwined. Everything was related: my father's tangling with a pharmaceutical company thirty years ago, evidence that some people high up in the justice system were in cahoots with the pharmaceutical company, Tomas's history of working for a similar company, Hal's sister's death—a death he was looking into right before he was killed—possibly being related to a drug similar to the one involved in my father's case, and Carolyn Abernathy's job working in medical billing.

Jeremy Prince had been the thread that tied all of this together, and we flushed him out by using a ruse. We had Alison Miller, who at the time was the Sorenson newspaper's ace photographer and reporter, do a news bite on TV claiming that someone responsible for the deaths of Carolyn, Hal, and Tina was talking to the police. As a result, Jeremy Prince had shown up at our house, nervous and jittery, and after a few harrowing moments during which I feared our family was about to become the next murder victims, Prince essentially turned himself in, confessing to three murders—though also intimating that there had been a fourth—and asking for protection for him and his family.

He claimed that somebody, or some entity—he never got to tell us who or what—had hired him to do some contract work that had started out only a little shady. The pay was good, and since Prince had two kids and a wife with multiple sclerosis whose health was declining, the money had been an irresistible draw. When the work he was being asked to do escalated to contract killings, he balked, but he claimed that the people who hired him threatened to harm his family if he didn't carry out their instructions. His fear that our news bite would lead to his employers carrying through on their threat convinced him to turn himself in. Sadly, just as Hurley was loading Prince into our car to take him down to the police station, a black SUV drove by and gunfire erupted.

I thank my lucky stars every day that Hurley and I weren't hit, since both of us were outside at the time of the shooting. Alison Miller was there, too, but she wasn't as lucky. Death came instantly for her in the form of a bullet to the head. Prince was also shot with a fatal blow, but he didn't die immediately. He lived long enough to tell Hurley where his family was, elicit a promise that his family would be protected, and then give Hurley one name—or at least that's what Hurley has claimed.

Hurley held true on the promise he made to Jeremy Prince as he lay dying in our driveway and had the U.S. Marshal's Office take care of hiding Prince's family and establishing new identities for them. But since then the case has lagged, or at least it seems that way because Hurley brushes off every question I throw at him about it. He does so again now.

"I did a little digging," he says vaguely. "But I haven't come up with anything."

He isn't looking at me, and I'm certain he's lying. "Why are you being so cagey about this case?" I ask him. "It's been a month since Prince was killed, and every day that Tomas Wyzinski spends in prison is eating at me. I need to know if I've helped convict an innocent man."

Hurley says nothing. He stares straight ahead and keeps driving.

"You're playing this one awfully close to the vest, and that's not like you, Hurley, at least not where I'm concerned. I thought we were a team." I utter this last part with a whiny tone that I hate hearing, but it's already out there.

Hurley shoots me a look, and I'm expecting it to be one of

irritation, exasperation, impatience . . . I don't know which. But it's a look of worry, and it makes my guts tighten a little.

"Tell me," I say. "What are you hiding from me, Hurley? I need to know."

He opens and closes his hands on the wheel, letting out a long, pursed-lip sigh. Then he chews on his cheek for a few seconds. I wait even though every inch of me is screaming on the inside, sensing that his resolve to stay silent is caving.

"I suspect this case is a lot bigger than either of us originally thought," he says finally. "I also think it involves some very powerful people, and it needs to be handled with kid gloves. If we go into it with guns blazing, I'm afraid we'll end up like Jeremy Prince."

"Are you implying that I'm a guns-blazing kind of gal?" I ask, feeling a bit wounded even though some part of me wonders if he's right.

Hurley shoots me an amused look. "I love you, Squatch," he says, using his nickname for me—a shortened version of *Sasquatch* and a commentary on the size of my feet—"but let's face it, you're not a subtle person most of the time."

"I can be subtle," I protest. "Especially if the safety of our family is at risk."

Hurley rolls his lips in, and I can tell he's biting back a retort.

"Come on, Hurley," I wheedle. "You can't keep me out of this investigation. It was my friend and coworker who was killed. It was my testimony that got Tomas Wyzinski convicted, probably wrongly. And I was there when Alison and Prince were killed. I'm deep in this already."

He says nothing, looking straight ahead. It irritates the crap out of me.

"If you think I'm some blithering idiot who can't be discreet, then why did you marry me?" I grumble. I have no idea how our getting married relates to the situation, but my mouth is firing off with only part of my brain feeding it. "I thought you trusted me. I thought we were a team. I thought we agreed to share everything now that we've joined our lives together. I thought . . ."

"Fine!" Hurley snaps, making me flinch. "I'll tell you what I know so far, or at least what I'm speculating. But it isn't much. You're going to be disappointed."

"Try me," I say, leaning back in my seat with a smug smile.

Hurley shoots me a dubious look, his eyes narrowing. "First you have to promise me that you won't go poking your nose into things without my knowledge."

"I promise."

"You need to run everything by me. And I mean before you do it, not after the fact."

Damn. "Okay. I promise."

"Right before Prince died, he gave me a name."

"I know that. Whose name was it?"

"Remember that boat Prince used to reach Hal and Tina?"

"Yeah, it was named *Court A'Sea.* You said it belonged to an attorney, and that it was stolen a day or two before the murders."

"Correct. The name of the attorney who owned the boat was Randall Kupper."

I run the name through my mental data bank. "Any relation to Judge Wesley Kupper?" I ask. "The judge who handled the Wyzinski case?"

"One and the same," Hurley says. "And I recalled something I read in your father's file at the U.S. Marshal's Office the day we went down there. The ADA involved in your father's case back in 1980 was Wesley Kupper, and one of the cops who was involved was Jason Kupper."

Judge Wesley Kupper is a scary enough figure without thinking about him being involved in something so nefarious. He stands six and a half feet tall, weighs in at around 350 pounds, and has a booming voice and an intimidating presence. When he walks into a courtroom with his black robe billowing out around him, it's hard not to make comparisons to Darth Vader.

"Okay," I say, frowning. "I still don't see where you're going with this."

"Remember the list of coded items we got from Hal's thumb drive?"

The coded items he is referring to is an odd list of letters and abbreviations that were in a document saved on a password-protected thumb drive we found in Hal's truck. So far, we have had no clue what any of it meant, or at least that's what I thought. I suspect Hurley is about to change that belief.

"I don't recall exactly what it said off the top of my head," I told him. "I'd have to refer back to the file. Why? Did you figure it out?"

"Maybe, at least a part of it. One of the lines Hal had typed out was *CP off JK.*" Before I have a chance to parse this clue, Hurley continues. "I think it meant Chicago police officer, Jason Kupper. One of the other lines Hal had typed was *ADA 1980 WK.*"

"And Judge Wesley Kupper was an ADA in 1980," I say, feeling a trill of excitement. "Was Kupper the name Prince gave you?"

Hurley nods, and this knowledge ties our current-day murders even tighter to my father's trouble thirty years ago. That trouble involved some memos my father found in a briefcase he stole.

My father is a Gypsy by birth, raised in a family that traveled around the upper Midwest conducting thievery, cons, and swindles to survive. The family typically arrived in a location—usually smaller towns, suburban spots, or rural areas—and stayed for a few months while they ran their "jobs." When things started to get hot, they would pack up camp and move to a new location, where they would start all over again. My father participated in these "jobs" from the time he was old enough to walk and talk. In fact, he met my mother when he conned her out of some of her money. He was strongly attracted to her, however, and came back the next day to return what he had swindled from her. Their relationship took off from there, but since my father's family was extremely protective and possessive of their own, it wasn't easy for him to conduct a relationship with a woman who was an outsider. He did it, however, essentially leading two lives, neither one aware of the other, for nearly five years. He married my mother in a small ceremony that was kept secret from the family. I came along nine months later, and my father spent the next four years on the road, running back and forth between his family's current location and my mother and me.

Right around the time I turned four, my father's family was encamped outside of Chicago and my father was participating in a con with a fellow family member named Constantine in which they swapped an empty briefcase for one that their target mark had. They would use a similar-looking briefcase and follow the mark around until the timing was right, and then one of them would act as a distracting shill while the other conducted the swap. According to my father, they got money, watches, jewelry, credit cards, and other items of value doing this. They would pocket the cash, use the credit cards for a few days before ditching them, and pawn whatever they could. The then-empty briefcase became part of a collection used in other swaps.

With this particular con, however, my father and Constantine got a briefcase belonging to an employee of a pharmaceutical company named Miller-Weiss. It didn't contain any cash, credit cards, or other items of value, so they thought it was a bust at first. But what it did contain proved to be much more valuable: a series of internal memos from Miller-Weiss detailing some problems they were having with a new weight-loss drug that had proved to have fatal side effects, and what they were doing to cover it up.

My father and Constantine realized these memos might be worth something to the company, who would want them back lest their cover-up go public. They contacted people at Miller-Weiss and tried to negotiate a deal—basically they attempted to blackmail the company. But they grossly underestimated the desperation, power, and determination of their corporate adversary, and things went horribly wrong. Constantine was shot and killed, and my father, who had been smart enough to hang behind, went on the run.

The Miller-Weiss company cleaned house quickly and thoroughly. Their headquarters shut down, documents were shredded, and the workers and management personnel all disappeared. Some were reassigned to jobs overseas, and others, like the man whose briefcase had been stolen, simply vanished, though my father's mark hadn't disappeared forever. His body was found floating in a lake a few weeks later.

There was an investigation, and it was discovered that Miller-Weiss was a subsidiary of a larger corporation, which was also a subsidiary, and so on, with a dozen or more shell companies and walls separating the top honchos from the scandal. Fines were charged and paid, but no one was ever forced to take responsibility.

My father, fearing for his life and supposedly still in possession of the memos, went into hiding. He was given a new identity and relocated by the U.S. Marshals. He invited my mother to come along, but she refused. Her goal back then, presumably, was to distance herself, me, and my sister Desi from my father's troubles as much as possible. She succeeded for thirty years, but now it looked like they had come back to haunt us.

While I was relieved to learn that my father wasn't a cop killer, our visit to the U.S. Marshal's office led to some other startling revelations that impacted my family even more. I learned that my sister, Desi, who I had always thought was my half sister, fathered by my mother's second husband, was actually my full-blooded sister, sired by the same man I was. My parents wove a very tangled web thirty years ago, one that has unraveled in bits and pieces recently, each revelation more startling than the next.

Marshal Washington told us that my father had gone to the DA's office after the attempted, disastrous handoff of the hot memos, and told them his name was Rick Novaceski. False names were commonly used by the family during their cons and swindles. Shortly thereafter, some goons showed up at my father's family encampment asking for Rick Novaceski, even though my father hadn't used that name anywhere but at the DA's office.

"Marshal Washington didn't come right out and say it in no uncertain terms, but he implied that someone, somewhere in law enforcement or the DA's office had to have leaked my father's name," I say to Hurley. "So are you saying you think the Kupper family is somehow involved?"

Hurley nods, looking somber.

"Is this Randall Kupper guy who owned the stolen boat a relative of the other two?"

"He is," Hurley says. "He is Judge Kupper's nephew, and Jason Kupper's son."

"Where is Jason now?"

"He retired from the force five years ago and is currently an Illinois congressman."

I lean back in my seat and digest this information. "So you think the boat Prince stole wasn't really stolen, don't you?"

"I do. I think it was set up to make it look that way. Randall Kupper was conveniently out of town when it happened, effectively distancing him from the act."

"Wow," I say. "My father kicked up quite the hornet's nest back then, didn't he?"

Hurley nods.

"So where do we go from here? Is there a way to expose the Kuppers if they really are involved in this mess?"

Hurley grimaces, and cocks his head to one side. "Not at this point. We don't have any evidence, just a lot of supposition."

"Maybe we should talk to Tomas Wyzinski," I suggest. "You know, when I was testifying against him, his eyes creeped me out. They looked dead, cold, and at the time I thought menacing. But given what we know now, I'm beginning to think that deadness was resignation, maybe even fear. He has to be worried about his brother, Lech. In fact, I wouldn't be surprised to learn that someone has threatened to hurt Lech if Tomas ever talks."

"If that's true," Hurley says, "and since Tomas was willing to go to prison for the rest of his life over the matter, what makes you think he'd change his mind and talk about it now?"

"What if we offered to protect his brother?"

"You mean like witness protection?"

I shrug. "That, or something similar."

Hurley sucks in his lower lip and then rakes his teeth over it as he lets it out. "If this thing goes as high as a congressman and a judge, I'm not sure any sort of protection offer will be enough to convince Tomas."

He was probably right. We needed to come at it from a different direction. "What about Hal's sister? It looked as if Hal suspected her death was tied to that weight-loss drug she was on, and someone covered it up to make it look like a suicide. Maybe we can find a lead there somehow."

"I already thought of that," Hurley says, looking as frustrated as I feel. "I tried to contact the ME's office that did her autopsy, but the doc who did it has left the country. He's in South America somewhere."

"That in and of itself is suspicious, don't you think?" I say, trying to swallow down my irritation over the fact that Hurley has been looking into the case but not sharing any of his findings with me until now.

"I do," he admits. "But even if we could find him, what are the odds that he's going to confess to some sort of cover-up?"

I frown and let out an exasperated sigh. All those innocent people dead, some of them people I knew and cared about, and all we have are a bunch of dead ends. It's frustrating. I slump down in my seat, sulking, running all the facts of the case through my brain. There has to be a way, some lead we haven't yet picked up on, or some person who will be willing to talk.

Then I remember something. "Hurley," I say, sitting up straighter. "What about the phone data with Hal and Carolyn?"

"Phone data?" he says, looking confused. "We scrubbed the phone records and didn't find anything useful."

"I know, but remember how both Hal and Carolyn made calls that pinged off towers in some suburban area of Chicago right before they were killed? I don't recall the name of the place off the top of my head—"

"Kenilworth," he fills in for me, and I notice that he has perked up.

"Right. Kenilworth. Coincidence? Maybe. But maybe not."

Hurley looks skeptical. "Kenilworth is a big area, and most of the people who live there are wealthy, positioned, powerful people. Even if we knew where to look, I doubt any of them will be forthcoming with any useful information."

"We could look up the names of the people who live closest to the tower Hal and Carolyn pinged off of, and research them. See if anyone who lives in that area has anything to do with the pharmaceutical industry. It would be a lot of work, but it's exactly the sort of thing Laura is great at and loves to do."

Laura Kingston is an evidence technician who works full-time but splits her hours between my office, where she assists Arnie, and the police department, where she assists Jonas. According to recent rumors, she also splits her off time between her two coworkers, both of whom have a romantic interest in her.

Hurley gives me a grudging nod. "It's worth a shot," he says about my idea. "I don't know if it will produce anything, but it can't hurt to try."

"I also think we should dig deeper into Carolyn Abernathy's life, specifically her work life. If she was involved in this and onto something, it had to be related to her work in the clinic billing office. If we could get a look at the files she was dealing with . . ."

"We already tried that, and we were promptly shut out," Hurley grumbles.

"Then we try again."

He gives me a tolerant smile this time. "Easy to say, but how? We don't have enough to get a warrant, and I'm sure they've disabled Carolyn's ID badge by now, so we don't even have access to the area where she worked."

"There might be a way," I tell him, thinking. "Give me a little time, and I'll see if I can come up with a plan."

By the time we arrive back in Sorenson at Meredith Lansing's address, I have most of my plan figured out. Unfortunately, I'm fairly certain Hurley isn't going to like it.

CHAPTER 5

The residences for Craig Knowlton and Meredith Lansing are on opposite sides of town. Craig's house is in one of the ritzier neighborhoods, with sprawling homes nestled on immaculately landscaped parcels of land. Meredith Lansing, on the other hand, lives in an apartment in an area of town that is largely comprised of businesses. Her immediate neighbors include a bank, a Laundromat, an auto supply store, a Quik-E-Mart, and a car wash. Her apartment complex is an eight-unit building, and hers is on the second floor. Since Meredith's place is closest to the end of town we come in at, it's also the first notification we decide to do.

Dawn is breaking as we pull into the lot of Meredith's apartment building, park, and get out of the car. We climb exterior stairs to a door with the number 3 on it, and Hurley knocks. After waiting a minute, he knocks again, harder and louder. There was a doorbell at one time, but now there's nothing but wires.

Hurley is about to knock a third time when we hear a chain lock slide. A second later, the door opens to reveal a dark-haired, sleepy-eyed man dressed in shorts and a T-shirt, both of which are rumpled. His hair is sticking up on top of his head like a rooster comb. He blinks at us, squeezes his eyes closed, and blinks again.

"Can I help you?" he says, scratching at one armpit.

Hurley flashes his badge. "I'm Detective Steve Hurley from the Sorenson Police Department, and this is Mattie, my assistant. Are you John Lansing?"

He nods and switches his scratching efforts to his chin, which has a couple days' growth on it. "May we come in, Mr. Lansing? We need to talk to you."

Lansing processes this request. It's not lost on me that Hurley didn't bother to announce what office I'm from, or give my married last name, lest he reveal our relationship. I haven't actually changed my name yet anyway, and I'm not sure I'm going to, even though keeping the last name of my ex irks Hurley. But keeping it makes it possible to avoid awkward explanations that occur at moments like this when we're working together.

Lansing eventually says, "Sure, I suppose." He steps aside, and we enter the apartment's living room. It has standard beige carpeting that is worn, and the walls are an eggshell-white. The furnishings look like garage-sale pieces: a scarred wooden coffee table, a gold fabric couch whose cushions are flattened to half their normal size, a green fabric love seat with a tear in one side, and a pressed-wood entertainment center with cockeyed doors and sagging shelves.

We make our way to the couch, and when I settle into it, I can feel a spring beneath my butt. I let Hurley take the lead, watching Lansing.

"Mr. Lansing, you're married to Meredith Lansing, correct?"

He nods. He's still standing a few feet inside the door.

"Do you know where your wife is right now?"

"She's at work," he says, scratching at his chin again. "She works the graveyard shift up at the hospital." An ironically apt answer, I think. "Why?"

Hurley had done his due diligence before leaving the motel by calling the hospital to make sure Meredith Lansing wasn't working, even though we were 99 percent sure she wasn't. "Your wife is not at work," Hurley says. "Why don't you have a seat?"

John's face is curious and concerned. He hesitates but then does as Hurley suggests, settling onto the love seat.

"Mr. Lansing, I'm sorry to inform you that your wife is dead," Hurley says in a soft, sympathetic voice.

John blinks rapidly several times. "She's dead?" he says in a tone of disbelief. "How? Where? Are you sure?"

Hurley doesn't answer any of his questions. Instead, he fires back with one of his own. "Do you know a man by the name of Craig Knowlton?"

John looks at the floor, his expression one of shock. After a few seconds, he shakes his head. "No," he says finally. Then he starts scratching at his head, making his rooster comb stand up even more. His eyes narrow in thought. "Though the name does seem vaguely familiar somehow. Who is he? Did he kill Meredith?"

"Your wife was shot in what appears to be a murder-suicide," Hurley says. "Mr. Knowlton was the other victim."

Lansing takes a few seconds to digest this before asking his next question, his expression a mix of confusion and distaste. "Are you saying this guy shot my wife?"

"It appears that way," Hurley says.

"Is he a patient, or someone who works at the hospital?" John asks. "Is Meredith at the hospital?"

Hurley shakes his head. "Your wife and Mr. Knowlton were found together in a room at the Grizzly Motel."

John shakes his head, as if trying to rattle something loose. "Grizzly Motel?" he echoes. "Where is that?" I'm sure he must have a hundred other, more important questions he wants to ask, but he looks to be in shock, and I'm guessing all he can focus on for now is this most recent revelation.

"It's about twenty miles outside of town," Hurley explains.

There is a period of silence as we give John Lansing some time to digest everything we've told him. I watch the expressions on his face change, from shock and disbelief, to sadness, and then to something that looks like suspicion. I know then that he has made the connection.

"You said you found Meredith and this man at a motel," he says. "Why? Were they having an affair?"

"It looks that way," Hurley says in an apologetic tone. "Did you have any suspicions about her seeing someone else?"

"No," he says, his tone wounded. "An affair? For how long?"

"We don't know," Hurley says. "Were you and your wife having marital problems?"

John huffs in disbelief and shrugs. "I didn't think so. I mean, we had the occasional spat. All married couples do. But overall, I thought our relationship was a good one." He looks perplexed, and after a moment, he says, "How did she meet this guy, this Greg whatever?"

"Craig," Hurley corrects. "Craig Knowlton. He's a financial adviser here in town."

A look of dawning comes over John's face, and he snaps his fingers. "That's where I've seen the name. Meredith was trying to figure out what to do with her retirement money from her last job. She wanted to roll it over." He lets out a humorless laugh. "She was all about planning for the future, especially since I lost my job."

"Where did you work?" I ask.

"I haven't worked for two years," he says, looking off to one side. "I was with an insurance company, but they had some cutbacks, and I was one of the ones they let go." He leans forward and runs his hands through his already mussed hair. "Money is tight for us. That's one of the things we argue about. Meredith keeps telling me to get any job I can, flip burgers if need be. But I've been holding out for something more in line with what I was doing before." He leans back and sighs, shifting his gaze to the ceiling. "I suppose that's what made her look elsewhere," he says. His face screws up like he's about to cry.

"Is there someone we can call for you?" I ask him. "A relative, or a friend?"

He looks at us, thinks for a moment, and then shakes his head. "My family is all back East. We've only been out here for a year."

"What made you move?" I ask.

"Her family," he says with a pained look. "They all live around here, and she was homesick." He pauses, wincing. "Oh God, how am I going to tell them about this? I'm not exactly their favorite person, and they'll blame me. I know they will."

"Blame you?" I say. "Why?"

"Oh, pick a reason," Lansing says churlishly. Then he switches to a mimicking, whiny tone. "Because I wasn't a good husband. Because I didn't support my wife the way I was supposed to. Because I'm a freeloader." He pauses and sighs. "Like I said, pick your complaint."

"I'm sorry," I say. I feel for the guy.

He leans forward and buries his face in his hands, rocking back and forth. We let him rock, giving him time to process. After a time, he leans back, his eyes wet. "So what happens now?" he asks. "Do I have to find a funeral home and all that?"

"Because your wife was the victim of a homicide, the medical examiner's office will need to perform an autopsy," Hurley explains. "At some point, her body will be released to the next of kin, and that would be you. So, yes, you will need to make some arrangements. The ME's office can help you with that, if you like."

He nods slowly, and I can tell he's back in shellshock mode. Hurley and I exchange a look, and then Hurley gets up and hands John one of his cards. "I'm sorry to have to deliver such shocking news to you this way," he says. "Please don't hesitate to call me if you have any questions."

I get up and do the same. "I work at the ME's office," I tell him. "We'll be in touch with you when our work is done. And I'll be happy to help you with the arrangements when that time comes. I'm very sorry for your loss."

John nods. He is leaning back in his seat, staring at our cards, looking lost and forlorn. I hate leaving him this way. "Mr. Lansing, are you sure there isn't someone we can call for you?"

He looks up at me with sad, wounded eyes. "I'll be fine," he insists. "I just need some time to digest all of this." He sighs heavily. "Thank you for . . . well . . . thank you." His voice falls off, seeming to realize that there really isn't anything to thank us for.

We take our leave, shutting the apartment door quietly behind us. Once we are back in the car, I say to Hurley, "Man, I feel sorry for him. This is bound to be one of the worst days of his life."

Hurley nods and starts the car up. "And now we get to go ruin someone else's day," he says grimly. "Some days I really hate this job."

CHAPTER 6

We hit up a drive-through after leaving the Lansings' apartment and grab a quick breakfast with more coffee before heading to the Knowlton house. Hurley drives slowly, eating his breakfast sandwich as we go. We don't say anything along the way. Neither of us is looking forward to our next visit.

We manage to scarf up our food and wash it down with a few swallows of coffee by the time we pull up in front of the Knowlton house. It's an attractive, two-story Craftsman with a stone façade on the front wall and tapered columns on either side of the steps going up to the front porch. The front yard is sloped down toward the street, and the climb up the sidewalk combined with my dread over what's to come makes me feel like I'm lugging a huge weight behind me.

This time there is a working doorbell, and when Hurley pushes the button, we hear a rich, four-note chime emanate from inside. Once again we wait, and once again no one comes to the door. Hurley gives the bell a second ring and then knocks as well, for good measure. After another minute passes, I'm about to go over and peer through the garage door windows to see if there is a car in there. Then we hear a man's voice from off to our right.

"If you're looking for the Knowltons, they aren't home." This comes from what I presume is the Knowltons' neighbor, a balding, elderly man who is holding his morning newspaper, fetched from his lawn. "They go into the office real early in the mornings," he says. "Something about the time of the overseas markets, or some such."

"Okay, thanks," Hurley says. We turn to head back to the car, but Hurley pauses and asks the neighbor a question. "Do they usually go into the office together?"

"Couldn't tell ya," he says. "I'm not usually up at that hour. But I've seen them come home in separate cars, so I'm guessing no."

Hurley thanks him again, and we get back in the car. "Let's hit up their office," Hurley says.

It takes about five minutes to make the drive. Carrier Investments is located in an office a block from downtown and the main drag. There is no traffic to speak of at this hour, and we have no problem finding a parking spot right in front of the office entrance. There is another car parked in front of ours, a beige Beemer.

"The Knowltons seem to be doing well for themselves," I say. "I think John Lansing might have been right about what attracted his wife to Craig. The lure of a well-to-do man must have been hard to resist."

Hurley shoots me an amused look.

"What?" I say.

"Was that part of what attracted you to David? His money?"

I frown at him and immediately dismiss the idea. "Of course not. I won't deny that it was a nice benefit, but it wasn't the reason I was attracted to him."

Hurley arches his brows at me.

"I'm not a gold digger, Hurley," I say, irritated.

"Come on, the money must have played some part in it."

I start to deny it again but hesitate. Had it played a role? The idea of being a doctor's wife had been appealing to me, and I couldn't deny that I liked the idea of a financially secure future.

"Okay," I say petulantly. "Maybe it played a small part, but it was a very small part. I like attractive, successful men who are well put together, and David fit that mold. Did his money have something to do with it?" I shrug. "Maybe. But it wasn't the main driving force."

"So are you saying you think I'm attractive, successful, and well put together?" Hurley teases.

I wink at him. "I love the way your parts are put together," I say in a low voice. "Particularly some parts."

We share a heated look for a few seconds, and then Hurley rolls his eyes at me. "Great! *Now* you're in the mood for morning sex."

On that happy, if somewhat inappropriate note, we get out of the car and walk up to the entrance for Carrier Investments. The door is made of glass, and there is a CLOSED sign hanging inside. Beyond the door is a reception area with a long desk, and to one side of it is a doorway leading to a back room. The reception portion of the office is dark, but there is light emanating from the back area. Seconds after knocking, we see a woman appear in the lit doorway, looking out at us with a curious expression. Hurley takes out his badge and holds it up for her to see.

The woman, an attractive, tall, slender brunette with a pixie haircut and huge, round, green eyes, walks over to the door, unlocks it, and cracks it a few inches. "Can I help you?" she asks.

Hurley does a quick introduction and then asks, "Are you Pamela Knowlton?"

"I am."

Hurley does a quick introduction, once again using only my first name, but this time including the fact that I'm from the medical examiner's office. "We need to talk to you," Hurley says. "It's about your husband."

Pamela's face takes on a worried look. She opens the door wide enough to let us in and then closes and locks it again as soon as we are inside. "I wondered why he wasn't here," she says. "I figured he was having an early breakfast with a client. Was he in an accident of some sort? Is he okay?"

"Let's sit down," Hurley says, gesturing toward some chairs in the reception area.

Pamela shakes her head impatiently. "I'm fine," she says, holding up a hand to forestall any more of our delaying tactics. "Please just tell me what's happened. Is Craig okay?"

With a sigh of resignation, Hurley says, "No, he is not. I'm sorry to inform you that your husband is dead."

Pamela's eyes grow wide and wet. She staggers back a step, but then seems to catch herself. There is a counter nearby, and she reaches out and grabs the edge of it, staring at Hurley. "He's dead?" she says, and Hurley nods. "What happened? How? Was it a car accident?" Her eyes flood with tears, and despite her earlier reassurance that she's fine, she makes her way over to a nearby chair and falls into it.

Hurley settles into a chair beside her, and when she leans forward, putting her head in her hands, he leans forward also, arms on his legs. He hesitates a few seconds before delivering his next blow. "It wasn't an accident," he says. "It appears that your husband killed himself."

For a few seconds, Pamela doesn't move, and the room is absolutely quiet. Then she rears back and gapes at Hurley. "Suicide? You're telling me Craig committed suicide?"

"I'm sorry, yes."

Pamela shakes her head vigorously. "No. No way," she says adamantly, clearly unwilling to even consider the idea. "Craig wouldn't do that. You're lying. Is this some kind of sick practical joke?"

"It's no joke," Hurley assures her. He pauses, giving her a little more time to digest the information before moving on to the next bit of bad news.

"How?" Pamela asks after another brief period of silence.

"He shot himself," Hurley says.

"Where?"

I'm not sure if she's asking where on his body he shot himself, or where he was when he did the deed.

Hurley answers one of the questions. "He was found in a room at the Grizzly Motel located about twenty miles out of town."

Once again Pamela shakes her head, looking confused and seeming adamant in her denial. "That doesn't sound like Craig," she says. "He wouldn't do that. He didn't even own a gun. Are you sure it was suicide? Could someone else have shot him?"

Hurley rakes his teeth over his lower lip and takes in a bracing breath. My heart speeds up a little in anticipation of what I know is coming next.

"Do you know a woman by the name of Meredith Lansing?" he asks Pamela.

She pulls her gaze away from his for a moment, staring off into space. "I don't think so," she says, but both her expression and her tone make it clear she isn't sure. Then her eyes grow wide. "Wait. Yes, I think I've heard that name before. I think she might be a client of his." She returns her gaze to Hurley. "Why? Does she have something to do with this?"

Hurley shifts in his chair. I know this whole conversation is an uncomfortable one for him. Death notices are never easy, and one like this is doubly hard, given both the nature of the death and the circumstances surrounding it.

"Meredith Lansing was also found dead," Hurley says. "In the same room with your husband." Before he can continue, Pamela makes the connection.

"Oh my God, you said he was found at a motel?" Hurley nods. "Why were they at some out-of-town motel? Were they having an affair?"

Pamela's tone suggests she finds this idea ludicrous, but

when Hurley says, "It appears so, yes," her expression turns incredulous.

"I'm very sorry," Hurley says. "I know this must be a huge shock."

Pamela is shaking her head yet again, but it's slower, more resigned this time. "That's an understatement," she says in an ironic tone. Her eyes have dried, but she looks pale and shaky. It's clear she is struggling to absorb everything. "Was it some kind of suicide pact or something?" she asks.

Hurley shifts again. "It doesn't appear that way," he says, clearing his throat. "We think your husband shot Mrs. Lansing because she wanted to break things off with him."

She's staring at him again, eyes agape. "*Mrs.* Lansing?" she says, seemingly grabbing at the first straw she can focus on. "Are you telling me she's married, too?"

"Yes," Hurley says.

Pamela leans forward once more and runs her hands through her hair. "I can't believe this," she says, and the tears start flowing again. "Oh my God. Oh my God," she sobs, rocking slowly.

Hurley gives her a moment before hitting her up with a request. "Mrs. Knowlton, I'm very sorry for your loss, and I know this must be very difficult for you. But because of the nature of your husband's death, we need to look into some things."

She turns her tear-stained face toward him. "What things?"

"Your husband worked here in this office with you?" Hurley asks.

Pamela nods.

"I need to take a look at his workstation. I assume he has a computer?"

"He does," Pamela says. She gets out of her chair and walks toward the back part of the office, her gait zombie-like. Hurley and I exchange a look before we follow her.

The back area of the office contains two desks, a half-dozen filing cabinets, and a small kitchenette. Pamela walks over to the closest desk, stops, and gestures toward the computer. Then she stands there, staring off into space.

I take out my camera and shoot a few pictures of the work area. Then, after donning gloves, I tap the space bar on the desktop computer and the screen springs to life, requesting a password.

"Do you know what Craig's password is?" I ask Pamela.

She nods. "It's the word *moneymaker*," she says. "All lowercase."

I type it in, but it doesn't work. Just to be sure, I type it again, but it's definitely not the right password. "That doesn't work," I tell Pamela. "Any other ideas?"

She stares at the screen, looking perplexed. "Are you sure?" she asks. "That's been his password for as long as I can remember. It's mine, too. We came up with them when we opened the office here."

"Maybe he changed his," Hurley says. There is a hint of innuendo in his voice, and Pamela doesn't miss it.

"Of course," she says with a pained expression. "If he was having an affair . . ." She drifts off, not stating the obvious.

Hurley says, "We'll need to take this computer with us. In the meantime, if it's all right with you, we're going to look through his desk to see what we find. Maybe he wrote down his new password somewhere."

Pamela frowns. "We have confidential financial information on these computers," she says. "I can't just let you take it."

"I'm sorry," Hurley says, though the softness in his voice is gone now. "But this is evidence in a homicide investigation."

While the two of them are debating the matter, I start looking though Craig's desk drawers, beginning on the right side. There's the requisite hanging-file drawer, and it's stuffed with manila folders, each one labeled with a name. I recognize a couple of the names when I scan the labels, but I'm only interested in seeing if there is one for Meredith Lansing. There isn't.

"I need some kind of assurance that the files on that computer will be kept confidential," Pamela says as I open the drawer above the one with the files. It contains a bottle of Scotch, a bottle of vodka—both of them high-end brands—and two highball glasses. I shut it and move to the drawers on the other side.

"I assure you the files will be kept secure," Hurley says. "There will be no need to expose any of the information on them unless it's pertinent to our investigation. And at this point, I can't imagine any of it would be unless we find a file belonging to or relating to Mrs. Lansing."

There is another file drawer on the left side of the desk that mirrors the first one. I once again scan the labels, and this time I strike pay dirt. There is a file with Meredith Lansing's name on the label. I pull it out and set it on top of the desk, moving the keyboard to one side to make room.

That's when it hits me. I look at the top of Craig's desk—his monitor, sitting atop a PCU, a wireless keyboard in front of it, and a wireless mouse off to one side of the keyboard. I flash back on the scene in the motel room.

"Don't you need a warrant or something like that before you can take Craig's computer?" Pamela is asking.

Hurley shakes his head. "Your husband left a note in the motel room," he explains. "It was computer generated, and that makes this computer, your office printer, and any other computers Craig might have key to our investigation. Does he have a laptop or a second computer at home?"

I make quick work of the remaining desk drawer, which contains a variety of office supplies: pens, pencils, staples, a staple remover, a letter opener, paper clips, and a couple of sticky notepads. I'm eager to get Hurley aside and tell him what I'm thinking, but I don't want to interrupt his debate with Pamela.

"He has a laptop at home," Pamela says in a resigned

tone. "You're welcome to it." She hugs herself, gazing about the small office. "How are you going to examine his computers if you don't know the password?" she asks.

"We have technicians in our lab who do this sort of stuff all the time," Hurley says.

I can't stand waiting any longer. I get up from Craig's desk chair, pick up Meredith Lansing's file, and tug on Hurley's shirt. "I need to speak to you," I tell him. "Privately."

Hurley looks mildly annoyed at my interruption, but when he sees the expression on my face, he nods and says, "Mrs. Knowlton, I'm going to ask you to have a seat out front in the reception area."

Pamela doesn't look happy at this directive, and for a moment, I think she's going to raise yet another objection. But then her shoulders sag, and she squeezes her eyes closed and lets out a perturbed but resigned sigh. "Fine. I need to make some calls anyway." She shuffles past us toward the front reception area.

I start to tell Hurley what's on my mind, but he puts up a hand, halting me. "Hold on. I want to get some help out here."

"You need to hear me out first," I say, grabbing his phone hand, "because you're going to need more help than you realize. I think Pamela might be right. I don't think Craig Knowlton killed himself."

His brow furrows, and he looks amused. "And you're basing this on what?"

"Look at his desk. Specifically, look at his mouse."

Hurley does so, and for a moment he looks befuddled. Then his face assumes a faraway expression, and I know he's recalling the motel room scene the way I did a few moments ago. After a few seconds, he purses his lips and rakes a hand through his hair. "His mouse is to the left of his keyboard," he says. I nod. "And the only reason it would be is because he was left-handed." I nod again. "And the gun in the motel room was by his right hand," Hurley concludes, and I can't resist looking a little smug.

"Damn," he says, punching in the number for the police station. "So much for quick and easy."

CHAPTER 7

After a quick discussion about how to proceed, I go out front to keep Pamela company and watch for our help to arrive, while Hurley remains in the back-office area. Pamela is on her cell phone, pacing back and forth in front of the reception desk, talking to someone in a tone that is half hysteria, half disbelief.

"They said he was having an affair with this woman," she says into the phone. "How could I have not known that?"

She listens to whatever the person on the other end is saying and then says, "I believed him when he told me he was meeting clients for lunch and dinner. And I know some of them were legit; I know they were." I wonder who she's trying to convince, herself or the person she's talking to. "Clearly, he had me duped," she concludes. "I just can't believe he would do this to me. I thought things between us were good."

I walk over and stand by the door, keeping an eye out for whoever is coming to help us out. Pamela doesn't say anything for a minute or so, then she says, "Yeah, I guess. It's a hell of a mess. What do I do now?"

As she listens again, I see Bob Richmond's car pull up out front, followed by a patrol car with a uniformed officer named Grant Culpeper behind the wheel. Richmond is a detective who was semiretired at one time, primarily due to his health. A couple of years ago, he was grossly overweight and sedentary, a heart attack waiting to happen. But a stray bullet in the gut and a new outlook on life got him to the gym and on a better diet, leading to a weight loss of nearly two hundred pounds. He also returned to work full-time and is in charge of a cornucopia of investigatory categories, including robberies, burglaries, fraud, auto thefts, and missing persons. Even with all these under his hat, he typically has time to assist Hurley whenever there's a homicide investigation. Culpeper is relatively new to the force, having come on board two years ago. So far, he's earned a reputation for being quite the ladies' man, as well as a natty dresser.

I throw the dead bolt on the door as they approach and let them both inside.

"Would you?" Pamela says behind me. "I'd really appreciate it. I'm at a loss here." As I greet Richmond and Culpeper, Pamela concludes her call with, "Thanks. I love you, too."

Pamela disconnects her call and stands there staring at the new arrivals.

"Pamela Knowlton, this is Detective Bob Richmond and Officer Grant Culpeper." Everyone nods. "They're going to help us with our evidence collection," I explain to her.

"Junior and Laura are coming, too," Richmond explains.

Junior Feller used to be an officer with the Sorenson PD, but he was promoted to detective two years ago. His primary focus is vice, but he helps out with homicides when needed. It goes both ways. This sort of cross coverage is common in small departments.

I briefly explain to Pamela who the other arrivals will be. "Detective Hurley and I will follow you back to your house so we can look at the rest of Craig's stuff," I tell Pamela. "The others will stay here and collect what we need from the office."

Pamela eyes Richmond and Culpeper. "Just how much are you planning on taking?" she asks, clearly upset. "You're not going to take all our paper files, are you?"

"We'll take the ones that seem pertinent," I say vaguely. "We'll record everything we take so you'll know what's gone, we'll keep it all secure, and once we are done with our investigation, we will return any items we can."

This seems to placate her, which is fortunate for me since I've left out the fact that we have come to suspect that Craig's death is a homicide, and this means she might not get anything back anytime soon.

"You should have someone with you," I say to her, hoping to distract her before she has too much time to think things through.

She nods. "My sister is coming by. She said she was going to meet me at my house." She gives me a questioning look.

"That should be fine," I tell her. I direct Richmond and Culpeper to the back-office area and then head for the front door when I see Laura's face peering in through the glass.

Pamela is back on her cell phone, so this time I forgo the introductions and point Laura toward the back room, eager to pass her off onto the crew there. Laura is a talker, and a fast one at that. I don't want to play interference to her infamous verbosity. Hurley once clocked her at over 100 words a minute, and on that occasion, she was relatively laid-back. If she only spoke for a minute, this wouldn't be too awful, but the woman talks nonstop. Fortunately, she's also a crackerjack researcher, a competent evidence tech, and smart.

Junior shows up as I hear Pamela leave a voice message for someone to call her back immediately. I send him into the back to join the others, and a few moments later, Hurley comes out.

Pamela looks at us with a lost, forlorn expression. "So how does this work?" she asks. "Do I have to ride with you to my house?"

"No," Hurley says. "We'll follow you. But can you give me a key to the office here so my people can lock up when they're done?"

She nods, takes a set of keys from her purse, and goes about removing one. "Will I be able to get back in here once they're finished?" she asks, handing him the key. "I've got a lot of work to do." She seems to realize the inappropriateness of this comment, and she bursts into tears. "What am I going to tell Craig's clients?"

Hurley and I both give her a sympathetic look, but we don't give her an answer, at least not to the last question. Hurley says, "We'll give you access to your office as soon as we can." He is holding what appears to be one of the many manila folders Craig Knowlton had in his desk drawers. "Mrs. Knowlton, is this your husband's handwriting?" he says, opening the folder and showing a page to her.

She looks at it and nods. "Why are you asking that? I thought you said his note was printed from a computer."

"I'm just establishing some facts," Hurley says vaguely. "Why don't you lead the way to your house, and we'll follow you in our car."

Pamela nods absent-mindedly and heads for the door. We follow, and once we're in our car and she is in hers, I ask Hurley why he questioned her about the file. He hands it to me.

"Look at the writing and tell me what you see."

I open the folder. The sheet inside has a name at the top that matches the name on the folder. There is other identifying information: an address, phone number, e-mail address, Social Security number, and birth date. Below that are boxes filled with letters that look like stock ticker symbols and, beside each group of letters, a series of numbers. All of it is written in black ink, and it doesn't take me long to see what Hurley is referring to.

"The ink is smeared on the left side of the page in places,"

I say. "Typical for someone who is left-handed. As their hand moves over the stuff they've already written, the areas where the ink is still wet tends to smudge."

Hurley gives me an approving look and smiles. "I've married myself one hell of an investigator," he says.

We follow Pamela Knowlton back to her house, and once there we park in the street as she pulls into the driveway. She doesn't put her car in the garage, but parks on the drive instead and gets out. Hurley grabs his video camera from the trunk, while I retrieve my scene kit from the backseat.

Pamela is utterly silent as we follow her to the front door. As we wait for her to unlock it, I see a curtain flutter at the window of the house next door where the neighbor we had talked to earlier lives. I wonder if he's always nosy, or if we aroused his curiosity when we showed up this morning.

We enter into a large foyer that leads into a great room with a high, cathedral ceiling. The décor is what I expected given the neighborhood and the house's exterior. The furnishings are plush and made of high-end materials: buttery-soft leather couch and chairs, mahogany dining table with heavy matching chairs, a kitchen with granite surfaces, stainless steel appliances, and travertine stone flooring. The other floors are a dark-stained wood that I think is bamboo, and there are thick, wool area rugs of the same muted colors that are on the walls. The overall effect is one of comfort—both aesthetically and financially.

Pamela directs us to the leather seating, but Hurley begs off with an apologetic look. "If you don't mind, I'd like to go straight to your husband's office area."

Pamela looks nonplussed by this request, but she nods and points to a closed door off the foyer. "We share the space," she says. Then she stands there.

Hurley and I head for the office space, leaving Pamela behind but within our line of sight. We open the door to reveal a pleasant room with an antique partner's desk that has computers and chairs on both sides. There is a built-in, wooden bookcase covering the wall opposite the door, and to our right is a window that looks out onto the tastefully landscaped front lawn. A healthy-looking, potted ficus tree stands in front of the window.

Pamela has joined us at the threshold to the room, and she is staring at the desk with tear-filled eyes. "Craig had the side by the bookcase," she says.

As Hurley turns on his camera and does a quick pan of the room, Pamela turns and heads into the main area of the house.

"Follow her," Hurley says in a low voice. "And let's swap cameras." As we make the trade, he adds, "Try to get a look at the bedrooms, and whatever bathroom Craig used."

I nod and exit the office area. Pamela is in the kitchen, getting ready to make some sort of concoction from a coffee machine that looks like it came straight out of Starbucks.

"Can I fix you something?" she says, looking over her shoulder at me. "An espresso? A latte? A cappuccino?"

The smell of freshly ground coffee beans is tantalizing and tempting, but I shake my head. "Pamela, I wonder if you could show me your bedroom. I need to have a look at Craig's personal spaces, like his bedside stand."

She winces at this, and I can't say I blame her. I'm asking to poke around in the most intimate, private parts of her home and her life. "Is that really necessary?" she asks. "Isn't it bad enough that Craig has done this awful thing? Do you have to go rooting through every aspect of his life?"

I open my mouth to answer, to give her the usual spiel about thoroughness and the importance it all has to our investigation, but the doorbell rings before I can.

"That's probably my sister," she says. And in the next moment, the front door opens without waiting for anyone to answer the bell. A woman rushes in, slamming the door behind her.

"Oh, Pammy," the woman says in an angst-ridden voice. "Are you okay?" She makes a beeline for Pamela and envelops her in a hug. The two of them stay like that for a moment, and I look away, wanting to give them at least the illusion of some privacy.

When they finally pull apart, the woman steps back and holds Pamela by the shoulders. "I can't believe Craig is dead," she says. "Are they sure?" She seems to remember me then, and she lets go of Pamela and turns to me. "Are you sure Craig is dead?"

I nod, giving her my best sympathetic expression. Now that I have some time to study her face, I can see the family resemblance. The newcomer is shorter, a tad stouter in build, and has thin, shoulder-length blond hair. But the large green eyes and the small pert nose are the same as Pamela's.

"Are you a cop?" the woman asks me. She eyes me up and down with a look of skepticism.

"No," Pamela says before I can answer. "She's with the medical examiner's office." She shoots me an apologetic look. "I'm sorry," she says with a shake of her head. "I don't remember your name."

"It's Mattie Winston," I say.

"Right," Pamela says. "It's Mattie. Sorry."

"Don't worry about it," I tell her. I shift my gaze to the sister. "And you are . . ."

"Penny," the woman says. "Penny Cook. I'm Pam's sister. Is it true what Pam said? Was Craig having an affair?"

"It appears that way," I say, hedging a smidge.

"And he killed the woman he was having the affair with?"

Pamela turns her back to us and starts messing with her coffee machine again.

I don't want to answer this question, so I use one of Hurley's tactics and come back with one of my own. "How well did you know Craig?"

Penny seems startled by the question. She rears back, her

eyes wide. "If you're asking me if I knew or suspected he was having an affair, then the answer is no."

"That wasn't what I asked," I say, trying to soften the harshness of my words with my tone. "Did you know him well?"

"I suppose," she says with a shrug. "He and Pamela have been together for nearly ten years."

I dismiss her then and shift my attention back to her sister. "Pamela, I know this is a difficult time for you, and the sooner we can get done with what we need to do here, the sooner we can get out of your hair. Do you mind if I take a look at the rest of the house?"

Penny ruffles at this. "Why do you need to go poking around Pammy's house?"

"We are in the middle of an investigation," I tell her in my best professional tone. "There are things we need to determine in order to understand exactly what happened to Craig."

Pamela looks over her shoulder at her sister. "Let it go, Penny," she says. Then she cranes her neck farther to look at me. "Go ahead and do whatever you need to."

Penny is not going to be so easily placated, however. "If you need to investigate Craig's death, why aren't the cops here?"

"They are," I say. "Detective Hurley is in Craig's office right now. You went past him when you came in."

Penny looks confused, then doubtful. Fortunately, Hurley chooses that moment to exit Craig's office and head for us. The change in Penny's expression when she sees him is a remarkable one. She sucks in a breath and arches one eyebrow. Her posture immediately slackens from her warrior stance to one that I can only describe as coquettish: chest out, one arm akimbo, head tilted down ever so slightly, a hint of a smile on her lips as she looks sideways at him. I wouldn't have been surprised to see her bat her eyelashes.

I can't say I blame her. Hurley is a fine-looking specimen. He's tall and lanky, with a thick head of black hair and eyes as blue as an October sky. Thanks to our middle-of-the-night call, he's currently sporting a five o'clock shadow. He looks sexy as hell as he strides toward us.

Penny wastes no time. She glides toward him, meeting him halfway, one hand extended.

"Hi. I'm Penny Cook, Pam's sister."

Hurley takes her hand, locks her in with his blue eyes, and says, "I'm Detective Steve Hurley with the Sorenson Police Department. Sorry to have to meet you under these circumstances."

Penny doesn't look sorry at all. "It's a horrible thing," she says with a dismayed expression. "Pammy said Craig not only killed himself, but someone else?"

Penny is still clinging to Hurley's hand, and he pulls it free. I'm curious to see how he's going to answer this question. Turns out, he doesn't.

"We're still investigating," he says.

"Can you tell me who this other woman is?" Penny asks.

"Right now, I need to focus on gathering as much information as I can," Hurley says, still dodging her inquiries, though since we've already given the name to Pamela, I imagine Penny will be in the know soon enough. Hurley looks at me. "Have you been anywhere else yet?"

I shake my head. "We were just discussing it when you walked up."

Hurley steps to the side, away from Penny.

Penny looks a little put out that she's been summarily dismissed. She pouts for a second, then brightens. "I'm sure Pammy has enough on her plate at the moment. I'd be happy to show you around."

The woman is persistent, I'll give her that. And apparently either oblivious or indifferent to the wedding ring Hurley is wearing.

"Hurley, I'm sure you have some more questions for Pamela. Why don't you talk to her while Penny and I look around the rest of the place?"

Hurley cocks one eyebrow at me. He hasn't missed my manipulations, and he's apparently amused by them. For a second, I think he's going to mess with me and turn down my offer, disappearing into the bedrooms with Penny. But he doesn't. I think she scares him a little.

"That will work," he says.

Penny's pout is back, and her eyes shoot daggers at me. I ignore them, smile pleasantly, and say, "Penny, can you show me where the master bedroom is, please?"

Reluctantly, and with one, last, longing look at Hurley, she leads me to a hallway off the great room. I follow her to the master bedroom, which is at the end of the hallway.

The room is huge—as big as the entire cottage I lived in before moving in with Hurley. There is a sitting area nearly as large as our current living room, furnished with a leather lounging chair and hassock, and a settee covered in a rich, embroidered gold material. There are tables beside each of the seating areas, and lamps on each of the tables. On the far wall, which would be the end wall of the house, is the king-sized bed, looking oddly dwarfed by the dimensions of the room. The ceiling above it is high and coffered, and there are windows above the bed covered with pleated blinds.

Off to the right of the bed is a hallway of sorts through a huge walk-in closet. At the end of this is the master bath. A quick glimpse as we pass reveals an expanse of the same travertine floors that are in the kitchen, marble-topped vanities, and a spa tub that looks big enough for four people.

Penny stops at the bottom of the bed, her arms folded over her chest. She gives me an exasperated look. "This is an awful invasion of privacy," she grumbles. "Is it really necessary for you to go digging around in their things?"

I force my expression into something I hope looks halfway

professional. I don't like Penny, and it's not just because she looked like she wanted to saddle up my husband and ride him home. I get the sense that she's a prickly person, the kind with a sense of entitlement and a no-holds-barred attitude when it comes to speaking her mind. So I decide to give like for like. "My husband and I try to be very thorough with every case we investigate," I say. I see her expression falter for a second, and her eyes dart toward my left hand. *Message received*, I think with a little smile. Then I turn on my camera to start filming and switch topics. "What kind of work do you do, Ms. Cook? Or is it Mrs.?"

"Ms. is fine," she says with a little pout that would look cute on a four-year-old but seems kind of pathetic on a woman Penny's age. "I'm divorced."

"And do you have an occupation?" I ask since she ignored that question.

"I have three kids and a house to manage. Does that count?"

Given what a challenge I've had managing a house with only two kids, I feel obligated to nod. Then, just to firm up my claim on Hurley, I say, "Detective Hurley and I have two kids, and that keeps me plenty busy, so I can imagine how crazy your life gets. Does your ex help out any?" I'm filming things in the room as I talk, trying to keep some level of conversation going to keep Penny distracted and talking.

"My ex-husband owns several car dealerships," Penny says. "He helps out when he can with the kids, but he's pretty busy most of the time."

"Any of the dealerships here in town?" I ask.

She nods. "He owns the Chrysler-Dodge place over on the south side of town, and two others between here and Madison."

"Whose side of the bed is that?" I ask, pointing to the right side.

"Pammy's," she says without hesitation.

I find this interesting. I couldn't tell you what side of the bed belongs to my sister or her husband. "You and Pamela are pretty close, I take it." I move to Craig's side of the bed as I say this and film the top of his nightstand. It's ordinary enough: alarm clock, reading glasses, a current thriller novel open and facedown, a remote for the blinds on the windows above.

"I more or less raised Pammy," Penny says as I reach down and open one of the two drawers in Craig's nightstand. It contains dozens of rolled-up pairs of socks. I rummage through them to make sure there isn't anything hiding in there and give most of the socks a squeeze. It's a surprisingly common hiding place.

"Our parents died in a house explosion when I was nineteen and Pam was twelve," Penny continues as I shut the top drawer and open the one beneath it. "There was a leaky gas line, and they think the gas ignited when my mother lit a candle. It killed them both instantly and destroyed the entire house. Fortunately, Pam and I had both left for school when it happened—I was attending a local community college at the time—or we probably would have been killed, too."

"How awful," I say, giving her a sympathetic look.

"It was," she acknowledges, looking sad. "At first, the authorities wanted us to go and live with some aunt in California, but I turned twenty a few days after the explosion, and I was able to convince social services that I could take care of the two of us. I still had a year to go to obtain an associate's degree in nursing, but I was able to get a license as an LPN."

"I'm a nurse," I tell her, an effort to bond. "An RN. I used to work at the hospital here in town. Did you ever go back and finish your degree?"

Penny's lips thin. "No," she says after a moment. "I meant to. In fact, at one time I had plans to transfer my credits to the university and pursue a four-year degree, but it never happened. I became a single mother literally overnight. Our parents had a nest egg of retirement savings between the two of them, and there was also a little money from the insurance on the house. So it wasn't like I had to become a big bread-winner right away. It gave me time to focus on getting Pammy and me back on our feet emotionally." She pauses and takes on a distant look, a hint of a smile on her face. "Our parents were both smart financial planners—I think that's where Pam gets her affinity for number crunching and finances."

The smile disappears, and she refocuses on me. "Anyway, we had a little money to tide us over for a while, and I found us a nice rental house just outside of town. I took some nurs-ing odd jobs here and there when I needed to, but I tried to be home as much as possible for Pammy. I got her through school and on to college, and basically ran the household until she graduated. Then she met Craig and moved out a couple of months later."

"When did you get married?" I ask as I survey the second drawer. It contains more books—spy thrillers—some sex lube, and a copy of the Kama Sutra. Craig was adventurous, it seems, and I wonder if he was sleeping with both his wife and Meredith Lansing, or if the marital bed had grown cold.

Penny has moved beside me and is watching everything I do. I shut the drawer and head for the walk-in closet, Penny on my heels.

"I got married not long after Pammy moved in with Craig," she says. "I'd known Chip for a couple of years, and he initially proposed to me when Pammy was still in college." She sighs. "I turned him down that time, telling him I felt like I needed to be there for my sister. Fortunately, or perhaps unfortunately, Chip was persistent and loyal. He hung in there and pro-posed again right after Pammy graduated." She pauses, sighs, and rolls her eyes. "And since I was five months pregnant at the time, I accepted." She looks wistful for a moment. "Wish I'd known then what I know now."

"It must have been difficult for you, taking on the role of

mother to your sister," I say as she follows me into the closet. The two sides are divided into his and hers: Pamela's stuff on the right, Craig's—perhaps fittingly given his left-handedness— on the left. After snapping pictures of everything, I paw through the shirts and sports coats hanging on Craig's side, giving any pockets I find a squeeze.

"It wasn't that hard," Penny says. "I mean, losing our parents that way was a shock, but the two of us were always close, and we leaned on one another for support."

I find nothing in the hanging clothes and move to the built-in drawers beneath them. These, too, provide nothing in the way of clues other than the fact that Craig was a boxer man. I move to the other side and do the same with Pamela's things.

"Divorce is hard," I say, working to keep the conversation going. "I went through one myself." Penny perks up at this, and I feel obligated to clarify. "We split up right before I met Detective Hurley," I add, "so I suppose it turned out to be a good thing. But it was quite the emotional roller coaster."

"Why did you split?"

"He cheated on me."

"That seems to be the male way," Penny says in a bitter tone, making me wonder if that's what happened to her marriage. "No kids?" she asks.

I shake my head.

"That's fortunate. It really complicates things. Chip and I are still fighting over custody of the kids."

Pamela's side reveals little of interest other than some fancy lingerie, so I move on, with Penny still at my heels. The bathroom is huge and luxurious. The towels are thick, beige cotton, and there are two robes hanging on hooks just inside the door. I guess the floral-patterned one is Pamela's. Craig's is a blue-and-red plaid number.

Penny stands by silently, watching me as I film, and then I look through the various drawers and cupboards in the vanity. Once I'm done with those, I look through the medicine cabinet.

"You're very thorough," Penny says, and I detect a hint of irritation in her voice.

"It's helpful to learn as much as possible about our victims. I know it seems intrusive, but it's necessary."

"Whatever," she says with a sigh. She glances at her watch.

The medicine cabinet offers up nothing helpful. There are no prescription medications, just the usual assortment of over-the-counter pain and cold remedies, along with some vitamin and mineral supplements.

"How long have Craig and Pamela been married?" I ask Penny.

"Eight, almost nine years now. They lived together for a year before that."

I do a quick mental calculation and figure Penny must be pushing forty. "No kids?" I ask.

Penny shakes her head. "It hasn't been in the cards for them. They've been trying for years. Pam has seen a fertility specialist, and apparently they are . . . were at the point where they were going to have to consider in vitro. It's quite expensive, but Pam was determined for a while. Then she said the stress of it all was starting to weigh on their marriage, and that Craig told her if they couldn't do it naturally, then it wasn't meant to be." She pauses and gives a half-hearted shrug. "Maybe that's what made Craig stray. Who knows?"

I leave the bathroom and go over to Pamela's side of the bed. The contents of her nightstand bear out Penny's story. There are books on fertility, some ovulation test strips, and a thermometer.

Satisfied, I leave the room and move back out into the hallway. There are two other bedrooms and another bathroom off the hall. One of the bedrooms is done up for guests; the other is nearly empty, boasting nothing more than a rocking chair and a dresser. I guess that the emptier room is, or was, designated to be a nursery, if and when the happy day ever came.

The main bathroom is clearly set up for guests as well, and it yields nothing of interest. We head back out to the kitchen, where we find Hurley and Pamela seated at the breakfast bar, sipping coffees.

"I was just explaining to Mrs. Knowlton about our evidentiary procedures," Hurley says. Pamela looks at her sister with a scared, confused expression. "Mattie, if you would please escort Mrs. Knowlton to her room, she is going to remove the clothes she is wearing so we can collect them as evidence. I've just checked her hands for GSR and that came up negative."

Penny, who looked like she was ready to resume her flirtatiousness when we first entered the room, now looks angry and startled. "What the hell are you doing?" she says, her hands on her hips. "You can't treat Pammy like this. Her husband just died, for cripes sake. Just because he's a murderer doesn't mean she is, or that she had anything to do with it."

I put out a hand to Penny and try to calm her. "It's merely routine. It's important to be thorough in any investigation we conduct. The woman victim's husband might come back later and say Pamela was involved somehow. If we don't have evidence to the contrary, then you've got a problem on your hands."

Penny gives me an impatient look, heads straight for her sister, and stands in front of her, looking her in the eye. "You don't have to do this, Pammy," she says. "You don't have to listen to them, you don't have to give them anything, you don't even have to let them in your house."

Pamela, tears welling in her eyes, gives her sister a pleading look. "I want to get this over with," she says in a small, quiet voice. "I've got nothing to hide."

"That doesn't matter," Penny says. "They might find a way to use evidence they collect against you later on. At the very least, you should call a lawyer."

Pamela drops her head, and a tear falls from her face to the floor. Silently, she sidesteps past her sister and heads for the bedroom. I follow, leaving Penny and Hurley in the kitchen together—not the greatest idea, in my opinion.

In the bedroom, Pamela walks over to her closet, grabs a T-shirt and a pair of shorts from a shelf, and then takes out a pair of panties and a bra from a drawer. Wordlessly, she carries them to the bed, tossing them on top of the spread, and then kicks off her shoes. She then strips herself down until she is naked, handing me each item of clothing as it comes off. I have brought my scene kit along and have bags at the ready for the items. As I bag, seal, and label, I also steal a few surreptitious glances at Pamela's body to determine if she has any wounds, bruises, or other markings that might be indicative of a struggle. There is nothing.

"I'm sorry to put you through this, Pamela," I say. "I know it must be humiliating."

She shrugs. "It's no different than being in the gym locker room," she says, pulling on her panties and then her shorts.

"Penny told me about your parents," I say. "What an awful experience that must have been for you."

Pamela stares at me as she picks the bra up from the bed. Her eyes look dead. She shrugs into the bra with her eyes still locked on mine. "It was definitely a shock," she says, reaching behind to hook the bra. When she's done, she grabs the tee, and slips it on over her head. "So is this. I can't wrap my head around the idea that Craig did something like this. I mean . . . an affair I could maybe understand. But killing someone? And then himself? That's not the man I knew. Or the man I thought I knew," she clarifies, her posture sagging. Tears well again, and she turns away from me. I finish my evidentiary duties and then stand there, staring at the floor, letting her have some semblance of privacy.

"Are we done?" she says after a minute or two. I look up, see her face is tearstained but dry, and nod. She heads back toward the kitchen, and I follow, carrying my evidence and scene kit with me.

Out in the kitchen, we find Penny and Hurley sitting at the breakfast bar. Hurley has his back to me. Penny is leaning on the bar with one arm bent, her face resting on the back of her forearm. She is smiling that coy little smile again. As soon as she sees me. she straightens up and adopts a guilty expression, something I suspect is a deliberate ploy.

After a few instructions on what to expect from here on out, Hurley and I load up our evidence, which includes Craig's laptop, the office printer, and some files from his desk, say goodbye, and leave. Outside, we have to walk past Pamela's car and a beige, older-model sedan that's parked behind it, which I assume is Penny's car. Once we have everything, including ourselves, loaded in the car, I give Hurley a summary of what I found in the house—which was essentially nothing—and what I learned from Penny.

"How about you?" I ask him when I'm done. "How was your time alone with Penny?" I tease.

Hurley looks at me and rolls his eyes. "That woman reeks of desperation."

"Understandable, I imagine. It sounds like her ex treated her like crap."

"Maybe. There are always two sides to these things."

"I guess."

"Jonas sent me a text while you and Penny were in the bedroom. The serial number on the gun we found in the motel room came back registered to a man named Philip Conroy, who reported it stolen a year ago. So that's a dead end unless we can find a connection between this Conroy fellow and the Knowltons or Lansings. I didn't see a file in Craig's home desk with that name on it. I've got the guys looking for one in the office files."

"I have to say, I found both Lansing's and Pamela's reactions very convincing. And the only motive I see so far is revenge for the affair. That means one or both of them is an excellent actor and liar."

Hurley nods, looking thoughtful. "Well, I did find a million-dollar life insurance policy in Craig's desk, so that's a possible motive."

"Does it exclude suicide?" I ask. "Most policies do for a period of a year or two after the policy is written."

"Good question," Hurley says. "I don't know. It's in that box in the backseat. Have a look."

I take off my seat belt and reach around to rummage through the boxes he has loaded into the car. Eventually, I find the policy and skim through it. "This is interesting," I say when I get to the second page. "Suicide is excluded for one year." I flip to the last page and check the signatures and the date the policy was signed. The first thing I notice is that the person who issued the policy is Patty Volker, my ex-husband's new wife. I log that in a mental file and then look at the dates. "Wow," I say. "This thing was signed one year and a day ago."

Hurley shoots me a look. I can tell he's intrigued. "We need to go back and have a longer chat with John Lansing and find out if his wife had an insurance policy, too," he says. "Now that we know this thing isn't what it seems, we need to take a closer look at him."

CHAPTER 8

John Lansing is clearly surprised to see us back. "What is it now?" he says. In the time we've been gone, he hasn't showered, dressed, or—judging from his breath—brushed his teeth. I get a sense that good hygiene wasn't high on his list before, and now that his wife isn't around to nag him on the topic, it will deteriorate even more. He looks tightly wound and ready to flinch at whatever news we have to deliver this time.

Hurley says, "We need to take a look at some of your wife's things, to help us clear up some questions about the case."

"Such as?" Lansing says irritably. "First you tell me my wife has been murdered by some love-struck asshole, and then you say the two of them were having an affair. Now you want to paw through my wife's things? What the hell for?"

As if Lansing isn't angry enough already, Hurley ramps up the man's ire with his next question. "Did Meredith have any life insurance?"

Lansing blinks at Hurley, staring at him in disbelief. "She has a small policy, nothing big. We both do. They're for ten grand each, enough to take care of a funeral and maybe pay off a few expenses. Though I think Mer also had some coverage through work, through the hospital. I think she said it was equal to a year's earnings, or something like that." He pauses and frowns. "How could that possibly have anything to do with this?"

"There are some irregularities in this case that we need to clear up," Hurley says with imminent patience. Lansing is still standing in his doorway, and he doesn't look inclined to invite us inside.

"Such as?" John asks again.

"I'm not at liberty to discuss that at this time," Hurley says. "May we please come in?"

Lansing scowls at the request, and I can tell he wants to tell us to get lost or put our request where the sun doesn't shine. Apparently, Hurley senses this, too, because he then adds, "I can get a warrant if you prefer." Hurley's blue eyes turn steely as he and Lansing engage in a stare-down. It amazes me how quickly that blue can change from friendly and welcoming to blood-curdling coldness.

John's whole body sags as he capitulates. "Fine," he says, stepping to one side and opening the door wider.

We go inside quickly before he can change his mind. As John shuts the door, Hurley and I turn to face him.

"Mr. Lansing, do you have a car?" Hurley asks.

"We do. But it's not here. We only have the one car, and Meredith took it to work." He stops, and his mouth drops open with dawning. He squeezes his eyes closed and looks like he's about to cry. "I guess she didn't take it to work last night though, did she?"

"What kind of car is it?" Hurley asks.

"It's a 2009 Ford Focus. Bought it used two years ago. It has a lot of miles on it, but it runs okay."

"Are you sure it isn't here?" Hurley asks.

John arches his eyebrows in surprise. "Why would it be?"

Hurley shrugs. "Maybe she was picked up?"

John makes a face. "That would be ballsy," he says. He walks over to the front window that overlooks the parking lot and pushes the curtain aside. "It's not here," he says glumly.

"Is the registration for it in your name or your wife's?" Hurley asks.

"It's in Meredith's name. She's the one who bought it. The title is in her name, too." John doesn't sound particularly happy about this fact, and it's not hard to imagine that he and his wife had a lot of arguments about money or the lack thereof. When it comes to motives for murder, love and money rank right up there at the top of the list, and John Lansing is steeped in both.

Hurley takes out his phone and hits a speed-dial number. "Hey, it's Hurley," he says to whoever is on the other end. I'm fairly certain it's Stephanie, the police department's day dispatcher. "Can you look up a 2009 Ford Focus registered to Meredith Lansing and give me a plate and VIN number?" While he's waiting, he reaches into his jeans pocket and takes out a pen and the small notebook he carries with him everywhere he goes. After a half minute of us standing around trying not to look at one another, Hurley says, "Yep, go ahead." He jots down the information while propping his phone between his ear and shoulder. When he's done, he says, "Got it. Thanks. Can you pass this info on to Junior and ask him to check the hospital parking lot? Devonshire already ran all the plates that were out at the motel, and this one wasn't among them."

He listens for a few seconds, says thank you, and then disconnects the call.

John rakes a hand through his hair and says, "Is there any way you guys can bring the car back here for me?"

Hurley gives him an apologetic look. "It's going to be seized as evidence for now."

John stares at him in disbelief. "What? Why? How am I

supposed to get around or do anything if I don't have any wheels?"

"Sorenson isn't that big a town," Hurley says. "Do you have a bike?"

John doesn't answer; he just stares at Hurley with an expression of incredulity.

"There's also the cab service," I suggest. "They'll take you anywhere in town for two-fifty."

John shakes his head in dismay. "Grrreat," he says, sounding like a pissed-off Tony the Tiger.

"Do you have a home computer?" Hurley asks.

John gives him a tired look. "It's in the spare bedroom, down the hall." He leads us in the right direction, walking like a man making his final march on death row.

As we follow, I notice that the rest of the apartment, like the living room, is neat but showing some wear and tear. The walls are in need of fresh paint, the hardwood floors are scuffed and scarred, and what furniture I see looks like mismatched hand-me-downs or garage-sale fare. The room in question is one of three off the main hall; the third is a bathroom. The master bedroom is at the end of the hall, and the door is open. The bed is unmade on one side, while the other appears neatly tucked. This makes sense given that Meredith worked the night shift. We do a quick but thorough survey and filming of the room, opening nightstand and dresser drawers—Meredith has a nice collection of lacy, frilly underthings, I note—and closets. It's standard fare for the most part, with nothing that would appear to be of evidentiary value.

It doesn't take long to scope out the bathroom. It is small, but adequate. We find the usual potpourri of hygiene products for both men and women, though John's are minimal. The medicine cabinet offers no surprises, just a few over-the-counter pain meds and one prescription. I take the prescription bottle out—it only has four pills in it—and take a picture of it.

It is for Meredith, a supply of sleeping pills. This doesn't surprise me since I know Meredith worked nights, and it's not uncommon for night-shift workers to have trouble sleeping during the day.

We move on to the second bedroom, which is clearly being used as an office. It has a battered wooden hutch with a desktop computer, a wicker chair that looks like a leftover from someone's lawn furniture, and a nicked, pressed-wood bookcase painted—badly—in white. There aren't many books in the bookcase, and most of them are textbooks related to laboratory training and the medical field. The rest of the space on the shelves is filled with knickknacks, photo albums, candles, and a handful of framed photos.

"Can you get me the life insurance policy for your wife?" Hurley asks John.

He nods and walks over to a corner of the room, where he picks up a metal lockbox from the floor. It isn't locked, and when he opens it, I see several hanging folders with tabbed labels. He pulls out one that reads INSURANCE and hands it to Hurley, who then hands it off to me.

"We also need to look at what's in the one labeled retirement," I say to John. "Given that Meredith was working with Craig on her plan." As her husband, John stands to inherit his wife's retirement fund as well as the life insurance. To a guy who's been unemployed for two years, living with a wife who likely controlled the purse strings, that has to be appealing.

John gives us a perturbed look but pulls the file and hands it to me. As I flip through the contents, Hurley starts rummaging through desk drawers. He finds more hanging files, the labels marked with items related to household bills. He pulls out the one for the phone bill and sets it on top of the desk.

I find the life insurance policy for Meredith and wince when I see that it was also issued by Patty Volker. John was correct about the policy, as well as his own, which is also in the folder. Both are for ten thousand, not a huge amount, but a major windfall for someone like John who is unemployed and broke, especially when you take into consideration the additional work policy. Not to mention that John might also have been mad as hell that his sugar mama was doing the nasty with someone else, someone with much better financial prospects.

I take Meredith's policy and set it atop the phone bill folder, then, after flipping through the financial forms and reports in the retirement folder, I add it to the pile as well. John stands to gain another seventeen grand from that fund.

Hurley wakes up the computer once he's done going through the drawers, and the monitor reveals a desktop filled with icons. I see several that are games and guess that this is how John spends a lot of his spare time—something I imagine he has plenty of. There are also icons for a variety of websites, including some gambling sites, a dozen or so word-processing documents, some financial software, and a number of online shopping sites.

"What did Meredith use for an e-mail server?" Hurley asks John.

"Gmail. That's what we both use."

Hurley launches the Internet, and it opens to the Google home page. He clicks on the Gmail icon and gets a prompt for a user ID and password. He turns and gives John a questioning look.

"Her user ID is MeredithL," he says, "Capital M, capital L." Hurley types it in. "The password is vampire, all lowercase," John adds at the appropriate moment. This makes me smile. It's the perfect password for a lab technician.

Hurley types it in and gets an error message. "Are you sure there aren't any capital letters in it?" he asks.

"I don't think so," John says, scratching his belly.

Hurley tries different variations anyway, using caps and adding numbers. None of the attempts work.

"She must have changed her password," John says, his face growing dark. "Makes sense, I guess, since she apparently had something to hide." He looks away, staring out the window, his cheek muscles twitching angrily.

Hurley's phone rings, breaking the tension a smidge, and both John and I stand by, staring at him, as he takes the call. Aside from his initial, "Hurley here," when he answers, he says nothing for a minute or so. Then he thanks the caller and hangs up.

"We found your wife's car in the hospital parking lot," he says, and I wince at his use of the term *your wife's car*, since I sense that John is already feeling battered and emasculated with regard to the marital financial situation. I wonder if Hurley is unaware of this jab, or if he did it intentionally. He likes to keep people emotionally labile during an investigation, but he can also get so focused on details at times that he doesn't think about how things might sound when he says them.

John digests the information for a few seconds. "So, this guy she was with probably picked her up at the hospital?"

Hurley nods.

"She was trying to hide her tracks," John says miserably. I don't think the man can get any lower, but I'm wrong.

Hurley changes topics and says, "We're going to need to take this computer with us."

John's look shifts to one of irritation. "Why? It's my computer, too."

"You can probably get it back at some point," Hurley says in an effort to calm him. He leaves out the fact that it might be months, or even years, if ever.

"Probably? I can *probably* get it back?" He lets out an irritated huff and shifts his feet like he wants to pace, except the room isn't big enough. "Do you know how long we had to save just to be able to buy that damned computer? First you confiscate my car, and now my computer. Do you people think I'm made of money?"

I feel for the guy, but there isn't much we can do to placate him. "You could use the computers at the library in the meantime," I suggest. "They're free."

"And almost always in use," he snaps. "Believe me, I've been there and done that."

"Sorry," I say with a shrug. "But I imagine that the life insurance money will be enough to buy you a nice new computer. And a car."

Hurley and I both watch John's face closely as he gives me a look of distaste, maybe even disgust. But something about it feels forced, and beneath the heat of our scrutiny, he suddenly turns away and storms from the room.

I give Hurley a look, my eyebrows raised. He nods. We now have a primary suspect. Hurley follows John, who has escaped into the bedroom. I hear him tell John he needs him to strip so we can collect his clothes as evidence. An argument ensues, during which John demands to know why he's the one being treated like a suspect when some asshole killed his wife, and what his clothing could possibly have to do with anything. But in the end, he capitulates and provides the clothing. Hurley also tests John's hands for GSR, a test that comes up negative. This doesn't mean John didn't fire a gun. He could have fired one and washed carefully afterward, or been wearing protective gear of some sort, like long-cuffed gloves.

While the clothing and GSR drama is playing out in the main bedroom, I shut down the computer, disconnect the peripherals, and label each piece with an evidence tag. I do the same with the files, placing them in evidence bags.

Hurley emerges from the bedroom carrying John's clothes,

and the two of us haul all of our evidence to the front door. We pass John along the way. He is leaning against the doorframe into the kitchen, his arms folded tightly over his chest, his lips drawn thin and tight. He is giving us what my mother calls the evil eye, and as we head out the door I hear him mutter a few choice words behind us.

CHAPTER 9

We load up the car with our evidentiary cargo and head back to the police station. Hurley pulls into the underground garage area where Jonas has his lab. Jonas pulls in with the PD's evidence van as we're unloading our booty from the car.

"I was just about to call you," Hurley says to him.

"Why?" Jonas asks, opening the van's side door and removing a box of bagged evidence. I can see the gun from the motel room, four cell phones, a couple of bullet casings, and several other bags that contain fibers of some sort.

"Four phones?" Hurley says, his eyebrows shooting up as he eyes the motel room evidence haul.

Jonas nods. "Turns out Craig and Meredith both had burner phones as well as their regular phones. I took a quick peek, and it looks like the burner phones were used exclusively between the two of them."

"I want you to do the phone forensics ASAP," Hurley says. "See what sort of train of contacts you can establish between the two of them. I want to know how long they've been seeing one another, and whether or not there was any animosity between them. I also want to know about any text messages between either victim and their spouse."

Jonas nods. "I'll do that first thing."

"I also want you to dust the casings you collected and any bullets remaining in that gun for prints. See if you can find any prints other than Craig Knowlton's."

"It sounds like you think the scene at the motel was a setup," Jonas says, looking intrigued.

Hurley nods. "We have several indications that suggest Craig Knowlton was left-handed," he explains. "And since the gun was found by his right hand, I doubt he shot himself."

"Any potential suspects?" Jonas asks, setting his box of evidence on a table and then removing its contents.

"Either of the spouses could have done it if they knew about the affair," Hurley says. "When you look at the phones, check to see if either of the victims had GPS activated. It would be helpful if we could track their movements. When is Knowlton's car getting here?"

"Should be any moment," Jonas says.

"It has GPS capabilities," Hurley says. "See what you can dig up from it, too."

Jonas nods again.

As if on cue, a tow truck arrives and idles just outside the garage door with Craig Knowlton's car loaded onto the bed. With both the evidence van and Hurley's car parked in the garage, it can't deliver its cargo. Hurley goes to move his car out of the way while I wait with Jonas. The tow truck's passenger door opens up, and Laura Kingston hops out.

"Hey, Mattie," she says, practically skipping into the garage. Laura is an annoyingly cheerful person. I've never seen her look or act depressed, or even serious. She's consistently bubbly, smiling, and upbeat. When I first met her, I found this trait charming. Now it grates on my nerves at times. No one can be that happy all the time.

"What a case, eh?" she says as she approaches. She manages to take a breath before releasing a rapid-fire barrage of speech. "Quite the intriguing situation. Clearly someone thought they had cooked up the perfect murder, but they weren't as smart as they thought they were, were they?" She doesn't give us a chance to answer. "Yep, they screwed up royally with that left-handed business, and now we get to catch ourselves a killer. Did you know that only ten to twelve percent of people in the world are left-handed? And it's twice as common in men as it is in women. In fact, four of our last seven presidents were left-handed. Being left-handed means you have a greater risk of developing psychosis, but it also means you are more likely to choose a career in the creative arts. Lefties also tend to drink more alcohol than right-handed people. And left-handers even have their own celebratory day. Did you know that? I love this job! I love nailing these smug bastards who think they're smarter than everyone else. And we will get them, won't we? We always do. It's foolish to think you can pull one over on us. We can—"

"Laura!" I say loudly, trying to be heard over the sound of the tow truck's winch and motor.

"Oops!" she says with a silly giggle. She clamps a hand over her mouth for a second. "There I go again," she continues, dropping her hand. "Sorry. I know I get carried away at times, but I just get so excited by this stuff and I can't seem to help . . ."

I give her an overly dramatic, exasperated look, and her self-awareness manages to kick in as she realizes she's rambling an apology about her rambling. The hand once again covers her mouth, and this time she leaves it there.

"It's okay," Jonas says to her. "I admire your enthusiasm."

Judging from his goo-goo–eyed expression, it's not Laura's enthusiasm that Jonas admires, or at least it's not the primary thing.

"Jonas," I say, "why don't you have Laura move your van? There's another car that's going to be here shortly. Meredith Lansing's car is being towed from the hospital lot."

Jonas nods and tosses Laura the keys, and we are granted a few minutes of blessed quiet.

"None of these phones is password-protected," Jonas says to me after a while. He has gloved up and removed Meredith's and Craig's phones from their evidence bags. "That should make this a snap," he goes on. "I'll let you know what I find."

"Those computers won't be quite so easy," Hurley says, nodding toward the Lansing and Knowlton computers. "They're all password-protected."

"I'll do what I can," Jonas says. "I might hand the computers off to Arnie. He typically has better luck with those than I do. If we can't figure them out, we'll have to send them off to Madison."

The reason Arnie has better luck with computers is because of his relationship with Joey Dewhurst, the slightly slow hulk of a man I tried to fix up with Cinder, the woman who runs the Grizzly Motel.

Hurley nods at Jonas and says, "Do what you can. And have Laura dig into the finances for both couples. I want to know who spent what, where they spent it, and when."

Laura returns from moving the evidence van, and with her comes the second tow truck hauling Meredith Lansing's car.

Hurley and I leave Laura and Jonas to their work, and make our escape before Laura can launch into another diatribe. As we're heading upstairs to the main part of the station, my cell phone rings. I see it's Emily, and a little worry worm squiggles in my heart.

"Hey, Em," I answer. "Is everything okay?"

"It is," she says in a chipper tone. "But I forgot I have a volleyball game this afternoon and a date tonight with Johnny. Sorry. I was so sleepy this morning when you woke me that I wasn't thinking straight."

"That's okay." I do some quick mental calculations. "What time do you need to be at your game?"

"By one."

"Okay. Either your dad or I will come and get Matthew and take him to Dom's before then."

"Thanks."

"No, thank you for stepping in at the last minute." Emily has been a lifesaver when it comes to the crazy hours Hurley and I work. While my sister and Dom are both available on short notice to provide childcare, the ability to leave in the middle of the night the way we did today without having to wake Matthew and drag him along somewhere is invaluable. It's been particularly helpful recently, as I've had to resume full-time—and then some—hours at work following Hal's death.

"What are you two going to do on your date?" I ask her.

"We're going bowling and then to his place, to watch some movies on Netflix."

This sounds safe enough to me given that I know Johnny's mother has other kids and is almost always home. I thank Emily again, disconnect the call, and follow Hurley into the police department breakroom.

"I should head over to the office so I can help Izzy with the autopsies," I tell him. "But someone needs to go pick Matthew up and take him to Dom's before one. Emily has a game this afternoon and plans this evening with Johnny."

Hurley frowns at the mention of Johnny, who has been Emily's boyfriend for going on two years now. While I quite like the boy, Hurley has his doubts. This stems in part from Johnny's family tree, which has branched into correctional facilities on multiple occasions for each generation preceding Johnny's. So far, Johnny and his mother seem determined to seed new plantings and leave behind the crime-ridden mighty oak, but Hurley remains skeptical.

"I can pick Matthew up and take him to Dom's," Hurley offers. "Can you pick him up from there later?"

"That shouldn't be a problem."

"Where are Johnny and Emily going tonight?"

"They're going bowling, and then they plan to watch some movies at his place," I say. "Emily knows she has to be home by eleven." This reassurance does little to relax Hurley's scowl. "Come on, Hurley," I say. "Give Johnny a break. He's been walking the straight and narrow for nearly two years now, and the only thing he's likely to knock over or up tonight are some bowling pins."

Hurley shoots me an exasperated look.

"What?" I say, irritated by his persistent suspicions.

"I think you're being a bit naïve," he grumbles. "Johnny already has Emily smoking. I know because I've smelled it on her before."

"Yeah, she tried it a few times. But she told me she hasn't smoked in several months. She doesn't like the habit, and she's nagging Johnny to try to get him to quit. Kids that age are going to experiment."

"That's what worries me," he says, his frown deepening. "What else are they going to experiment with?"

"Well, Emily has already tried pot a couple of times, but that was before she came here. Johnny is adamantly against any kind of drugs."

Hurley shoots me an incredulous look. "How do you know that?"

"Because Emily told me. We've had quite a few frank discussions in the past year or so. We also discussed her sexual activities. Would you like to know the details of that, too?"

Hurley gapes at me, managing to look both frightened and angry. "She's having sex?" he says, his mouth curling in distaste.

"She is. But she's on the pill, and they also use condoms."

Hurley rakes a hand through his hair and blows his cheeks out. "How long has this been going on?" he asks. "And why didn't you tell me about it before now?"

"I had a talk with Emily a year and a half ago when she

was recovering from her broken leg," I tell him. "She and Johnny hadn't had sex yet at that time, but she said she didn't know how much longer that would last."

"He was pressuring her into it?" Hurley growls.

"No, not at all. In fact, Emily admitted that she was the one doing most of the, um, provocation, and Johnny kept stopping things before they went too far."

"So you just condoned their promiscuous behavior?"

"No," I say, trying to be patient. "But they're teenagers, Hurley. Their hormones are raging, they genuinely care for one another, and their attraction is a strong one." I pause and shrug. "It would have been foolish to risk trusting them to not take things further and then end up with a pregnancy or an STD. And your daughter has been very responsible about the whole thing."

"I should have been consulted on the matter," he says, his face red with anger.

"You weren't exactly open to such discussions," I remind him. "I suspect you still aren't," I add pointedly. "And Emily felt more comfortable discussing some of the more intimate details with another woman."

"Another woman?" Hurley says, askance. "Emily is a girl, not a woman." I'm about to argue this point with him, but he goes on before I can get a word in. "And what kind of an example did you set, having an unplanned child out of wedlock?"

I stare back at him, not believing he has just said this. The words are like an ice pick jabbed into my chest, snaking between my ribs, and piercing my heart. "You can be such an ass at times, Hurley!" I snap. Then I spin around, make for the exit, and storm out.

CHAPTER 10

I mutter to myself as I walk the two blocks to my office. I can't believe Hurley said what he did, but in spite of my anger, I also feel a twinge of guilt. He's right, to a degree. And while I hadn't planned my pregnancy with Matthew, I was slack in my vigil when it came to taking my own birth control pills. I missed a couple, and I didn't take them at the same time every day. For months, I felt guilty, and worried that Hurley would think I was trying to trap him, or would feel obligated to marry me because of the pregnancy. He convinced me otherwise, or I wouldn't have married him. But here we are, less than a month into our married life, already dredging up this bit of our past. So far, our road to marital bliss has been as smooth and painless as petting a porcupine.

I shove my thoughts aside as I enter the office. Our receptionist/secretary/file clerk, Cass, is seated at the front desk.

"Hey, Mattie," she says. She isn't wearing any sort of costume today, a definite departure from her usual practice. Cass belongs to a local thespian group that puts on plays several times a year, and she has a habit of dressing, acting, and speaking like whatever character she is scheduled to play. Her most recent one was Sigmund Freud.

"No costume today?" I say, curious.

Cass shakes her head, looking glum. "We're taking a break for a while," she says. "We've lost some of our key members, like Dom, and right now we don't have enough people to put on a decent show. So we decided to wait until the fall before we start up again."

Though I hadn't realized Dom had given up his acting interests—understandable since he and Izzy adopted a baby girl four months ago—it makes sense. Now seven months old, Juliana takes up a lot of Dom's time and energy. Plus, he takes care of Matthew for me on most of my workdays, though my sister occasionally fills in.

"I'm sorry, Cass," I say. "I know how much you enjoy your acting."

She wags her head from side to side, a grudging look of acceptance on her face. "Hopefully, it's only temporary. In the meantime, we're trying to recruit some new members." She pauses and gives me a hopeful look. "I don't suppose you—"

"Sorry, no," I say before she can finish her sentence. "It's not something I'd be good at, and besides, since Hal's death I've been putting in so much time at work that I wouldn't be able to do much anyway."

"Yeah," she says glumly. "Of course. And speaking of work, Izzy and Arnie just finished checking in those bodies from the Grizzly Motel. In fact, Izzy told me to call you if you didn't show up or call on your own by ten."

"Well, I'm here for the duration," I say. "Is Izzy in his office?"

"Not sure. But he's here somewhere. Oh, and I have a message for you." She hands me a pink slip of paper with the name Marvin Holmes written on it, along with a phone number. Marvin is the contractor in charge of building our new house. "Did Mr. Holmes say what he wanted?" I ask her.

"Something about your house—the one they're building, that is."

I stuff the note in my pocket, deciding it can wait, and then head into the back area of the office, taking out my cell phone along the way. I place a call to Dom, who answers with, "I was hoping you'd call soon. Juliana is feeling kind of lonely. Tell me you're bringing Matthew by."

"I'm not, but Hurley will be later. I'll be the one picking him up at the end of the day. It might be a late night, though. Is that okay?"

"Of course it is," Dom says cheerily. "And my offer to leave him here overnight anytime you need to still stands."

"Thanks, Dom," I say, thinking this sounds mighty tempting about now, and then feeling an immediate twinge of guilt. "I might have to take you up on it at some point, but for now I want to spend as much time with him as I can. As it is, my mommy time is much too short."

"They grow up fast, don't they?"

Indeed, they do. Matthew is changing every day, right before my eyes, it seems. At just shy of two, he is achieving new physical and developmental strides every day, sometimes every hour. His vocabulary is rapidly increasing, his motor skills grow more adept each day, and his brain is rapidly absorbing and processing the world around him. This is not always a good thing, as in when he decides he can't eat certain foods because they're too soft, or gets artistic with his poop, or refuses to wear certain clothes because they're too red, or blue, or green . . . pick a color. He is definitely a strong-minded kid who doesn't like it when he doesn't get his way, and he isn't afraid to show it. Several people in town have been witness to his tantrums in the grocery store, one of his favorite places to stage a meltdown. I actually begged the store manager to create one checkout aisle that didn't have gum and candy displays in it . . . just one. But the evil bastard just smiled at me and muttered something about impulse sales, which gave me an impulse to sail something up the side of his head. Clearly, the guy doesn't understand that kids are the epitome of impulsiveness. Or he does understand and puts all these items within cart-riding reach on purpose.

"Don't worry about when you get here to pick him up," Dom says. "Juliana and I will make sure he's well taken care of."

"Thanks, Dom. I don't know what I'd do without you. Speaking of which, I just spoke with Cass, and she says your thespian group is on hiatus for a while because so many people have dropped out. She misses you."

"Yeah, I know, but now that we have Juliana, I just don't have the time or the interest anymore."

"Are you sure you don't have the interest? Because I can get my sister to watch both Juliana and Matthew anytime if you want to get back into it." He hesitates just long enough to let me know that I've hit on something. "You'd like to get back into it, wouldn't you?"

"I don't know. Maybe. I did enjoy it."

"Well, think about it, okay? Desi is always willing, and hopefully, things with my work schedule will get more manageable once we find a replacement for Hal. You don't have to shoulder the entire childcare burden yourself."

"It's no burden," he says, and once again I feel like a terrible mother. "I love these kids."

I know he does. It's evident in the way he handles them, the way he smiles at them, and plays with them, and dotes on them. The man was born to be a parent.

"Listen, Dom," I say. "Why don't you work up a schedule of days when my sister can take the kids for you so you can go back to the acting group? I know Desi loves taking care of the kids as much as you do." Like Dom, my sister was born with a nurturing, mothering instinct that I think skipped my genetic roll of the dice. "We can talk more about it tonight when I see you. Right now I need to find Izzy and get to work."

"Okay. See you later. And don't let Izzy overdo it, okay?"

"I got it covered," I assure him.

I disconnect the call and head for Izzy's office. He's not there, so I make my way to the autopsy suite, where I find him standing on the step stool he needs to use in order to reach the autopsy table and whoever is on it. Izzy is the antithesis of me: dark hair to my blond, swarthy complexion to my paleness, barely passing five feet tall when I'm a smidge over six. Spread out on the table in front of him is Craig Knowlton, still dressed in the clothes he was wearing at the motel.

"Ah, perfect timing," Izzy says as I approach. "I'm just getting started. I already X-rayed both victims. I'll get all the basic measurements and start undressing him while you change."

"Okay, be right back."

I head for the locker room, where I grab a pair of scrubs and change out of my street clothes. My cell phone rings, and when I look at the caller ID, I see it's Hurley. I'm too angry to talk to him yet, so I let it go to voice mail.

By the time I return to the autopsy suite, Izzy has Craig's shirt unbuttoned, though it is still on him, and he has cut the undershirt Craig was wearing up the middle front. He has also removed Craig's shoes and socks.

"How are you doing on your third day back to work?" I ask as I step up next to the table. "I was hoping you could ease into things a little slower than this."

"I'm fine," he says dismissively.

I scan him closely with my nurse's eye, trying to determine the truth of his statement. His color looks normal, but there are dark circles under his eyes that didn't used to be there. "You look a little tired," I say, bagging the socks and shoes he has removed.

He shakes his head as if he's about to deny this, but then he pauses and stops what he's doing, looking at me from across the table. "I am a little tired," he admits. "That heart attack took something out of me."

"Are you sure you're okay to be back at work?" I ask, worried. "Doc Morton said he'd be happy to fill in for as long as we want."

"My cardiologist said I'm fine to return to work, though he did say I should start out part-time for now. And I agreed with him. In fact, I've decided to stay part-time."

I stare at him, parsing this last statement. "You mean forever?" I ask, feeling a mix of satisfaction, relief, and sadness. While I'm happy to hear him say he's going to cut back a little, I know that I will miss him. Over the nearly three years we've been working together, Izzy and I have achieved a comfortable rhythm.

"Yes, forever," he says with a little smile. "I've given this a lot of thought over the past few weeks, Mattie. That heart attack was a wake-up call for me. I'm not getting any younger. And I've got Juliana to consider now. These past few weeks at home have been such a delight with her, watching her grow and change. I want to be there for her as much as I can."

His face lights up as he talks about his daughter, and I wince inwardly, once again feeling conflicted about my own state of motherhood. "I think that's a great idea," I tell him, and I truly do, though the news is making my heart ache. "I won't lie to you. I'm going to miss working with you all the time, but Otto Morton is easy enough to work with."

"Good," Izzy says with a sigh of relief. "I was hoping you'd be okay with it. Otto can stay on for a while, but eventually we'll probably start rotating MEs through on my days off. Unless I can find someone to job share."

The idea of rotating MEs makes me groan. We've done this a couple of times in the past when Izzy took time off, and some of the docs who filled in were quite an adjustment.

There was a guy from the Milwaukee area who insisted we zip-tie the ankles together on all of our bodies, just in case there's ever a zombie apocalypse. And there was a woman from up north somewhere who told me how she spent a year back in the seventies living with some cannibal tribe, and then proceeded to tell me what every organ we removed tasted like.

But the awkwardness of these two paled in comparison to Dr. Nick Roman, who I later learned was better known by his regular colleagues as Dr. Necromancer, thanks to his habit of casting spells over any bodies he worked on before touching them, and a macabre collection of mummified objects he had acquired over the years.

"How much are you going to cut back?" I ask Izzy.

"I've talked to Otto, and for now we've agreed to split our weeks. I'll work two days one week, and three the next. We'll each take calls on our working-day nights, and we'll alternate weekends."

"Sounds reasonable," I comment. I help Izzy lift Craig Knowlton's upper body so we can take off his shirt. "Any progress on finding a replacement for Hal?"

Izzy nods. "As a matter of fact, we have a couple of candidates coming in for interviews tomorrow morning, one at eight and one at eight-thirty. Are you doing okay with the extra hours in the meantime?"

"I'm surviving," I say, "but I'll be glad when there's someone else to share the load."

"Why don't you sit in on the interviews with me, give me your take on them since you'll be job-sharing with whomever I hire."

"Thanks," I say. "I'd like that."

Fifteen minutes later, we have removed, bagged, and labeled all of Craig's clothing, and his body is laying naked and exposed on our autopsy table. I'm conducting tests for gunshot residue on his hands; while we had a positive result on the right hand at the motel, I want to retest it here.

Izzy examines the bullet's entry wound more closely. "The stellate tears in the wound are consistent with a contact injury," he says.

"And we're positive again for gunshot residue on his right hand," I say. "Negative on the left."

"Whoever staged this did a good job of making it look like a suicide," Izzy observes.

"Except for the hand thing," I say.

Izzy gives a half-hearted nod, but then appears to capitulate. "Discovering that he's left-handed was a lucky break for us," he says. "Although I suppose one could argue that the man was ambidextrous and we misinterpreted things. Hopefully, we can find some other evidence beside the hand thing to support our theory."

"Speaking of misinterpretations, I'm beginning to wonder if we're ever going to be able to prove that Tomas Wyzinski didn't kill Marla Weber. The case seems to be stagnant, and my guilt increases with each passing day."

Izzy shoots me a look. "You have no reason to feel guilty. All you did was recite the facts. How they were interpreted wasn't up to you."

"Perhaps not, but I did interpret them, pretty much the same way the prosecution and the jury did. I can't help but feel like I've contributed to an injustice."

"Has Hurley made any progress with the investigation?"

"A little," I say in a frustrated tone. "Not as much as I'd like, and what he has uncovered is a little unsettling."

"Fill me in," Izzy says.

"Well, he figured out a possible meaning for some of the items on that cryptic list Hal left behind on his thumb drive." I share Hurley's theory about the Kupper family.

Izzy lets out a low whistle. "A judge, a congressman, and a lawyer? That's a big can of worms."

"No kidding."

"So what is he going to do now?"

"We're going to look into the people who live in the Kenilworth area near the cell tower that picked up calls both Hal and Carolyn Abernathy made while they were in Chicago. Maybe it's a coincidence they were both there not long before they were killed, but you know how Hurley feels about coincidences."

"The same as I do. But that's a rather large field to search. How is he going to narrow it down?"

"For now, we're going to look to see if any familiar names or titles pop up. Maybe we can find someone with a connection to the pharmaceutical industry."

"It sounds like a long shot," Izzy says with a grimace.

"It probably is, but it's the best we have for now. We're going to put Laura on it. She's good at mining information like that, and it ought to keep her busy for a while. I told Hurley I thought we should make a run at Tomas Wyzinski, too, to try to get him to talk. But Hurley doesn't think we'll get anywhere."

"I'm inclined to agree with him," Izzy says in a grudging tone. "If the man is willing to spend the rest of his life in prison to stay quiet, I doubt he's going to open up simply in the name of justice."

We work in silence for several minutes as we finish undressing, washing, and scouring Craig Knowlton's body for clues. When we turn him over, Izzy's face takes on an "Aha!" expression.

CHAPTER 11

"What?" I ask Izzy, knowing he's hit on something important.

"I thought it seemed odd that these two victims were laid out so peacefully in that motel room. Look at the lividity here." He points to Craig's backside. "What does it tell you?"

I examine the dark purple coloring in Craig's back, which is consistent with the blood in his body settling in the most downward spots, pulled there by gravity. Except there is a greater amount of the purplish hue in the upper part of his buttocks and his lower back, and almost none along the bottoms of his butt cheeks. And there is also a blanched line that runs across his upper thighs, indicating that something linear applied pressure there after he died. I point to this line first. "Anything on the bed that would have caused this mark?" I ask.

Izzy shakes his head, the start of a smile creeping over his lips.

"And the lividity seems more in keeping with a body that was in a sitting position, at least part of the time," I say.

Izzy's hint of a smile breaks into a full-fledged grin. "Bingo," he says with a touch of pride.

I shift my gaze from Craig Knowlton's backside to Izzy.

"He didn't die in the bed," I say. I flash back to the motel room, envisioning the other furnishings and the scene in the bed, and frown. "But there was blood and brain matter splattered on the bed and pillow, and on Meredith Lansing, if I remember correctly."

Izzy nods. "He was shot in the bed, there's no doubt about that. I'm guessing someone held the gun in his hand, put it to his head, and pulled the trigger. But he was already dead when it happened. Not long dead, however. Just long enough to give us that flawed lividity pattern, which I think is likely from him being sat up in a car seat."

"If we can find the car with a line on the seat that matches the one on his thighs . . ."

Izzy nods.

"So what killed him?"

"I'm guessing he was sedated with something, and whatever it was turned out to be too much for him. It will be interesting to see if we find any similar evidence on Meredith's body. In the meantime, we'll likely have to wait for the tox screen. We should analyze the stomach contents and take a close look at his skin to see if we can find any puncture wounds."

We do so, hunting for any tiny bruises or pinpricks, but if there are any, we can't find them. Once that is done, we proceed with the rest of the autopsy. We find nothing unusual in the body itself, and when we empty his stomach, we find what appears to be some sort of pasta with a red sauce and, judging from the smell, a good amount of alcohol. We package it up to send off to Madison along with the vitreous fluid from the eye, blood, and the small amount of urine that is in his bladder. We keep samples of each here, as well. Arnie can analyze all the fluids, but he is essentially a one-man show, even though Laura Kingston kicks in to help him at times. Laura isn't trained or certified to run the various diagnostic and analytic equipment. She has some very useful other talents, however, thanks to her past indecisiveness when it came to career choices. She had an MBA before she decided it was too boring and switched her focus to forensic science, where she specialized in forensic botany and toxicology. For this particular case, she might be able to help Arnie analyze the bodily fluids, and she'll also be able to help Jonas with the forensic accounting, thanks to her MBA. This thought gives me an idea, and I make a mental note to mention it to Hurley, assuming I ever speak to him again.

As if he is reading my mind, Izzy says, "How is wedded bliss treating you?"

I flash back to the comments Hurley made earlier and suppress a shudder. "It's okay," I say.

"Just okay?" Izzy narrows his eyes at me. "You're married less than a month, and already the glow has worn off?" He arches his eyebrows at me as he finishes making an incision around the sides and top of Craig's scalp.

"Things have been a little tense lately," I say, proving my astounding talent at understatement. "We're breaking ground on the new house, and I think once we get it built and our work schedules settle down a little, it will be better."

"Any plans for a honeymoon?" Izzy asks as he dissects Craig's scalp away from the skull, peeling it forward so that it ends up lying inside out over the man's face.

"Sure," I say in a highly sarcastic tone. "Just as soon as Matthew grows up, our work schedules calm down, and Hurley gets his head out of his ass."

Izzy arches his eyebrows again. He has picked up the bone saw in preparation for opening the skull, but he pauses, the saw held in one hand. "Uh-oh," he says. "What has the heathen done now?"

I reiterate the conversation Hurley and I had earlier, finishing it off with the snide comment Hurley made right before I stalked off. When I'm done, Izzy turns the saw on, and the noise he makes snuffs out any chance to continue our conversation until he finishes.

"Give Hurley a pass on this one," Izzy says, once he's done with the saw. "I'm sure he said it out of frustration and fatigue. It can't be easy for him adjusting to fatherhood the way he's had to, and I can promise you he didn't marry you just because of Matthew."

"I didn't say he did," I say, annoyed at Izzy's ability to read my mind.

"No, but you were thinking it."

"You men all stick together," I mutter irritably.

Izzy cocks his head to one side and gives me a sardonic look. "I'm not saying that what Hurley said was right or even justified. But sometimes, when things get really stressful, we lose our filters and say things to the ones we love that are meant to hurt. It's not nice, it's not pretty, but we all do it. I've done it to Dom, you've done it to Hurley, Dom's done it to me . . ." He pauses and winces before continuing. "Though I have to admit I've been the more frequent offender between the two of us." He shrugs this off. "Mostly it's a defensive move, or a way to postpone talking about difficult topics. Hurley is a smart guy, and he's in love with you, Mattie. I'm willing to bet he'll come around and apologize."

"Indeed I will," says a voice behind me, and both Izzy and I look toward the door to the suite and see Hurley standing there. "I had to come anyway to see what, if anything, you've turned up on the autopsies, but I'm also here because you didn't answer my call." He is looking directly at me when he says this.

"I was in a hurry," I say, looking away from him. Izzy rolls his eyes. "And I admit I was angry, and a little hurt by what you said."

"I know, and I'm sorry." He sounds genuinely remorseful. "I'm tired and frustrated by these unsolved cases, and trying to balance work with family. And I feel like I'm failing at both. That's not an excuse for what I said; there is no excuse for that except to say that I can be an ass at times. And while I have to admit that the way everything happened in my ac-quiring a family wasn't the way I would have liked for it to go down, I can honestly say that you, Emily, and Matthew are the best things that have ever happened in my life, and the most important."

He has walked over to the head of the autopsy table while talking, and he stands there now and calls my name.

"Mattie? Please look at me."

I do so.

"I love you. I love our family. And I wouldn't trade it for anything in the world." He shoots me an air-kiss, and at that very second, Izzy opens Craig's skullcap, exposing the brain. The bone comes loose with a sucking noise, followed by a distinct *pop* that is perfectly timed with the kiss.

Someone's exposed brain is not the most romantic setting for exchanging air-kisses, I'll grant you, but my heart does a little flip-flop anyway, much the same way Craig's heart did not too long ago when I almost dropped it before getting it onto the scale. When you have the kinds of jobs and hours we do, you take your intimate moments however you can get them.

"I don't know what I'd do if something ever happened to you," Hurley continues.

"Most likely twenty-five to life."

Izzy lets out a little huff, and I can't tell if he's amused or dismayed. But Hurley's eyes take on a twinkle, and I see the corners of his mouth twitch. That's why I love this man. He gets me. He gets me in a way no other person on earth does.

"So are we okay?" he asks me.

"We're better than okay," I say. "That sweet little apology of yours is going to get you something special tonight." I give him a wink and hear Izzy huff again, louder this time. The blue in Hurley's eyes darkens, a wicked grin curls his lips, and it's all I can do to keep my mind on the job at hand.

"You guys have dirty minds," I say in a chastising tone, focusing on tissue and bone. "I'm referring to Matthew's bath. You haven't done one with him in a long time, and since you're in this loving family mode today, I figured I'd let you have that fun experience all to yourself tonight."

Hurley's wicked smile fades, and his mouth forms into a pout. Izzy snorts back a laugh. A few seconds of rebooting silence follows, and then Hurley gets back to business.

"Got anything of interest for me yet?" he asks.

"We found GSR on Craig's right hand—no surprise—and there is stippling around the entry wound consistent with a contact wound like you'd find in a suicide," Izzy says. "However, I don't think the head wound is what killed him."

"What?" Hurley says, sounding shocked.

"Hold on," Izzy says. He removes Craig's brain and examines it. "Yep, this confirms it," he says. He points to the damaged tissue where the bullet entered and exited. "There is hardly any bleeding here. This wound was delivered postmortem."

"He was already dead when he was shot?" Hurley says, still sounding like he thinks he isn't hearing things right.

"He was," Izzy says with a definitive nod. "I suspected something was off at the motel when I saw how little bleeding there was from the wound. Head wounds typically bleed very heavily. Once I got Mr. Knowlton back here and was able to look at his body more closely, I noticed that the lividity suggests he died in a sitting position. What's more, I don't think he died in that motel room."

Hurley blinks hard and scratches his head. "Explain that to me more," he says, and Izzy does, reiterating the evidence he and I discovered earlier, including our theory that the man was drugged with something, and that he died in a car on the way to the motel. "Based on his stomach contents, he had consumed a lot of alcohol," Izzy says. "It, combined with whatever was used to drug him, may have been fatal."

I think about Laura's comment regarding how lefties tend to drink more than righties, and wonder if that held true for Craig.

Hurley takes a moment to digest things as Izzy starts slicing sections of Craig Knowlton's brain. He then takes out his phone and calls Jonas, telling him to take pictures of all the seats in both of the cars we confiscated and swab them for DNA evidence. After disconnecting the call, he looks at Izzy and asks, "What about Meredith Lansing? Did the bullet wound kill her?"

"I don't know," Izzy says. "We haven't gotten to her yet."

"How long do you think it will be?" Hurley asks.

"We're almost done with Mr. Knowlton here," Izzy says. "Give me half an hour to record some notes on our findings, and then we'll get started on Mrs. Lansing. Give me two hours for that one."

Hurley nods, takes out his ever-present notebook, and starts writing things down.

"Any progress on your end?" Izzy asks.

"Some," Hurley says. "Jonas was able to run a forensic analysis on the victims' cell phones. I don't know if Mattie told you this or not, but we found four phones total, two burners—one for each of them—and two others that appear to be their day-to-day phones. They definitely had contact with one another through calls and text messages on the burner phones, going back about a month. And the most recent text messages suggest that Meredith was having second thoughts about the affair and wanted to end it. Craig, on the other hand, wanted to move things along, so much so that he claimed he was willing to leave his wife."

"So they were having an affair, and one of the spouses found out about it and decided to kill them, not knowing that Meredith was trying to end things?" I suggest.

"Maybe," Hurley says. "Your theory answers one thing that was bothering me. I couldn't figure out how the killer managed to get the drop on the two of them so easily. There's no hint of any struggle or resistance from either of the victims. But if they were drugged, that explains it."

"We'll run a full tox report on them both, including the stomach contents," Izzy says. "But it will take some time to get the results back. Depending on how obscure the drug is, it might take a week or more."

"I understand," Hurley says, sounding resigned but unhappy. "Give me what you got when you got it." His phone dings with a text message, and he looks at it, swiping at his screen. After a moment, he holds it up so we can see it and swipes through a series of pictures Jonas sent him of the car seats.

Izzy studies the pictures and shakes his head. "I don't see anything in either car that would have caused that mark on Knowlton's legs," he says. "Maybe it was a piece of furniture somewhere."

"We'll keep looking," Hurley says.

"We should let Laura have a run at the finances of both couples," I say. "Jonas is capable, but Laura has more knowledge in that area. While it seems likely that jealousy was a primary motive here, there might have been others. So I'd like to dig a little deeper into the insurance policies that were in place. We know the one policy on Meredith wasn't for that much money, but combined with the work one and the retirement money, it is more than enough to give her husband a new start. And the fact that Craig was killed one day after the suicide clause expired seems like too much of a coincidence. We could chat with the agents who issued the policies, see if they recall any conversations that might have taken place when the policies were taken out."

"Agreed," Hurley says. "I suppose I can put Laura on that, too."

"I'll do it," I say. Technically such inquiries fall within the realm of my job as a medicolegal death investigator, but I also know I'm motivated as much by personal curiosity as I am our case, given that Patty Volker is the agent on both policies. But I keep this to myself.

Hurley considers this. "That should be okay," he says. "At this point, I'll take all the help I can get."

After another brief silence, Izzy says, "Mattie tells me you've made some progress on the investigation into Hal's case."

Hurley makes a frustrated grimace. "Not enough," he says. "I talked to a friend of mine who's with the FBI because I think it's too involved for us to handle alone, but he didn't think there was enough for them to go on. We already know who killed Hal, Tina, and Carolyn Abernathy, and he's dead, so as far as they're concerned, those cases are closed. And they think Marla Weber's killer has been caught and convicted, as well."

"You told your FBI friend that Prince was blackmailed into it?" Izzy asks.

"I did," Hurley says with a sigh of resignation, "but there isn't any proof of that other than the man's dying declaration to me. I've already given Laura the task of trying to match up names of people who live in the Kenilworth area near the cell towers that both Hal and Carolyn pinged off of to see if any connections pop up."

"Yeah, Mattie mentioned that," Izzy says. "Sounds like a long shot."

"Maybe," Hurley says, though he seems relatively upbeat about the idea. "I've also got Arnie and Laura digging into the Big Pharma industry to see if they can sort out the corporate maze and find anything useful, but it looks like these guys cover their tracks all too well."

"Mattie told me your theory about the Kuppers," Izzy

says. "Those are some high-powered suspects you're dealing with."

Hurley nods, a sober expression on his face. "It might help if we could definitively decipher Hal's cryptic notes, but we haven't had much luck with that other than my suspicions about those initials. I can't be sure I'm right, and unless we can find something that clarifies it all . . ." He shrugs, letting us reach the conclusion on our own. "We've searched everything in Hal's house, in Tina's house, and on both of their phones and computers. If there's a clue in there anywhere, we didn't find it."

"Or perhaps you just didn't recognize it," Izzy says.

Hurley shoots him a bemused look.

"Sometimes we see what we expect to see," Izzy says. "Try thinking outside the box."

Hurley gives Izzy a look of amused tolerance. I can tell he thinks Izzy is just spouting some clichéd phrase he heard somewhere. In fact, I'm almost positive I read something just like that on a fortune cookie I got from Peking Palace a while ago. But the longer I think about what Izzy just said, the more I feel like there's something to it. I sense a tiny niggle in my brain, a nudge that I know means those words have triggered something, some memory or connection that is deeply buried. But I can't quite unearth it yet. I make a mental note to take another look at that list Hal left.

"I'd like to stay for the autopsies," Hurley says in a tired, resigned tone, "but I need to go get Matthew and drop him off with Dom. Plus, I've got tons of stuff to do at the station. Let me know what you find when you're done."

Izzy nods, and with that, Hurley leaves us to our grim duties.

CHAPTER 12

As soon as Hurley's out the door, Izzy gives me a look.

"What?" I say.

"He *is* a bit testier than usual."

"I know. We both are. I think it's a combination of the usual stuff . . . worries about money, worries about the kids, worries about the job, worries about the new house . . . there's a lot on our plates right now."

"It will get easier," Izzy says.

I hope he's right. I've already racked up one failed marriage; I don't want to become a serial divorcer.

We finish Craig's autopsy—Izzy lets me sew Humpty Dumpty back together again while he goes to dictate and write down his findings—and when I'm done, I bag Craig up and move his body back to the morgue fridge.

We decide to take a quick lunch break before starting on Meredith. I grab a BLT sandwich from a shop two blocks down and top it off with a bag of Cheetos—the lunch of champions. We eat together in the breakroom, and Izzy eyes my meal with an expression that looks disturbingly like lust. His lunch—lovingly prepared by Dom, he mentions—consists of some carrot sticks, some rye crackers with something that looks like either chicken or tuna salad to go with them, an apple, and a low-calorie yogurt for dessert.

"I'm glad to see you're eating healthier," I comment.

Izzy drops a rye cracker back into the cute little multi-sectioned Tupperware container it came in with a puff of disgust. "If I have to eat like this for the rest of my life, I think I'd rather be dead."

"Izzy," I admonish.

"I mean it, Mattie." He picks up the rye cracker he dropped a moment ago and bangs it on the tabletop, crumbling it. "This is like eating wood. And the chicken salad wouldn't be so bad except Dom made it with low-fat mayo, and there's no taste to it. I might as well be eating that white paste they give kids in kindergarten."

I know the change must be hard for him. Dom is an amazing cook, and his specialties are Italian dishes that are typically rich with creams, sauces, and all kinds of bad fats that taste spectacularly good. It dawns on me then that Izzy's new diet means the likelihood of my getting to enjoy one of Dom's yummy creations anytime in the near future is small, if not nonexistent. My stomach growls in protest at the thought.

"You're looking good," I tell Izzy, trying to provide encouragement. "I can tell you've lost some weight."

"Of course I have," he grumbles. "How could I not, given that all I eat is cardboard, roots, paste, and sticks? Not to mention that cardiac rehab tyrant who keeps running me through the paces. That witch seems determined to turn me into Arnold Schwarzenegger. The other day she made me sweat so much on the cycling machine that someone nearby suggested they put a kiddie pool beneath me."

I snort back a laugh, and Izzy shoots me a mean look. Though in my defense, I do have some sympathy for him. When I was going to the gym with Bob Richmond in support of his weight-loss efforts (trying hard to ignore the fact that I needed my own efforts in that regard), I experienced some torturous moments at the hands of my personal trainer, Gunther. I spent many a workout session imagining how easy it would be to use those exercise machines as torture devices on Gunther for revenge. It's not easy for me to admit it, but I loathe exercise simply for the sake of exercise. And these days, I get plenty just chasing my son around, trying to maintain a household, and working full-time.

Izzy looks so miserable that for a moment I seriously consider offering him a piece of bacon from my sandwich. But then I envision his mother, Sylvie, finding out about it and seeking revenge. Izzy's mother is a tiny woman who looks quite frail, but looks can be deceiving. I've seen her sport her walker like a weapon, and her verbal barbs are capable of piercing the strongest armor.

Once we're done eating—or in Izzy's case, kvetching and mourning—I go and fetch Meredith's body from the fridge and wheel her into the autopsy room. By the time Izzy joins me, I have her on the autopsy table ready to go.

Our autopsy process is a routine one, and that can get boring at times. But the routines are in place for a reason. Skipping or skimming over any one step might mean missing a critical piece of evidence. For me, the hardest trick is to not let the tedium of the routines lull me into a state of inattention. It would be easy to let muscle memory take over and lose focus.

We carefully remove Meredith's blouse and shorts, and I dutifully bag and tag them. But when it comes time to remove her underwear, I pause, frowning.

"Izzy, this is all wrong," I say.

"What do you mean?"

"Her underwear. Look at it. Her panties are plain white cotton, obviously old because the material has separated from the elastic in places and they look like they've been washed hundreds of times. And her bra isn't any better. It's basic 18-hour Playtex kind of stuff: white, ordinary, and, again, old. You can tell from the wear and tear on the straps, and the underarm stains."

Izzy stares at the underwear for a few seconds and then shakes his head. "I guess I'm not seeing what you're seeing," he says. "Help me out."

"It's a girl thing, or a girl hooking up with a guy thing," I say. "That's why you don't see it, although I would imagine guys hooking up with guys do it to some extent. Maybe." Izzy stares at me over the top of his glasses. "Or maybe not. Let me paint you a picture. Meredith and Craig just met, what, a month ago or so? She went to him about her retirement plan; the texts and e-mails only go back a month, so I think it's a safe assumption. That means their affair is a relatively new one. Except I'm not convinced they were having one."

"You don't think Meredith and Craig were having an affair?" Izzy says, his voice rife with skepticism.

"I can't say for sure, but I have my doubts because of this underwear. When a girl hooks up with a new guy, whether she's single, married, or somewhere in between, she's going to wear her very best lingerie, not the ragged, old, washed-a-million-times, only-wear-them-during-my-period undies. She's going to have on the colorful, racy, Victoria's Secret kind of stuff, not this." I wave a hand over Meredith's body. "And Meredith has that kind of underwear. I saw some of it when we were in her apartment. This is the stuff you wear when you've been married or living together for a long time, when you're more comfortable with one another, and when you have a kid and a job that suck up every spare minute of your life, leaving you exhausted and feeling about as sexy as a barbed-wire fence."

Izzy shoots me a wary side glance, and I realize my voice grew a little shrill toward the end of my last statement.

"I take it you're wearing undies like Meredith's," he says finally.

"I am, and I'm not proud of it," I tell him. "I think it's important for couples to keep some fun and interest in their sex life. I got too blasé with David, and I'm determined not to let that happen again. But lately I'm just so damned tired all the time that the idea of sex seems like work, just one more duty I have to check off on my to-do list."

Izzy's eyes widen. He looks away and makes duck lips while he tries to think of something to say.

"Too much information?" I ask, wincing.

"No, not exactly," he says, looking back down at Meredith's underwear. "In fact, in the context of what we're doing here and the investigation, it's very valuable information, at least in the general form. I'm just not sure what to say about your personal issues."

"I shouldn't have said anything. Sorry. It just blurted out."

"If you need to talk about it, I'm willing to listen," he says. "But maybe we should shelve it for later? When we're done here?"

"Right. Yes. Of course." My cheeks are burning hot, and I know my face is turning as red as a baboon's ass, which is what I feel like I am right now.

"Your point about the underwear is an interesting one," Izzy says. "I'm just not sure how it plays into the overall picture. And if Meredith and Craig weren't having an affair, what motive have we got?"

He has a point. Even if the murder-suicide thing was staged by someone else, we've been working under the assumption that Craig and Meredith were likely killed by a jealous spouse who discovered the affair. If they weren't having an affair, what motive is left? Just money. I start backtracking on my theory.

"The text messages did seem to hint at Meredith wanting

to end the affair," I say. "So maybe she wore her old undies as a way of making a statement to that effect."

"Unless she wanted one last roll in the hay for old time's sake," Izzy suggests.

I sag and gape at him. "Which side of this debate are you on?" I ask him.

"Whatever side gets us to the truth. You make a valid point. I think we need to keep it in mind."

With both of us placated for the moment, we remove the suspect underwear and bag it. Then I help Izzy examine Meredith's skin closely, looking for any puncture marks, wounds, or unusual bruises. Unlike Craig, Meredith's lividity is in keeping with the scene at the motel, her death occurring in the bed from the gunshot to her chest. The entry wound has a stellate pattern with a minimal ring of gunpowder stippling around it, meaning it was likely a contact wound. The exit wound on her back has more of a torn appearance.

We move on to the internal exam, and the stomach contents are a mirror image of Craig's: pasta, red sauce, and some sort of alcohol-based drink. At first blush, Meredith's internal exam doesn't seem to reveal any more surprises or significant finds other than the known bullet wound.

Then Izzy says, "Look at the bullet track. What do you see?"

I look at the area, studying it closely. The bullet's trajectory is an upward one, entering just to the right of her sternum—our right, not hers—between two ribs, shattering part of one and tearing the cartilage in between them. From there, it passes through the right ventricle, exiting to the left of her spine—or what would be her right—just below her scapula. I run through some scenarios in my head, recalling the scene in the motel. "It's a slight upward trajectory," I say, "and also from right to left as we're looking at her. It looks like whoever fired the bullet was probably straddling her in the bed, and firing with their right hand."

Izzy nods, looking pleased. "Let's assume for a moment that Craig was ambidextrous and did fire with his right hand. If he was straddling Meredith in the bed when he shot her, what other evidence might we expect to find?"

I wrack my tired brain, thinking, and imagining the scene. "Gunpowder residue?" I say. "On his clothes. On his pants."

Izzy smiles. "Very good," he says. "We need to do GSR testing on Craig's clothing."

"Should I do it now?"

"Go ahead."

I back away from the table, strip off my gloves and gown, and head for the evidence locker. Once I find the packages containing the appropriate clothing items, I bring them back into the autopsy suite, don fresh gloves, open the seals, and remove the clothing. Then I take pads out of a GSR kit and start wiping along the surfaces of Craig's shirt, and then his pants. I dedicate one swab to each specific area of the clothing—doing the lapels of the shirt first, then the right and left sides of the collar, then the shoulders, then the fronts of the short sleeves, and finally six different sections of the shirt front. I spray the reactant on each swab and watch for a reaction.

The only one that comes up positive is the test I do on the right side of Craig's collar, shoulder, and sleeve, which is not surprising given that the gunshot wound was on the right side of his head. We already know Craig was left-handed, so the whole right-sided thing is a major red flag. But just in case someone tried to argue that Craig might have fired with his right hand, the lack of GSR on the rest of his shirt is damning.

Izzy watches me as he continues with Meredith's internal exam, and I give him a running dialogue of my results. I move on to the pants, swiping sections along the front with another dozen swabs. None of these tests positive for GSR.

"So there it is," I say when I'm done. "No GSR on Craig's clothes where we would expect to find it if he had straddled Meredith when he shot her."

"This case just gets curiouser and curiouser," Izzy says.

"We need to test for GSR on the clothes John and Pamela were wearing," I say. "And any other dirty clothing we can find in their houses. I need to call Hurley right away."

CHAPTER 13

Hurley answers on the second ring. "What have you got for me, Squatch?" he says.

I fill him in on our findings: the bullet trajectory, the underwear, and the GSR testing.

"I'll get on it right away," Hurley says.

A few seconds of silence stretch between us until I say, "Thank you for the apology, Hurley. It meant a lot to me. What you said to me earlier, I know it was born out of frustration and exhaustion. I know you didn't mean it."

I hear him sigh on the other end, and a second, more uncomfortable silence ensues. I wait him out.

"Look, Squatch, I'd like to discuss this more, but I can't do it now. So suffice to say, I love you. And in my mind, that's all that matters. It's enough to get us through whatever life throws at us."

I can't swallow; there's a huge lump in my throat. And for a moment I can't speak either. But I finally manage to eke out a few words, and I think they're enough. "I love you, too, Hurley. More than you know."

With that, I disconnect the call, letting him go do what he needs to do. Izzy, who has overheard the entire conversation, says nothing as I once again don a paper gown and a fresh pair of gloves. When I return to my spot at the autopsy table, there is a satisfied smile on his face.

Half an hour later we are almost done with Meredith's autopsy when Cass pokes her head into the room. "You guys have another call," she announces, and I squeeze my eyes closed in frustration.

"I can go if you want to stitch up Meredith," Izzy offers.

I shake my head. "You've done enough today. You need to rest. You're not that far out from your heart attack. I'll get Doc Morton to come with me." I glance at my watch. "He's taking call tonight anyway, right?" Izzy nods. "So we'll put him to work a little early. I'm sure he won't mind."

Cass says, "You can debate which doc takes this call all day long, but either way I think Mattie has to go."

In unison, Izzy and I both turn to her and say, "Why?"

"Because the body is on the property you and Hurley bought. Your contractor unearthed it when he was digging for your foundation. Hurley said he'll pick you up out front in ten minutes." She pauses and looks at her watch. "And that was almost five minutes ago."

Well, isn't this just grand? Not only does this mean that our whole construction schedule will likely be pushed back, it also means we're planning to build our house on potentially haunted ground. Not that I believe in ghosts—at least not the menacing, harmful kind. I find the living to be much scarier than the dead. I do believe there is an energy inside all of us that gets released when we die, and what happens to it is anyone's guess. But the idea of living in a house built above a burial ground is a little creepy. And if it turns out to be some sort of historic or Native American burial site—they are scattered all over Wisconsin—we might not be able to build at all.

Just when I think life can't get any more complicated, Cass proves me wrong. "And I should probably warn you, it isn't just any dead body. According to Hurley, the contractor says it's the body of a space alien."

Izzy and I stare at each other with matching expressions of incredulity. "You go," Izzy says with a hint of a smile. "I can sew Meredith up faster than you can. Give Otto a call and see if he's available. If he is, let him go. If he's not, let me know, and I'll come out there."

I step away from the table and peel off my gloves. "You're afraid it's real," I tease Izzy, though to be honest, I'm glad he's playing things safe and sensibly. He looks tired, and he's been on his feet for two autopsies and five hours now, and it's only his third full day back at work. I'm worried about him.

Izzy shoots me a cautionary look. "Just don't let Arnie get wind of it," he says. "If you think his conspiracy theories have been crazy up until now, I'm betting this will make those look tame."

"Um, about that," Cass says with a sheepish look. "Arnie already knows about it. He was at my desk when the call came in. That's why it took me a few minutes to get back here." She shrugs and gives us an apologetic look. "I'll go call Doc Morton for you and let you know what he says." With that, she beats a hasty retreat from the room.

Izzy wishes me luck as I head for the bathroom to change into some fresh scrubs. I don't have time for a shower, much as I'd like one, but I do a quick sink washup before heading out front. Hurley is there waiting for me.

I hop in the car and give him a tentative smile, some small part of me hoping this is some kind of practical joke. But judging from the tired, worn look on his face, I feel certain it is real.

"This may be a late night for one or both of us," I say. "We should run by the house so I can get my car."

He says nothing; he simply nods and pulls into traffic.

"Cass said the contractor thinks the body is a space alien?" I say in a half-joking tone, still clinging to a meager hope that

Hurley will break into a smile and say "Gotcha!" But all he does is look over at me and roll his eyes.

"Arnie knows," I tell him.

This makes him let out a long, heavy sigh. He shakes his head woefully.

"Helluva day, isn't it?" I say, trying to sound chipper. Still he says nothing. Exasperated, I turn toward him as much as my seat belt will allow. "Hurley, what's going on? Why aren't you talking to me? I thought we fixed things earlier."

"Sorry," he says, flexing his fingers on the steering wheel. He flashes me a meager smile. "It's not you or us. I'm just tired and frustrated. And angry with myself for not collecting the extra clothing from our suspects earlier, or doing a more thorough search at Lansing's place. I should have been on top of that right away."

"Okay," I say with a shrug. "So we move on. We'll figure it out."

"Maybe not," he says. "Junior called me a bit ago to tell me that John Lansing is refusing to let anyone in his apartment at this point. He told Junior we've taken enough of his stuff and that literally taking the clothes off his back was going too far, particularly since it was someone else who killed his wife. So now we're trying to get a warrant, but I'm not sure we will. I want to search both houses for potential sedating agents, too, but without knowing what it is we're looking for, and with no definitive proof that the victims were sedated, I doubt that's going to happen. And just to add to the fun, guess what judge is on call for the warrant?"

"Who?"

"Judge Kupper."

"Oh." I frown at this.

"Yeah," Hurley says. "If he's involved in this case with Hal and Tina, then he has to suspect that Jeremy Prince talked to me before he was killed, especially if they've tried to find his family. I don't know that he'd be blatant about making my life miserable, but it wouldn't surprise me if he tested me a bit, to see what shakes out.

"And on top of all that," he goes on, "I think both John and Pamela are beginning to suspect that this wasn't the simple murder-suicide we told them it was. At the rate things are going, they'll probably both lawyer up any minute now." He rolls his lips in and shakes his head.

"Don't beat yourself up over it," I tell him. "Mistakes happen. We're both exhausted. And I goofed up, too. I searched the medicine cabinets in both houses. There was a prescription for some sleeping pills at Meredith Lansing's place. I forgot about that." I slap myself upside the head, both literally and figuratively. "I need to tell Arnie so he knows to look for that drug in our victims."

I've never seen Hurley this down before, this defeated-looking. I know we're both exhausted and stressed out, but Hurley has been under more stress in the past, and he handled it just fine. I'm worried about him. I reach over and gently massage the back of his neck. The muscles there are hard and taut beneath my fingers, so I continue for the short ride to our house.

Hurley pulls up to the curb behind my hearse to let me out. He shifts into park, reaches behind his neck, and grabs my hand, kissing the back of it. It's a sweet gesture that makes my stomach flip-flop.

"Hey," I say with a wink, "at least all this chaos in our lives will cure you of those thoughts you've been having lately about us having another kid."

He breaks into a sly grin and winks at me. "Nope, I still want another one."

I gape at him and pull my hand back, narrowing my eyes at him. "Okay, where are you hiding the stuff?"

"What stuff?" he says, cocking his head to the side.

"Your whips, chains, and leather," I say. "Clearly you're a

closet masochist. There's no other explanation for this level of insanity."

He breaks into a loud belly laugh, and it does my heart good to see his mood improved, even if only for a minute or two. I get out of the car, climb into my hearse, and then follow Hurley as he drives out to our new home site.

The land we bought is a total of five acres that belonged a farmer in the area who no longer farms and is selling off parcels to finance his retirement. It's a quick ten-minute drive, through and out of town, five of which we spend at stoplights that I hope aren't an indication of how the rest of my day is going to go. Along the drive, Cass calls and tells me that Doc Morton will meet me at the site. "And you should probably know that Arnie is already headed out there, too," she adds. "He thought you might need some help processing the scene."

This elicits a smile from me. Arnie hates doing scene work. He's a lab rat by nature, and he likes his machines, and his slides, and his reference books, and his clean, sterile work area. But given that the man can find a conspiracy hiding inside a roll of toilet paper, it's not hard to figure out why he's offering to help out with this particular scene. His paranoia, while amusing, is also useful in his job. I've seen him suss out clues so obscure and well-hidden that most people would never find them. But given his hard-held beliefs in things like aliens, I fear it may be difficult to rein him in with this case.

The road up to the top of the bluff is a rutted dirt track for now, though we plan to grade it and maybe even pave it at some point since it will be our driveway once the house is done. I follow Hurley up it, eating his dust both literally and figuratively, until we reach the flatter area above.

I see that Arnie is already there when we arrive. There are four construction workers and the head contractor, Marvin Holmes—a moniker that makes me wonder if his name helped him decide on his career—standing around. Marvin has met me before, and he knows I drive a hearse. His workers, however, who all look like members of a third-world chain gang, stare at my car with wide eyes and gaping mouths.

Marvin came highly recommended by several doctors I know who have used him to build their own homes, so I hope his workers only look like criminals and lowlifes because of the hard work they've spent their lives doing on other job sites. At the moment, they are all standing around an excavator that is sitting near the edge of a large, raw wound in the ground, a rectangular area that is some fifty feet wide and seventy long.

As I approach this gargantuan hole, I see that the depth of it varies. On one end, it goes down nearly twelve feet, but on the other, the end where the excavator is currently parked, it is only about five feet deep. Since that's where everyone else is standing, I make my way there and peer into the hole.

I can see why the body was reported to be an alien. There is an entire skull lying cockeyed on a small shelf of dirt about five feet below the edge. It's abnormally shaped. Despite appearing small, like a child's skull, the top is large and bulbous-looking, the jawline narrow. The eye sockets look larger than usual, and they are set far apart. A few feet away I can see what appears to be a rib cage half embedded in the dirt.

Marvin says, "The skull came out of the ground, caught on one of the bucket teeth. It fell off as my guy started to swing the bucket around, and as soon as we realized what it was we stopped digging and called you guys." He pauses, and winces. "I think Lenny—he's the scoop operator—might have scraped over the skull with the bucket."

Otto arrives and walks over to where the rest of us are standing, and I fill him in on what Marvin just told us. When I'm done, we all fall silent as we stare at the bones. I can tell from where I'm standing that the rib bones don't look normal either. The cage is small and narrow—almost forming a cylindrical shape—and the sternum is misshapen.

A minute or so goes by before Hurley says, "Is it a child?"

Arnie, who has been shifting back and forth from one foot to the next, clearly excited, says, "It's an alien skull. I mean, just look at it! It's like the Starchild skeleton."

"Starchild?" Hurley asks, making me wince. The last thing Arnie needs is any sort of encouragement, but it's too late now.

Arnie gives Hurley a disdainful look and then brings us all up to speed, whether we want him to or not. "The Starchild skull was unearthed in 1930 from a mine about a hundred miles southwest of Chihuahua, Mexico. They found it with another, normal skeleton. The Starchild skull looks just like this one, bulbous and big on top, flat in the back, with the eyes close-set. And I'm betting our skull won't have any frontal sinuses, just like that one."

Arnie pauses and gives his rapt audience a distrustful look. "Supposedly," he goes on in a skeptical tone that makes it clear he doesn't believe what he's about to say, "DNA testing proved the Starchild skull was human, because they found both an X and a Y chromosome. But that was based on a minimal amount of partially degraded DNA. It doesn't mean it wasn't an alien hybrid. For all we know, the aliens might have Y chromosomes just like ours. Or perhaps they somehow altered the fetus in a woman who was already pregnant."

The chain gang members all take a couple steps back, though I'm not sure if they're trying to distance themselves from the skull or from Arnie.

I give Arnie my best skeptic's look.

"Come on," he says, seeing the same expression on Hurley and Otto. "Are you going to tell me that ancient men were able to build things like the Egyptian pyramids and the Mayan temples without some form of advanced technological assistance? And is it a coincidence that ancient drawings from these areas feature men with large, bulbous heads and small facial features? What about the geoglyphs, the Nazca lines in Peru, giant figures that can only be identified if you're looking at them from up in the sky? They look like landing strips, and those ancient people had no way to make such a thing, not to mention a need for it." He pauses and his eyes grow wide. "Or did they?" he asks in a dramatic, suggestible tone.

Otto, who has stood by with admirable patience up until now, says, "Arnie, I hate to burst your bubble, but odds are this skeleton is from a child who may have suffered from hydrocephalus."

"Hydro-what?" one of the chain gang members says. "Is it contagious?" They all back up another step.

Otto shakes his head. "Hydrocephalus simply means fluid on the brain. It's caused by a birth defect, not a disease."

I look at Otto and say, "I'll snap some pictures from here, but we need to get a closer look at it, see if there are other bones in there."

He nods. "We'll need a ladder of some sort so we can get down there without disturbing the scene any more than it already is."

"Gotcha covered," Marvin says. He snaps his fingers at one of his workers, a skinny, sinewy guy with a glazed, stoner expression in his eyes and long hair that looks like it hasn't been washed in weeks. "Hank," Marvin says, and then he nods in the direction of the parked vehicles.

It takes Hank a few seconds to glean Marvin's meaning, and the dopey, clueless look he has on his face makes me fear our new house—assuming it ever gets built—will be about as sturdy and straight as the one my son built out of pots and pans on the kitchen floor the other day. Hank finally discerns what he's supposed to do and scurries toward a large, blue pickup truck. He grabs an extension ladder out of the back bed, carries it over, and starts to set it in the hole, aiming it right at the skull.

"No!" I yell, nearly dropping my camera and making the poor guy jump. His cohorts snigger and snort at this. "Not there." The skeleton is resting on a small ledge that is only a couple of feet wide, five feet below ground level, and bordering part of the twelve-foot-deep area of the hole. "We need to put it down in the deep part so we can stand on the ladder below the level of that ledge where the bones are."

Hurley steps toward Hank, and does a *gimme* gesture with his hands.

Hank hands the ladder to Hurley, who then—with some help from Marvin—releases the latches that hold the sliding parts in place. Then they carefully lower the ladder into the hole, extending it past the ledge with the skeleton.

I have my scene kit with me, and after setting down my camera, I search through it for the fine-bristled paintbrush I know is in there. I'm not sure it will be all that useful because the dirt around the skeleton appears to be wet and muddy, so I also grab a few other tools, stuffing some into the pockets of my scrubs and handing others, along with my camera, to Hurley.

"Ladies first," Hurley says, waving a hand toward the ladder.

I survey the scene for a moment. "There's no point in more than one person going down there."

"You're not going to just start digging those bones loose, are you?" Arnie asks, looking askance.

I consider his question, wondering if I've overlooked some bit of procedure or protocol. I can't think of any, so I shrug and say, "Yeah, why wouldn't we?"

"Shouldn't we call someone first, like the FBI, or national security, or SETI?"

"How about the *National Enquirer*?" Otto suggests. "I hear they'll pay big bucks for something like this."

"Or what about the men in black?" I toss out with more than a hint of sarcasm.

"Fine," Arnie says in a snide tone. "Mock me if you must, but those guys exist. They don't look or act like the movie characters, but I promise you, they exist. And we should call someone. This could be a groundbreaking, historic find."

The chain gang members start whispering back and forth between themselves, and seconds later the cell phones come out. They inch back toward the edge of the hole.

Hurley sees this, too, and takes action. "Marvin, tell your men they can go home. I assume it's close to their usual quitting time anyway, and there isn't going to be any more work here today, maybe not for several days."

Sensing that their opportunity to take a potentially valuable picture is fading fast, the workers hold their phones out, and I hear several clicks.

"*Now*, Marvin," Hurley snaps, clearly growing impatient.

Scowling, Marvin directs his men to back up and go home. They do so, but several of them get in a few more clicks before they leave. Their retreat is accompanied by the sputtering sounds of an engine approaching, and seconds later an older-model white panel van pulls up, parking on the grass beside Marvin's pickup. I half expect to see Will Smith and Tommy Lee Jones jump out in their tidy, black suits. And if Arnie's wide-eyed expression is any indication, he expects this, too. Though this type of windowless van is more in keeping with a kidnapping pedophile than an alien hunter.

"What's up with the creeper van?" I ask, as we all watch. We can't see the person behind the wheel because Marvin's pickup is in the way, but a moment later a young man who looks like he's all of twelve comes hurrying around the end of the pickup toward us. He's wearing large, dark-framed glasses that sit crooked on his nose, and his face is pockmarked with zits. His light brown hair is cut short, spiking up in places, and he's wearing a stunning outfit—and I mean stunning in a Taser sort of way, not a fashionably chic sort of way: Bermuda shorts, a hideous Hawaiian shirt, sandals, and mid-calf, black socks. The footwear is uniquely Wisconsin. A clue to his identity is the camera he has hanging from a strap around his neck.

"Howdy there, folks," he says as he approaches, pushing his glasses up his nose. He stops a few feet away and gives us a goofy smile. "I'm Cletus Barnes, the new photographer and reporter for the Sorenson paper. I hear you guys found a dead body?"

His spinach-colored eyes look huge behind those glasses, making me guess that his vision without them is somewhere in the 20/1,000 range.

"You're Alison Miller's replacement?" I ask. Just saying Alison's name makes my heart clutch inside my chest.

"I am," he says with enthusiasm. "Bummer what happened to her, but hey, life goes on, right?" He glances into the hole. "As does death."

"That's a bit cavalier," I say.

"Sorry," he says with a shrug, not looking sorry at all. "I didn't know the woman. Was she a friend of yours?"

I'm not sure how to answer this. My relationship with Alison Miller had been a mixed one. We knew each other in high school, though we weren't close friends, and when I first met Hurley, she became something of an enemy for a couple of reasons. One was the fact that she was competing with me for Hurley's attention and affections. The other was the fact that she photographed me several times in very unflattering, half-naked circumstances, and those pictures appeared in our local paper and, on one occasion, in a national rag much like the *National Enquirer*. She was also incredibly nosy and a bit of a pest when it came to our investigations.

Over time, we sorted things out with her and hit upon a working relationship that was satisfying to all parties involved. And when her mother was diagnosed with ALS—forcing Alison to pass up on a cushy job offer in Chicago—I helped her care for the woman until she died.

Alison's death had hit me hard, and now she had been replaced by this pimply-faced, nerdy, Jimmy Olsen character. "Yes, she was a friend of mine," I say.

Cletus Barnes again apologizes, concluding with, "Sorry for your loss." His obvious lack of sincerity is annoying, but he doesn't offer me a chance to chastise him any further. He is gaping at the bones in the hole, close enough to the edge that he's at risk of falling in.

I suppress an urge to give him a shove. "Stand back, please," I say.

Cletus ignores me and starts shooting pictures. "That skull doesn't look normal," he observes. "It looks like an alien or something." He turns and gives us a wide-eyed look. "Is it an alien?"

"No," I say.

"Could be," Arnie says at the same time, and I roll my eyes as I hear Hurley cuss under his breath.

Cletus looks back down at the bones and snaps a few more pictures. Finally, Hurley grabs him by the arm and pulls him away from the edge. "Back off," Hurley grumbles. "This is a potential crime scene."

Cletus allows himself to be pulled back, but he doesn't go far. And I can tell he has no intention of leaving. He takes out his cell phone and makes a call. To my relief, he walks off a little way so he can talk. The fact that he's whispering into the phone makes me suspect that rumors of an alien skeleton will soon be rampant. In fact, given that an edition of the paper comes out tomorrow, I'm betting it will be the headline.

Time is ticking away, and even though we're blessed with the late sunsets of summer, it will be dark sooner than we'd like. "We best get to it," I say to Otto and Hurley.

They both nod their agreement, and after moving the ladder a little closer to the bones, I position myself on it and make my way down to where I can easily reach the rib cage. With my brush, I try to remove some of the dirt around the skull, but it's too wet and packed too hard for me to move much. I stick the brush back into my pocket and take out a small hand rake and a trowel. I spread my feet as far apart as I can on the step I'm on and stick my left arm between two rungs, wrapping it around the side of the ladder. Holding the small rake in my right hand, I start clawing away as gently as I can at the surrounding soil. Above me, Hurley is making a videotape of the scene and my efforts.

About ten minutes in, I have exposed a neck bone and part of what appears to be a shoulder. So far, these look quite ordinary and human. Fifteen more minutes and I've exposed all of one arm, and I'm working on what appears to be the hand. This is where normalcy stops. There are only three fingers: a thumb-type of appendage, and two other digits that are easily the width of two or three normal fingers. The bones don't look like anything I've ever seen before.

"What the hell?" Otto says when he sees it. This draws the attention of Cletus, who takes advantage of everyone's distracted state to once again encroach on the edge of the hole. I hear the subtle *click, click, click* of his camera.

Arnie, who has been standing by and pacing, stares at the bones for a second before saying, "See? I told you it was an alien." He pauses, cocks his head to one side, and looks up at the sky. "And here they come," he says in an ominous tone.

That's when I hear the soft *whump, whump, whump* of an approaching helicopter.

CHAPTER 14

Just as the helicopter comes into view, another van comes up the drive and pulls to a stop. It's a TV van from one of the stations in Madison. I shoot Cletus a dirty look, convinced he's the reason the TV people have shown up. As the helicopter draws closer, we can see that it, too, is from a TV station, not the feared—or in Arnie's case, revered—men in black.

Hurley mutters another curse under his breath. The helicopter closes in and hovers above our dig site, hanging there and sending down a whirligig of wind that forces me to stop what I'm doing and hang on to the ladder for dear life. Hurley and Otto both try to wave the copter off, but if the pilot sees either of the men, he's ignoring them. From the TV van, two men emerge, one carrying a camera, the other a box of some sort.

"Hi, there," shouts the man carrying the box. Even with his loud tone, it's hard to hear him over the loud *whump, whump* of the helicopter blades above us. "I'm Adam Wagner from the Madison FOX TV affiliate. I heard a rumor that you found an alien skeleton out here."

Hurley stops the man's progress by stepping into his path and putting his hands on his hips with his elbows out to the sides—the human equivalent of the frilled-neck lizard. "Hold it right there," he says loudly. "This is a crime scene, and as such, I can't allow anyone else to be here."

Adam frowns at this, but it's a calculating frown that tells me he isn't going to give up easily. "Really?" he hollers back. "What crime?"

"Until we finish unearthing these bones and get them examined, I can't tell you," Hurley yells.

"So, it's not technically known for sure that it's a crime scene?" Adam says. He doesn't wait for an answer. "And I've heard that the bones you found aren't normal ones, that they might be from a space alien?"

"They're not from a space alien," Hurley says through gritted teeth. This softens his voice to the point that Adam can't hear him.

"What's that?" Adam asks, cupping a hand behind one ear.

Hurley repeats what he said, louder this time. And sharper. I can tell his patience is wearing thin.

"Oh, so you *have* been able to examine them, then, to rule that out?" Adam yells back with a grin that is a perfect mix of smugness and innocence. None of us is fooled as to which emotion is the true one.

Hurley's face becomes a thundercloud. His head rolls back on his shoulders, and he glares at the helicopter overhead, which now has someone hanging out a side door, aiming a camera down at our hole. For a moment, I wonder if Hurley is going to take his gun out and shoot the damned thing.

"If there is even a small possibility that those bones aren't human," Adam goes on, "the public has the right to know, before the government steps in and tries to cover it up."

Arnie nods vigorously at this comment, and I suspect he's just made a new friend.

Hurley lowers his head and glares at Adam. "If you don't turn around right now and head back to your vehicle, I'm going to arrest you."

"Arrest me?" Adam scoffs. "For what?"

"For trespassing, to start with," Hurley says.

Adam weighs this threat for a few seconds, and then says, "I'll get permission from whoever owns this land." He takes out his cell phone, presumably to search for who it is who owns the property. I can't help but smile.

"*I* own this land," Hurley says in a loud, menacing voice. He takes his gun from its holster. "And you, sir, are trespassing. I tend to shoot first and ask questions later."

Adam pales at this, and his cameraman shifts nervously, waiting to see what's going to happen next.

The helicopter, its occupants apparently satisfied with whatever footage they got, suddenly takes off, giving us some relief from the noise and the downdraft. I look over at Hurley, point toward the retreating copter, and say, "Whoever that was got pictures, and you can bet this is going to be on the news tonight and in the morning. So why not let these guys get a picture or two as well?"

"Because it's going to feed into the fantasies of the crazies out there who believe in this space alien crap, and they're going to be swarming all over our land before you can say ET."

I see Arnie shoot Hurley a wounded look.

"So we post a couple of guys to keep people away," I say. "It's a done deal, Hurley. You're fighting a battle that's already been lost, thanks to that helicopter. Besides, maybe someone out there will know something about these bones. It could help us identify the body."

Hurley considers this and seems to realize I have a point. He holsters his weapon, and with a perturbed but resigned shake of his head, he waves Adam and his cameraman over toward the edge of the hole and the ladder I'm standing on.

"Thanks, man," Adam says, hurrying over before Hurley

has a chance to change his mind. "I don't suppose you'd be willing to give us a sound bite, answer a question or two on camera?"

"You are really pushing your luck," I tell him in a low, warning tone, thinking Hurley is already mad enough to push Adam into the hole.

Adam waves his cameraman over and points toward the bones. As the guy starts filming, Adam looks around at all of us and says, "Who are you people?"

Otto, who has stood by quietly, looking more amused than annoyed, does the introductions. I go back to doing what I was doing before all the interruptions. When Adam has been adequately informed, he shifts his attention back to the bones, staring at them.

"So if that's not an alien body, what the heck is it?" he asks, staring.

"Most likely the body of someone with some serious birth defects," Otto answers.

Adam contemplates this answer, still staring at the bones. After a moment or two he says, "You know, my aunt claims that she was abducted by aliens four years ago. She drew a picture of the creatures, and I have to tell you, it looked exactly like those bones you have there. We all assumed she was crazy at first, but there were some things that were hard to explain."

Arnie jumps on this. "Like what? What was her story?"

Adam pulls at his chin. His photographer, whose name we learned during the earlier introductions is Hans Larkin, stops filming the bones and lowers the camera.

Adam begins his story, and as he speaks, he has the rapt attention of everyone there. "She said she was watching TV, and it was late at night, around midnight, she thought. She and my Uncle Lou lived up on Madeline Island at the time. It's one of the Apostle Islands in Lake Superior near Bayfield. Anyway, the island population is small, and as you might guess, it's a relatively secluded place, particularly in the late fall, which is when this happened. Aunt Gertrude said Lou had gone to bed already, and she was sitting in a recliner watching TV when all of a sudden, all the lights in the house went out. At first, she didn't think anything of it because it was windy outside, and the electricity on the island is always going out. She got out of the chair, intending to head up to bed, when a bright light suddenly came in through the window. Several windows, actually. She said it was like someone had turned their yard into a football field with all those klieg lights they use at night."

I glance over at Arnie and see that he is spellbound by Adam's story.

"Curious," Adam continues, "she walked over toward the front door and window, and looked outside. The light was so bright, it was blinding. She tried to shield her eyes some and look again, but all she could see was bright white light that seemed to be coming from above. The whole thing spooked her, so she turned around to head for the kitchen, thinking she should at least arm herself with a knife or something. They owned a shotgun, but it was upstairs, and she didn't want to turn her back on the lower level to go up and get it."

Adam pauses and looks around at his audience. All eyes and ears are focused on him and his story. "She says she remembers thinking about getting the knife and heading for the kitchen, but she has no memory of actually reaching the kitchen or getting any sort of weapon. In fact, the next thing she remembers is waking up in the living room the next morning."

Hurley rolls his eyes. "Easy enough to explain. She fell asleep in the recliner and had a dream. A very vivid dream, I'll grant you, but still."

"Yeah," Adam agrees, "we all came up with the same explanation. Except she didn't wake up in the recliner. She was on the couch."

"So she walked in her sleep during her dream," Hurley says dismissively.

"Maybe," Adam says. "But that doesn't explain the other stuff."

"What other stuff?" Arnie asks, his eyes wide, his expression eager. He looks like a dog waiting for its owner to throw a ball.

"When she woke up, she felt groggy, like she'd been drugged or something. And she swore she didn't take anything. She had some vague memories of small, short creatures touching her and looking at her. She drew pictures of them. They had big heads and big eyes, but the eyes were close-set. The lower part of the face was small and narrow, and the hands were like claws, she said. With two fingers and a thumb." He pauses and casts a pointed look down toward the bones.

"Still all explainable as a dream," Hurley says.

"But I'm not done yet," Adam says with an arch of one brow. "Outside in the front yard, about where she said the bright light seemed to have been brightest, there was a large, circular burn mark in the grass. She and Uncle Lou swear it wasn't there the night before. And when she continued to feel off throughout the day, she went to her doctor for an exam. And her doctor found this weird piece of metal embedded in her back, just below her shoulder blade. There was a tiny, healed scar around it, and when Aunt Gertie insisted that the doc remove it, he did. He said he had no idea what it was. It was a small, perfectly round piece of some strange blue metal, with a grid pattern on one side. The doctor sent it off to a lab to be analyzed, but it never got there. It simply disappeared. No one has seen it since, and no one was able to trace what happened to it."

"Convenient," Hurley mutters.

Arnie gives him an impatient look. "Bury your head in the sand if you want," he says. "But all the denial in the world doesn't change the fact that they're here. They've been here for centuries, and they're still here."

Hurley rolls his eyes in disgust and takes out his cell phone. "I'm going to check on some things," he says. And with that, he walks off toward the parked vehicles, leaving the rest of us behind.

I've now managed to unearth the entire skeleton, along with several small pieces of something that looks like cloth. Most of these are tiny and rotted to the point that they disintegrate if I even touch them, but there is one intact piece that is about the size of a quarter, its edges frayed and caked with mud and dirt. It's folded in half, and I have Otto shoot some footage of it—Hurley has handed off the filming duties—before I gently separate the layers. In the fold, I can see a gold-colored surface.

"That's odd-looking," Otto says.

"It looks metallic," Arnie says. "Like a uniform of some kind," He looks like a kid who has just been set loose in a candy store with a twenty-dollar bill.

Cameras start snapping away, and a few minutes later, all of the newsy people are gone, dashing back to their offices to report on the find.

Over the next half hour, the last of the construction workers leave, too, so that the only people left are me, Hurley, Otto, and Arnie. Arnie has been busy tapping away on his smartphone, no doubt contacting whatever group of alien-embracing conspiracy theorists he hangs out with online.

"I think we can expect a lot of extra company on this case," I say to no one in particular. "Once this hits the news, people will be flocking here."

"There won't be anything here for them to see once we get the body out," Otto observes.

"Assuming it's the only one," Arnie says, eyebrows raised. This thought makes all of us exchange pained looks of realization.

"Damn," Otto says, massaging his temples. "He's right. We need to excavate this area more thoroughly. There could be other bodies buried nearby."

"Or parts of a spaceship," Arnie says.

This makes Hurley groan.

But Arnie is not deterred. "Come on," he says. "We find a malformed body and bits of some sort of metallic cloth. Tell me you aren't considering the possibility that this might be something otherworldly."

In unison, Otto, Hurley, and I say, "We're not."

Arnie shakes his head in disappointment. "You people are in denial. And you have no imaginations. You need to open your minds to other possibilities."

At the moment, the only other possibility I can focus on is how tired and dirty I am, and how much longer this work is going to last. "Arnie," I say, feeling annoyed, "since you're so intrigued by this site and what we've found here, the least you can do is get down here in the dirt and help."

If I expect this to daunt him in any way, I'm disappointed. Arnie rubs his hands together gleefully.

"Happy to help," he says. And then he grabs a nearby shovel left by the construction crew and starts digging in to the edges of the hole near our find.

I'm glad he's willing to help, but even if all of us start digging in—literally—I know we're likely in for an all-nighter.

CHAPTER 15

My human alarm, otherwise known as my son, Matthew, wakes me just after six thirty the next morning. I'm not as happy to see him as I should be, primarily because I didn't get to bed until well after two. I called Dom around suppertime to explain that we might be late picking up Matthew, and Dom kindly offered to keep him all night. I was tempted to take him up on the offer, but Hurley called Bob Richmond and had him and a couple of off-duty officers come out to the site to help. Then Hurley went to pick Matthew up somewhere around seven.

We finished digging up the skeleton and a reasonably large area of the surrounding ground a little after one. At that point, Richmond called it a night, saying that the likelihood of finding any other bodies was negligible at that point. I transported our bones and the piece of fabric we found with it back to the morgue and went about checking it in. There wouldn't be any autopsy to perform, at least not in the usual sense, and Otto said he would decide how to proceed later in the day after we'd all had a chance to get some sleep.

I crawled home and entered the house as quietly as I could, not wanting to wake anyone. Everyone was in bed asleep, including Hurley, though I knew from text messages he sent me that Emily had come home around ten, and he had gone back to the station to work on the Lansing-Knowlton case, staying there until well after midnight.

Though I thought Hurley might be awake by the time I made it upstairs and took a much-needed shower, he was snoring loudly when I emerged from our bathroom. I felt a tinge of relief that I wouldn't have to spend any time talking to him—precious time that I could spend sleeping instead— and immediately afterward felt a smidgen of resentment that Hurley was getting more sleep than I was. Both of these thoughts triggered a twinge of guilt, but I tossed it aside and was out like a light the second my head hit the pillow.

"Momma, up!" Matthew commands, reminding me that my brief respite is over. Just to make sure I understand his directions, he peels back one of my eyelids. There is something on his fingers—they are wet—and I pray it isn't anything too disgusting.

"Matthew, don't do that," I grumble, pushing his hand away.

I sit myself up and look over at Hurley's side of the bed. He isn't there, and I wonder if he's downstairs or already back at the station. I knew from a quick telephone chat with him before he left the station last night that he and Junior Feller has followed up on all the plates in the Grizzly Motel parking lot—a few of which delivered potential blackmail material if we were the type to do such a thing. They called and interviewed most of the guests who had been there, eventually deciding that whoever had killed the couple had probably escaped through the woods behind the motel as opposed to in a vehicle parked there. Presumably, they didn't want to risk any witnesses to their departure who might later be able to provide a description of the vehicle or, even worse, a license plate number. It was a smart move, actually, because it left us with very little in the way of leads.

I crawl out of bed and shuffle into the bathroom to pee. Matthew follows me, and when he sees me sit down on the toilet, he promptly walks up between my knees, pulls down his pull-up, and aims his penis at me.

"Maffew pee, too," he says gleefully, and before I can stop him, he proceeds to tinkle all over my thighs.

I suppose I should be glad he's grasping the idea of peeing in the toilet, but I'm a little too tired at the moment to see the glass half full. My first instinct is to yell at him, but I manage to swallow the words down just before they leave my lips. In a calm, rational voice that is the exact opposite of the way I feel, I tell him, "Matthew, we don't share the potty. You have to wait your turn."

He pouts at me, clearly annoyed that I haven't praised the fact that while he didn't pee in the toilet, he was in the neighborhood and did manage to pee on it. I grab a wad of toilet of paper and wipe the urine off my legs. Then I get up and kick off my pajama bottoms, which were also hit. Matthew needs to work on his aim. He gets so enthralled with the sight and feel of his own penis that he tends to stare at it and not focus on where it's pointed. I reach over and pull a washcloth off the towel rack and wet it under the faucet so I can wash my legs off. When I'm done, I turn and see that Matthew has done his part in the cleanup. He has kicked off his pull-up, tossed it into the toilet, and unrolled a long length of toilet paper, which he has draped over the toilet, the floor, and his feet.

"Matthew, honey, no," I say. I'm hit with an overwhelming urge to cry out of a combination of fatigue and frustration, and I squeeze my eyes closed and count to ten. When I open them again, my son is standing a few feet away, stark naked, sucking on his thumb, watching me with big, loving eyes. Despite my irritation, it makes me smile, and I bend down, scoop him up, and give him a big kiss and hug. The feel of his tiny arms hugging me around my neck makes everything right with the world again, at least for a short while.

Unfortunately, it doesn't last long. After I set Matthew down, I look in the mirror and nearly gasp at the sight. My hair, which is currently cut in a short bob—an accommodation that makes the hot summer weather more tolerable—is sticking out from my head like Medusa's snakes, thanks to the fact that I went to bed with it wet. My eyes have dark circles under them, and my face has given birth to a large, feral zit that is sprouting out from the center of my forehead like a Cyclopean eye.

I grab a brush from the countertop and try to coerce my hair into something less frightening. There isn't much I can do with the zit, but I brush my teeth, figuring that taming my fire-breathing-dragon breath will help make me feel more human instead of like a CGI monster in a movie based on some ancient mythology.

As I bend over to spit in the sink, I hear the toilet flush, and look over to see Matthew holding the handle, staring into the bowl. All of the toilet paper, other than a few remaining soggy pieces that are stuck to the wetter areas of the floor and toilet seat, have been picked up. Matthew has put all of it in the toilet. I quickly realize as I see the swirling mass come to a standstill amid rising water, that all that paper, on top of the pull-up he dropped in there, is too much for the toilet to handle. Water starts to overflow the sides, running onto the floor. I grab for the tank top, take it off, and promptly drop it on my foot.

I bite back a scream of pain as I reach into the tank and stop the bowl from filling. I mutter several curses under my breath, and Matthew starts to wail. Behind me, I hear feet running up the stairs and down the hall. A moment later, Hurley bursts into the bathroom, looking panicked.

"What the hell?"

My foot is throbbing in agony, and it's a struggle to get any words out between my tightly gritted teeth. "Take him," I finally say. "Take him *now*!"

Hurley looks at my expression and makes a split-second decision. He grabs Matthew into his arms and makes a hasty retreat from the bathroom.

I sit on top of the dirty clothes hamper and bury my face in my hands. I'm so tired that I seriously consider just crawling out of the flooded bathroom and back into bed. Instead I cry, indulging myself for a good five minutes before the water-works—mine, anyway—dry up. Then I muster up the dregs of my strength and clean up the bathroom.

Forty minutes later, I have unclogged the toilet, washed and dried the bathroom floor, showered again, dressed, and put on a minimum of makeup: some eyeliner, a few swaths of mascara, and a swipe of blush on each cheek. I don't need any lipstick—my lips are already flaming red from chewing on them in an effort to bite back the raging soliloquy that has been on the tip of my tongue the whole time.

Satisfied that I have done as much as I can, I head down-stairs. On my way down the hall, I see that Emily's bedroom door is closed and feel a pang of envy. Oh, what I would give to be back in the lazy summer days of my teenage years, when I was able to sleep away half the day and my biggest worries were whether or not any of the boys had managed to grow enough to pass me up in height, whether or not I could get tickets to the upcoming Pearl Jam concert, and where I could go to get the Rachel haircut.

Downstairs, I find Hurley and Matthew in the kitchen eat-ing pancakes. Both of them look up at me with wary expres-sions as I enter the room, as if they are afraid I might explode any moment. Their wariness irritates me even more than I al-ready am, because I realize their fears may be justified. I need to get a grip . . . and about a week's worth of sleep.

I pour a cup of coffee and sit down at the table to Matthew's left, with Hurley across from me.

"You okay?" he asks.

I shake my head, feeling the burn of tears behind my eyes. "Something's got to give, Hurley. I'm so tired."

"I'm sorry," he says. "I didn't know Matthew was awake or I would have come upstairs to get him." He pauses, sees my look of frustrated irritation, and adds, "We can get through this. Things are a little crazy right now—okay, a lot crazy—but it's not going to last forever."

"At this rate, neither am I," I say, running a hand through my wet hair. I look over at Matthew, who is dropping syrup-soaked pieces of pancake onto the floor for our dog Hoover to eat. I know the sugary content will give Hoover a case of the squirts, but I'm too exhausted to care. "Izzy has a couple of interviews lined up this morning, and I hope one of them pans out. If they don't hire a replacement for Hal soon, I'm going to lose it." I pause. "Not that Hal can ever be replaced."

"What can I do to help?" Hurley asks. Even as he says this, he grabs Matthew's arm just as he is about to drop yet another piece of pancake onto the floor. With a stern look Hurley says, "No, Matthew. I've told you before, we don't feed the dog at the table."

Matthew dutifully returns the piece of pancake to his plate, much to Hoover's drooling disappointment.

I don't have an answer to his question, so I simply shake my head and take another sip of coffee.

"Look," Hurley says, "why don't you go on to work, and I'll take care of getting Matthew ready and off to Dom's, okay? I have a lot of things on my agenda for today, but nothing with a time frame this morning, so I'm not in any rush."

I nod, sipping more coffee.

"Did you guys determine anything useful about the bones last night?" Hurley asks.

With a side look at Matthew, who is busy drawing a finger-paint picture on his plate in a pool of maple syrup, I say, "Based on the size, it's probably a child. But you already knew that. Otto said the bones appear to be old—we're talking decades—but he also said that the metals and other stuff in the soil leaching into the bones can make them look old when they're not. He plans to have a bone specialist from Milwaukee come in today to look at them."

"Well, keep me posted on what you find," he says. "Until we get this thing resolved, our building plans are on hold. What are you going to be doing in the meantime?"

"Izzy invited me to sit in with him on the interviews, so I need to be there by eight." I glance at my watch and get out of my chair, chugging one last gulp of coffee as I carry my cup to the sink. "And that means I need to get going. What do you have planned?"

"I'm going to check in with Jonas and Laura to see if they have come up with anything new on our motel case, and then I'm going to try to track both of our victims' activities over the past week. The text messages on the burner phones certainly support the affair theory, although there was an odd one on Meredith's that I found."

"Odd how?"

"It came through on the afternoon of the murders, and it was the last one she received. It said something about meeting under the double arches."

"McDonald's?"

Hurley looks doubtful. "McDonald's is typically referred to as the Golden Arches. But I'll see if I can find any evidence of the two of them being there on that day. I'm hoping Jonas will have some GPS info by now, so I can track all their activities leading up to the Grizzly. And I'll check with Arnie to see if he has come up with something in the computers, though given his fixation with the 'alien skeleton' "—he makes little air quotes when he says this—"I'm not sure if he's been as focused on his job as he should be."

"Are you going to let the surviving spouses know that it wasn't a murder-suicide?" I ask, grabbing my purse.

"Not yet," Hurley says, his brow furrowing. "I want to do a little more digging first. I'm going to go back out to the motel and search those woods behind it."

"I can probably help you," I tell him. "If no autopsies come in, I should be relatively free. There isn't much for me to do with the bones we found on our property."

"I'd love the company," he says with a wink.

I walk over, kiss both him and my son good-bye, and then start for the front door. But I turn back before leaving the kitchen. "What about the Tomas Wyzinski case?" I ask. "Any progress with that?"

"It's on a back burner at the moment." I frown at this, and he gives me an apologetic look. "I'm still working on it," he says, "but for the moment these other cases need to take precedence."

I'm not sure I agree with him, but there's little I can do about it.

"You've got to stop blaming yourself for Wyzinski," Hurley says in a soft voice.

"How can I? It was largely my testimony, my findings that put him away. The idea that he's sitting there in jail because of me when he is likely innocent is a huge weight on my shoulders."

"It's not your fault," Hurley insists.

"I appreciate your sentiment, but you know I bear some of the burden. We both do."

"And we'll get there," Hurley says. "You have to be patient."

"Let me help you," I say, giving him a pleading look.

"You've been keeping this thing to yourself for the past few weeks. Two heads are better than one."

"You just finished telling me how overwhelmed you are with the stuff you already have on your plate. Let's get these current cases settled, and then we'll take another look at things, okay?"

I give him an exasperated look. "Are you reining me in on this case because of my father?"

His eyes dart toward Matthew, and I know he's about to lie to me. "No," he says. "I'm worried about the level of danger involved. Clearly the people behind this thing have no compunctions about murdering to protect their dirty little secrets. I don't want our names to end up on that list."

"And my father?" I ask.

He shrugs. "Whether or not you want to meet and talk with him is up to you. That's a personal thing."

I sense the last part of his comment is a subtle reminder to me that I can talk to my father about our personal relationship, but not the case. "I haven't seen or heard from him in weeks, not since we interviewed him down at the station," I tell him. "I'm not even sure he's still in the area."

I head for the front door but hesitate before opening it, something I do every time now. The memories of the night when both Alison and Prince were shot and killed in our front yard are still fresh and painful. I brace myself for a moment, and then open the door.

There are no bodies, no dark SUVs cruising by, no bullets raining down on me. It's a gloriously sunny, clear morning, and it feels like the stifling heat and humidity have taken a holiday. I take this meteorological bellwether as a harbinger of good things to come. And then I look down at my feet.

The Sorenson paper is on the front stoop. It's not a big paper—about twelve pages folded in half. The headline side is facing down, but on the lower half of the page I see a picture that I recognize immediately. It's a shot of our property and the dig site. I pick up the paper and unfold it.

Blazing across the top of the front page is this headline: ALIEN SKELETON UNEARTHED ON NEARBY FARM? Below that is a picture of the skull.

I fold the paper back up and tuck it under my arm. I'm going to need more coffee, I decide, because I suspect it's going to be a very long, very trying day.

CHAPTER 16

The office is a zoo. There are TV vans parked around the block and a throng of people milling outside the front door. I use my key card to gain entrance to the underground parking garage beneath the office and manage to get inside without being waylaid.

Upstairs, I find Otto in the library along with Arnie. They are munching on pastries that I suspect Otto picked up from the local bakery. One of my favorite things about having Otto on board is his compulsive need to bribe his fellow workers with sweets. After greeting both of them, I quickly scan the bakery box, grab a cheese-filled Danish, and then head for the coffeepot.

"It's crazy out there," Otto says. "I really didn't think this thing would attract this much attention."

Arnie looks askance. "Why wouldn't it? It's a historic find, proof that there were aliens here at one time, perhaps even now."

Otto gives Arnie a look of patient tolerance. "It is not an alien," he says. "My guess is it's a child who had some sort of genetic problems involving craniofacial deformities."

"I don't know," Arnie says, shaking his head and pursing his lips. "It bears a strong resemblance to the bones they found in Atacama."

"Those bones were only six inches long," Otto says.

I have no idea what they're talking about, so I settle in at my desk, wake up my computer, and do a Google search for Atacama. My page instantly fills with articles and pictures of the tiny, mummified bones that were unearthed in this desert climate.

"The skull of the Atacama skeleton is more elongated than ours," I say, looking at the pictures.

"That's because the bones were mummified and the desiccation torqued the bones out of shape," Arnie says, walking over and looking at my screen. "Check out the Starchild skeleton."

I do another Google search, and find more articles and pictures purporting the discovery of an alien, or rather a human-alien hybrid.

"It looks like the skull of a child who suffered from hydrocephalus," says Otto, who has also approached my desk and is now peering over my shoulder. "Nothing more."

I click on an article and scan the text. "It says here they tested the bones for DNA and concluded it was human," I say.

"Poppycock," Arnie says. "They only tested for mitochondrial DNA, which comes from the mother. The father might not have been of human origin."

"But they found enough DNA to identify a Y chromosome," I say, still reading. "So the skeleton belonged to a boy, and since the Y chromosome comes from the father, he must have been human."

"The simple fact of a Y chromosome doesn't prove anything," Arnie argues. "Who's to say what alien DNA looks like? Why couldn't they have some DNA that's similar to ours and some that's not? Maybe they interbred with us thousands of years ago, and the progeny later returned to see how things were going and breed some more."

Otto and I both eye him skeptically.

"Come on, guys," Arnie says. There is a gleam in his eye that tells me how excited he is about this whole thing. "Think about it. Aliens from space had to have visited earth in the past. There's all kinds of evidence that proves it. How else do you think ancient man was able to achieve such remarkable feats of technology and science as the pyramids? Or the airstrips in Nazca, Peru? Or the cave paintings, carvings, and petroglyphs dating back thousands of years that can be found all over the world, images that depict beings with reptilian heads, or what appear to be helmets, or even some that look like they're wearing some sort of protective suit? Where did these images come from? Huh? Why do ancient images that appear in Kiev, and Africa, and Utah, and Ecuador all have these common elements, even though the people who lived back then were isolated from one another? Those ancient people thought these images were gods from heaven." He pauses and points toward the ceiling, giving us a knowing look. "Heaven . . . as in space. Get it?"

I suspect Otto has sensed that further discussion with Arnie on the topic will be an exercise in futility, because he says, "Well, let's wait until we have a chance to analyze the bones we found before we go labeling them as alien." He glances at his watch. "I have an osteologist named Mark Schmitt coming up today from Chicago to take a look at them. He should be here around nine."

"He'll have a hard time getting through that crowd out front," I say.

Otto nods. "I've arranged with the local PD to have a couple of officers out there to assist him. While we're waiting, let's get the bones on the table for him." He gives Arnie a pointed look. "And I think you have some things to work on with our other active cases, don't you?"

Arnie frowns, looking defeated. "Yeah, yeah," he says, and then he turns and skulks away.

"You've broken his heart," I tease.

Otto chuckles. "You have to admire his sense of conviction."

"Could he be right?" I ask. I'm curious to test Otto's skepticism on the matter. How open is he to the possibility of those bones not being entirely human?

He looks over at me with an enigmatic smile. "There are still many things in the world we don't fully understand or know of," he says. "I'm open to possibilities, but I'm also a realist. And I've seen too many human anomalies to jump onto the alien bandwagon this soon."

"Glad to hear it," I say. "But whatever else those bones may be, they are a thorn in my side. We can't continue with the construction on our house until we clear this case."

"Sorry about that," he says. "Of course, we'll do what we can to get to the bottom of things as quickly as we can, but I'm afraid it's going to take time. Those bones will have to be aged, and depending on the results of that, we might have to do a little more looking around out there on your land."

This is not good news. Postponing the construction means more time living in our current cramped quarters. And who knows how long our contractor is going to sit idly by waiting for a green light? I'm not a happy camper along about now.

We go about getting the bones laid out and ready for Schmitt to examine when he arrives. Once that is done, Otto says, "If you want, you can check in with the PD and see if there's anything we can help with in regard to the other cases. You can be here when Schmitt does his thing if you like, but you don't have to be. What would you prefer to do?"

My preference would be to go home, crawl back into bed, and take a nice long nap. But I don't say so. "Actually," I say, glancing at my watch, "I'm expecting Izzy any minute. He has a couple of interviews set up this morning to look for

Hal's replacement, and he's invited me to sit in on them. After that, I think I'll check in with Hurley and help him with some investigative stuff we need to do on the motel case. I'm afraid if I'm around when your Mr. Schmitt arrives, I might try too hard to persuade him that those bones are nothing to be concerned about. I'm not very objective on the subject."

"I'll give you a call if something comes up," Otto says. "And I'll give you a call after Schmitt is done with his initial examination and let you know what his findings are."

With that settled, I grab another pastry, figuring a sugar rush will help me keep my energy levels up. This is just one of the gazillion justifications I have in my repertoire for eating things I know I shouldn't. I have to be careful not to use them too often lest I end up with a body that requires a large circle should I ever be murdered and someone has to draw a chalk outline around me. But it's hard. I love food. Sometimes I feel like the only way I can stick to a diet is if someone handcuffed my arms behind my back, and then put one of those cones of shame around my head—you know, the little funnel-shaped things dogs get to keep them from chewing and licking on parts of their bodies. Plus, the combination of dietary deprivation and my current sleep deficiency has left me with the personality of a serial killer, and my first victim would be some skinny chick I see eating a banana split.

If cynicism burned calories, I'd be as thin as a Victoria's Secret model.

This train of thought is not a good one, because now I have a wicked craving for ice cream. I try to suppress it as I take another bite of my second pastry—a raspberry-filled, glazed delight—and take out my phone to call Hurley.

"Hey, what's up?" he says when he answers.

"Are you at work yet?" I say, trying not to sound like I have a mouth full of gooey deliciousness.

"Hardly," he says. "I'm still at the house. Matthew has decided that his blue shorts with the red buttons are the only ones he'll wear, but he was trying to get them on and one of the buttons fell off. Now he's having a meltdown."

I can hear my son crying in the background. "You might have to sew it back on," I tell him. I'm half teasing him, because I know he hasn't a clue about how to sew on a button. But it's only half a tease because I also know how persistent and determined our son can be once he has his mind set on something.

"Actually, I tried to superglue it," Hurley says. "Now my fingers are fuzzy, because I picked up Matthew's socks without realizing I had glue on my fingers."

I bite back a laugh. Hurley sounds genuinely frustrated, and I know I would be if I was in his position. But when it happens to someone else, there is a certain level of hilarity to it all. "Nail polish remover," I tell him. "That will get the glue off your fingers. There's some in our bathroom medicine cabinet."

One thing my nursing career taught me is a variety of tricks and tips for removing various stains and other unwanted "gunk" from one's body or clothing: hydrogen peroxide for blood, hairspray for ballpoint pen ink, toothpaste for iodine, and acetone—aka nail polish remover—for any type of gummy adhesive.

"Okay, thanks," Hurley says.

Izzy walks in and waves at me. I hold up a jelly-smeared finger to indicate I need a minute. Izzy nods and then his eyes shift to the box of donuts, his gaze longing.

"Izzy is here," I tell Hurley, and at the sound of his name, Izzy finally tears his gaze away from the pastries. He licks his lips and then leaves the room. "I have to run, Hurley, but when I'm done with the interviews, I'll be free to help you with whatever you need. Otto has a bone specialist coming in to examine the skeleton we found last night, but I don't need to be here for that. In fact, I should probably try to distance myself from it lest I drop to my knees and beg the man to dismiss the bones as nothing so we can get back on schedule with the house."

Hurley chuckles. "There's plenty to do," he says, and then he starts listing items that need to be followed up on, most of which are things I can't do alone without an officer or detective present. But then he hits on one I can do.

"I want to follow up on your idea of checking into the life insurance policies and chatting with the agent who issued them," Hurley says.

"The agent on both policies is Patty Volker," I say, finally letting that cat out of the bag because I figure Hurley will figure it out himself sooner or later. "I'd be happy to go and talk to her."

There is a moment of silence on the other end. "Are you sure you want to do that?" he asks finally. "Won't it be . . . awkward?"

"Not particularly," I say, hoping I sound convincing. The truth is, it *will* be a little awkward, but my curiosity is outweighing any reservations I might have at the moment. "I'm long over David," I tell Hurley. "And I knew Patty before she married him. She's a nice person. Besides, this will be a strictly business visit, so there shouldn't be any cause for awkwardness."

"Okay," Hurley says, and I can hear muffled, hiccupping sobs in the background that tell me Matthew is over the worst of his tantrum, though the start of a new one is always a possibility. "By the time you do that, I should be at the station, and we can reconnoiter there."

"Consider it done," I tell him. "And good luck with that missing button."

I disconnect the call with a slight twinge of guilt, but also with a sense of relief that he's the one dealing with the button debacle rather than me. I settle in behind my computer, and while keeping one hand free to continue feeding my face, I search for Patty Volker's contact information, typing with my free hand. Once I pull up her number, I take out my cell phone and dial it, still using only one hand. I've always been a good multitasker, particularly when food is involved.

Patty answers on the third ring, sounding chipper and far more awake than I am. I'm licking the remnants of raspberry jelly from my fingers by the time she finishes her greeting spiel.

"Hey, Patty, it's Mattie," I say.

"Oh, hi," she says, sounding a little less chipper.

"This is a business call," I tell her to put her mind at ease. "It's about a case we're working on. I wonder if I could come by and talk to you about it?"

"Of course," she says.

"What time does your office open?"

"Um, I'm not in my office, or at least not the one downtown. I let it go, and I work from home now. I have an office here at the house."

The house. The rebuilt version of the one I used to share with David.

"Would it be okay if I dropped by?" I ask her.

"Sure. What time is good for you?"

I glance at my watch. It's almost eight, and I figure the interviews won't take more than an hour. Just to make sure I'm on time, I give myself a cushion. "Would nine-thirty work?"

"It would."

"Great."

"Can I ask what it's about?"

"I want to chat with you about some life insurance policies that were taken out on a couple of people who are now dead under suspicious circumstances." Izzy reappears with a short, squatty woman beside him. "I have to go, Patty, but I'll fill you in on the details when I get there. Thanks, and see you in a bit."

She says good-bye, and I disconnect the call. Then I look over at Izzy and the woman with him, who I'm assuming is our first interviewee. I put on my friendliest smile as hope swells in my chest that this woman will be perfect for the job and I might get caught up on my sleep in the not too distant future.

CHAPTER 17

Myrna Nesbitt is one of those women whose age is difficult to guess. Her hair is a basic brown color, cut in a classic pageboy style. I don't see any gray there, but these days it's so easy for women to fight off the gray that it's an unreliable cue. She is a round woman, short in stature, with nary a wrinkle anywhere. This would seem to imply youth, but there is an expression of knowledge, wisdom, and confidence on her face that suggests some years of experience behind her. That, and her somewhat dowdy business jacket, basic skirt, and sensible pumps.

Izzy makes the introductions, and we all settle in at the library table. With another longing look at the box of pastries, Izzy pushes it across the table to Myrna and invites her to help herself.

She thanks him and shakes her head. "I need to maintain the girlish figure," she says with a wink.

Izzy slides Myrna's résumé over to me, and I give it a quick once-over as he starts in with a basic description of the job she is applying for. Based on the dates I see for her educational experience and previous jobs, I do some quick math and estimate Myrna to be somewhere in her mid to late forties. She has a master's degree in pathology and has spent the past seven years working for a private medical research lab in Chicago that is currently focused largely on stem cell research. She lists necropsy—the animal kingdom's version of a human autopsy—as one of her primary duties there.

Prior to this job, she worked at a variety of hospitals and clinics all over the country—California, Virginia, Vermont, Florida, Montana, Tennessee, New Jersey, and Arkansas—changing jobs every two years or so.

Izzy finishes with his description and asks Myrna why she's interested in the job.

"I find I need more challenge in my work life," she says. "In my current job, I spend most of my day cutting up dead animals. It's tedious, monotonous, and depressing. I had hoped to eventually become more involved in the research end of things, but all I do is cut and report, cut and report, cut and report." The singsong quality of her voice gets across her bored feelings well. "My understanding is that this job involves some investigative work as well as the cutting, and I find the opportunity to get away from the dissection for a while, to challenge my brain in other ways, very appealing."

It's an articulate, intellectual, and satisfactory answer. Myrna speaks in a reasoned and intelligent way that suggests she is a bright, well-educated woman. So far, so good.

"You do understand that this job is only part-time," I say to her. "You and I will be sharing a full-time job."

She nods and smiles at me. "I have some money saved up," she says. "I find that at this stage in my life I'm more interested in using my spare time to explore other interests. I need to make up for lost time."

"Lost time?" Izzy says.

"I've dedicated my life thus far to two things," Myrna says. "One of those is my career. I had hoped it would follow a different track than it has, and I also hoped it would be more rewarding to me than it's proven to be. I don't really feel like starting over in a new field or career at my age, so it makes sense for me to find something different to do with my talents, something that lets me explore other areas of my brain and other areas of life.

"The second thing I've dedicated my life to is my abusive, cheating, drunken, scumbag husband."

Her words come as a shock to me, and judging from the way Izzy has leaned back in his seat, I'm guessing they are a shock to him as well.

"Like my job," Myrna continues, "I had high hopes for my marriage—things like children, a nice house, and a husband who loved and adored me. Unfortunately, none of those things came to be." She pauses and sighs. "I'm sure you're wondering why my work history includes so many different positions in so many different places for such short periods of time."

Again, she pauses, looking back and forth between me and Izzy. Neither of us says anything, but I give Myrna a grudging shrug of acknowledgment because I had noticed this peculiarity in her job history, and I am curious about it.

"It's because my husband couldn't hold down a job. He also had a hard time getting along with people. When it comes to burning bridges, my husband—or rather my ex-husband—is a first-class arsonist." She makes a pained face. "He also happens to be sterile, hence no children, although in retrospect I suppose that was a good thing." She flashes a smile at us before continuing. "Anyway, it took me longer than I like to admit to get smart and leave him, but I finally wised up. I thought my current job would offer enough challenges and diversity to fill the void, and for a number of years, I guess it did. But not anymore.

"Now my primary focus in life is me, and what makes me happy. My current job no longer makes me happy for the reasons I've already explained, so I've decided to look for something different. I believe this job can offer me that."

"It appears that most of your career *cutting*, as you call it, involved necropsy," Izzy says. "Do you have any experience with human anatomy?"

Myrna rakes her teeth over her lower lip. "Hands-on experience? No. But I studied human anatomy as part of my degree, so I think I have a good handle on it, and I don't think the necropsy procedures are all that different from what you do. Plus, I'm a fast learner."

Izzy chats with her some more about her past jobs, the time frame she's looking at for making the move if we offer her the position, and whether we can check with her current employer for a reference.

"I'd rather you didn't say anything to my current employer until you're ready to offer me a spot," she says. "They don't know yet that I'm looking."

"Not a problem," Izzy tells her. He asks her if she has any questions.

"Regarding salary," she says, "the range was posted along with the job description on the online site, but it leaves a fair amount of wiggle room. Can you give me any idea where I'd start?" She then quotes him her current salary, which makes me think I'm in the wrong business.

"Obviously we can't match that," Izzy says.

"I realize I will be taking a pay cut," Myrna says. "I'm just trying to figure out how much of one it will be. I'm sure the cost of living here in Sorenson is a lot less than it is in Chicago, so that will help some, but I do need to plan."

"I'm not prepared to offer you a specific number at this point," Izzy says. "But I imagine we'd be talking somewhere in the lower third of that range."

Myrna frowns at this, and I want to nudge Izzy and try to convince him to bump his estimate up. Myrna is ready to work and can start in just two weeks. While she won't hit the ground running, I get a sense that she's the quick learner she says she is and would be up to speed relatively quickly. Relief for me is in sight, and I want to grab it so it doesn't get away.

Izzy offers to give Myrna a quick tour of our office—an offer she quickly accepts—and while they are doing that, I hang in the library to wait for the next interview. Curious, I head over to my desk and do a Google search for Myrna Nesbitt. I don't expect to find much, but I find plenty. And what I find dashes my hopes of a quick hire.

Izzy returns ten minutes later. "So what did you think of Myrna?" he asks me. "I like her. She seems motivated, eager, and smart enough."

"But not open-minded enough," I say with a sad, apologetic look. I then show him what I've found online. Myrna Nesbitt is a major leader in a group that calls themselves CADS, which stands for Christians Against Depraved Souls. And a large part of their rhetoric involves an anti-gay movement that labels gay people as immoral, wicked, and damned to hell, put on earth to undermine society's good Christian people.

"Damn," Izzy says. "I had high hopes for her, too."

"So did I," I say with a tired sigh.

We change subjects and spend a few minutes discussing the skeletal remains unearthed on our property, with Izzy saying he's eager to see what the bone specialist has to say, and me bemoaning the indeterminate delays the find will cause for our building project. Then Cass pokes her head into the room.

"Your next interview is here," she says.

"Great," Izzy tells her. "Bring him on back." Cass disappears, and Izzy hands me the résumé for our next candidate. "Here's hoping this one is better," he says.

The next person in line is a man named Norman Gates, who looks to be in his mid to late thirties. The similarity in his name to the infamous *Psycho* character is unfortunate, particularly since the guy bears a striking resemblance to the late actor Anthony Perkins.

According to Norman's résumé, he has a bachelor's degree in biology, and his previous work experience, starting from the most recent, includes five years at a funeral home in a town about forty miles from here, a brief stint of two years as an orderly and OR tech at a hospital in Milwaukee, and a few years spent working on a dairy farm up north while he was going to school. At least with his hospital and funeral home experience, he should possess the basic skill set necessary to do the job.

Izzy once again does the introductions and offers Norman a pastry. Unlike Myrna, he accepts, opting for a glazed fritter I had my eye on as an after-lunch dessert. This makes me lower my opinion of him several notches, not just because he stole my donut, but because his willingness to eat during a job interview is a professional faux pas that makes me think he isn't all that serious about wanting the job.

"Thank you," Norman says, accepting the donut. "I normally wouldn't do this during an interview, but I ran into a traffic jam on my way here and didn't have time to grab something to eat." With that, he takes a bite and chews while Izzy does his spiel describing the job.

Once Izzy is done, he asks Norman, who has wolfed that fritter down, why he wants to work here.

"I think it would be a good combination with my skill set," he says. "I have experience with handling bodies and have assisted with the embalming procedures. I also have experience with seeing the human body cut open, thanks to the time I spent working as an OR tech. Plus, I enjoy puzzles, and the investigative part of the job would fit nicely with that."

They are all good answers, and I begin to consider forgiving Norman for his donut grab.

"Let's get over the elephant in the room thing," Norman says. "My name. I'm used to the *Psycho* references, and I know I bear a passing resemblance to Anthony Perkins. I get teased about it all the time."

"The name thing is interesting," Izzy admits. "But I don't see how it would interfere with your ability to do the job. Why are you looking to leave the funeral job?"

"Hmm, yeah . . . about that," he says hesitantly. "My current employer got a little upset with me because he found out I have a hobby that made him uncomfortable."

This piques my interest. "What hobby?" I ask.

"I've always had an interest in ancient Egypt and mummification," he says. "I have a collection at home that is . . . well . . . unusual."

Izzy and I both stare at him, waiting for him to continue.

"They are mummified animals, two of which I bought online, and one of which I did myself when my pet cat died."

Okay, this is a bit odd, and creepy, but when I weigh this against my need to find someone to relieve me workwise, I'm not sure it's a deal breaker. Then Norman explains further.

"We had a body at the funeral home, a man who died of natural causes and whose only surviving relative was a homeless person. Since we couldn't find any other living family members, and the one relative we did have was broke as broke can be, my boss offered to cremate the remains for free. I've been wanting to try out my mummification process on a human, and I thought this particular body might be the perfect candidate. So I asked the relative if he would be willing to give me permission. He was fine with it—to be honest, I think he just wanted the whole thing to go away whatever way it could—but my boss freaked out and told me I was morbid and inappropriate. And ever since then, all he lets me do is oversee ceremonies and sell coffins. That's not enough for me. I want more hands-on experience with the corpses.

And to be honest, I've run out of cozy metaphors to help me sell those overpriced death boxes to people who can't afford them half the time."

I glance over at Izzy to see his reaction to this, and judging from the stunned expression on his face, it's similar to mine.

Norman is sitting across from us, looking serene and pleased with himself, as if he'd just told us he likes to bake cakes as opposed to experiment with dead bodies.

Izzy finally collects himself, thanks Norman for coming in, and offers to show him out. I notice he does not offer to give him a tour of the place, which tells me all I need to know about Norman's chances of receiving a job offer.

Out of curiosity, I do a Google search on Norman while waiting for Izzy's return, but surprisingly, I don't find much of anything other than the obvious corrected finds for Norman Bates and some info on a character actor who also has the name Norman Gates.

Izzy returns, still looking a little shocked as well as apologetic. "Sorry about that," he says. "We'll keep looking."

I let out a sigh of disappointment, and nod. "I suppose it was too much to hope we would find someone quickly," I say, feeling my sense of exhaustion increase merely at the thought of having to continue at the rate I've been going. "And on that happy note, you should go home and get some rest. I've got some investigating to do."

"What are you looking into?"

"For starters, I'm going to pay a visit to Patty Volker to talk to her about the life insurance policies on Meredith Lansing and Craig Knowlton."

Izzy arches his eyebrows at this. "That could be . . . interesting."

"Tell me about it. And just to make it more interesting, I'm meeting her at her house, *the* house, the new one David built."

"Are you sure you're up for that?" Izzy asks, looking concerned.

"Hell, yeah," I say, waving away his concern. "I'm dying to see what the inside of the new place looks like. And I'm not worried about Patty. She's always been easygoing and nice."

"Be careful," Izzy says. "Curiosity did kill the cat."

Words to die by.

CHAPTER 18

I make my way down to the garage and my car. This requires me to walk past the pastries one more time, and my eyes are drawn to them as if they're magnetized and my eyes are made of metal. I lift the lid on the box and eye the remaining specimens. A particularly attractive donut with maple frosting on it skewers my attention. For a full minute I argue with myself, knowing that I don't need it, that the calories in it would take me an eternity to burn off, and that I really should eat something a little healthier. Then I realize that just by standing this close to it I've probably absorbed some of the calories already and throw caution to the wind. In a last-ditch effort to show some restraint, I break the donut in half and leave one of the pieces in the box—the slightly smaller piece, of course. By the time I reach the garage, I'm seriously considering retracing my steps back to the library to get the second half, but I manage to make it to my car. I'm a stress eater—justification number five thousand and twenty-one—and I promise myself I'll do better tomorrow.

I drive to a local coffee shop and order a latte with a double shot of espresso, skim milk, and sugar-free almond flavoring. Then I give myself kudos for doing better with my diet already. As I'm waiting for my concoction, I mentally prepare myself for the visit ahead, for the inevitable flood of old memories that will likely hit me, and the awkwardness of having to deal with my ex-husband's new wife. The stress it all triggers makes me seriously consider adding a piece of coffee cake to my order, but I stay strong.

Driving down the road to my old house, which also happens to be the road to the cottage I lived in after David and I split up, I feel a twinge of nostalgia. It's not for the McMansion life I had with David, but rather the solitary, cozy, relatively uncomplicated life I had while living in the cottage. Though I suppose *uncomplicated* isn't a true description considering that I underwent a separation, a divorce, the start of a new job, the discovery of a new love, the near loss of that new love, a pregnancy, and the birth of my first child while living there. Still, compared to the life I have now, it seems so peaceful and idyllic to me. I guess it's all a matter of perspective.

When I look back on the past couple of years, it amazes me how many changes have occurred in my life. Chief among them is the dissolution of my marriage to David, which wasn't a smooth ride, but also wasn't as acrimonious as some I've heard of.

I want to resent or dislike Patty on some level, though I can't come up with a rational reason why I feel this way. There is a level of awkwardness between us now—how could there not be?—but it's minimal in my mind. Patty's a nice person who has always been kind and friendly toward me. Her only transgression—and it's a suspected one, not a proven one—is that there were some shenanigans that took place in the settlement of our insurance policy after the fire that burned down our old house, shenanigans that might have let David benefit a little more from the settlement than I did.

Despite my suspicions, I am happy enough with what I got at the time—and the lesson I learned about establishing credit in one's own name—and I considered it a reasonable payment to be released from a marriage that had suffered a fatal blow.

Despite the fact that my relationship with David ended painfully, I still harbor a fair number of fond memories, memories of good times we shared when our love was still new and strong. David isn't a bad person, in general. After all, he chose an occupation that dedicates him to trying to better or save other people's lives. But like all of us, he isn't perfect, and his inability to keep his one-eyed monster in his pants cave was an imperfection I couldn't overcome.

My mother, whose primary goal in life has always been to see me and my sister, Desi, married to rich, influential men, regardless of any shortcomings they may have, couldn't believe I was willing to walk away from a marriage to a doctor . . . a surgeon, no less. The fact that I then hooked up with a lowly cop only made things worse in her eyes. To my mother, infidelity wasn't nearly reason enough to give up on a marriage that assured one a financially secure, somewhat prestigious future. The irony of my mother giving marital advice to anyone, given that she has been married and divorced four times and is currently living with a man I once dated, is lost on her.

Then again, my mother isn't always playing with a full deck when it comes to her mental health. She's a hypochondriac with a serious case of OCD and a warped way of looking at the world. It is due in part to her hypochondria that my divorce from David was such a blow to her. He was a key player in this part of her illness, and she consulted him endless times regarding whatever imagined symptoms she was having and the possible diagnoses that went with them.

While growing up, my mother's hypochondria led to a sense of instability for me, because before I understood her illness, I believed she was likely to die any day, any time. Gradually, I came to realize that most of her illnesses—at least the physical ones—were imagined, and any real ones she had were hugely overblown. As it turned out, this quirk had a positive spin to it in my later life because my mother's cumulative acquired medical knowledge and her library of medical textbooks was so extensive by the time I started nursing school that it gave me an advantage in learning all I needed to know to ace my classes.

Recently, I've started to wonder if some of my mother's mental health issues stem from the way my father handled things back when he left us. Learning the true circumstances around his disappearance has shed a new light on my mother's issues for me. But while I may have a better understanding of why she is the way she is, it doesn't make her any easier to live with. The last time I visited her house with my son in tow, she nearly had a heart attack—maybe even a real one. Matthew, in his typical style, left a trail of detritus everywhere he went: cookie crumbs, spilt juice puddles, jellied finger-prints, and the ultimate crime in my mother's eyes, a major dump in his drawers. My mother, whose skin is normally the color of alabaster, turned so white at the smell of Matthew's poo that she would have been invisible in a snowstorm. And by the time I had plopped Matthew down on my mother's bathroom floor to change and clean him and put his new clothes on, my mother had dressed herself in full biohazard gear. She was wearing a Tyvek bodysuit with a hood, rubber gloves, a gas mask, and rubber boots. I suspect the only rea-son she wasn't wearing a CDC-level respirator is because she hasn't figured out how to get one yet. She came armed with no less than six bottles of various cleaning agents. If she'd had a flamethrower, I suspect she would have brought that, too. As soon as I had emerged from the bathroom, my mother en-tered it and locked herself inside. I waited nearly an hour, and when she still hadn't emerged, I packed up my son and left.

In retrospect, my marital woes with David fit in well with my family history of dysfunction, and in a way, my childhood tribulations have helped to prepare me for the meeting I'm about to have with my ex's new wife. I became an expert at dealing with awkward at a very young age.

As I pull up in front of David and Patty's house, I marvel at the newness of it—how clean the exterior is, how fresh the trim paint looks, how young and green the landscaping appears. It triggers a twinge of envy in me (one I quickly quash) since I know that the building of my new house is now on hold indefinitely.

I park and head up the stone front steps to the porch. The front door is a massive, wooden, arched affair with a small, grated window near the top. There is a large, wrought iron knocker on it, but I forgo it in favor of the doorbell. When I push the button, I hear a rich, melodious chime from inside.

Patty answers quickly, and as always, she is gracious and kind, greeting me with a warm, genuine smile and a cheerful, "Good morning, Mattie. Come on in."

As I step over the threshold, I expect to be hit with a flood of memories, but it doesn't happen. The interior of the house is a stark contrast to the medieval-looking front door, probably because David picked out the house plan and started building it before he and Patty got serious. Everything about the house is vastly different from the one I had lived in. The structure is different, the colors are different, and the furnishings are all new and strange to me. My taste in design tends toward the traditional, or at least transitional, and I favor warm colors and soft, cushy lines. This house, however, is very modern in its design, with lots of smooth, sleek lines, monochromatic walls, floors, and furnishings touched by tiny splashes of scattered color in the accessories, and lots of open spaces. It's a relief in a way, because it bears no resemblance to the house I once called my own. But it's also a little sad.

"Good morning, Patty," I say. I stand a moment and take in my surroundings. "Wow! You've done an amazing job with the place."

"Thanks," she says, looking a little abashed. "Why don't we go into my office?" She waves a hand down the central area of the house. "It's the second door on the right."

I walk down the hall, hearing the cold echo of my steps on the stone floor. I glance in at the first room on the right and see that it is David's office. I can't resist a smile at the décor. It's a sharp contrast to the rest of the house and more in line with the office David had in our old home: lots of dark wood, plush carpeting, a warm, peach color on the walls, and bookcases filled with medical texts. I move past it to Patty's office, where the modern design is once more in play. Her desk is a glass-and-chrome affair that faces the entrance to the room; the floor is the same whitewashed-looking wood I saw in the living area, accented by a small area rug in a faux zebra pattern in front of the desk. Three of the walls are basic white, dotted with a half-dozen black-framed pictures. The fourth wall is an accent wall, with a pattern of horizontal panels in varying shades of gray. Sitting in front of this wall is a metallic credenza with four storage drawers—two on either end—and a second desk area in the middle. Atop this desk area is a row of manuals and books, bookended with two L-shaped slabs of stone, a multifunction printer/copier/scanner, and a Keurig coffeemaker.

The chair behind Patty's desk has a chrome frame with a molded mesh body, and a matching one sits on the side of the desk near the door. Behind the desk is a large window that looks out onto the side yard and the woods that separate this house from Izzy's.

I walk over and settle into the chair closest to me while Patty heads around behind the desk and sits in hers. The only items on top of the desk are a laptop and a peacock-blue pencil holder that looks completely out of place in the otherwise gray room. As I examine the pristinely clean glass top of the desk, I can't help but imagine what it would look like in my house, covered with Matthew's sticky fingerprints and the remnants of whatever was on those fingers, Hoover's nose prints, and trails of tiny cat prints crisscrossing the glass. That's not to mention all the stray fur that would likely be adhering to every surface.

"How have you been doing?" Patty asks me once we're both settled. "It's been a while."

She, like her house, is modern. She is sporting one of those stacked, layered haircuts with one side longer than the other, and it looks great on her. Her clothing is chic and sophisticated: narrow black slacks topped by a red T-shirt, and a red-and-black jacket with a mandarin collar that has a narrow strip of material across the middle front that brings the two sides together. She has earrings and a bracelet in the same black and red. I feel a little frumpy by comparison. Okay, a lot frumpy.

"I'm doing great," I lie. "Life is busy, what with the job, the kids, and whatnot."

"Yes, I imagine it is," Patty says. She smiles, but this time, it looks a little forced.

"How are things with you and David?"

"They're great," she says quickly, perhaps a little too quickly. "We're great."

I narrow my eyes at her, my gut alarm clanging loudly. She looks back at me, and that smile falters a smidge. She opens her mouth, and then shuts it again, looking away. Something is bothering her. I'm certain of it.

"I have some news," she says with an edge of wariness in her tone.

"Oh?" I say, unsure if she's referring to her and David, or my inquiry into the insurance policy.

"I'm pregnant," she says, the words rushing out. Her face blushes. "I mean, we're pregnant," she adds.

She rolls her lips inward and stares at me, sitting poker-straight in her seat, waiting for my reaction.

It's a mixed one. On the one hand, I'm very happy for her

and David and think it's great that their relationship has moved on to this next step. But there is also a lingering part of me that still mourns the loss of the future hopes and dreams that David and I once shared, which included a family.

"Congratulations, Patty!" I say with as much enthusiasm as I can muster. "I'm very happy for you."

She sags visibly, so I gather my enthusiasm must have seemed genuine enough. "Thank you," she says, sounding relieved. "I was worried how you might take the news. David didn't want to tell you ahead of time, but I felt it was only fair."

"I appreciate that, Patty," I say. "I confess that some small part of me feels a little shocked . . . and sad, I guess, that this final seal has been applied to the story that I once thought was mine. But David and I are long in the past, and I'm very happy now with Hurley and my son."

"As well you should be," Patty says with a warm smile. "He's adorable."

"Who?" I say in a teasing tone. "Matthew or Hurley?"

"Both," she answers without hesitation, punctuating it with an arch of one brow. "Your son is the cutest little rug rat I've ever seen—I hope my kid looks half as adorable. And let's face it, your husband is pretty easy on the eyes."

"He is that," I say. And just like that, all the tension leaves the room. "When are you due?" Like I said, it's hard not to like Patty. She's genuine, kindhearted, and sweet by nature.

"Not until early February," she says, an unconscious hand rubbing her tummy. "I'm a little over twelve weeks at this point, so we're past the danger zone."

"Oh, but there are many more dangers to come," I say with a wink. "There's the whole peeing every five minutes thing, and having boobs that leak all the time, and feeling like a beached whale."

She smiles and nods, but she looks eager rather than wary to experience these problems. Naïveté can be a blessing.

184 Annelise Ryan

"But it's all worth it in the end," I add.

She nods again, more eagerly this time. "So what can I do for you?" she asks, having gathered her sunny persona around her again.

"I'm interested in a couple of life insurance policies you issued. One for Craig Knowlton and one for Meredith Lansing. I'm sure you've heard about their deaths." It dawns on me then that I never read the rest of the paper this morning to see if the murder-suicide had been mentioned. I was so taken aback by the alien body headline that I forgot about the other case. But even if the deaths weren't mentioned in the paper, odds are Patty has heard about them. Sorenson is small enough that news like this leaks out faster than blood from a ruptured aortic aneurysm.

Patty nods, a soberer action this time. "I did," she says. "I heard it was a murder-suicide thing."

I don't affirm or deny this. "Have either of the spouses contacted you yet to cash in on the policies?"

"As a matter of fact, John Lansing called me right before you got here," she says.

This doesn't surprise me. "I saw that the policy on Meredith was taken out fairly recently," I say. "She and her husband both got one. I'm curious as to what you can remember about that. Were they here together? And what, if any, discussions took place regarding the policies?"

Patty frowns. "Why are you asking?" she says. "Were the deaths not what they appeared to be?"

Add not dumb to Patty's list of attributes. I don't answer her right away, debating how much to tell her.

"I'm sure the company investigator will be looking into it," she adds during my silence. "That's customary."

I nod. "You might put a bug in his ear to stall paying on the policies for now. There are some things about the case that don't quite add up. I would suggest that the investigator—or investigators, as the case may be—take a long, careful look at both cases."

"Good to know," Patty says. She gets up and walks over to the credenza, opening one of the drawers. A minute or so later, she returns to her desk carrying two manila folders. "As I recall, Craig's policy has a suicide preclusion," she says. "Most such policies do. I assumed that was why I hadn't heard from his wife yet."

I sigh and give her a warning look. "The bad news is the policy, at least the copy we saw, has a one-year suicide exclusion, and it was signed one year and a day ago. Although it may turn out to be a moot point."

Patty looks confused. "Are you saying Craig Knowlton didn't kill himself?"

"We're not clear yet," I tell her. "Like I said, there are some things that don't add up just yet. We're still investigating."

Patty scans Craig's policy, reads the suicide clause, and then leans back in her seat, her eyes wide. "Interesting timing, all right," she says.

I nod. "What, if anything, can you recall about either couple and the establishment of these policies?"

"Well, I remember the Knowltons came in together. They said their business was doing well, and they felt it was important to ensure the business survived if either or both of them didn't. The decision to insure themselves seemed like more of a business decision than a personal one. They debated over the amounts some. At one point, they were considering a higher amount in case they started a family. But I talked it through with them and assured them they could increase their coverage later on if necessary. They were both young enough that they still had plenty of time to do that before the rates grew prohibitive." She pauses, shaking her head for a second as if trying to shrug off a chill.

"I have to say," she goes on, "that when I heard about the

murder-suicide thing with Craig, it surprised me a little. Granted it was a year ago when I saw them, but I wouldn't have pegged either of them as the type to have an affair. They seemed very happy together. They were affectionate with one another, casting doe eyes and touching one another all the time; their body language suggested a strong intimacy between the two of them. Plus, they both seemed very uncomfortable whenever the death of either of them was mentioned."

"A lot can happen in a year," I say, thinking about how quickly my marriage to David had imploded. Then I remember who's sitting across from me and immediately regret having said it. If Patty picked up on my train of thought, she doesn't show it.

"With regard to the Lansing policy," she went on, "John came in by himself to talk with me initially, and he opted for both policies that same day. He said he used to work in the industry and knew the importance of having adequate insurance. I had to make a separate appointment for Meredith to come in and sign her paperwork. They both treated it like it was an everyday thing in the beginning, but that changed recently."

"How so?"

"John is no longer the beneficiary on Meredith's policy."

"What?" I say, leaning forward. "Tell me!"

"Meredith came in a couple of weeks ago and changed things up. She seemed upset, but she didn't say much. Just that she wanted to change the beneficiary."

"And who did she change it to?" I ask, reaching for the folders on the desk.

"Her niece and nephew," she says.

For a moment there, I thought she was going to say it was Craig Knowlton. "Wow, that's interesting," I say, digesting this information. "I don't think John was aware of that change."

"You're probably right. Meredith said she wanted me to keep a copy of the policy here in my office but declined to take one with her."

This information has me rethinking our case. Why had Meredith changed the policy? What had triggered her decision? "I'm curious," I say. "When John called here a bit ago, did you tell him that?"

Patty shakes her head. "I told him he would need to come into the office. I also told him that it would take some time to process the policy, that we needed certain things, like a death certificate, and that we would need to wait for the police investigation to be officially closed."

"That was smart thinking," I tell her.

She shrugs my compliment off. "It's standard procedure."

"Can you give me copies of these policies?"

"Sure. I can scan them and e-mail them to you later today, or if you want to wait around while I copy them, I can do that now."

"E-mail is fine," I say. I rise from my chair and hand her a business card with my work e-mail address on it. Then I turn toward the door as she comes around the desk to see me out. When we reach the main hallway, I take another look at the décor of the place and turn to her.

"Patty, I'm going to ask you something, and I want you to feel free to say no if it makes you at all uncomfortable."

"Okay," she says, her smile tentative.

"Would you give me a tour of the house? Normally, I wouldn't ask, given our history and all, but Hurley and I are just now starting on building a house, and I'm still trying to put together ideas for the interior. And you clearly have a great eye with a good sense of both space and design."

Patty looks relieved at my request, and I can't help but wonder what she thought I was going to ask. Even so, I feel a twinge of guilt. While it's true that I'm still trying to put together some of the interior design for our new house, Patty's sense of style is the polar opposite of mine, and little in this house is likely to help me much. I'm simply curious. Some might call it nosy.

"I'd love to," she says, and if she has any reservations at all about my request, she is hiding them well.

"Can we start with the kitchen?" I ask. "That seems to be my biggest bugaboo when it comes to planning."

Patty leads the way, and I follow her into a magnificent kitchen that looks like it belongs to an award-winning chef. There is a huge cast-iron stove with two ovens, a griddle, and six burners. A cylindrical chrome tube with a black flange at the bottom hangs over it—presumably the exhaust fan. The refrigerator doors are masqueraded to match the white upper cabinets that run along two walls. The lower cabinets are done in a dark wood, and there is a gigantic island—nearly as big as my entire kitchen was in the cottage—in the middle of the room with a huge slab of gray-and-white granite on top of it, more cabinets beneath, and a small prep sink. Six stools line the side closest to us, sleek black-and-chrome affairs with scooped seats. They are facing the sink, a stainless behemoth set beneath a window that looks out into the backyard and the woods beyond. Lining the walls along the countertops, which arc some sort of white, slick-looking material, is a gray, black, and white backsplash. The flooring is a dark-colored wood—almost black—done in wide planks.

All this monochromicity would be boring if not for the touches of color: yellow pendant lights over the island, red towels hanging by the sink, a bright red Keurig machine, yellow oven mitts hanging beside the stove, and on the countertops, a set of red canisters, a giant bowl of lemons, and a colorful array of cookbooks. Off to one side is a breakfast nook that is built out from the house as a sort of sunroom, with three big windows and a glass roof. It's furnished with a black wooden table surrounded by four white cushioned chairs that make me grimace when I think about Matthew's grubby little hands touching them.

It's a beautiful space, no denying that, but I wonder how practical it will be once Patty and David start raising a family.

I make all the necessary complimentary comments, taking note of a few items that I think I might want to incorporate into my own kitchen design. I hardly ever cook, so the stove holds little appeal to me, but I love the pot-filling faucet built into the wall behind the stove. And when Patty shows me a few of her cabinet features—a nifty, narrow little spice rack that rolls out, shelves that pull out, a pot cabinet with both racks and hooks, a pull-out pegboard organizer under the sink for gloves, sponges, dish soap, dishrags and cleaning supplies, and bins designed for trash cans as well as storage of things like onions and potatoes—I start building a mental wish list.

We move on to a guest bathroom, a second, less-formal living area where the furniture is a little less starkly modern in design, and then to David's office.

"I'm guessing David had a say in the design of this room," I tell Patty as we stand by the heavy wooden desk.

Patty gives me a tolerant little smile. "You could say that," she says. "He's not a huge fan of my modern tastes, and he said he wanted a room that he could call his own. So he got to pick everything in here, from the flooring to the wall color and all of the furnishings."

As she talks, I'm scanning the top of David's desk. There is one of those large blotter calendars on it, something David always had on his desk in our old house. Scribbled in on the days are various surgeries, meetings, and appointments, all of it in David's angular scrawl that is so familiar to me. For the first time, I feel a twinge of nostalgia. Then I zero in on today's schedule and see that David has three surgeries planned, including a late one that won't start until four o'clock. These off-hour surgeries are something David has always done to accommodate his patients—patients who have kids they need to pick up and drop somewhere, people who need to wait until a spouse is off work, patients who simply aren't morning people. David has never minded working these late hours, and sometimes he schedules surgeries this way simply to get his quota of procedures done all in one day and have a free day before or after. Neither the OR staff nor the hospital administrators are overly fond of these weird hours, but given that David is the only general surgeon on staff—a fact that is likely to continue, given that the hospital has been trying unsuccessfully for two years to recruit a second surgeon—the hospital is willing to bend and cater to him in this regard.

I used to staff a lot of David's evening surgeries; unlike the other nurses, I didn't mind the hours since it gave me more time with my husband. And I kind of liked the off hours because all of the administrative dinks and department managers were gone for the day, and this gave the hospital a more informal, relaxed feel.

As this memory hits me, so does an idea. And like a lightning strike, something else comes to mind, an idea that is both frightening and exciting at the same time.

CHAPTER 19

When Patty and I reach the living area of the front hallway, I glance at my watch and thank her for her time and her tour. I don't know if she's willing to show me the upstairs part of the house, but it doesn't matter because I've decided that would be too much of an invasion of privacy. Besides, I'm eager to pursue the idea I had while we were in David's office.

Once I'm underway in my car, I call Hurley and let him know I'm on my way back to the station. He arranges to meet me behind the station, and he's already in his car, idling, when I pull in. I park my hearse, grab my scene kit, toss it into the backseat of Hurley's car, and then climb into the front seat.

"Ready to do some Grizzly Motel reconnaissance?" he asks me.

"Ready as I'll ever be," I say as he pulls out of the police station lot.

"Heard anything on the bones yet?"

I shake my head. "It might take a while."

"The contractor called me a bit ago and asked how long it was going to be before they could resume work," Hurley says with a pained expression. "I told him a day, maybe two. Think that's possible?"

"I doubt it," I say with a grimace. "The DNA testing alone will probably take a week."

Hurley sighs.

"We're just going to have to be patient," I tell him. "I know it won't be easy. Believe me, no one wants to see that house built more than I do, but it is what it is."

He nods, looking morose. "How did things go with Patty?"

"It was easier than I thought it would be. She's such a nice person, and she was not only gracious, but helpful. And she had some interesting news to share. She and David are expecting."

Hurley looks over at me. "Really? How do you feel about that?"

"I'm happy for them."

"Is that it?"

I give him a bemused look. "What do you mean?"

"Well, it's kind of a closing chapter on your life with David. Any regrets?"

I dismiss the idea readily with a little *pfft* and an adamant shake of my head. But then I stop. Hurley looks at me again, then at the road, then back at me.

"I suppose there was a twinge of something," I admit. "I don't know what to call it. Not regret, certainly, and not jealousy or anything like that. I'm long over David, and I love you. I love our life together, our kids, and our house that may never get built. But at one time, building a family and a life with David was my dream, and I guess I feel a tiny sense of loss—or maybe nostalgia is a better word—for a dream that was never realized. And for my naïveté."

Hurley nods slowly, a hint of a smile on his face.

"What's so funny?" I ask.

"Nothing," he says. He reaches over, grabs my hand, and

kisses the back of it. "I'm just happy that you love our life. And speaking of life, what did you find out about the insurance policies?"

I summarize my conversation with Patty regarding the policies and the people attached to them. When I get to the part about Meredith changing her beneficiary, Hurley arches his brows.

"That's interesting," he says. "I wonder what made her do that?"

"I don't know, but if John found out about it, who knows how mad it might have made him."

"We might need to have another chat with Mr. Lansing," Hurley says. "In fact, I think we should do that as soon as we get back to town."

"Do you plan on telling him about the insurance policy?"

"We'll see. I'll play it by ear. Want to sit in on it?"

"Heck, yeah." Another brief silence ensues before I switch topics. "Speaking of chats, I think we need to talk to Tomas Wyzinski."

Hurley purses his lips. "It's not going to help," he says. "The man isn't going to talk. If we're right about our theory in that case, the ears are numerous and high-reaching. He's not going to trust anyone, especially a cop."

"What if I talk to him alone?"

Hurley looks at me like I'm crazy.

"I can record it if you want, but I think we'd have better luck if we didn't."

"And what, exactly, do you want to say to him?"

"That I'm working with him, or at least for him. That I've come to believe in the possibility of his innocence. I can talk to him with his lawyer there if necessary."

Hurley tips his head to the side, his lips expressing his disapproval of the idea. After a few seconds, he says, "You're not going to give up on this notion until I let you do it, are you?"

"You don't have to let me," I say, irritated. "I don't need your permission to visit with and talk to the man. But I want to do it with your support and knowledge."

He shakes his head in frustration, flipping on his turn signal as he pulls into the parking lot of the Grizzly Motel. "Fine," he says. "But I'm telling you, you're wasting your time."

I table the topic for now, not wanting to push the issue. Hurley pulls around to the back of the motel and parks his car along the far edge of the rear parking lot where it borders the woods. Hurley turns off the engine, and I grab my scene kit while he fetches a video camera and a flashlight from the trunk. Then the two of us walk over to the start of the path I saw when we were here the other night.

Even by the bright light of day, the trail is kind of creepy. The trees here are thick, and the foliage is heavy. Only dapples of sunlight manage to eke their way through the canopy of trees to the path below, which is little more than a dirt trail.

"After you," Hurley says, handing me his flashlight.

I take it, turn it on, and head into the copse feeling like we're Hansel and Gretel. There is trash scattered on and alongside the trail, items like empty plastic bottles, plastic drink cups, food wrappers, and even a used condom. I start to think we should have put on some protective gear. The path winds and wends its way through the trees, and after a few minutes I stop in my tracks, staring up ahead.

"Hurley, look at that," I say, pointing. About twenty feet ahead, the path splits into a fork. Half of it veers sharply to the left, while the remainder continues to meander deeper into the woods. On the path to the left is a tree with a split trunk, both sides of which are bowed over, their tops nearly touching the ground, the trunks arching over the path to the other side. "Does that look like a double arch to you?"

Hurley stares at it for a second, blinks hard, and then smiles. "Like in the text message," he says.

"I say we follow the left path first."

"I agree." He reaches over, takes the flashlight from me, and picks up the lead.

Five minutes later, our path emerges from the woods, right alongside a road with a sign a few hundred feet to our right that informs us it's County Road P.

"This road intersects with Morals Road just past the Grizzly," Hurley says. He holds a hand out at his side to indicate I should stand still, and he shifts his attention to the ground at our feet. "Scan this area carefully," he says. "There might be evidence here."

Together, we spend the next twenty minutes walking a grid between the edge of the woods and the shoulder of the road, searching the ground for anything that might be relevant. We find a gum wrapper, a bottle cap, and two cigarette butts, none of which are likely related to our case given that all look like they've been out here a long time, but we collect and bag them anyway. When we reach the shoulder, however, our luck changes. There in the mud alongside the road are tire tracks.

"These look fresh," Hurley says, filming the length of the mark. "And it's a good impression. It rained the day before the murders, so this ground was nice and wet when whoever was driving pulled over here. We need to get a casting."

"I can do that," I say, setting my scene kit down. I open it and remove the necessary materials. Ten minutes later, the cast is solidifying, and we use the time to walk the shoulder a hundred feet or so in each direction, looking for more clues.

My phone rings while I'm searching my end, and I see that it's the office calling.

"This is Mattie."

"Hey, Mattie, it's Otto."

"You have some news on our bones?"

"I do. But you're not going to like it." I roll my eyes and brace myself. "Schmitt thinks the bones are fifty to sixty years old. And there is some evidence of possible blunt-force trauma in the skull bones."

"What about the weird shape of the bones?" Hurley has overheard enough of the conversation that he knows what it's about, and he's coming toward me at a fast lope.

"It's hard to say at this point," Otto equivocates. "We're going to send a sample to Madison for a DNA analysis. The abnormalities are curious, and though I mentioned hydrocephalus, nothing points to a specific genetic defect that we know of. And much as I hate to say it, Arnie was right about one thing. There are no sinuses in the skull."

"Oh jeez, don't tell him that."

"He already knows. He trumped up a gazillion dumbass excuses to pop in on us while we were examining the bones. And every time he showed up, he asked what he had found so far. Unfortunately, Schmitt was more than happy to oblige with information and updates."

"Are we going to have to dig some more?"

"I don't think so, but we need to preserve the area as a crime scene for now until we can determine the cause of the skull injuries."

"So our building project is on hold," I say, giving Hurley a sad look.

"Looks that way."

"Great."

"Have you and Hurley made any progress on the motel case?"

"Maybe." I tell him about my visit to Patty, and the information I learned about the life insurance policies. Then I fill him in on our hike and what we found there. "Hurley's thinking that whoever shot Craig and Meredith did so and then left the motel room on foot, disappearing into the woods behind the motel. We followed a path that merges with an intersecting road, and we suspect someone had a car here, either with an accomplice behind the wheel or parked on the side of the road. We have some decent tire tracks to work with, so maybe that will lead to something."

"Sounds good. Tell Hurley he might want to start investigating these bones. Who did you buy that property from? And for how long did they own it?"

"It belonged to a farmer who owns a bunch of other acres out that way," I tell him. "As far as I know, the land has been in that family for several generations."

"Then he should probably start there, talk to them, see what they might know about it."

"I'll pass that on. Need me to come in to the office for anything?"

"Nah, things are relatively quiet. Keep working with Hurley, and I'll call you if I need you."

"Thanks, Otto." I disconnect the call and summarize what Otto said for Hurley.

"Just what I need," Hurley says, raking a hand through his hair. "Another case."

"Let's wind this up and get back to town," I say, glancing at my watch. "It's lunchtime, and I'm hungry." I leave out the information that my hunger is likely from a precipitous drop in my blood sugar brought on by my donut gorging earlier.

We collect the tire cast and follow the path back into the woods. When we reach the intersection, we follow the other branch for ten minutes and emerge on the edge of a field. Since there is no other evidence to be had, we head back to the motel and the car.

Next on our agenda is lunch, turning in our evidence, checking in with Jonas to see if he and Laura have come up with anything new, and then paying another visit to John Lansing. I have a feeling it will be an eventful day by the time all is said and done.

CHAPTER 20

The trip back to town is a mostly silent one as Hurley and I mourn the loss of our completion date on the house. My thoughts drift back to my visit with Patty, and the idea I came up with when I saw David's surgery schedule. I debate whether or not to share the idea with Hurley. I'm reluctant to do so because I suspect he'll tell me I'm crazy and forbid me to do what I want to do.

These thoughts lead to a nag that is tickling my brain. There is something else in there, some clue or connection that I know I'm close to figuring out but just can't see. I need a mental jog, so I turn to Hurley and ask, "Do you have a copy of that list we found on Hal's thumb drive in your notebook?"

"I do," he says, shooting me a curious, sidelong glance. "Why?"

"Can I see it?"

He reaches into his shirt pocket and pulls out the notepad. I take it and flip through the pages, scanning his notes. This particular notebook is almost full, and it contains notes on our current case, the bones case, and the Jeremy Prince case. He has headers on the pages to signify what the notes refer to: *Knowlton/Lansing* for the motel case, *Jeremy Prince* for that case, and, much to my amusement, I see he has *Alien Body* as a header for the bones case.

"You're not as much of a skeptic as I thought you were," I say, showing him a page with the *Alien Body* header.

He shrugs and grins. "It seemed like a logical title at the time."

"Do you believe aliens have visited us here on earth?" I ask, flipping through more pages until I find the one I want.

"Not really," he says. "But I try to have an open mind. I think there are some things in the world that can't be explained by any other logical means, at least not yet, including some of those things Arnie pointed out."

"Don't tell him that. His theories don't need any fodder." A silence falls between us as I scan the notes from Hal's thumb drive. I see where Hurley has scribbled in the Kupper names next to the applicable abbreviations, with a question mark after each one. As I scan the remaining items, one jumps out at me.

"Hurley, this MW equals KP note, do you think MW might be code for Miller-Weiss?"

He nods but does so hesitantly. "I already thought of that, but I have no idea what the KP stands for."

"Both Marshal Washington and my father said that Miller-Weiss was a subsidiary of a much larger corporation, a Medusan type of business model with a number of shell companies and branch-offs. Maybe KP is an abbreviation for one of them."

Hurley nods, and this time it's more encouraging. "That's a good thought," he says.

"And the K in KP, maybe it's related to the Kuppers. I mean, it might be a coincidence, but then again . . ."

His brow furrows as he considers this. Meanwhile, I take out my smartphone with the intention of googling to see if there are any businesses out there with the Kupper name attached. But we are still too far from town, and I can't get a signal for Wi-Fi access. I relay both the idea and the fact that I can't research it yet to Hurley.

"You're on a roll," he says. "Keep it in mind for when we get back to town."

I set the phone in my lap and pick up the notebook again, scanning the list. And then something else strikes me. And when it does, some of the other abbreviations start to make sense. I feel a trill of excitement in my chest.

"Oh my God, Hurley, I think I know what these letters by all the locations mean."

Hal's note had a list of four pairs of initials, each one followed by several geographic locations from around the world:

> *RO: France, Switzerland, New York*
> *DW: Miami, Florence, London*
> *PQ: London, Sydney, Belgium*
> *TR: Edinburgh, Prague, Mykonos*

"Tell me," Hurley says.

"Do you remember me telling you how David and I went to Miami for a conference where he was speaking? It was where I first went scuba diving."

"Yeah, so?"

"One of these entries, the DW, has Miami listed after it. And the other two locations are London and Florence."

Hurley ponders this and shakes his head. "I'm not following you."

"Don't you remember me telling you how David and I might have benefited from some of the pharmaceutical company monies disguised as speaking fees? We went to London for a conference as well, and—"

"And he went to Italy, too," Hurley says, his tone finally

excited. "You said you weren't able to go on that trip because you had the flu or something."

"Yes." I don't say anything else. I just stare at him, waiting for him to figure it out.

"You think DW is David Winston," he says.

"I do."

"And those other initials? Do you have any names to go with those?"

"One of them. When we were in London, we went out to dinner one night with another couple, an internal medicine doctor and his wife. His name was Peter Quinn. And London is listed in Hal's note after the initials PQ."

Hurley digests this. "So you think Hal's notes are referring to doctors who might have accepted kickbacks in the form of speaking fees for prescribing their drugs? And that David was one of them?" Before I can answer him, he takes one hand from the wheel and snaps his fingers. "Kickbacks!" he says, giving me an excited look. "The number, and the initials AKS, that could stand for the Anti-Kickback Statute! I think that number might reference a particular law."

His excitement is contagious. "We'll have to look it up as soon as we get back to town," I say. "And I think I need to have another chat with David."

"You mean we should."

I give him a look that says that's not what I mean at all. "I think I might be able to get further with him than you will, given that I might have been a part of it."

At least he doesn't dismiss my objection outright. "I don't think David knowingly participated in anything illegal," I tell him. "If you're there when I talk to him, he might get defensive."

I can tell he's not wild about the idea. So I figure I might as well hit him up with the thought that came to me earlier, though I'd rather not, since acting on it will mean skirting the law and compromising some evidence. But I did promise I would tell him everything. So I bite the bullet and go for it.

When I'm done detailing my plan, I fully expect him to tell me I'm crazy, or reckless, or just plain dumb, but he does none of those things. He opens and closes his hands on the steering wheel a few times, his brow furrowed in thought. Finally, he speaks.

"It's not a bad idea," he says. "It could give us some valuable leads. But it isn't completely aboveboard, and it could end up costing you your job."

"It's a risk I'm willing to take," I tell him. "Please, Hurley, we have to do something. We're getting nowhere with this Prince case as it is."

"It might compromise our case in the end."

"If we handle it right, I don't think it will." I explain to him what I mean.

"Okay," he says with a reluctant nod. "Let's do it. And for the record, you and I never had this conversation."

I'm surprised by his capitulation, but also pleased. As we have now reached the outskirts of town, I try again to access the Internet on my phone. This time I'm successful. The first thing I do is a search for the number referenced in Hal's notes. Sure enough, it comes back to a federal anti-kickback statute. I share this news with Hurley.

"Maybe we're finally going to get a break in this case," he says, sounding hopeful for the first time since Prince's death. Then I improve his mood even more when I search for the Kupper name and businesses.

"Hurley, here it is!" I say excitedly. "There is a company called Kupper Products. It says they are a medical research company. Kupper Products jibes with the initials KP in Hal's note."

To my surprise, his reaction isn't the cheerfulness I'd expected. Instead, he frowns.

"I thought that would make you happy," I say. "What's wrong?"

"What's wrong is that it makes it even more likely that the Kupper family is tied in to this thing. And they're a powerful family. We're talking about a judge and a congressman, Mattie. That's not going to be easy."

"We'll figure out a way. Together we're an indomitable team, Hurley."

He gives me a meager smile, one that suggests I'm delusional.

We have reached the police station, and Hurley pulls into the underground entrance to Jonas's lab area. We drop off our evidence and give Jonas the details of where we found it and what we hope to get from it. In exchange, Jonas informs us that he found a partial print on one of the bullets in the gun found in the motel room. It's a match for John Lansing.

This is both good news and bad news—good because we're closer to solving our case, bad because I was hoping we could go for some lunch now. But Hurley says, "I want to talk to John Lansing right away. He might decide to run if he suspects we're on to him. I want to nail things down before he can."

My stomach lets my disappointment be known by grumbling in protest once we're in the car.

"I take it you disagree with our schedule," Hurley says with a smile as I rub my complaining stomach.

"I'll survive," I say. "Hell, I can live off the fat in my thighs alone for at least a week."

"I like your thighs," Hurley says with a salacious eyebrow wiggle. He starts the car and pulls out of the lot. "It's been a while since I've had the chance to see them up close and personal."

He's right. It has been a while. Sex has kind of fallen off our radar of late, mainly because our schedules are so crazy, but also because I'm so exhausted lately and we never seem to have any time alone when Matthew isn't vying for our attention.

"I know," I say with a wistful sigh. "We need a date night."

"What we need is a honeymoon," Hurley says.

"That would be nice," I agree. "But until Izzy can hire on someone to help, it's not going to happen. Plus, I don't know if I could leave Matthew to go anywhere."

"He'd be in good hands if we left him with either Dom or your sister," he says.

"I know, but I'd miss him."

"I miss you," Hurley says in a quiet voice.

I know he's right, but I also know it will be a struggle for me. And since it isn't going to happen anytime soon, I decide I'll cross that bridge when I get to it.

We arrive at John Lansing's apartment complex and make our way up to his door. Hurley knocks and we wait, but nothing happens. He knocks again. There is a window off to the right, but the blinds on it are closed.

"He can't have gone far," I say. "He didn't have any wheels. He and Meredith shared a car, and we have it impounded."

"He could have taken a taxi," Hurley says. "Maybe he's already flown the coop."

I sense his agitation, and out of curiosity, I try the doorknob. It turns easily, and I give Hurley a look. He chews on his lip for a second, debating. Then he shrugs and gives me a nod. I push the door open.

Inside, we see John Lansing lying on his couch. "Mr. Lansing?" Hurley hollers. Lansing doesn't move. We step inside, and as we venture deeper into the house, we see the stuff on the coffee table: an empty bottle of pills, an empty highball glass, a near empty bottle of vodka, and a single sheet of white paper with some writing on it. Now that I can get a closer look at Lansing, I see that his color is pale . . . too pale.

I hurry over and touch his neck, feeling for a carotid pulse. But as soon as my fingers feel the cold, hard skin, I know we are too late.

"Don't touch anything else," Hurley says. He takes out his cell phone but stops before punching in a number. Instead he leans over and reads the note on the table, done in pen, the letters printed in all caps.

I can't go on without Meredith. I'm so sorry. Please forgive me.

At the bottom, scrawled in a wavering hand, is the name *John.*

I look at the bottle of pills and see it is the sleeping pill prescription written for Meredith that I'd seen in the medicine cabinet on our first trip here. Except that bottle had only four pills left in it. I bend down and peer more closely at the container and see that the date on it is seven days ago and there were fifty pills dispensed. I remember looking at the bottle in the medicine cabinet and noting the medication and who it was for, but did I notice the date? Unlikely, because it would've struck me as odd that so few of the pills were left. That's assuming the bottle in front of me now is the same one that had been in the medicine cabinet.

"Hold on, Hurley," I say. "I need to check on something." I go back to the bathroom and open the medicine cabinet. There is no prescription bottle in there. Next, I take out my phone and call the dispensing pharmacy. They tell me that the most recent refill was seven days ago and there were none before that for almost six months.

I tell Hurley what I've learned. "I'm certain there were only four pills in that bottle when I saw it before, so he must have taken a bunch of them out and stashed them somewhere. There are a total of forty-six pills missing."

Hurley looks at the bottle, then at me, then at John Lansing's body. "This ties everything up with a neat little bow," he says.

"Maybe a little too neat," I say. "This feels off to me."

Hurley shoots me a quizzical look.

"That signature at the bottom of the page doesn't look at all like John Lansing's, assuming he signed the life insurance policy taken out on him. And Patty mentioned that he came in specifically to sign it. I remember thinking the handwriting was very tight, heavy, and angular, as if whoever wrote it was angry. This"—I point to the signature on the supposed suicide note—"is a good attempt to imitate it, but it lacks the heaviness and the angularity of the signature I saw."

"He might have been well under the influence when he signed it. That could affect the way he wrote."

"Maybe," I admit, though I don't agree. "But then why block print the note? That takes concentration."

"You don't think this is a suicide, do you?" Hurley asks.

"I don't. John Lansing didn't strike me as the suicidal type. For one thing, I think he was too much of a narcissist. He considered himself smarter, better than the average Joe. That's why he wouldn't settle for a job that was, as he put it, beneath him."

"So give me your theory," Hurley says. This is unlike him. He normally develops his own theory of a crime scene soon after seeing it and is typically skeptical, if not reluctant, to consider opposing views. The fact that he is so open to my opinion on this one makes me think the lack of sleep and hectic schedules are getting to him as much as they are getting to me.

"Okay," I start, "if we assume that John Lansing killed both Craig and Meredith, how did he get to the motel and back? Meredith's car was at the hospital, and Craig's was at the motel. Supposedly, Craig drove out to the motel, but we know Craig was already dead when he was shot. So how could John Lansing get Craig's car to the motel and then get back to town? He could have driven Meredith's car to the hospital and walked home from there, but the motel? That's way too far."

Hurley nods. "He had to have had an accomplice," he says. "We already surmised there were probably two people involved."

"And perhaps that accomplice wanted to eliminate the only person who could point a finger at her."

Hurley shoots me a look. "Her?"

"It had to have been Pamela Knowlton. Who else has a motive here?"

"So we have another murder on our hands," Hurley says, finally punching a number into his phone. He looks toward the heavens as he puts the phone to his ear. "This case is really starting to tick me off."

CHAPTER 21

I call Otto and ask him to meet us at John Lansing's apartment. While we're waiting for him and the other cops to show up, I head out to the car and grab my scene kit. As I'm coming back into the apartment, Bob Richmond pulls up. Right behind him is Brenda Joiner.

Once I'm back inside, I don some gloves and start poking and prying at John's face, neck, torso, and limbs. "Judging from the fact that rigor is present in his face, neck, and upper torso, but not his abdomen or limbs, I'm guessing his time of death was somewhere between midnight last night and four this morning," I tell the assembled group. "We can be more precise once we open him up."

I snap pictures of the scene, including a close-up of the prescription bottle. Something tugs at my mind, a nag that I can't quite identify. After a few seconds, I shrug it off and continue.

Hurley fills Richmond in on our findings and then tells him to go and get Pamela Knowlton and bring her down to the station. "Once Jonas and Otto get here, I want to have a chat with her. I'm beginning to think she was the mastermind behind this thing. I think she set it up so that she could collect on her husband's life insurance policy, and she used John Lansing to help her. Then she killed him to ensure he wouldn't rat on her. I think they set up the whole business with the burner phones, making it appear as if Meredith and Craig were having an affair. Then they set up the motel scene to make it look like a murder-suicide. Odds are Pamela promised John Lansing part of the proceeds if he helped her, then she made sure he wouldn't be around to collect."

Richmond stares at the scene a moment, nodding slowly. "How do you think she did it?" he asks.

Hurley looks at me. "How many of those pills would it take to kill someone?"

I think a moment. "Rough guess, ten, maybe fifteen. The effect would be greater if alcohol is involved. The combination of the two would slow the respiratory drive until the person stopped breathing altogether."

"I'm betting we'll find traces of that same medication in both Craig and Meredith," Hurley says. "She used what she had left on John. I think she came over here and shared a drink with him, only she spiked his to get him extra drunk, crushing up those pills in it. With fifty pills in that prescription, there would have been plenty to go around. If anyone saw her car here, or saw her here, she could always say that she came by to talk to him, to find out if he knew about the affair her husband was having with John's wife. And that when she left John, he was morose but still alive. Easy enough."

"And it was smart of her to use Meredith's prescription," I say. "I didn't find any scripts in the Knowlton house, so this gives her one more degree of separation."

The others nod. I look at the prescription bottle again, feeling that same nudge in my brain. Something . . . but it eludes me.

Otto arrives then, and we fill him in on how we got here and what we found.

"The sleeping pills aren't a surprise," he says. "Arnie informed me just a bit ago that he found the same drug in both Craig's and Meredith's stomach contents."

After examining the body, Otto agrees with my estimate on the time of death, telling the others the same thing I did, that we can be more precise once an autopsy is done. I help him bag John's body for transport, and while we're waiting for the Johnson sisters to arrive to pick up the body, I assist Jonas, who has also arrived, with bagging and tagging evidence. Richmond stays until Otto and I are done packaging Lansing's body, before heading out to find and pick up Pamela Knowlton. Otto then takes Hurley into the kitchen and has a chat with him. I try to overhear what's being said but can't.

When they return to the living-room area, Hurley gets a phone call. "It's Richmond," he says just before answering. "Have you got her?" he says into the phone, bypassing such niceties as a simple hello. He listens for a moment, says thanks, and then disconnects the call. "Richmond is on his way back to the station with Pamela Knowlton. He said she came willingly, without any objection, though she looked puzzled as to why we wanted to talk to her." Hurley focuses on Otto. "I'd like to have Mattie sit in on my chat with the woman, if possible. She has a keen sense with people, and she knows Mrs. Knowlton from our previous dealings with her. But if you need her to assist you with the autopsy, I'll understand."

Otto says, "It will be an hour or more before the body gets to our morgue and gets checked in. I can do that part if you want to borrow Mattie until then."

"That's great," Hurley says. "Thanks, Doc. I'll get her back to you as soon as we're done."

While this conversation leaves me feeling a bit like chattel that is being passed back and forth, I'm glad Hurley has asked for me to come along. I love the interrogation process, and Hurley is right. I'm good at reading people. That stems in part from my years working as a nurse in the ER. Patients I saw there lied all the time, sometimes about serious things, sometimes about innocuous things. I learned early on to double any amounts the patients admitted to when it came to their smoking, drinking, and drug use habits. And I also learned all the manipulative behaviors people use to get what they want, whether it be narcotics, an unnecessary CT scan, or antibiotics for what is clearly a viral infection. After a while, I learned all the little tells that so often give people away, the subtle shifting of the eyes, a certain hesitation before answering a key question, a fidget here or a squirm there. Most people don't lie very well, though there are exceptions.

Hurley and I head back to the station a few minutes later, both of us dismayed as we drive past my office, where the assembly of newspeople and vehicles is still gathered by our front door. We enter the police station break room through the back door from the secured parking area and head down a hall that passes between offices and the interrogation/conference room. Richmond is sitting at his desk, and when we enter the office—one he shares with both Hurley and Junior Feller—he spins around in his chair to give us an update.

"Your suspect is in the conference room, and I tested the recording instruments to make sure they're working."

"Did you tell her anything about why we wanted her to come in?" Hurley asks.

Richmond shakes his head. "Not really. I just told her you had some more questions to ask her about her husband's death. I implied it was routine. I didn't Mirandize her."

"Okay, thanks." Hurley turns to me and waves a hand toward the door. "Shall we?"

I lead the way—I've been in that room enough times that I could find my way there blindfolded—and enter the space. I settle into a chair close to the door, right beside the audiovisual equipment switch. Hurley closes the door behind us and settles into the seat next to me on the other side of the switch. Pamela Knowlton is sitting on the opposite side of the table, doing something on her cell phone—a game or texting, I can't really tell—and she doesn't acknowledge our entrance until we're both seated. Arrogance or innocence, I wonder.

When Pamela finally looks up at us, she smiles warmly. "Hello again," she says, shifting her gaze between me and Hurley. "That other detective said you needed to talk to me more about Craig." There is a hint of a question in her voice, telling me she's confused as to what else we could possibly need to know.

Hurley always takes the lead in these sorts of things, and I wait for him to do so. He reaches down beneath the table and flips on the AV equipment. Then he starts things off by stating the date, the time, the case this is in reference to (he refers to it as the suspicious deaths of Craig Knowlton and Meredith Lansing, sidestepping the whole murder-suicide declaration), and who is present. When that's done, he gives Pamela his most charming smile and informs her that our session is being recorded and that he needs to cite the Miranda warning to her as part of the procedure. He does so, and she doesn't seem bothered, though she does look a little puzzled by it. When Hurley is done, he asks Pamela if she understands her rights.

She nods and says, "Yes, of course."

"Mrs. Knowlton, I need to inform you of some things we have discovered about your husband's case."

This gets a reaction. Her expression looks like Matthew's did the first time he tried—and spat out—broccoli. "What more could there possibly be?" she says. "Isn't it all sordid enough already? Our clients are asking all sorts of questions, and I don't know how to answer them."

"Yes, I imagine that must be difficult," Hurley says, sounding genuinely sympathetic, though I'm fairly sure he's not. "But some irregularities turned up when we performed the autopsies, and it seems that your husband's death wasn't a suicide after all."

Pamela stares at him, blinking several times. "What are you saying?" she manages after several seconds. "Did that woman he was with kill him?"

"No," Hurley says. "But someone did."

I watch the play of emotions over Pamela's face as she considers what Hurley just said. I see confusion, disbelief, skepticism, horror, and then what looks like anger. "Are you telling me my husband was murdered?" she says, her voice tight.

"It appears that way, yes," Hurley says.

"Who? Why? How?" Pamela looks genuinely confused and overwhelmed by this new information. If it's an act, it's a good one. Her eyes tear up, and her chin starts to quiver.

Hurley doesn't answer any of her questions. "Mrs. Knowlton, I noticed that your husband's life insurance policy had a suicide clause in it, one that expired exactly one day before he was killed. The fact that you are the beneficiary of that policy, and your husband's death was staged to look like a suicide, makes me want to look at you a little closer. Do you understand why?"

Pamela again goes through a gamut of emotions, starting with confusion, then quickly moving on to disbelief, and ending with offended. Her next question comes out tightly controlled, her anger boiling just below the surface. "Are you suggesting that I killed my husband, staged it to look like a suicide, and apparently killed some woman as well, all so I could collect on Craig's life insurance?"

"You have to admit, the timing in relation to the life insurance policy is rather uncanny," Hurley says with a shrug.

Pamela squeezes her eyes closed and exhales her frustration hard enough that I can smell her mint-scented breath from across the table. When she opens her eyes again, she zeroes them in on Hurley's like a laser beam. "I did not kill my husband, Detective," she says, enunciating slowly and carefully. "I loved my husband. And I don't need his stupid life insurance. Our business has done very well over the past few years, and we have a healthy nest egg set up. The life insurance policies—and yes, I have one on me, too—were to cover the business value of our services to our company. I can show you our financial reports, if you like."

Rather than respond to this challenge, Hurley says, "Where were you between the hours of eleven last night and five this morning?"

If Hurley's aim is to unsettle Pamela with this sudden change of subject, it appears to have worked. She shakes her head, as if trying to loosen something in her brain, and stares at Hurley with her mouth agape.

"What the hell?" she says. "What has that got to do with anything?"

"Please answer the question," Hurley says calmly.

Pamela rolls her eyes and shakes her head in disgust. "I was at home, Detective. I spent most of the day there. Our office is closed because I needed some time to absorb Craig's death. I forwarded the office phones to my cell. I didn't take or make any calls, but I did monitor those that came in, and I listened to the messages. Most were condolence calls, but a few were work-related, mostly from clients who don't know about what . . . about Craig yet. I left the house this morning at five to go into the office and get some files for the clients who called needing services. Much as I would like to shut the business down indefinitely, Craig and I are that business. There is no one to take over for me, no one to fill in. And I have a fiduciary duty to our clients." Her eyes have filled with tears, and she stops, leans her head back, and closes her eyes for a few seconds. "Besides," she says, once she lowers her head and looks at Hurley again, "the work takes my mind off of . . . this." She waves a hand over the table and does the broccoli face again as a single large tear rolls down her cheek.

"Can anyone verify that you were home during those hours? Is there anyone who can provide you with an alibi?"

"An alibi for what?"

"I take it that means no?" Hurley says.

Pamela's anger is growing fast now. I can see a spark in her eye, the tension in her muscles, the increase in her respiratory rate. "Detective, I don't know what kind of game you're playing with me. First you tell me that my husband was murdered and that I'm a suspect because of his life insurance policy, and then you ask me for an alibi for a time period that has nothing to do with Craig's death. And what about the husband of that woman, Meredith what's-her-name, that you said was killed by my husband? If I'm a suspect, why isn't he? If Meredith and Craig were having an affair, he'd be angry and jealous, too, right?"

"Are you saying you're angry and jealous about Craig and Meredith's affair?" I ask her.

"Of course I am!" she snaps. "Wouldn't you be angry if you discovered your husband, the man you loved, the man you thought loved you, was having an affair with another woman?" Pamela's emotional control is tenuous at best at the moment. Her voice hitches on the last few words, her face is screwed up in a contorted expression as she tries not to break down in tears, and her breathing is irregular. Her pain looks utterly and completely genuine.

"Yes, I would," I say emphatically, and I feel Hurley's leg nudge mine beneath the table.

Pamela takes a moment to gather herself together. I slide a box of tissues over to her, and she takes two out, giving me a grateful look. After dabbing her eyes and swiping at her nose, she says, "So why aren't you questioning Meredith's husband?"

"We talked to him," Hurley says.

"And?"

Hurley doesn't answer her. He just sits there and stares.

Nearly a full minute passes in complete silence before Pamela says, "What the hell is going on here? Do I need to get a lawyer?"

"I don't know," Hurley says. "Do you?"

There have been a lot of emotions playing over Pamela's face while we've been in here, but this is the first time I see pure, unadulterated fear.

"Yes," she says, jutting her chin out in an attempt to look more confident than I know she feels. "I think I do. And I think I'm done talking to you. Am I free to leave?"

"You are," Hurley says.

Pamela lunges out of her seat and comes around the end of the table toward us. As she steps behind Hurley and opens the door to the room, Hurley says, "Don't go anywhere without checking with me first."

"I wouldn't dream of it," Pamela says with a pronounced sneer. Then she slams the door closed behind her.

CHAPTER 22

As soon as Pamela Knowlton is gone, Hurley gets out his phone and places a call to Jonas, switching the call to speaker. "Hey, Jonas, I know you're busy processing that scene at the apartment, but I need an update on the financials for our suspects, particularly Pamela Knowlton."

"Laura has been working on that," he says. "I know she started looking into it, but I don't know how far she's gotten. We've been working a lot of opposite hours lately, so I haven't had much of a chance to talk with her. You'll have to call her."

"Okay," Hurley says, sounding less than enthused. He disconnects the call and pulls up his contact info for Laura. But rather than call her, he sighs and gives me a sad look. "I don't want to call her. I don't think I have the patience." He looks and sounds exhausted. There are dark circles under his eyes, and his voice is hoarse and weaker than usual. I have a sudden urge to hug him or put his head in my lap and tell him to go to sleep for a little while. But I do neither.

"Just be firm with her if she starts to go off on any tangents," I say. "She's actually pretty self-aware when it comes to her verbosity, and in my experience, she responds well to reminders."

"Then you call her," Hurley says, and he slides his phone over to me.

I push his phone back toward him but take out my own. "Okay," I say. I dial Laura's number, and she answers on the second ring, sounding sleepy. I put the call on speaker.

"Hey, Laura, it's Mattie and Hurley. Sorry if we woke you."

"That's okay," she says, sounding very subdued for Laura.

I start to think I might have found the trick for managing a conversation with her: call her when she's sleeping. "We wanted to check with you to see if you've made any progress on the Lansing/Knowlton case with regard to the financials or the GPS analysis."

"Um, haven't gotten very far with the financials yet. The banks are being stubborn. But I did discover some oddities regarding the GPS stuff. I put a report online in the case file about it."

"Oh, sorry," I say, grimacing at Hurley. "We haven't checked the file today. Can you give me a summary?"

"Sure. I downloaded cell tower and GPS info from all four phones and the GPS info from Craig Knowlton's car. In general, it all seemed normal enough, but then I noticed that a call Craig made from his burner phone to Meredith's burner phone bounced off a cell tower on the far east side of town at the same time that his car GPS showed him being near the Dells."

"So maybe his wife was driving his car," I surmise. "Maybe Craig was with Meredith. What did Meredith's phones show for the same time period?"

"That's the thing. Meredith's regular cell phone shows she made a call at the same exact time and the GPS on that phone puts her at work at the hospital. The call was to a friend of hers, a coworker named Jeannie Howe. And yet the burner cells show a phone call lasting between the two burner phones for fifteen minutes."

"Maybe one or the other of them was merely listening on their end," I surmise.

"But I'm not done yet," Laura says. "Craig's regular cell phone also made a call during that time, one that started about a minute after the burner calls. And the GPS on his phone as well as the cell tower it bounced off of show he was in the Dells. So both his car and his regular cell phone were in the Dells, yet his burner phone called Meredith's burner phone from somewhere in town. Unless the man had powers we don't know about, he couldn't have been in two places at one time."

"Okay," I say slowly, thinking. "Who did Craig call on his regular cell phone?"

"His wife, Pamela," Laura says. "They talked for just over ten minutes, and it looks like her end of the call pinged off the tower closest to their house. That's a different tower than the one Craig's burner cell pinged off of."

"So clearly someone else was using Craig's burner phone," Hurley says.

"That's what it looks like, yes," Laura says, stifling a yawn.

"Is there any way to know exactly where Meredith's burner phone was?" Hurley asks.

"No, sorry," Laura says. "I can tell you it was in the vicinity of the hospital and her regular cell phone, but I can't say exactly where. However, I did notice that Meredith's apartment is in an area that would bounce off that same tower. So maybe her husband made the call? You should ask him."

"Can't do that," I say. "John Lansing is dead."

"What?" Laura says, the question coming out like a gunshot.

In my mind's eye, I visualize her bolting upright in her bed.

And I realize that this shocking news might be just the thing she needs to wake up fully. I sense our clock is ticking. "What happened?" Laura asks.

"It looks like someone killed him and tried to make it look like a suicide," Hurley says.

"Oh jeez," Laura says, her Midwestern accent coming through strong. "I need to get going. Don't worry. I'm up now, and I'll get to the office as soon as I can. I'll get on those financials and wring it out of the banks if I have to sell my soul to do it. And don't think I've forgotten about the Prince case. I'm working on that every spare second I have. I'm trying to allot at least two hours out of every shift to that particular project."

Laura's voice is breathless and irregular, and I can tell she's running around doing things on her end. Despite this, she shows no sign of letting up on her current train of thought, and I can tell we are going to have to derail her.

"I've got an extensive list of homes near that cell tower, and I'm wading through the tax and census records for the area to see who lives where. I've got a string of names already, but I still have to run those through some search engines to see if I can tie any of them to the pharmaceutical industry. It's going to take some time, but I promise you I'm working on it. And as soon—"

"Laura!" I say loudly. "We got it. You get yourself ready for work, and we'll touch base with you later, okay?" I jab at the little red hang-up icon on my phone, not giving her a chance to answer.

I look at Hurley, my eyes big as if I'm stunned. He smiles and shakes his head. "It's a good thing she's good at her job," he says. "I wish we'd known about the GPS phone thing when we talked to Pamela. I'm going to have to remind Laura to call or text me as well as upload information when she has evidence like that."

"She usually does," I say. "I wonder if we've scared her

away from doing that by complaining about her talking too much, too fast, and too often."

"Perhaps," Hurley says. "I guess listening to her babble is a price we'll have to pay in the future."

"Help me understand what this whole phone thing she came up with means," I say to Hurley, switching topics.

He squeezes his eyes closed and pinches the bridge of his nose. "Near as I can tell," he says, dropping his hand and opening his eyes, "our theory of this case is all wrong. And I'm going to have to try to talk to Pamela again."

"Good luck with that," I say, making a face. "I don't think she's going to be too inclined to cooperate with us at this point." I glance at my watch. "I need to get to the office so I can help Otto with John Lansing's autopsy. Is it safe to assume you won't be attending?"

"I can't," Hurley says tiredly. "I've got too many other things to follow up on. Call me if you find anything significant, okay?"

"Of course." I get up from my chair and kiss Hurley on the cheek. "I'll talk to you later."

I leave via the break room door and the secure parking lot, intending to take some back streets to my office so I can avoid the media cabal gathered out front. I haven't gone far before my stomach reminds me that it's waging a major protest. It feels like it's trying to eat itself, and I'm so hungry I feel nauseated. There is a sandwich shop a couple of blocks down past my office, and I decide to detour there and order a sandwich to go. I can get there and back using side streets that will help me avoid the media.

I make it to the shop without incident, and while I'm waiting for my food, my cell phone rings, and I see that it's my sister, Desi.

"Hey, Des, what's up?"

"Have you got a moment to chat?"

I glance at my watch. "Maybe five. Is that enough?"

"It will get us started," she says. "Let me begin with the fun stuff." I wince, knowing this means that whatever she has called about won't be all happy news. "I've decided to throw myself a birthday party," she goes on.

I curse silently, realizing I've forgotten all about my sister's birthday on August first—tomorrow. "Okay," I say, mentally adding the purchase of a card and gift to my mental to-do list. "That sounds like fun." I hope my voice sounds convincing because a party is the last thing I need in my life right now. Not that I don't enjoy them. Typically, I do. But my life is hardly typical right now, and this party is just one more thing I have to fit into a schedule that is already bursting at the seams, much like my thighs will be if Otto doesn't quit bringing pastries to work.

"I'm thinking of having it early in the evening tomorrow, around six," Desi says, sounding enthused and excited. "I'm going to whip up a bunch of fun hors d'oeuvres I've recently found recipes for. Erika has agreed to babysit, so you can bring Matthew, and Dom and Izzy can bring Juliana. I'm happy to keep both kids overnight if you like so you adults can have some adult time."

"Hold on," I say, chuckling. "This is supposed to be your celebration. You should be on the receiving end, not the giving end. You're throwing your own party, fixing your own food for it, and providing overnight babysitting services? I don't think that's how it's supposed to go, Desi."

She laughs. "I know, but I also know that your schedule right now is crazy hectic, and I really, really, really want you to come. It's been a long time since we've done anything fun."

"We had a wedding just three weeks ago," I remind her. "Mine, remember?"

"Oh, yeah," Desi says with a little chuckle.

"Hold on a sec," I say. "I need to pay for my sandwich so I can get back to the office." I set my phone down on the counter, pay for my food, grab both my lunch and my phone, and head outside, walking fast. I don't want to make Otto wait for me.

"Okay, I'm back," I say once I have my phone back to my ear. I try to wedge the device against my shoulder so I can have my hands free to unwrap my sandwich. I can practically feel my stomach trying to push its way through my skin to get at it. "How many people are you inviting? Are you inviting Mom? Is that why you're doing this at the last minute? Are you planning some sort of intervention or confrontation with Mom?"

"I've invited her, but I doubt she'll come," she says. "By the way, what's this thing about an alien body being found out on your new property?"

"It's not an alien body," I say, rolling my eyes. I've managed to unwrap most of my sandwich, but as I'm trying to remove the last bit of cellophane, it slips out of my hand and drops to the sidewalk. "Damn it!" I say, looking at my damaged lunch and trying not to cry. Part of it has landed on top of the cellophane, the bread slices sliding only halfway off. I give it a second's worth of consideration before bending down and picking up the part of the sandwich that isn't covered with dirt and gravel. I almost drop my phone while doing this, so I grab it with one hand, and end up grabbing only the top portion of the sandwich. I put it in my mouth, the bread hanging halfway out, and then reach for the rest of it.

Distracted as I am by my attempts to walk, talk on the phone, and eat at the same time, I forget that I should be taking the slightly longer back streets to the office. When I stand up, I see Cletus and two other reporters in front of me, their cameras posed and ready. I hear several rapid clicks, and then Cletus flashes me a smile.

"Our tax dollars at work," he says. The other two reporters turn and run back toward the crowd a block away.

I use the back of my hand to push the part of the sandwich that is hanging from my lips into my mouth, and chew quickly.

"Damn it, Cletus," I mumble around half a mouthful of food. "You are not going to use those pictures."

He shrugs and his smile widens. "Why not?" he asks. "I think the public would be interested in knowing that the assistant to the medical examiner not only has an alien body on her property but also eats off the sidewalk." He spins around and hurries off after the others, leaving me fuming. I'm mad enough that I consider tossing the sandwich remnant I'm still holding in my hand, but after a second I think better of it.

I hear Desi's voice calling to me from my phone. "Mattie? Are you still there?"

"I'm here," I say, coddling the sad remains of my lunch. "I had an accident with my sandwich."

"An accident?" Desi says, sounding mildly alarmed. "Are you okay?"

"Physically, yes. But my pride has sustained a fatal blow. As will yours when you see my picture in the next issue of the paper. You might want to think twice about admitting that we're related."

"Oh my," Desi says, now sounding amused rather than worried. "Speaking of being related, that's the other part of my news I wanted to share with you. I met my father . . . our father . . . yesterday. He just showed up on my doorstep, though it was the back door, not the front one."

"Really? Did you let him in?"

"I did. We had a very nice chat, in fact. And he met both Erika and Ethan. Erika wasn't particularly impressed, but Ethan really took to him. Go figure. That kid doesn't relate well to many people."

"What did you talk about?"

"Mostly about the past, when he left Mom, and how he didn't know she was pregnant with me. He discovered she'd had another child eventually, but he always assumed, as we did, that I was the daughter of her second husband."

"Did he explain to you why he left?"

"He did, though it was in vague terms. He didn't offer any specifics, just said that he got mixed up in something dangerous and had to enter the Witness Protection Program. He also said that he'd like to keep in touch, get to know me and the kids a little better, but that he still had to keep a low profile."

"Yeah, that's basically true," I say. "You're better off keeping your distance from him, Desi."

There is a brief silence, and I squeeze my eyes shut, bracing myself. I can sense what's coming. To further brace myself, I shove the rest of my sandwich in my mouth.

"About that," Desi says, sounding apologetic. "I told him he was welcome to come back any time, or that we could meet somewhere else if necessary. He seemed agreeable to that. He was really very sweet, and he seemed genuinely upset that he didn't know he had a second daughter all these years, not to mention two more grandchildren."

I start to swallow my sandwich, but what Desi says next makes it stick in my throat.

"So I invited him to come to my birthday party tomorrow."

I want to yell at my sister, to chastise her and tell her she's crazy, but I can't speak because I have a doughy mass of sandwich stuck in my throat.

"Mattie?"

"Hmph," I manage before I'm able to swallow.

"Are you mad at me?" Desi asks.

"No, not mad, just a little upset."

"Look, I know you have mixed feelings about the man, and you spent most of your life thinking he had abandoned you. But it's obvious that he really cares about you, about us. His eyes teared up several times when we were talking, and he sounded sincere when he said he wished he hadn't missed out on our lives, all the little accomplishments and celebrations. I think we need to give him a chance."

"Desi," I whine, "this isn't just about him missing out on

things, or trying to make up for lost time. This thing that made him disappear years ago is still a danger. He's a danger. And he's not sharing what he knows about it so that we can get to the bottom of it."

"Yeah, he said that you were angry with him and that all he was trying to do was protect you."

"That's a load of crap," I say. I have reached the entrance to the underground parking garage behind our office, which is also where the funeral home brings in our bodies. I know the area is a dead zone for cell signals as much as it is for bodies, so I stop, wiping my hand on my slacks to remove a few sandwich remnants lingering there. "If he really wanted to put an end to this, he'd tell me and Hurley what he knows. But he's being stubborn and controlling."

"Yeah, he said you likely thought that about him," Desi says. "Tell me you'll still come, even though he might be there."

"Yes," I say, resigned. "I'll be there. I doubt he'll show up anyway. Do you need me to bring something?"

"No, I've got it covered," Desi says, and while her answer makes me feel a little guilty, it also makes me feel a lot relieved.

"Okay, I'll see you tomorrow. Love you."

"Love you, too."

I disconnect the call and enter the garage, feeling a host of conflicting emotions. Tomorrow I need to go to a party I haven't the time or energy to enjoy, to be with my sister whom I love and adore. But I might also have to spend time with my father, a man I want to trust but can't, a man I never want to see again and desperately want to have in my life, a man I both loathe and love.

Life is full of curveballs.

CHAPTER 23

By the time I make it into the office and change into my scrubs, Otto already has John Lansing on the autopsy table, ready to go.

"Perfect timing," he says as I enter the autopsy suite. "I got our friend here checked in, weighed, and x-rayed, and I'm just about to begin."

"Sorry if I'm late," I say. "I needed to grab a quick lunch, and then I got accosted by the press."

"Did you give them any information?"

"No information, just an entertaining picture, I'm afraid, one that might embarrass me and everyone in the office." I explain to him what happened, but if I'm expecting any sympathy from Otto, I'm disappointed. He lets out a belly laugh that only enhances his resemblance to Santa Claus.

"That should prove to be a classic if they actually publish it," he says once he has his laughter under control.

"Yeah, well unfortunately, I have a few of those in my repertoire already."

As we get to work, I tell Otto about Alison Miller, about my quicksilver relationship with her over the years, and about some of the photos of me she had published in the past, including two in which I was in a state of undress. Otto is amused, and I find his attitude both cheering and a smidge annoying.

John Lansing's autopsy is straightforward. We don't find any indications of diseases, disorders, or injuries that could have killed him; he was a healthy man in his thirties with the rest of his life ahead of him. That leaves us with the tox screen, which is relatively straightforward as well, given that we know what drug to look for.

Arnie runs the specimens we give him—gastric contents, vitreous fluid, urine, and some bits of liver—through his various machinery, and he finds a high content of the sleeping pill that had been in the prescription bottle present in all four specimens. But when he does a routine drug screen, he finds something else, too. John had some sort of benzodiazepine in his blood. The sleeping pill was not this type of drug, so this means John was further sedated by some sort of tranquilizer. Identifying the specific one will take more time, but it makes sense to me when I finally recall the nag that had bothered me back at the apartment.

"I knew there was something about that scene that didn't seem right to me," I tell Otto. "Those sleeping pills have a strong, bitter taste to them. I know because I remember patients who took them complaining about it, and I took one myself once right after my split from David. If someone was going to try to spike a drink, even something as potent as vodka, that bitterness would be bound to come through and make whoever was drinking it suspect it was tainted. I'm guessing John was sedated with something else first. But disguising the taste of the pills in food like the pasta and red sauce we found in the stomachs of Craig and Meredith would be easier, especially since the amounts might have been smaller. The goal with Craig and Meredith was sedation, even though Craig's amount proved fatal."

"Makes sense," Otto says.

The brain nudge comes again—something about the prescription bottle. But I can't figure out what it is. I thought the bitterness thing might've been what was bothering me, but now I sense it's something else.

"Do you want to close him up?" Otto asks.

"Sure. I just need to give Hurley a call to see if he can pick up Matthew for me. I'll inform him of our findings." I strip off my gloves and grab my phone from a side table. I call Hurley and get his voice mail, so I leave him a message with our autopsy findings and a reminder that I need him to pick Matthew up and call Dom if he's going to be overly late. With that done, I re-glove and spend the next hour sewing up the incisions we made in John Lansing's body. When I'm done, I return him to the storage cooler, do the necessary paperwork, and then head for the shower. Normally, I would put on my street clothes at this point, but today I don a pair of fresh scrubs instead. Then I head upstairs to Arnie's lab, where I find him with his eye glued to a microscope.

"What are you up to?" I ask him.

He waves me in without lifting his face from the lens. "Come on in. I've got something to show you."

I walk over to him and wait a moment while he adjusts the focus on the scope. Finally, he lifts his head and points to the eyepiece. "Have a look," he says.

I put my eye to the lens. It takes me a moment to focus, and when I do, I see some shiny gold fibers on the slide. "What is this?" I ask.

"They're threads from that piece of cloth we found with the bones out at your place," Arnie says. "It's some sort of metallic material."

I lift my head and look at him. "You're not going to start in on the space suit theory again, are you?"

He looks disappointed and shakes his head. "No, sadly, these threads are very earthly in their origin. It's a gold thread like the kind used in lamé. It was used in clothing a lot in the sixties and seventies, though it was more commonly seen in costumes."

"So do you think the aliens made use of our gold thread here on earth for their uniforms?" I say with a sardonic smile.

"Go ahead and mock me," Arnie says, pouting. "Just because this isn't otherworldly doesn't mean that the bones aren't, or that aliens didn't visit our planet at one time or another. And I'm still holding out hope on those bones. We'll just have to wait and see what the DNA tests come up with."

"Good luck with that," I say. "Personally, while I'm open to the possibility of alien visitation, I hope those bones are plain old human ones. Otherwise I may never get my new house built."

"Yeah, sorry about that," he says, managing to look genuinely sympathetic.

"Me too. Listen, I'm here because I need a favor, Arnie. I need to get in touch with Joey Dewhurst."

"Joey? Why?"

"It's best if you don't know why," I say cryptically. Of course, this just piques Arnie's interest even more.

He narrows his eyes at me. "What are you up to, Mattie?"

"I have a little project I need to do, and I need Joey's help to do it."

"Is this related to our current case?"

Since the Prince case is still open, technically it's a current one. But I'm fairly certain Arnie is referring to the Knowlton/Lansing case. "It has nothing to do with the motel murders," I say, saving myself from an out-and-out lie. "It's personal."

Arnie shrugs and grabs a pen and paper. "Okay, here's a number where you can reach him." He scribbles the information down and hands it to me.

"Thanks, Arnie. I owe you one."

I can feel his eyes watching me as I leave, and I can almost feel his suspicion as a palpable heaviness in the air. His curiosity is likely killing him about now.

I head downstairs, check out of the office, and make my way to the underground garage. For once, I'm not happy to be driving the hearse because it makes it hard to be incognito. That's when I remember that my hearse is parked in the police lot. I start to walk that way, but as I leave the garage area and emerge into the early-evening light, a car pulls up beside me. I look over and see Cletus behind the wheel.

"Is that body you brought in this afternoon the husband of the woman victim in that murder-suicide thing?"

"I'm not at liberty to discuss anything with you regarding that case, Cletus," I say.

"Oh, come on," Cletus pleads. "Give me something."

"I'm sorry. You'll have to wait for the official announcement." I continue walking toward the police station, worried that Cletus will follow me. When I get in my car, I pull out of the police lot and then drive a serpentine route up and down side streets, pulling through an alleyway and circling around a time or two. Once I'm sure I don't have anyone on my tail, I make a beeline for the local hospital and pull into the back lot behind the building, out of sight from the road. At least here the hearse won't look so out of place, since this is also where the funeral homes park when they come to pick up bodies. After turning off the engine, I take out my cell phone and call Joey's number. At first, I'm afraid he isn't going to answer; the phone rings six times. But then I hear the deep, slow rumble of Joey's voice. "Who is this?"

"Hey, Joey, it's Mattie Winston. Remember me?"

"Of course, silly," Joey says, and I can hear the smile in his voice. "I always remember pretty girls."

"Hey, you better watch yourself, Joey," I tease. "You have a girlfriend now, don't you? Rhonda, I think you said her name was. You don't want to make her jealous."

"Okay. Don't tell."

There is a moment of silence, and I can't help but smile at Joey's childlike response. Joey is mentally challenged, and I suspect he's also autistic to a certain degree, albeit high-functioning. But I don't need him for his clever conversation, social abilities, or intelligence. I need him because he's a computer savant. I need HackerMan.

"I won't tell," I promise him. "I have something I need you to help me with. Any chance you're free this evening?"

"I just finished a job," he says. Joey does consulting work as a freelancer for a number of individuals and companies, both in and out of town, troubleshooting their computer hardware and software problems. Despite his intellectual limitations and superhero quirkiness, he is very good at what he does. Word of his abilities spread quickly around town and grew from there. "I'm eating my dinner. Then I'm going to watch TV."

"That sounds like fun," I say. "Can you take a break from your TV for a little while to help me?"

"Okay."

"Can I pick you up in about an hour?"

"Okay." Joey isn't big on conversation.

"Where?" I have no idea where Joey lives, but he recites his address to me in a robotic voice. "Okay, I'll see you in about an hour. If it's going to be any later than that, I'll call you." I disconnect and glance at my watch. It's almost 5:30, a perfect time for what I need to do.

I climb out of the car and make my way around the side of the building to the front entrance. I walk inside like any other employee, and no one pays me any attention. People in scrubs always look like they belong in a hospital, and fortunately, the scrubs we use in my office are the same color as the ones the nurses here at the hospital wear. There are elevators near the entrance, and I take one up to the third floor, a medical-surgical unit. Once there, I look down the first hallway I come to and frown. I don't see what I'm looking for, so I head down it to the intersection of a second hallway—the unit is shaped like a rectangle, with a nurse's station at either end—and here I strike pay dirt. Sitting in the hallway outside a patient room is an isolation cart.

After checking the hallway in both directions to make sure no one is watching me, I quickly rummage through the cart, removing a mask, a hair bonnet, and a pair of booties. Stuffing these under my shirt, I head back for the elevator and the first floor.

I've donned the mask, cap, and booties by the time I exit the elevator. I do a quick detour past the cafeteria and peek in to see who is taking a dinner break. I'm hoping to see one face in particular, and when I do, I turn and head in the opposite direction.

My next stop is the valet area by the main entrance. No one is there at this hour, and a half dozen wheelchairs are lined up alongside the valet desk. I grab one, and then I also grab a clipboard from the desk, placing it facedown in the seat of the wheelchair. Then I steer the chair down several hallways to the surgical wing.

Access to the operating rooms requires an ID badge. I still have my old one stuffed in a drawer somewhere, but it will no longer work. The badges are deactivated anytime an employee resigns or is fired. So I perch with the wheelchair just around the corner from the entrance to the surgical suite and wait. I take out my cell phone and hold it at the ready.

I worked in the OR long enough to know the routines. It's the dinner hour, and while most of the OR staff is gone for the day, there will be a few who are working later. I know this because David is in surgery at the moment, performing a ventral hernia repair. I saw it on his desk calendar when I was meeting with Patty earlier. That means there are not only surgical nurses on duty, but recovery room nurses as well, though these days it's called the PACU—the Post Anesthesia

Care Unit. When they have an evening case, the PACU nurse will typically take a dinner break while the case is in progress. My peek into the cafeteria confirmed this, so now I simply need to wait.

Five minutes later, I hear her coming. I put my phone to my ear and start a conversation with no one, pretending I'm on a call. As the PACU nurse rounds the corner and swipes her badge in front of the reader that gives her access to the OR area, I lean against the wall by my wheelchair, chatting away, my back to the woman. The doors swish open and the nurse enters and immediately turns left toward the PACU. The doors hang open for a moment, and as they begin to close, I grab the wheelchair and dash through them. A quick glance to my left tells me the PACU nurse is in her area and out of the hallway. I go the opposite way, turning right and heading for the staff lounge.

I park the wheelchair in the hallway and open the lounge door, prepared to continue my phone call ruse should anyone be inside, but the room is empty. I hurry toward the locker I know David likes to use, and when I open the door, a huge wave of relief rolls over me when I see his lab coat hanging there. His ID badge is clipped to the pocket where he always has it, and I grab it, stuff it in my pocket, and head back the way I came.

Five minutes later, I'm in my hearse, headed for Joey's apartment. I've never been to Joey's place before, and I'm surprised by how small it is. Joey is a huge hulk of a man, and I always imagined him living in a comparably huge hulk of a house. But instead he lives in a small studio apartment with a tiny kitchen area that consists of a normal-sized fridge, a two-burner hot plate, a microwave, and a sink. There is a large recliner chair just off the kitchenette facing the far wall, where there is a credenza with a TV on top. Also on top of the credenza are several piles of videos, the computer tower, and a gaming console. Not surprisingly, given Joey's alter ego of HackerMan, the vast majority of the videos are superhero movies.

Next to the recliner is a table with a laptop on it. To the right of the credenza is a large chest of drawers, and on the wall to the right is a double bed. It's a cute little place, *little* being the operative word. Joey dwarfs the room and the furnishings. I assume the door just to the right of the entrance leads to a bathroom, but judging from how much space there is available behind that door, I can hardly imagine Joey being able to get in there, much less have a shower he can fit into.

Still, the place is Joey's. He pays his own rent, buys his own food and clothes, and holds down a job. Given his mental limitations, it's quite an accomplishment, and one that he is unabashedly proud of. He waves me in and offers to let me sit in the sole chair in the room. I thank him and tell him I'm okay to stand because we need to get going soon. The look of disappointment on his face makes me feel bad, so I try to temper the situation by asking him to show me the place—as if I can't see it all from where I'm standing. This has the desired effect. Joey beams a broad smile and actually gives me a tour, a journey that involves us standing just inside the door and slowly revolving as he points to different areas of the room.

"This is a great home, Joey," I tell him.

"Thanks," he says, still beaming. "I really like it." His smile falters. "Except I wish I had another chair for Rhonda."

Joey's new girlfriend is someone I've heard about but haven't met. According to Arnie, who sort of adopted Joey as his younger brother when Joey's mother died (Joey's father died when Joey was three) and keeps an eye on him to make sure he's okay, Rhonda is a young woman with Down syndrome who works at the local grocery store. Arnie gives me updates regularly, and the most recent one had Rhonda, who lives with her mother, and Joey going on a few "dates." These excursions were to the movies, or a restaurant, or the local bowling alley—both Joey and Rhonda love to bowl—all with Rhonda's mother in tow. The couple has progressed from holding hands to hugging and even sharing a chaste kiss on the lips on one occasion, something Arnie said has Rhonda's mother a little freaked out. As far as I know, Rhonda hasn't been to Joey's apartment.

"Does Rhonda come here to visit with you, Joey?"

"Not yet, but I want her to. Her mom came here once to see where I live, and she said it wasn't good enough because there was no place for Rhonda to sit. So I need to get another chair."

I suspect Rhonda's mother objected for reasons other than the seating, though I'm guessing she didn't share this with Joey. She might be forced to address the issue, however, because while Joey has a childlike personality and level of intelligence, he also has a grown man's drive and sense of determination. He is very goal-directed and good at getting jobs done. That's part of what has made him successful enough to live on his own like this.

"Maybe you can work something out," I tell him. "I'll help you find another chair."

The beaming smile returns, and Joey then startles me by grabbing me in his huge bear arms and hugging me. "Thank you, Mattie. You're a good friend."

When he releases me, I glance at my watch and say, "We need to get going. But first let me tell you what I want you to do, not only to see if you can do it, but also because it won't be strictly legal, and you could get into trouble for helping me."

"You mean go to jail trouble?" Joey says.

"Maybe," I say, wincing. I don't actually think Joey would go to jail if what we are going to do is discovered, but I can't be totally sure. So I feel honesty is the best policy.

But Joey not only doesn't look intimidated by this; if anything, he looks excited. "I will help you because you are my friend," he says. "And this sounds like a job for HackerMan."

"That it is," I say with a smile. "Here's what I need you to do." I spend ten minutes explaining exactly where we're going and what we're going to do when we get there. "All you need to do is follow me until we get to the actual computers," I explain. "Then I need your expertise, assuming you can do what I want."

"It will be easy," Joey says with a hint of bravado. I hope he's right.

We head out, and I drive back to the hospital, parking in the rear lot again so as not to draw too much attention to the presence of the hearse. Joey and I get out and walk around the building, across a grassy expanse and part of another parking lot, until we reach the back door to the clinic building. While the clinic is on the same grounds as the hospital, it's in a separate building with its own parking lot and is run by the physicians whose offices fill it. At this time of night, the clinic is typically empty, particularly since it's a Friday evening. But just to make sure, Joey and I walk around the building, checking the windows for any light emanating from within.

The coast appears to be clear, and when we return to the back entrance, I use my old key to gain access to the building. I had a key to the office when I was married to David; it made sense at the time, and I used it often so I could visit him in his office without having to go through the patient waiting area. When we split up, I should have turned the key in to someone, but no one ever asked for it, and I never offered. It has been on my key ring—unused and more or less unnoticed—ever since.

Inside, all the main lights are off, but there are a few night-lights, enough to see by.

"I don't want to turn any lights on," I tell Joey. "Someone might see them and come investigate. And this needs to be a top-secret mission."

"Okay," Joey says eagerly. "Top secret." He reaches back

and tugs at his waistband. A moment later, his red cape appears, and he lets it hang down the back of his pants.

I glance at my watch; it's a little after 7:30. "There's a security guard who comes through the building every evening," I tell Joey. "He typically comes at nine, so I'm hoping we can be done by then."

Roger Deighton has been a weekday evening security guard for the hospital and the clinic for more than twenty years. I know him well, both from when I worked in the hospital and from when I was married to David and would hang out in his office late at night. I know Roger is a creature of habit, following the same routines shift after shift, and I'm counting on that routine being the same.

Once we are inside, I lead the way down the main hallway to the elevator. The clinic building is two floors of physician and dental offices, but there is also a basement that houses the billing and medical records office for all of the building's occupants. Hurley and I went down there once before, right after Carolyn Abernathy died, hoping to access her computer workstation and see what files she might have been working on. That time, we gained access to the area by using the dead woman's ID badge. It didn't help us much. The office supervisor essentially laughed in our faces and then told us to get lost. Threats of a search warrant didn't faze her in the least, and since we didn't really have enough evidence to justify getting a warrant that would allow us to search private, personal medical records of who knows how many people, our visit proved to be a frustrating and irritating waste of time. I'm hoping to remedy that situation tonight.

Using David's ID badge, Joey and I take the elevator down to the basement level. I'm hoping there isn't anyone here putting in overtime hours, and I'm relieved to see the area is dark and deserted when the elevator door opens.

"Come on, Joey," I say. "I don't think it will matter which computer we use." We head for the nearest cubicle and computer station, and I sit down in front of the monitor. I say another silent prayer that David hasn't changed his computer password—he's used the same one for years—and I boot up the machine and prepare to log in. I type "DWinston" in for the username—the clinic and hospital both use a first initial and the last name for all logins—and when I get the prompt for a password, I type in "A1Surgeon." A tiny spinning circle at the center of the screen appears and continues to spin for several seconds. I fear the dreaded warning that my username or password is incorrect, but suddenly the screen fills with the home page of the electronic charting program used by both the clinic and the hospital.

"Okay," I say, getting out of the chair and gesturing for Joey to take it. "See if you can work your magic. I need you to find all the records that were reviewed by Carolyn Abernathy during the past three to four months."

Joey drops into the seat, and for the next few minutes, he just stares at the screen, studying the various icons and drop-down menus. I stand at his side, chewing my lip, wondering if I've overestimated his abilities. Finally, he settles his hand over the mouse and starts clicking. He pulls up a screen for requesting reports and then starts filling in blanks for his search. He types and clicks, types and clicks, types and clicks. A variety of new screens pop up, followed by some tables and lists. He continues clicking and typing, and I see graphs and spreadsheets pop up and then disappear. I pace for a bit, looking back at Joey every minute or so. He studies the screen intently, his eyes moving rapidly, his hands busy with the keyboard and mouse. He looks totally involved and focused, and though every fiber of my being is dying to start firing questions at him, I bite my lip and stay quiet. I do a complete circuit of the office area three times, and when I glance at my watch, I see that it's ten past eight.

My hopes are starting to flag, and I'm about to break my silence when Joey says, "Is this what you want?"

I hurry over to him and stare at the screen. He has a spread-sheet displayed with columns that include service dates, patient names, dates of birth, diagnoses, physician names, insurance information, and some financial data. The very last column, which is labeled "Reviewer," lists the name Abernathy after each row.

"Yes!" I say, giving Joey a pat on the back. "That looks like it." I reach down and take over the mouse, using it to scroll through the list. I click several times, and more rows appear with each click. "How many entries are there?" I ask.

Joey points to a number at the bottom of the screen. It says 1,456, and I groan. "That's way too many," I say. "We have to figure out a way to winnow it down."

Joey gives me a perplexed look. "Winnow?" he repeats.

"Sorry," I say, waving my hand in the air as if I'm trying to wave away the word. "We need to find a way to make this list smaller, to find the charts that might have the information I'm looking for."

"What are you looking for?" Joey asks.

I think about this, studying the column headings. "We can sort these results using these column headings, can't we?" I ask him.

He nods.

"Let's start with the diagnoses," I say.

Joey takes the mouse, clicks on the header for the diagnosis column, and the results are then sorted alphabetically. I think about a weight-loss drug, and the sorts of maladies a person might have if they were prescribed one. My mind ticks off a mental list: diabetes, heart disease, stroke, and the most obvious one, obesity.

"Can we sort this list by more than one column?" I ask Joey.

"Sure. Just tell me what you want."

Over the next fifteen minutes, we sort the list first by diagnosis, then by physician, and finally by age. Joey shows me how we can hide all the charts that aren't relevant to our search—young children, unrelated diagnoses, and doctors who are specialists in areas such as orthopedics, urology, and neurology. While some of those doctors might have a patient or two who would require weight management, I know they aren't likely to prescribe a weight-loss drug. Specialists tend to leave that sort of thing up to primary care doctors. But I have included David in the list since his initials match one of the ones listed in Hal's notes. Eventually, we end up with a more manageable list of 386 charts. But it's still too many.

I glance at my watch, undecided how to proceed. I don't want to linger down here. The risk of discovery is too great, and while I'm not that worried about getting caught myself, I don't want to get Joey into trouble. Then I remember Hal's list, and Hal's sister.

"Joey, is there a way to search these remaining charts for a particular item, like a drug that might have been pre-scribed?"

"No," he says, looking thoughtful. "But I can do it an-other way."

"You can?" He nods and smiles. "Okay then, search for Leptosoma," I tell him. This is the name of the weight-loss drug that Hal's sister, Liz, had been taking. "But save this spreadsheet result. I might want to look at it again." Then I remember something else: the nudge regarding the prescrip-tion bottle that was nagging me earlier. Now I know why it was bothering me. I take out my phone as Joey starts tapping away, and call Arnie. He answers on the second ring.

"Hey, Mattie, what's up?"

"Any chance you're in the office?"

"I am. Laura and I are here working on something to-gether."

Thank goodness for Arnie's crush on Laura, I think. "I

need you to look something up for me," I tell him. "Remember that prescription bottle we found with Liz Dawson's name on it? The one for Leptosoma?"

"Yeah, what about it?"

"Can you look at it and tell me who the prescribing doctor was?"

"Sure. Hold on." He puts me on hold, leaving me listening to static. I watch Joey, slightly alarmed to see that he is no longer in the software program that provides the electronic medical charts. Instead he is on a screen where lines of what looks like jibberish are scrolling by.

"Mattie?" Arnie comes back on the phone.

"I'm here."

"It was a Dr. Richard Olsen."

A light goes on in my mind. "Thanks, Arnie. One more thing. What were the items in the list that Hal had on his thumb drive, specifically the letters that were followed by the locales?"

"One sec," Arnie says. "I need to pull it up on my computer."

I grab a pen and a notepad on a nearby cubicle and prop the phone against my ear, waiting.

"You ready?" Arnie says a moment later.

"Go ahead."

"RO is followed by France, Switzerland, and New York, DW is followed by Miami, Florence, and London, PQ is followed by London, Sydney, and Belgium, and TR is followed by Edinburgh, Prague, and Mykonos."

"Great. Thanks."

"What are you doing?" he asks, sounding suspicious, which is how he sounds 99 percent of the time.

"I'll tell you later if it pans out," I say. "I have to go." I disconnect the call before he has a chance to ask any more questions because I don't want to explain where I am, and also because I see the screen in front of Joey is no longer scrolling. It's displaying a list.

"Is this what you want, Mattie?" he asks.

On the screen is a list of about twenty names, all of them physicians. Included in the list are the names of my ex-husband, along with Peter Quinn and Robert Olsen. And as I scan the remaining seventeen names I see one that fits the final pair of letters in Hal's note: Timothy Rutledge.

"Can you print that list for me?" I ask Joey.

"Sure." He taps a few keys, and I hear the sound of a printer come to life somewhere off to my right. Thanks to my earlier pacing, I know where that printer is. But as I turn to head for it, I hear something else as well, something that makes my blood turn cold. Someone has called the elevator.

CHAPTER 24

"Joey, quick! Turn off the computer."

While Joey does as I say, I dash over to the printer and grab the sheet of paper in the tray, folding it and sticking it in my pocket. Then I glance at the numbers above the elevator. The car has stopped on the first floor. I hear the doors open, and a moment later, I hear them close. Then the machinery starts running again. I can't be sure, but it sounds like the elevator is headed in our direction.

"Come on, Joey," I say, grabbing his arm. "We have to get out of here fast."

I pull him toward the stairwell, knowing we can get out of the basement that way, even though access to the stairs from the first floor requires a badge. For fire safety reasons, one can exit the basement into the stairwell without a badge. But from there the only way out is through an alarmed exit to the outside or the badged doorway at the top of the stairs on the first floor.

I push the door open and hurry through, with Joey close on my heels. Just as the door is about to close, I see the B above the elevator door light up and hear a ding. I point up the stairs, and then put my finger to my lips, indicating the need for quiet. Joey nods his understanding, and I set off up the stairs as quietly as I can. I'm afraid that Joey, as huge as he is, won't be able to be as furtive, but he is surprisingly lithe on his feet, making almost no noise at all. At the top of the stairs, I peer through a glass window in the door and see that the hallway is empty. Then I wave David's badge in front of the reader, wincing when a buzzing sound emerges from the box, followed by the click of the door lock. That click sounds like a bomb blast to me now, but I don't wait to see if it has attracted any attention. I push the door open and wave Joey through ahead of me.

Though I know it will use up potentially valuable escape time, I hold the door as it closes, easing it back into place, wincing again when I hear the latch engage. Then I point down the hall toward David's office and the back exit to the clinic. Joey hurries down the hall, and I follow after him, smiling despite my anxiety as I see his red cape billowing out behind him. When we reach the end of the hall and David's office, I pause and tell Joey he needs to head back to the car and wait for me. Then I open the door and peek outside, to see if anyone is around. The area looks deserted, so I wave Joey on and tell him I might be a little while because I'll need to wait for the guard to leave.

Joey nods, a concerned expression on his face. "Be careful, Mattie," he says, looking very serious. "I don't want you to get into trouble."

"Believe me, neither do I," I say with a smile. "I'll be fine. Now go."

He turns and heads off at a lope toward the back of the hospital. I watch as his red cape flutters and waves in the night breeze, disappearing into the darkness. Then I ease the door closed and turn toward David's office.

Once inside, I settle into David's chair behind his desk and boot up his computer. It takes a minute or so for the thing to fully come to life, and I keep my eyes focused on the thin band of light beneath the door to the hallway, watching for any shadows that might indicate feet. I remember Roger's nightly routine. He always started on the first floor at the end by David's office, and after making his way to the opposite end, he would then take the stairs up to the second and third floors. The basement was always his last place to check, and from there he would return to the first floor and exit out the back entrance.

My hope is that he not only still practices this routine, which never varied during the years I knew him, but that he will simply go by David's office and exit without checking it out since he already would have done so. Worst-case scenario, I hope to be able to convince him that my presence here is nothing to be alarmed about. I'm sure he knows David and I are divorced, but I figure I can argue that my current job requires me to do some research on one of David's patients. Why I am sitting here doing it in the dark will be a little harder to explain, but I'll deal with that problem if and when it happens.

I stay as quiet as I can, and when the computer is done booting up and prompts me for a password, I type in David's "A1Surgeon," thanking my lucky stars that my ex is a creature of habit. I hit the mute key and then find the one that darkens the screen, lowering the light as much as I can. Off in the distance I hear the ding of the elevator returning to the first floor, and I freeze.

I listen as Roger's footsteps draw closer, and then I see the shadow appear beneath the door. The shadow pauses, and for a few seconds I figure I'm done for. He's coming into the office. But then I hear him say, "Hey, Marty, it's Roger. What are you up to?" This is followed by the sound of the back door opening and closing, and Roger's voice growing suddenly distant.

I breathe a sigh of relief and shift my focus back to David's computer. I open his Outlook mail program and scroll through the most recent messages he has sent, reading the subject lines to see if anything looks pertinent. None of them do. Next I do a search for Leptosoma, targeting his recent e-mails as well as his archives. Five e-mails pop up, all of them from last year. I open the first one and read it. It's from David to a man named Jim Horner, who works at a company named Drake Industries. David starts by saying how nice it was to meet this Mr. Horner at the conference in Seattle and then goes on to say he has someone who might be a good candidate for the trial. What the trial entails is never referred to, but it's not hard to guess after reading the remainder of the e-mail. David writes that he has a male patient in his thirties named Freeman Kohl who is suffering from morbid obesity, weighing in at just under 600 pounds. David goes on to say that Mr. Kohl came to him requesting gastric bypass surgery, but he is too great a risk because of a preexisting heart problem. After explaining this to Mr. Kohl, David then explained about the Leptosoma study, and Mr. Kohl indicated a willingness to participate. He understands that this will require him to either relocate or travel to Madison on a weekly basis.

The second e-mail, which is dated two months later, is a short thank-you to Mr. Horner for making the necessary arrangements to get Mr. Kohl into the Leptosoma program. The third e-mail is an inquiry dated three months later—a year ago almost to the day—asking how Mr. Kohl is doing. This e-mail apparently went unanswered because the fourth one, sent a month later, was a second request for this information, mentioning the previous inquiry.

David's final e-mail was a bit of a shocker. Mr. Horner's reply to the previous e-mail was attached to David's final message. In it, Mr. Horner regretted to inform David that Mr. Kohl had suffered a fatal case of liver failure, brought on by a secret drinking habit he had apparently hidden from everyone. But when Mr. Kohl was found dead in his hotel room in Madison, an autopsy was performed that revealed a severely cirrhotic liver. A subsequent investigation by the ME's office in Madison had revealed a trail of receipts to a variety of liquor stores over the past eight months, indicating a significant level of consumption. They also discovered a large stash of empty booze bottles in Mr. Kohl's house.

Horner's e-mail goes on to say that because of this discovery, Mr. Kohl was excluded from the trial results, but that Drake Industries was open to any other candidates David might want to send their way. He also mentions that David can keep the professional fees paid to him for his role in getting Mr. Kohl into the program. Horner then goes on to say that there is a weeklong conference in Hawaii coming up the following spring, and if David is open to doing a presentation on the benefits and risks of the various weight-loss surgery options, Drake Industries would be happy to provide him with a generous honorarium as well as hotel and travel accommodations.

David's reply to this e-mail is a two-parter. First, he expresses his sorrow that Mr. Kohl died and his shock regarding the drinking problem, stating that he never had a clue the man was hiding such a habit. The second part of his e-mail thanks Mr. Kohl for the invitation to speak but says he will have to pass for now. He closes with a request to keep him in mind for future opportunities.

There is an attachment to the e-mail, and when I click on it, I see it's the medical examiner's report on Freeman Kohl. I print this last letter and the report, stashing both in my pocket along with the list I had from downstairs. I do an additional search of the e-mails, looking for any mention of Drake Industries, but the same e-mails are the only ones that come up. I close the e-mail program, and I'm about to shut down the computer when I see an icon for a financial management software program. Curious, I open it.

I scan the current year's info, finding little in the way of surprises. I go to the file menu and find many other years of data, going back more than a decade. I pick last year's and open it. When I scan the fee data entered during the time that Kohl was in the program for Leptosoma, I see several monthly entries for fees earned from Drake Industries, and it's a tidy little sum. Curious, I launch the electronic chart program and use David's login and password to access Mr. Kohl's medical record. I scroll through the info until I find the entries made by David: notes on his current weight-loss progress, which was significant—the man dropped nearly fifty pounds in a matter of a few months—some lab test results, and a couple of physical exams. The last exam done, according to the chart, was three months before Kohl died. Some routine lab work was done at that time, and sure enough, the man's liver enzymes were slightly elevated. According to David's note, he believed this to be a by-product of the drug; the numbers were low enough at that point that they failed to raise any concern. He also documented that he told Mr. Kohl about this information and cautioned him against using alcohol and certain drugs, including over-the-counter pain relievers, lest the numbers worsen.

I shut down his computer, but not before printing the financial data relating to Drake Industries. Then I drop David's ID badge on the floor next to his chair, and leave the office and the clinic building.

Back outside, I make my way through the grounds and the front parking lot, alongside the hospital building and into the back parking lot. I find Joey sitting inside the hearse, chewing on his fingernails, which I note are gnawed down to the skin.

"Are you done?" Joey asks me in a voice that sounds like it's on the verge of panic.

"I am. Thank you for helping me, Joey. And remember, this has to remain a secret between the two of us. No one can know what we did tonight, okay? That's very, very important."

Joey nods vigorously. "Okay," he says.

My phone buzzes with a call, and when I look I see it's from Arnie. "Hey, Arnie. What's up?"

"I have some interesting news for you. Laura and I got a hit on that investigation she was doing into the homes around that cell tower in Kenilworth."

"A good hit?"

"I think so. We found a home near the cell tower that is owned by a man named Desmond Townsend, who happens to be the CEO of a company called Drake Industries."

At the mention of the company name, my heart speeds up a notch.

"So we did a little research into Drake Industries and discovered they specialize in R&D for a number of other companies, including a pharmaceutical company called Algernon Medical. And Algernon Medical happens to be the company that produces Leptosoma. What's more, Algernon Medical is also a subsidiary of a company called Kupper Products, which according to their website specializes in medical research and product development. And the CEO of that company is Marilyn Townsend. Marilyn (née Kupper) Townsend."

"Oh my," I say, feeling a thrill of excitement. "Who is she in relation to Judge Kupper?"

"His sister, which makes her Jason Kupper's sister also."

"Wow," I say, thinking. "This is great info, but I'm afraid

it only complicates things for us. How on earth are we going to bring down a family as powerful as the Kuppers? Especially if we don't have any direct evidence connecting them to anyone else involved. I mean the phone thing is neat, but it's hardly concrete evidence of their involvement in anything."

"We're still working on digging into the corporate relationships," Arnie says. "Maybe we'll come up with something that connects them to Miller-Weiss."

"Okay. Let me know if you find anything. This is good work, Arnie. Thank you, and tell Laura thank you for me, too, please."

"I will, but don't hang up yet. I have something for you on the Knowlton/Lansing case, too."

"Arnie, you are just full of surprises."

"Arnie is very good," Joey says with exuberance. He punctuates the compliment by clapping his hands.

"Is that Joey I hear?" Arnie asks.

"It is."

"Should I ask?"

"You should not. Tell me what you have on the Knowlton/Lansing case."

"I should let Laura fill you in because she's the one who came up with it."

"No!" I say quickly. "You tell me, please. I don't have the patience for Laura's rambling right now."

The phone is quiet, and for one horrifying moment I think Arnie has already handed Laura the phone and she is now stunned into a rare silence by my rude comment. But then Arnie says, "Yeah, there is that. So here it is. She did some digging into the financials for both parties, and she discovered that Pamela Knowlton is quite well off. It looks like the business she and Craig ran was doing quite well, and she has a substantial savings account that should hold her over just fine even if she doesn't cash in on the life insurance. We're talking well over a million dollars."

"Interesting," I say.

As I try to puzzle out the meaning behind this, I stifle a huge yawn. I'm so tired, and I realize I'll be able to think things through better after a few hours of sleep.

"That's all I have for now," Arnie says. "But we'll keep digging."

"Thanks, Arnie. You've been a big help, as always. And do tell Laura thanks, too."

"I will," he says with a hint of suggestiveness in his tone. It makes me wonder just how he's going to reward Laura for her job well done.

"I have to go," I say. "I'll talk to you in the morning."

After bidding one another good night and letting Joey holler a raucous good night to Arnie, I drive Joey home, reminding him once more that our little escapade tonight needs to remain top secret. He assures me he will keep quiet, and as a way of saying thanks to him for his help, I lean over and give him a kiss on the cheek. This makes him blush three different shades of red, and he takes on an *aw shucks* look that is utterly adorable.

I watch him go inside to make sure he's safe and then head home. When I arrive at the house, I find Hurley in the kitchen at the table, his laptop in front of him, papers scattered around him.

"Hey," he says with a tired smile. "How did it go?"

"Good," I say. "Are both of the kids upstairs?"

He nods, and since we have the room to ourselves, I fill him in on what I found and show him the printouts. "I realized something earlier tonight," I say. "When we were at Lansing's apartment, I kept looking at the pill bottle and getting this nagging feeling there was something there that I was missing. I think I know what it was now. The doctor who prescribed the Leptosoma was named Richard Olsen. His initials are R.O." I wait to see if Hurley makes the connection. It takes him a second or two, but I see his face light up when he gets it.

"The initials on Hal's thumb drive," he says.

I nod. "How much do you want to bet that if we look into Richard Olsen we'll find that he had speaking engagements"—I make air quotes for those last two words—"in the places Hal noted."

Hurley nods, his smile broadening. "Good work," he says. "We're getting there, slow but sure. But we still don't have any solid proof we can use."

"Let's switch gears," I say, wanting to keep the mood upbeat. "Did Arnie call you with his information?"

Hurley shakes his head, so I fill him in on that, too. He listens but makes no comments. He looks as exhausted as I feel.

"You look tired," I say.

"I am. And I'm frustrated. I'm beginning to think we've been looking at this motel case all wrong. Jonas and I compared the tire tracks we found on the side of the road out by the motel to the tires on Meredith Lansing's car as well as Craig's and Pamela's cars."

"And?" I say hopefully.

He gives me a glum look. "No match."

I feel my hopes and, with them, the last vestiges of my energy flag. "Let's go to bed," I say, walking over and massaging his shoulders. "We can start fresh in the morning."

He leans back, his head resting against my chest, his eyes closed. "That feels exquisite," he says. He opens his eyes then and looks up at me. "I'd love to return the favor. I can make many parts of you feel exquisite." He wiggles his eyebrows at me suggestively.

I walk around and take him by the hand, leading him toward the stairs. We tiptoe upstairs and down the hall to our bedroom, shutting the door behind us. A moment later, we fall into the bed, wrapped in each other's arms. We share a long, heated kiss, and I feel Hurley slowly stroke my back, his hand eventually working its way around to my chest.

It's the last thing I remember until we both awaken the next morning, still in our clothes, our sexual appetites overruled by physical and mental exhaustion.

CHAPTER 25

We manage to get up before either of our kids, so we take advantage of this brief respite and sneak downstairs to share a quiet cup of coffee together. Our failed attempt at intimacy the night before goes undiscussed, but we make up for it some by touching hands frequently and playing a little game of footsie under the table. It's a Saturday, not a normal day for either of us to work, but with all we have going on at the moment, it's going to be like any other workday.

Though I know the cases we're working are uppermost in both of our minds, we avoid discussing them through some unspoken agreement, reveling instead in a half hour of peace and quiet that we spend reading the morning paper, checking out the news online, sipping our coffees, and enjoying one another's company.

I know it can't last, and sure enough, I eventually hear the pitter-patter of little feet overhead and give Hurley a wan smile. "Rock, paper, scissors?" I say.

He gives me a grudging nod, sets down his coffee cup, and cups his fisted hand. I do the same and then count it out. "One, two, three."

Hurley's hand is flat, while mine stays fisted. "Paper beats rock," he says with a smug little smile. Then he picks up his coffee cup and turns his attention back to his laptop.

"I don't suppose you'd consider two out of three?"

He gives me an amused look, one eyebrow arched.

"Didn't think so," I say. I slurp one more sip of my coffee and then head upstairs.

Matthew is in the bathroom sitting on his potty chair. I'm both surprised and impressed, until I realize he still has his PJs on.

"Matthew, are you going potty?"

"Potty!" he says excitedly.

"You need to take your pants off first," I say, bending down to help him. But as my face gets nearer to his little body, a whiff of something tells me I'm too late. "Oh, Matthew. Did you go potty already?"

"Potty!" he exclaims again.

I suppose I should be happy he gets the general concept, but I really can't afford the ten minutes it takes me to clean him up. When we're done, we return to the bedroom so I can get Matthew dressed. This turns out to be another exercise in frustration when my son starts to cry because his right sock feels funny. I bite back the snapping retort that is brimming at my lips and spend a minute or so manipulating the sock on his foot in an effort to make the bad feeling go away. Matthew, however, is not so easily mollified, and in the end the only thing that makes him happy after he throws himself on the floor crying, rips the sock off his foot, and throws it to the dog, is letting him wear two mismatched socks: one blue and one orange.

I'm sure this duo will attract attention at some point during the day, most likely from some well-meaning, judgmental professional mother who will look at the socks and *tsk* with a sad little shake of her head, a head she'll be lucky to have afterward lest I bite it off and spit it out. Hopefully, I'll be able to head off any such smug judgments because I've honed that warning expression—the one that says, *Go ahead and criticize my mothering skills, and I'll demonstrate just how good my homicidal ones are.*

Breakfast proves to be equally challenging as Matthew decides to play chase around the kitchen table with Hoover rather than eat his cereal and fruit. Just to keep things interesting, he runs with his milk in his hand. It's in a sippy cup, so I think it'll be okay at first, but Matthew somehow manages to get the lid off and spill milk all over the floor and me.

"Matthew!" I yell. "Stop it right now! Get up in your chair and eat your breakfast before I paddle your bottom."

This gets me a look from both Hurley and Matthew. Not only have I never paddled Matthew's bottom, I've never threatened to do so. So Hurley is looking at me to see if I've finally gone over the edge, and Matthew is looking at me with confusion, unsure what this new threat means. I can tell he's gauging me, trying to decide if he can push me a little further, but either the tone in my voice a moment ago or the look in my eye now convinces him that it's time to start behaving.

The rest of the meal goes by without a hitch, and I leave Matthew with Hurley while I go upstairs to shower and dress. When I return downstairs, Hurley has Matthew packaged up and ready to go. "Are you going to your sister's birthday party tonight?" he asks me as I gather up Matthew's things and prepare to head for my car.

"I am," I say. "She said Erika volunteered to watch Matthew for us while we're there. You're going, right?"

Hurley makes a face. "I suppose. Though to be honest, I'd rather spend the time working on these cases."

"I know, but we need to take some time for us, too," I remind him. "And Desi has done so much for us lately. I mean, look what she did to put together our wedding and reception. The least we can do is attend her birthday party, one she's planned and arranged all by herself. Besides, a little R and R is good for the soul. Not to mention cake and ice cream."

"Ice cream!" Matthew says with his classic childlike exuberance. His love for this particular dessert is another thing he inherited from me, so it shouldn't surprise me that it's one of the things he learned to say with perfect clarity early on.

"There you go," I say with a smile. "It's two votes in favor of going, so you're outnumbered."

Hurley gives me a resigned smile.

"We don't have to stay late," I tell him.

His phone dings, indicating there is a text message. He takes it out, looks at it, and his eyebrows arch in surprise.

"What is it?" I ask.

"I'm not sure yet. But I may have a surprise for you later. I'll let you know." He kisses me on the cheek and then ushers me and our son out the door.

I drive to Dom and Izzy's place to drop Matthew off. When I get inside, I find Dom in the kitchen whipping up something that smells sweet and delicious.

"What's cooking?" I ask, though the presence of a waffle maker on the counter gives me a good idea. A fresh bowl of berries next to it makes my mouth drool.

"I'm whipping up some waffles with berries and cream," Dom says, opening the waffle maker and removing two golden-brown waffles. He scoots them onto a plate and then proceeds to spoon the berries, which are floating in an abundance of their own juice, on top of each one. Then he tops them off with a dollop of whipped cream. "Want one?" he asks, turning around with a plate in each hand. "One of these is for Izzy—the whipped cream is a low-fat version, but don't tell him that—and I was going to eat the other one, but you're welcome to one of these if you want. I can make more."

"Awful," Matthew says in my arms, stretching toward Dom and one of the plates.

"I think he's asking for a waffle, not judging your efforts," I say with a wink.

Dom smiles at him and then at me. "Trade you," he says.

"Deal."

He sets the plates down on the counter and holds his arms out to Matthew, who goes to him without hesitation. I grab the two plates and some forks, and as Dom is seating Matthew at the kitchen table, I head to the living room, where I find Izzy playing with Juliana.

"Breakfast is served," I say.

"Hey, Mattie," Izzy says, eyeing the plates eagerly. He puts Juliana in the playpen and then comes over to take one of the plates from me. "I was hoping to see you this morning. I have some news for you."

We settle down in our respective chairs, resting our plates in our laps, and I dig in without hesitation while Izzy explains what he means.

"Two things," he says. "First, I have another job candidate coming in for an interview at eight-thirty this morning."

"On a Saturday?"

Izzy shrugs. "The guy seems eager, and Lord knows we are. Want to sit in?"

"Of course."

"Good. The other thing is regarding Hal's case. I know the case isn't technically mine since Otto was the one in charge at the time, but I've been looking it over." He nods toward a side table, and I see a file there.

"Izzy, you're supposed to be relaxing on your days off, not working."

"This isn't anything physical," he says. He cuts a bite of waffle and puts it in his mouth, closing his eyes as he relishes the flavors. "Mmm," he moans, chewing slowly. He swallows and opens his eyes. "It's low-fat whipped cream, isn't it?"

I nod. "Don't tell Dom you know. He thinks he's out-smarting you."

"It's not that bad," he says with a conciliatory shrug. "It beats the hell out of that cardboard toast I've been eating lately." He takes another bite. I do the same, and the two of us enjoy a silent moment of gustatory ecstasy.

"Anyway," Izzy says after he has consumed two more bites, "as I said, I was looking over the file, and I noticed the name of the ME who did the autopsy on Hal's sister."

I nod, chewing quickly. "Yeah, it was a Dr. Farmer, as I recall," I say around half a mouthful of waffle. I swallow and add, "But he's in South America somewhere, and no one has been able to find him or get hold of him." I punctuate this depressing news with another bite of waffle.

"I found him," Izzy says, which stops me mid-chew. "And I spoke to him."

I stare at him, chewing like a munching machine because I'm so eager to speak. "What?" I manage, choking down a half-chewed piece of waffle. "How?" This last question comes out a bit hoarse because my food has stuck halfway down my throat. I can feel it there—a giant lump of pasty goodness that is starting to make my esophagus spasm like it's having a leg cramp. I try to swallow again, but not only doesn't the lump move, I find my spit won't even go down. Great, I think. I'm about to become one of those patients who presents to the ER with what medical folks call a food bolus, a giant wad of undigested food too big for the esophagus to handle. Food bolus is a euphemism for you haven't learned how to eat slowly and politely and thoroughly chew your food, and the remedy is typically getting something that looks like a toilet snake with teeth pushed down your throat.

My chest aches as my esophagus spasms even harder in protest. I now know how John Hurt felt when that alien creature came busting out of his chest. For an insane moment, I wonder what an alien waffle creature would look like, then I come to my senses and look around for something to drink. I grab the only thing I see: Juliana's half-finished juice bottle.

It works, but as I lower my head and feel the waffle bolus finally give way and slide into my stomach, I see Izzy staring at me, a forkful of waffle midway between his plate and his mouth, his expression both stunned and amused.

"Sorry about that," I say, giving my chest a pounding with my fist, just to make sure any waffle vestiges are gone. "I swallowed too much too soon, and it got stuck there for a few seconds." I look at the bottle in my hand and then set it aside. "I'll get her another bottle in a minute," I say. "Tell me about Dr. Farmer."

I have to wait a few seconds because Izzy has eaten his pending forkful, and he hasn't yet swallowed. I set my plate aside, done for now thanks to my bolus episode.

"Well, for starters," Izzy says finally, "I know him because I went to medical school with him years ago, and then we worked together for a short time in Madison. Eventually he went north and I came here. I haven't spoken to or seen him in probably twenty years, but at one time we were good friends. So I figured it was worth a shot to try and find him—something I had an idea about—and if successful, to talk to him about the case. I remembered that back when we were in medical school together, Chuck—that's his first name—had a friend who moved to Brazil when he was in high school because of his father's job. Chuck and this friend were pretty close, and they stayed in touch for a number of years. The friend, whose name was Ike—apparently his mother had a thing for Eisenhower—started up a charter fishing business in Brazil after he finished high school, and he kept inviting Chuck to come down and work the boats with him. Chuck used to talk about it whenever we got frustrated, or tired, or overwhelmed with med school stuff or later with work-related stuff, saying that one of these days he was going to do it."

Izzy pauses to take another bite, and it's all I can do not to knock the fork out of his hand. He takes his time chewing, and I roll my eyes. I suspect he's torturing me on purpose.

"Anyway, I got to thinking that if Chuck went to South America, where else would he go? So I searched for fishing charters with the name Ike, and sure enough, I found one operating out of a little seaport in Brazil called Tibau do Sul. So I called last night, said I was in the States, that I was a doctor, and that I needed to get in touch with Chuck Farmer regarding a family emergency. Sure enough, he called me back early this morning."

"Izzy, you are brilliant!" I say. "Did he talk at all about the case with Hal's sister?"

"Not at first. He claimed he had no idea who I was or what I was talking about. But then I assured him of who I was by telling him some things that only the two of us would know, things we went through in med school, and that I was desperate for information because a very close friend of mine was killed, and I feared for myself and my family. That got to him. It was threats to his family that got him to leave. It's also why he falsified the autopsy report on Hal's sister, Liz. There was no suicide."

"He admitted to that?"

"He did."

"Can he name names?"

"Probably," Izzy says, "but he won't."

My hopes sag. "Damn," I mutter.

"But he did tell me one thing," Izzy says. "We know Tomas Wyzinski worked for a pharmaceutical company a few years ago. And Farmer gave me the name of that company. It's Drake Industries."

Now I've perked up again. "Arnie and Laura came up with someone related to the Kuppers who lives near that cell tower in Kenilworth," I say excitedly. "His name is Desmond

Townsend, and he's the CEO of Drake Industries. His wife just happens to be Marilyn Kupper, Judge Kupper's sister."

"That's progress," Izzy says, looking pleased.

"It is. And not only that, I have evidence that someone from Drake Industries was involved in the Leptosoma trial with a patient of David's. A patient who later died of liver failure."

"That's great," Izzy says. "That could lead to some concrete evidence."

I make a face.

"What?" Izzy says.

"I'm not sure we'll be able to use it, given how I came by the information. And it looks as if someone covered the tracks like they did with Liz, making the man's death appear to be from something other than what it was."

Izzy narrows his eyes at me, slowly chewing on a bite of waffle. I can tell he wants to ask me how I came by this information, but in the end, he wisely defers.

Eager to move on, I say, "I also think it's time to have a chat with Tomas Wyzinski."

"I suppose it's worth a try," Izzy says.

I take out my cell phone and call Hurley, filling him in on what Izzy has just told me. "I really think we need to talk with Tomas," I conclude. "Today, if possible."

"As I've told you, I doubt it will do any good," Hurley says. "Besides, if he's afraid of the Kuppers and their involvement, he isn't going to trust someone from a police department."

"Then set it up so I'm the only one he talks to," I say. "Maybe he'll open up more if it's just me."

"You're still a part of law enforcement," Hurley says. "Granted, it's less of a direct line, but . . ." He trails off, and I can tell he's thinking. "You're not going to let this go until I let you talk to him, are you?"

"You know me too well, Hurley."

"Okay," he says, his voice tinged with resignation. "Let me see what I can set up, and I'll call you back."

"Thanks." I disconnect the call, eyeing the remains of my waffle longingly, but a lingering twinge in my chest helps me decide to leave it. "Gotta run," I tell Izzy. "But I'll see you in the office for the interview at eight-thirty."

I head back out to the kitchen and deposit my plate in the sink. Dom eyes it curiously. "I've never seen you leave food on your plate uneaten. The waffle wasn't good?" he says, looking wounded.

"On the contrary, it was delicious," I say. If there is any doubt to this testament, my son's delighted, sticky, strawberry-stained face eliminates it. "In fact, it was so good, I inhaled it . . . literally. I had a chunk stuck in my esophagus, and now it hurts to swallow."

"Sorry," Dom says.

"Don't be. Unless you're apologizing for being a kick-ass cook, in which case you're forgiven."

"Kick ass!" Matthew says loudly, his enunciation perfect.

"Hmmph!" I hear behind me, and when I turn I see Izzy's mother, Sylvie, standing there. "Such language you teach your boy," she says, shaking her head forlornly. "And his table manners aren't much better, I see."

"Good morning, Sylvie," I say, ignoring her jibes. "How are you today?"

She dismisses my question with a wave of her hand and a look of disgust. She wrinkles her nose, and at first, I think it's yet another commentary on my inquiry, but then she says, "Whatever that mess is, it smells good. And an old lady like me needs good fuel in the morninks, yes?" In addition to her unique pronunciation of the word *mornings*, she says the word *fuel* as two distinct syllables. She plops herself in a seat at the end of the table opposite my son and folds her hands on the tabletop, looking at Dom expectantly.

"Coming right up," Dom says, and as he turns back to the waffle maker, he gives me a roll of his eyes, followed by a wink.

"I need to get to work," I say. I give my son a kiss on top of his head in the square inch of hair that isn't sticky and full of crumbs. Matthew seems to enjoy playing with his food as much as, if not more than, eating it.

I head for the door, but before I leave, I turn back. "Are you and Izzy coming to Desi's party tonight?" I ask.

"Party?" Sylvie asks in a voice that sounds mildly wounded as well as curious. She squares her shoulders as if she's preparing for a blow.

Belatedly, I realize my faux pas. Desi probably didn't extend an invitation to Sylvie. "Yes, it's to celebrate her birthday," I say, giving Dom a wide-eyed look. "It's something she planned very last minute. Can you come, Sylvie?"

"I will check my schedule," she says, looking haughty.

I have to stifle a laugh. The busiest Sylvie's schedule gets these days is right after she takes her Lasix, which then requires her to pee every thirty minutes for the next several hours. "Well, I hope to see you there," I say, and before the conversation can get any worse, I take my leave.

CHAPTER 26

On the drive to the office, I call my sister and wish her a happy birthday. Then I explain—though it comes out more like an apology—that I've invited Sylvie to her party.

"That's fine," Desi says with her usual good humor. "I didn't even think to invite her, but I should have."

"I'm not sure Dom and Izzy will be happy about it," I say. "But it is what it is. See you later."

When I arrive at the office, I see that the media throng out front has thinned, but there are still some people milling about. Unfortunately, my hearse makes it hard for me to be clandestine, and as I prepare to pull into the garage, I see one eager and energetic female reporter break free of the group and come running toward me. I have to stop and use my key card to gain entrance to the garage, and this gives her enough time to catch up to me.

"Ms. Winston," she says in a loud, commanding voice. She is an engaging young woman whom I'd guess to be somewhere in her late twenties. She has perfect makeup, a wild mass of curly dark hair, and huge blue eyes. She also has a tape recorder in one hand, which she holds in front of her face. "Susan Simons," she says. "I'm a stringer for one of the

FOX affiliates. Can you tell me anything about the bones that were found out on your property? Do we know yet if they're extraterrestrial?" She thrusts the recorder at me and waits expectantly.

"We don't have the DNA results back yet and probably won't for a week or so," I say. "However, we are fairly certain the bones are human."

"Really?" says the woman, pulling the recorder back, her tone suggesting she thinks I'm giving her a snow job. "Then how do you explain their unusual appearance? And what about the piece of material that looked like some kind of metallic uniform that was found with the bones?"

As she once again thrusts the recorder in my direction, I ponder the fact that she knows about the material. Someone has been talking. It was probably Cletus, but I wouldn't put it past Arnie to fuel this particular rumor fire.

"We are looking into the origin of the bones, but we haven't come up with any definitive answers yet," I tell her, ignoring the question about the fabric. "I would suggest you check back in a week or so when we have the DNA results." With this, I pull into the garage, half expecting the woman to follow me in. While the card requirement at the drive-in entry to the garage limits who can pull in and park here, there's nothing to keep pedestrians from entering, which is why the elevator from it to our office also requires a key card. Fortunately, the reporter turns back and returns to the group by the front office entrance.

Upstairs I find Otto, Arnie, and Laura in the library, standing beside a new, fresh box of pastries on the table. Today, I'm going to have to be strong and pass these goodies by. I don't want to eat anything more just yet, not after my waffle incident. But it isn't easy. The warm, sweet, yeasty aromas are making me drool. Or maybe my food bolus isn't gone after all.

"Otto, you have to stop bribing us with these pastries every time you work."

"No, he doesn't," Arnie says, taking a bite out of a donut that leaves his mouth and part of his face dusted with powdered sugar. He looks over at Otto. "Don't listen to her," he adds, his mouth full.

"Any word on our alien bones?" I ask Otto.

He shakes his head. "Don't expect there will be until sometime next week."

Arnie says, "I have some information that might be helpful. I did some research on that piece of material we found with the bones. It's nothing too spectacular, just some gold-colored thread known as Lurex. It came into use somewhere in the late fifties and was quite popular in the sixties. That gives us a window of time to look at."

"Of more than fifty years," I say. "That's a pretty big window."

"Ah, but I'm not done yet," Arnie says with a wink. "The piece of fabric we found was somewhat protected from the elements due to its location in relation to the body habitus, but also because Lurex thread isn't very biodegradable. However, I found remnants of some plain nylon threads around the edges of it, implying there was a garment composed of nylon that decomposed, and our piece was a small part of that larger garment, maybe some type of badge or insignia or appliqué. Nylon takes around thirty years to decompose in these conditions, so I'd say our body was buried sometime between 1960 and 1987."

"That's still twenty-seven years," I say.

"That's the best I can do for now," Arnie says. "But I'll keep digging."

"Speaking of digging," I say, "wait until you hear what Izzy dug up." I fill Otto and the others in on what Izzy told me earlier about Dr. Farmer. "Hurley is going to try to arrange for me to have a chat with Tomas Wyzinski," I tell them when I'm done. "And I think we're going to have to visit Drake Industries, too."

"I'm fine with you working on investigative stuff for the day, particularly since it's a Saturday," Otto says. "We had a call right before you got here for a nursing home death, but it sounded routine, and the guy was ninety-eight, so I signed off on it over the phone."

"I'm going to be here most of the day, so I can assist you with an autopsy if one comes in," Arnie says.

Otto nods.

"I'll be here for a little while," I say. "Izzy will be here shortly to conduct another job interview, so I'll be in the office for at least that long. If you don't need me for anything else in the meantime, I'll probably try to catch up on some of my paperwork."

"That's fine," Otto says, and with that we split up and head for our respective workstations. It's only after everyone is gone and I'm alone in the silence of the library that I realize Laura didn't say a word the entire time. I am both relieved and bothered, relieved for the obvious reason, and bothered because it is so out of character for her.

A few minutes before 8:30, Izzy appears in the library doorway. He tosses a folder onto the table and says, "Here's the résumé and info on our candidate. He's out front, so I'm going to go get him." Rather than do so, however, he stands in the doorway, eyeing the pastry box.

"Don't even think about opening that box," I tell him, getting up from my desk and walking over to the table. "It's infested with diet demons, little waiflike creatures that get into your brain and convince you that the sugar in that box is necessary to life."

Izzy looks at me, amused. "Diet demons?" he says with a healthy dose of mockery.

I ignore him, pick up the box of pastries, and carry it to the far end of the room, leaving it on the desk that used to be Hal's. Izzy watches me for several seconds with a longing expression on his face before turning away and heading for the front lobby.

I grab the folder and glance at the résumé inside. Christopher Malone, thirty-four, bachelor's degree in criminal justice, attended a police academy and worked as a cop for a year in Ventura, California, and then traded that job for one working as a diener—an industry term for an autopsy assistant—for a medical examiner in Ventura. He kept that job for five years and then took one as a medicolegal investigator for King County in the state of Washington for six years before moving here. He is currently unemployed.

Izzy returns with Christopher in tow. He is an attractive fellow, about five-eleven with a full head of thick, dark hair, hazel eyes rimmed with dark lashes, high cheekbones, and three dimples—one in his chin and one in each cheek. I, too, have dimples in my cheeks—and not just the ones on my face.

Christopher remains standing until Izzy introduces me and then shakes my hand with just the right amount of firmness. As soon as Izzy indicates he can sit, he does, directly across from me. "Pleasure to meet you," he says. "Thanks for giving me an opportunity to interview with you." His voice is even, steady, and low-pitched, but not overly so. He folds his hands on the table in front of him and looks from me to Izzy with a patient, warm smile that makes his dimples even deeper. No one says anything for several long seconds, but if this makes Christopher uncomfortable at all, it doesn't show.

Finally, Izzy starts in with his spiel regarding the job description, hours, and requirements. When he's done with that, he looks at the résumé and says, "It looks like you spent a lot of time out on the West Coast. What brings you here to Wisconsin?"

"A divorce," he says. "I'm actually from this area, and my parents and my brother still live here. My wife left me because of . . . well, because of a problem we couldn't get past. Isn't that always the way?" he asks with an apologetic smile and shrug. "We lived out west for her job, so when the divorce happened, I decided to come back home."

There is a noise then, a subtle sound like a chair leg scraping on a wooden floor. But none of us has moved, and the room is carpeted.

Izzy asks Christopher to talk a little about what he did on his last job, the one in Washington, and as I'm listening to him, I become aware of an odor that gets stronger and fouler as the seconds roll by. I realize then what the sound was earlier. Mr. Malone has let loose a fart.

I put my hand up to my face, not only to stifle a giggle but also to block out the smell. I'm feeling sorry for Malone—interviews are nerve-wracking enough without losing control of one's gases—when I hear another long, low sound. This time it's unmistakable, and sure enough, seconds later the smell hits.

Over the next five minutes, Malone cuts loose with three more farts. If he is aware of them, he doesn't show it. His expression hasn't changed, and he appears calm and composed. Izzy, however, has started to squirm in his seat. The air in the room is quite rank at this point, making me wonder what the hell Malone ate for breakfast. When Malone cuts loose with fart number six, Izzy gets up from the table and offers to give him a tour of the office. I'm grateful for this, because I've been holding my breath for so long I'm about to pass out.

Don't get me wrong. I've smelled all kinds of bodily emissions during the course of my careers and motherhood, not to mention the horrific odors that accompany sick and decomposing bodies. But there is something about the foul, acrid smell of Malone's farts, not to mention the frequency of them, that is not only sickening, it's making my eyes burn and water. I get up and follow the two men out of the room, turning left when they turn right and making a mad dash for the front office.

I burst into the reception area and suck in a breath of clean air. Except it's not clean air. I can still smell that smell, albeit less so than I did in the library. I look around, puzzled, and clamp a hand over my mouth.

"Is he still doing it?" Cass says from behind her desk.

I give her a questioning look.

"Is that poor man still passing gas every few minutes?" she asks. "He must have been awfully nervous because he tooted four times while he was waiting out here for Izzy." She grimaces and waves a hand in front of her face. "I think the guy needs to consider a serious dietary change."

"No kidding," I say. Behind me, I hear Izzy's voice approaching and realize that he and Mr. Malone are already headed back to the front area, their tour done. I look at Cass, desperate to escape. I can't go back the way I came, but when I look out the front door, I see the remnants of the media people lingering out there. It's a tough choice, but one I make quickly. I run for the front door and escape to the outside.

Cletus has joined the morning throng, and as soon as he sees me, he hurries over to ask me who the latest visitor is. "Is he here regarding the alien body investigation? Is he from NASA, or SETI, or some top-secret government branch that investigates extraterrestrial phenomena?"

I stop and stare at the remaining journalists, presumably those low on their respective totem poles if they have nothing better to do on a Saturday than wait around here for a space alien story that's never going to happen. Just then, Christopher Malone comes out, and it's all I can do not to turn and run.

"Why don't you ask him yourselves?" I say, arching my brows in a manner that suggests Christopher might be willing to dish something juicy. The crowd closes in around him, and I hear another telltale sound.

I turn and walk as fast as I can, heading for the underground garage and a back way into the office. I'm just entering the garage when I hear one of the reporters say, "What on earth is that godawful smell?"

Back inside, I stop in the autopsy suite and grab a mask, putting it on. Then I head back to the library, passing Otto, who is sitting in Izzy's office behind Izzy's desk. He eyes me curiously as I go by but says nothing. Izzy is back in the library, seated at the table, talking on his cell phone. He waves me in, and I take a seat.

"I see," he says to whoever is on the other end. "Yes, of course." More listening. Then a worried sounding, "Really?" More listening. My head is about to burst with curiosity, or maybe it's about to explode from the smells.

Finally, Izzy thanks whoever is on the other end and disconnects the call. "Well," he says, leaning back in his chair. "That was interesting."

"Interesting isn't what I would call it," I say. "What the hell was that? A bad case of nerves combined with a bad choice of meals?"

"Apparently not," Izzy says, tilting his head. "Our Mr. Malone has a metabolic disorder, an inherited one that affects the way his body processes food. It results in the production of lots and lots of really foul-smelling flatus."

"Oh. Wow. Poor guy," I say. "Isn't there a treatment or a cure for it?"

"Not according to his past employer."

"Is that who you were just talking to?"

Izzy nods. "It was. He filled me in on Mr. Malone's rather

sad history. The reason Malone has a degree in criminal justice is because he wanted to be a cop. But no one could ride with him in a squad car for any length of time, so after going through all the potential partners they had, they told him they were going to have to let him go."

"Ouch," I say wincing. "That had to have been a hard one to take."

"Malone didn't take it," Izzy says. "He sued the police department for discrimination, claiming he has a disability. He said it didn't interfere with his ability to do his job; his superiors and coworkers disagreed. They settled."

"Wow."

"The Ventura ME's office where he worked—that's who I was just talking to—said they heard about the police department thing after they hired him, so they were afraid to try to deal with the problem. Having him in the autopsy room with the fans going wasn't too bad, but they had to give him his own office and install an exhaust fan in it, too. The guy said Malone's work was exemplary, so there wasn't any other reason to let him go. When Malone's wife got a job promotion and had to move to Seattle, everyone in Ventura was relieved."

"I'll bet." I slip my mask down and sniff the air, testing it. It seems tolerable, so I remove the mask. "It's too bad," I add. "He seemed easygoing and qualified."

"He is qualified, very much so," Izzy says in a cautious tone. I frown at him. "And he can start immediately."

"You are not seriously considering hiring him," I say, staring at Izzy appalled.

"I can't not hire him," Izzy says with a shrug. "Unless we turn up something in his background check, criminal check, or references, there is absolutely no reason why I shouldn't hire him. If I don't hire him, he might sue us for discrimination."

I stare at him in disbelief. "Izzy, you can't . . ."

"I can, and I might have to." I continue starting at him, and he gives me half a smile. "He can start immediately," he says.

I'm speechless and, quite honestly, torn. My first impression of Malone was a good one, and the fact that he can start right away is a definite feather in his cap. A mental image fills my brain of Malone wearing a cap with a jaunty feather in it that then wilts when it comes in contact with that toxic gas. That gas . . . it's rather daunting, and while I feel some sympathy for Malone, I don't know if I can survive it. Then I realize I won't have to most of the time. If we hire Malone, he'll be working opposite me since we'll be job sharing. So my exposure will be minimal. It's the rest of the office that will suffer.

"Do you have any other candidates?" I ask Izzy.

He shakes his head. "There aren't a lot of people clamoring for this job. Cutting up dead people isn't as popular as you might think."

"Okay," I say with a shrug. "Get to checking those references." I'm not sure if I'm hoping Malone's references will or won't check out. The fact that he lasted several years at his other jobs makes me think we can make it work. There are air fresheners, and exhaust fans, and masks. But how much will that smell linger in the office? Will it be there even when he isn't? And what about when he has to interview people? How will that work if he's gassing them the entire time? But he can start *immediately*. Tomorrow even. That means a full night's sleep might be just over the horizon. That means some semblance of a normal life might be possible sooner rather than later. Isn't that worth a little odiferous suffering? I mean, come on, I deal with a kid who fills his pants regularly with something resembling toxic waste, and I've managed to get through some pretty horrific smells on this job. How bad are a few toots going to be?

The rational, more scientific part of my brain is knocking on the door of my idealistic part, trying to get in and remind me that this sort of thinking is the same kind of thing that happens to women when they contemplate having another child after experiencing the so-called joys of childbirth. Labor is painful. Not stub-your-toe-and-now-it-throbs kind of painful, not splitting-headache kind of painful, not burned-myself-on-the-oven-rack kind of painful (which was painful enough the one time I tried to bake something that I never tried again). No, childbirth is push-a-Volkswagen-through-an-opening-the-size-of-a-mason-jar painful . . . and the Volkswagen is on fire. And yet women seem to forget or minimize this pain soon after experiencing it. I think it's a survival tactic, because if we remembered the pain for any length of time as vividly as we experienced it, our legs would be forever crossed with DO NOT ENTER tattooed on each knee.

My phone rings then, saving me from having to debate this moral dilemma any longer, and I see it's Hurley. "What's up, love of my life?"

"I just got off the phone with Wyzinski's lawyer, Joan Mackey. She said she'd be happy to let you talk to Tomas, and she's eager to hear what you have to say. But she also said she doubted you'd get much out of him."

"Well, at least I can give it a try. When can I talk to him?"

"Mackey said she's free this afternoon if you want to meet her at the prison. He's at Waupun Correctional, which is only an hour's drive away. She can meet you there at one. There's some paperwork you'll have to fill out, so you might want to get there about fifteen minutes early. She said she'll meet you inside in the lobby area; they tend to frown on people sitting in their cars in the parking lot."

"Got it. In the meantime, if Otto doesn't have anything for me to do here, I'm going to try to have a chat with David this morning about those trips the pharma companies paid for."

"Want me to come along?"

"No, but thanks. I think David will be more willing to talk to me alone, particularly if I come at it from a personal level as opposed to a professional one."

"Maybe it should be professional. Maybe you should record your chat."

I consider this for a second but quickly dismiss it. "Hurley, if David is the DW referred to in Hal's notes, and I think he is, then all of those trips that are mentioned in the locales that come after his initials are trips he took when I was married to him. In fact, I went on two of them with him, so if he was doing something illegal, we both benefited from it. I honestly don't think he was doing anything illegal, at least not intentionally. And if he was, I'm not sure we can prove it. So I think we need to not think of him as a suspect."

There is silence on the other end for longer than I expect. "Hurley? Are you still there?"

"I am. How much of what you just told me is you trying to protect your ex?"

I sigh. "And how much of your desire to see David punished is because you resent my past relationship with him?"

"Don't be ridiculous," Hurley says, but I detect a hint of doubt in his voice.

"Look, if you take David down you might take me down with him. Not to mention that Patty is pregnant and she doesn't need this right now."

"That's no reason to excuse criminal behavior," Hurley grumbles.

"I don't think David is guilty of anything criminal, but if it turns out I'm wrong, we'll deal with it when we get there. Given past relationships, the case should probably be handed off to another jurisdiction, if it comes to that."

Silence again. I suspect this is because Hurley realizes I'm right. "Are we good?" I ask him.

"Yeah."

"Okay then. I'll talk to you later when I'm done with my prison visit. Love you."

"Love you, too," he says, and I quickly hang up before things can get tense again.

CHAPTER 27

I know from seeing David's calendar the other day, and from past experience, that he will spend some time in his office this morning. It's a Saturday, so he has no scheduled surgeries or appointments, but he will make the rounds of his hospital patients and then spend some time on paperwork. I call his cell phone, and he answers on the first ring. I can tell from the way the call hesitates a second before connecting that he is answering via the Bluetooth connection in his car. This might be a good thing for me since he didn't wait long enough before answering to see who the caller was.

"Dr. Winston," he says.

"David, it's Mattie."

"Oh. Hi." Instant indifference.

"I need to talk to you about something, and it's urgent. I wonder if I might be able to drop by your office this morning."

"I suppose. What is this about?"

"It's about a case I'm working on. I can explain more when I get there."

"Fine. I'm about to run through the coffee drive-through. I'll meet you at my office in five or so, if that's okay?"

It is, and I tell him so. The line at the coffee shop must have been longer than anticipated because even after checking in with both Izzy and Otto to tell them where I'm going and then driving to the clinic, I arrive seconds before David does. I see him pull in, driving the Mercedes he bought after his last car was burned up along with the house we used to share.

He gets out and gives me a distracted smile, fumbling with his keys as we walk to the back door of the clinic building. I wait as he unlocks the door, then follow him inside. As he enters his office, I hear him say, "Ah, there it is." Then I watch as he bends down and picks up his ID badge where I'd tossed it the night before. He clips it to his shirt and then moves behind his desk and boots up his computer.

"I lost my badge yesterday," he explains. "I could have sworn I had it on me when I went in to the OR because I used it to gain access. At least I think I did," he says with a frown. "Maybe that was the day before." He shakes his head and gives me a little smile.

This minor confusion over a task one performs routinely every day is what I had hoped for. David might have used his ID badge to gain entrance to the OR yesterday, or it might have been one of those days when the doors were already open because someone was coming out or someone ahead of him had already badged in. Days tend to blur together when you get used to doing things over and over again, and people don't always remember each individual action or task when dealing with common, everyday routines.

"What did you want to discuss?" David asks as I settle into a seat across the desk from him. He eyes his computer screen as it boots up and then types in his username and password.

"Before I get into that, let me say congratulations to you and Patty. I met with her the other day and heard the good news. I'm very happy for the two of you."

David looks away from his computer screen and scrutinizes me long enough to make me squirm a little. That intense gaze used to titillate me; now it just makes me uncomfortable. "I take it you're referring to the baby?" he says.

"Of course," I say. "What else could it be?"

He doesn't answer me and looks back at his computer screen. Then he opens the top drawer of his desk and removes a pair of glasses. He slips them on and starts tapping at his keyboard.

"I like your new house," I tell him. "It's quite different from the one we had, very modern, but I really like it."

David shoots me a look over the top of his glasses and shakes his head. "Come on, Mattie, I know your sense of style. You must hate that place."

"Not hate, no," I say. "I will admit it's not my style, but Patty has done a nice job with the design."

David says nothing, his focus back on his screen.

"Your office looks a lot like it did in the old house," I say, watching for a reaction. "Was that your choice or hers?"

David looks at me and cocks his head to one side. "Mattie, why are you here again? I have patients I need to round on." He glances pointedly at his watch.

"Okay, sorry. I'm here because I'm a little worried about Izzy. He's recovering from his heart attack nicely, but I think he needs to take some time away from the job, time he can spend with Dom and Juliana. But you know how stubborn he can be with that kind of thing. So I was thinking that if I could somehow arrange a vacation of sorts disguised as work, he might go for it."

"A vacation disguised as work?" David echoes. His tone suggests he thinks I've lost my mind.

"Yeah, remember that trip we took to Florida right after we were married? To the conference where you did your talk? The one where we went scuba diving in the Keys?"

He nods and smiles. "That was a fun trip."

"It was." I leave out mentioning that the scuba diving certification I got for that trip came in handy a few weeks ago while investigating Hal's murder. "And then there was the trip we took to London a year or so later."

"Another fun time," he says, looking almost wistful. But he shakes it off quickly. "What about them?"

"Who sponsored you for those trips? Who arranged the speaking engagements?"

His eyes narrow. "I don't recall off the top of my head. Those trips were years ago. Why do you want to know?"

"Because I was thinking something similar might be a way for Izzy and Dom to get a vacation of sorts. I don't know if Izzy will take a vacation otherwise. But if he's being paid to do a lecture and can convince himself it's work, then . . ." I shrug and give him a conspiratorial smile.

David scoffs at my idea. "Those trips are typically sponsored by pharmaceutical companies, and I don't imagine Izzy's patients have much of a need for drugs."

"There might be a way to tie something in to the benefits of a certain drug. I'm sure we could find some sort of relevant lecture Izzy could do. I just need some leads, some companies where I can maybe name-drop a little."

David arches an eyebrow at me. "You want to use my name to get an in? Is that what you're saying?"

"If it will help," I say, trying to look sheepish. "You've been invited to several of those conferences, so clearly you're someone they respect."

David never could resist ego stroking, and I see that hasn't changed. He smiles, shaking his head and looking pleased. "I suppose."

"Do you have a strong relationship with any one company in particular? Who invited you to speak at the London and Miami conferences?"

David shrugs. "I don't remember, and I'm not sure it matters. All those companies are intertwined anyway. It's an incestuous little business with one big head overseeing dozens of Medusas, who oversee all their little snake offspring."

"You sound kind of cynical."

"Well, they *are* in the business of selling their drugs," David says. "That's why I think your idea to get Izzy a speaking engagement isn't likely to work. You'll have a hard time convincing them to support him."

"Is pushing their drugs an understood agreement?" I ask. "Did they pressure you to push a certain drug when they offered you these speaking engagements?" I make air quotes around the words "speaking engagements."

"Not exactly," David says. "I mean, they always have some new drug on the market that they're hoping to get the most out of before their licensing runs out and the generics start hitting the market. They educate and encourage, but they don't force you to prescribe anything."

"What kinds of drugs do they typically push to you?"

"Pain meds, mostly. A few GI drugs, anxiety drugs, some clotting aids, that sort of stuff. To be honest, as a surgeon I'm not someone who offers them a lot of return on their investment. I'm not a big prescriber, particularly over the long term. They tend to prefer the internists and family practice docs. If they have a specialty drug they're pushing, they might target the specialists in that field, but for the most part they go after the generalists."

"I suppose that makes sense from a sales and marketing perspective."

"I do remember one drug they were pushing when I got invited to speak at that conference in Italy. Remember that one? You were sick with some kind of stomach bug and had to cancel at the last minute, so I went alone."

"Oh, I remember it well," I say. "It broke my heart that I couldn't go on that trip." This was true. The fact that I didn't go was a testament to how sick I was. If I'd been hemorrhaging or on my deathbed with cancer or suffering from any number of other ailments, I would have dragged myself on that trip anyway. Not only did I desperately want to tour and visit parts of Italy, Italian is my favorite food group. But I was stricken with a vicious GI bug that had fluids exiting my body through every orifice every half hour for three days straight. I practically lived in my bathroom and spent hours worshipping the shiny porcelain god. By the time that bug was done with me, I was so weak I could barely manage to get from my bed to the bathroom, and I had my nursing buddy, Phyllis (aka Syph), come by the house and start an IV on me to give me some fluids. It took me the better part of a month to fully recover.

"I recall the drug they were peddling for the Italy trip," David goes on, "because I remember joking with the rep about how the only reason he was sending me to Italy was so I'd get fat on all that delicious Italian food and end up needing this drug myself. It was a new weight-loss drug called Leptosoma."

"Did you prescribe this Leptosoma for anyone?"

"I did on a few bariatric patients who needed to lose some weight before I'd consider them for gastric bypass surgery or banding, or who didn't qualify for the surgery at all. It worked well for the most part."

"Interesting. It sounds like a huge moneymaker if it really works."

David goes wide-eyed a moment. "It does have potential. In fact, I instructed my stock market guy to buy a bunch of shares in the company that makes it."

"Really? Maybe I should invest as well. Have you heard of any problems with the drug? Any serious side effects?"

"I had one patient who died while taking it, but I don't think it had anything to do with the drug."

"What's the name of the company that makes it?"

David squints in thought. "Can't remember off the top of my head," he says with an apologetic look. I wonder if he's telling me the truth or trying to keep a great stock tip to himself.

"What about a rep? Do you remember the name of the one who contacted you about the Italy trip?"

"It was a guy . . ." He rubs his temples, squinting some more. Then he snaps his fingers. "Wait, I think I have his card here somewhere." He opens his desk drawer and drags out a rubber-banded stack of business cards nearly three inches thick. "I'm pretty sure it was one of these." He removes the rubber band and starts sorting through the cards. "I think his name was Derrick something or other," he says, still sorting. Then he stops and smiles. "This is it," he says, handing me a card.

I take it, half expecting to see the name Drake Industries on it. But instead it just says Algernon Pharmaceutical Products, with the name Derrick Hutchins on the bottom. I tuck the card into my purse and get out of my chair. "I've taken up enough of your time," I say. "I'd best get going."

David shoots me a bemused look. "You're going to keep that card?" he says. "What possible topic could Izzy lecture on that is in any way related to a weight-loss drug?"

"The epidemic of morbid obesity in our country," I say. "He sees the end results of it all the time on our autopsy tables."

"Yeah, I guess I can see that," David says. "Good luck."

"Thanks. And congratulations again on the pregnancy," I say. I walk over and glance out the window toward the back of the clinic, wanting to ask more, but not wanting to look David in the eye when I do. "Are you excited about it?"

There is the briefest hesitation before he says, "Of course. I mean, it's all happened kind of fast, but then we're not getting any younger, are we?"

Before I can answer, his office door opens. I'm not visible to the person who opened the door, nor can I see who it is. But I recognize the voice. It's David's new office nurse, Glory, an attractive brunette in her mid-thirties.

"Your first patient is ready, Doctor," she says in a sexy,

teasing tone. "I have a serious ache right here between my legs, and—"

David bursts out of his seat. "Thanks, Glory. Let me just finish up here with Mattie, and I'll be right with you." He makes a pointed look in my direction.

I can't see Glory, but I swear I can feel the heat of her blush radiating through the door.

"Of course, Da . . . um, Doctor," she says, and then the door quickly closes.

I look over at David and shake my head. "Really, David? Your wife—your relatively new wife, mind you—is pregnant. And you're cheating on her?"

"It's . . . I'm . . ."

"Oh, for heaven's sake, David. Spare me the lies and denials. I've been there, remember? I know the signs."

To his credit, he doesn't try to deny it. Instead, he hangs his head, at least having the decency to look embarrassed, though I suspect his embarrassment stems more from the fact that he was caught rather than from what he actually did. Or is doing. "I guess I shouldn't be surprised," I say to him. "A snake may shed its skin, but on the inside, it's still a snake. You haven't changed a bit, have you?"

With that I walk out of the office, head held high, glad I escaped the marriage when I did. I'm tempted to go find Glory and say something to her, but I decide not to. It's not my business anymore. The bigger question I have to deal with is whether or not to say something to Patty. When I was in her position, others knew what was going on and didn't say anything to me. Would it have made a difference in the outcome if I'd known sooner? Probably not. But given the shocking and embarrassing way I found out, I would have preferred something a little lower on the adrenaline-release scale.

But my situation was different from Patty's. She's pregnant. And I know from having been pregnant myself and essentially single at the time that it's not easy. I like Patty. I harbor no ill will toward her. She didn't cheat with my husband. She started her relationship with David long after our marriage had blown apart.

Didn't she?

I realize then that I have no way of knowing if the two of them were carrying on before David and I split. And then I realize I don't care. David is not a part of my life anymore, at least not a significant part. I have a sexy husband I adore, a son I cherish more than life itself, and a stepdaughter who I've come to love like my own. Granted, my life has been exhausting and complicated lately, but that's about to change. With a new house coming and a new coworker on the horizon, life is about to get even better.

I just need to figure out how to deal with DEFCON Level 1 farts, overeager alien enthusiasts, and paranoid construction workers. Piece of cake.

CHAPTER 28

The drive to Waupun is a surprisingly peaceful time for me. Despite where I'm headed and why, I am alone in my hearse, the windows down, the warm summer wind blowing my hair into a riotous mess, the fragrance of late summer tickling my nose. It's a rare moment of solitude, peace, and quiet, and it's definitely the happiest fifty minutes of my day.

When I arrive at the prison, I park and show my driver's license to a guard at an outside gate, and then proceed through a metal detector at the main entrance to the building. As I step through, it squawks, and I check my pockets to make sure I've removed everything. I took my watch and earrings off out in the car and left them, along with my cell phone, in the glove box. The man at the gate had warned me that cell phones weren't allowed.

I also left my purse in the car, and it has all of my money. There is no change in my pockets, no other jewelry, no clips in my hair, no belt around my waist. Puzzled, I step back around and walk through the metal detector again. And again it squawks. I give the guard a puzzled look and shrug.

"Step over here please," he says, indicating an area off to his left. There are two other people behind me, and he sees

them through the metal detector—they get through just fine—
before turning his attention back to me.

"We're going to need to search you," he says. "I don't
have a female guard here at the moment, so you'll have to
wait."

"Are we talking about a basic pat down?" I say.

The guard, whose name tag reads BRAD ADAMS, nods.

"Listen, Brad," I say, hoping that a first-name basis will
help me bond with the guy. "I'm from the medical examiner's
office in Sorenson. I have a badge, but I left it in my car because . . . well, because of that thing." I point to the metal detector. I hold my arms up, making my blouse tighten over my
bosom. My pants, which are typical lightweight summer
fare, cling to my legs and butt. "Look at me," I say. "Where
could I hide anything?"

Brad gives me a tired look of impatience that tells me he
isn't the type to cave in. Then he looks directly at my bustline, and I realize he has a point. My boobs are quite large,
and I have enough cleavage to hide quite a few things, including a weapon or two. Hell, my bras are weapons by
themselves. If David had had one of my bras to use as a sling-
shot, he could have flung a larger rock at Goliath and done
him in more quickly.

And that's when it hits me.

"Brad, hold on," I say. "I think I know what the problem
is." I look around in search of a bathroom or a nook where I
can do what I need to. But there is nothing. Resigned to either doing what I need to do here or walking back out to my
car, I decide to go for broke. I reach up under my left sleeve,
grab my bra strap off my shoulder, stretch it down my arm as
far as I can, slipping my elbow and then my hand through it.
I then do the same thing on the other side. With that done, I
reach behind my back, using that awkward arm pose that
only women and people who are resisting arrest are familiar

with and unsnap my bra. Then I reach up under my blouse, grab the bottom of the bra, and tug it down and out.

Brad watches this with an amused expression, his eyebrows arching when I remove the bra. I'm not sure if it's the size of the bra that has surprised him or the significant drop in the height of my bustline. When I'm done, I hand him the bra, which he holds by one strap like it's state's evidence he's afraid to contaminate. I go back to the start of the metal detector and walk through it. This time it stays quiet. I give Brad a smug smile and go to grab my bra from him.

"I'm sorry," he says, snatching it away from me. "You'll have to get it on your way out, or else remove the metal stays in it."

"They aren't stays, Brad, they're underwires. And I need them in my bra."

"Doesn't matter what you call them, they're potential weapons in my book," he says. Now it's his turn to look smug. He walks over, grabs a plastic tray, and drops my bra into it.

I decide it's not worth fighting this battle and move on. It's a decision I come to regret rather quickly as the fabric of my blouse, which is made of a nubby cotton fabric, slides up and down over my nipples with every step. As I enter the main lobby and head for the check-in window, I realize my high beams are on. I roll my shoulders forward, trying to minimize the display, but I swear my nipples are more erect now than they've ever been. I show my ID again, and I'm given a clipboard with a form I have to fill out: a visitor's application.

Wyzinski's lawyer shows up just as I'm finishing the form. Joan Mackey manages to look both cute and professional, with her petite build, short blond hair, designer suit, and leather satchel. She checks in—making it through the metal detector just fine with those perky little breasts of hers—and I come up right behind her with my paperwork.

"Hello, Mattie," she says.

The last time I saw her, we were adversaries, so I wasn't sure how friendly things might be today, but her warm tone and smile seem genuine.

"Is it okay if I call you Mattie?" she asks.

"Sure."

"And please call me Joan."

I nod, and then our conversation ceases as we are buzzed through a door and led by a guard down a hallway to a small room with a table, four chairs, bare concrete walls, and a second door on the far wall. Joan and I take the two closest seats, her on the left, me on the right.

Joan sets her leather bag on the floor and turns to face me. "Detective Hurley, your husband," she adds pointedly, letting me know she's done her homework, "said you have reason to believe my client was wrongly convicted and that you want to ask him some questions."

"Correct," I say.

"Well, I've believed in Tomas's innocence all along, so I'm willing to hear what you have to say or ask, but I also reserve the right to stop you at any point or tell my client not to answer. Though I suspect he'll be reticent enough without any action on my part."

I nod my understanding. "Is it true Tomas took and passed a lie detector test?"

"It is," Joan says with a regretful expression. "Unfortunately, those tests aren't admissible as evidence. Nor should they be. They can be notoriously unreliable. May I ask what questions you intend to ask my client? Because—"

She is interrupted when the door across from us opens. Tomas Wyzinski shuffles into the room, his wrists, waist, and ankles shackled, a guard on his heels. Tomas is wearing dark green scrubs, his name sewn onto the right breast with a gold thread that makes me flash back on our alien bones for a moment. He drops into a chair across from us after the guard pulls it out for him, and then the guard stands, hands clasped, back rigid, right behind him.

Joan smiles at the guard and says, "This is a privileged meeting with my client. Would you please step out?"

The guard nods, shrugs, and goes out the door he came in.

I focus on Tomas. His eyes still look creepy to me, but instead of frightening me like they did before, they now make me feel sad and guilty. I can't help but wonder if I had something to do with the sorrow I see reflected there.

"Hello, Tomas," Joan says. "Do you remember Mattie Winston? She works with the medical examiner, and she testified at your trial."

Tomas looks up at me, but there is no expression on his face. He might as well be dead, or at the very least stoned out of his mind. I half expect him to snarl at me or to see a spark of anger in his eyes, but there is nothing. His gaze doesn't linger on me long; his eyes drift off, glazed and unfocused.

Joan continues. "Mattie is here to talk with you. She says she has uncovered some evidence that leads her to think you might be innocent. I think we should hear her out."

If I was expecting any sort of reaction to this declaration, I am disappointed. Tomas doesn't move, doesn't blink.

I lean forward, my hands on the table. "I think you were set up, Tomas," I say. "I believe Marla's death was arranged by the same people who had my coworker and his fiancée murdered last month. We know the person, the individual behind those killings, but we have reason to believe he was a killer for hire. We think he killed Marla, too, and then framed you for her murder."

Still no response.

"This man committed those killings for the same reason I believe you are willing to take the rap for Marla's murder, because the people who hired him threatened to hurt or kill his family if he didn't do what they wanted."

I think I see a slight shift in his eyes when I say this, but I can't be sure. Encouraged, I continue. "I think the day I found you at your house, you were supposed to die. I don't think you self-administered the insulin that almost killed you. And because you didn't die, the people who wanted you dead had to find another way to ensure your silence."

Still no reaction.

"They threatened to harm Lech, didn't they?" I say. There is a flinch, a tiny, subtle twitching of his facial muscles. "They're watching Lech very closely," I go on. "His caregiver, the woman who visits during the week, said that some strange men have been coming around and talking to Lech. Your brother is convinced of your innocence, and he tells anyone who will listen all about it. I think the people who framed you are getting worried that Lech won't shut up. They don't want him making a lot of noise, stirring up trouble."

I have his attention now. He turns his head and looks straight at me. I see a glimmer of something—fear, anger, distrust—in his eyes.

"I'm worried for Lech," I tell him.

His Adam's apple bobs up and down, and his eyes narrow slightly. The muscles in his cheeks twitch.

"If he keeps talking like he is, I'm afraid the people who framed you are going to do whatever they have to do to shut him up. And then they're going to arrange an accident for you because once they've eliminated the thing they're holding over your head, they're going to be worried that you'll start blabbing."

Tomas takes in a slow deep breath, easing it out. "I have no idea what you're talking about, lady," he says. "My brother isn't right in his head, and he has a very vivid imagination. I wouldn't worry too much about what he says. And while I appreciate your faith in my innocence, I'm afraid you're wasting your time. I killed that bitch, Marla, because she dumped me. And I'd do it again." The level of venom in his voice as he says this is shocking, and I wonder if I have this all wrong.

The two of us engage in a stare-down, and Tomas wins because I blink first. I smile, look over at Joan, then back at Tomas. "I get it," I say. "You don't trust me. You think I'm one of them, or that I'm testing your commitment to the party line."

His expression doesn't alter one whit.

"But I promise you, Tomas, I'm on your side here. Yours and Lech's. These puppet masters have killed a lot of innocent people, and let's face it, Tomas, they meant to kill you, too. If Richmond and I hadn't found you when we did, you'd be dead. Clearly these people will do anything to keep you quiet." I pause for effect. "You and your brother."

Tomas shifts in his seat, and I sense that I'm finally starting to get through to him.

"We can provide your brother with protection," I tell him.

Tomas's withering look of doubt tells me what he thinks of this idea.

"Not us, per se, but the U.S. Marshals." I clarify. "You know, the Witness Protection Program?" I think I see a gleam of interest in his eye, so I continue. "They can relocate your brother, and you, if we can get you out of here. Give you both new identities. You could go back to taking care of Lech, and it would be just the two of you."

I have his full attention now, but I also sense a lingering wariness in him. I suspect he doesn't trust me fully, though I think he wants to. He's still not convinced I'm not part of the enemy group, here to test his willingness to keep his mouth shut.

"You used to work for a pharmaceutical company called Drake Industries," I go on. "Were they . . . are they a subsidiary of the same parent company that once owned Miller-Weiss?" He doesn't answer me, but he doesn't look away, either. "Why did you leave your job there?" I ask, making him shift his position again. I sense I'm closing in on a nerve, so I keep going. "Let me guess," I say. "You caught wind of some shady dealings there with regard to a new weight-loss drug the company was testing, outcomes that were unacceptable but were either buried or disguised as something else."

I pause, giving him an opportunity to respond, but he remains quiet. "This drug is killing people, Tomas, but the company is covering it up, making the deaths look like they're attributable to something else. And once you figured out what was going on, you became uncomfortable with it. Maybe you talked to someone, or maybe you simply started asking questions. Whatever the circumstances were, they were enough to get the company concerned and bring you up on someone's radar. I'm guessing someone had a stern chat with you about it, perhaps with some thinly veiled threats thrown in for good measure. You resigned, thinking that leaving the company would end the problem. But they didn't let you go that easily, did they?"

Tomas's breathing is faster, and his feet are shuffling back and forth on the floor. I know I'm hitting a nerve, so I keep going.

"They delved into your life, looking at every aspect of it. My guess is they were hoping to find something they could use to blackmail you, but when that didn't work, they seized upon your brother and your girlfriend. Did they hint at what they were going to do, or did they just do it and leave you for dead?"

He blinks three times, really fast.

"My guess is they gauged the strength of ongoing threats to both your brother and Marla and figured your loyalty to your brother would carry the greater weight. That made Marla the first victim. They killed her, cut off her head, put it in your refrigerator to frame you, and then gave you an overdose of insulin, assuming you'd be found dead and the assumption would be that you had killed Marla."

I pause again and give a shrug of grudging admiration. "I have to say, the fact that these people thought things through well enough to use your brother as their contingency plan shows we aren't dealing with your everyday, common criminals here. These people are smart, they're desperate, and they're keen to make sure their tracks are well covered. How long do you think they're going to let your brother live if he keeps on babbling about your innocence?"

Though the man across from me is essentially still from his shoulders down, there are all kinds of subtle movements above his shoulders that tell me how worried he is: His carotid artery is bounding away in his neck, the muscles in his cheeks are twitching and dancing, and his Adam's apple is sliding up and down, up and down.

"Lech showed me your diabetic log, Tomas. You were meticulous in managing your insulin and your diet, so unless the overdose of insulin you received was your attempt to commit suicide, there's no way you can convince me it was an accident."

I see Joan shoot me a curious look, but she says nothing.

"Stay away from my brother," Tomas says. I suspect he's trying to sound angry, maybe even threatening, but there is a slight hitch in his voice that reveals his true underlying emotions.

"Lech misses you, Tomas. He's worried about you."

There is a very quick, very subtle shift of Tomas's eyes to my right, toward Joan, before he is back at me, staring unblinkingly. "I have nothing to say," he says, straightening in his seat.

Something in my brain starts niggling at me, a clue, something that I'm missing here. And then I think I have it figured out. I reach into my pants pocket, take out a pack of gum I have in there, and remove a piece. I turn to offer it to Joan, and as she looks over at me, I let it drop to the floor.

"Oh, crap. Sorry," I say as she bends down to pick up the piece of gum. I turn and look at Tomas, nodding my head toward Joan and then giving him a worried, questioning look. His nod is subtle but unmistakable. I give a quick nod back, and by the time Joan has retrieved the gum, straightened up, and handed it back to me with a polite, "No thank you," I am looking at her, an apologetic smile on my face. She hands me the gum with a tolerant smile and immediately turns her attention back to Tomas.

I unwrap the piece of gum and fold it into my mouth. After chewing for a few seconds, I look at Joan and sigh. "It doesn't seem like I'm getting anywhere, so I suppose I'm done here. Thanks for letting me talk to him."

"No problem," Joan says. She hollers, "Guard!" so loudly that it startles me. I'm amazed that much noise can come out of such a little body.

The guard reenters the room.

"We're done," Joan says.

Tomas pushes himself out of his chair and shuffles toward the door. But just before he turns away, I catch his eye. Joan has her back to us, already heading for our door. Tomas looks at me, and for a split second his expression is a pleading one. It's there and gone so fast that later I'd wonder if I imagined it.

I follow Joan back out to the front reception area.

"That went about how I expected it would," Joan says. "Sorry if you've wasted your time."

"It wasn't a waste at all," I say, and Joan looks surprised. "Talking with him today has convinced me that the man is guilty. Clearly we've been barking up the wrong tree."

Joan smiles. "That's how it goes sometimes. You work in this business long enough and you learn not to trust or believe anyone."

"Well, thanks for giving me the chance all the same," I say.

We part ways, and I head back out to my car, stopping

along the way to retrieve my bra. As soon as I'm inside my car, I call Hurley.

"I'm more convinced than ever that Tomas was framed," I tell him. I then reiterate every detail of my visit, what was said, what wasn't said, and the body-language cues I observed.

Hurley is less than impressed. "It sounds like you're interpreting things the way you want them to be," he says.

"You wouldn't say that if you'd been there," I argue. "I'd agree with you if not for the exchange Tomas and I shared when I dropped the gum on the floor."

"Also consider the possibility that Tomas Wyzinski is guilty as hell and manipulating you to his advantage."

I start to give him a quick and adamant denial, but stop myself. Was I being as open-minded as I should? Could Hurley be right? But then I flash back to the subtle but distinct gestures and expressions Tomas and I exchanged, and I feel certain I've read it right.

"You're going to have to trust me on this one, Hurley," I say. "What's more, I think his lawyer, and perhaps her firm, is in cahoots with whoever's pulling the strings. Tomas is afraid of her. I think we need to do something with Lech, take him into some sort of protective custody."

Hurley sighs.

"And maybe not tell anyone about it," I add. "It might be interesting to see what happens if Tomas thinks his brother has suddenly disappeared."

"That's kind of mean if you're right about him," Hurley says.

"Yeah, I suppose it is," I say. "But in this case, I think the end may well justify the mean."

"Means," Hurley corrects.

"Nope, I said what I meant." And with that I disconnect the call.

CHAPTER 29

By the time I get back to town, it's closing in on four o'clock. I check in at the office and chat with Otto, telling him about my visit with Tomas. I'm almost done when my phone rings, and I see it's Emily calling.

"What's up, Buttercup?" I say, answering the call.

"I wondered if you will have time to take me to Desi's party," Emily says. "I was going to ride my bike, but it has a flat tire."

"Um, sure," I tell her. "One of us will be by to pick you up."

"Thanks!" With that she hangs up. Short and to the point.

"We need to get that girl some wheels sooner rather than later," I tell Otto, shaking my head. "Some days I feel like I have a second job as a chauffeur."

Otto heads home, and I start to do the same, but not before grabbing a donut from the pastry box I'd moved to Hal's desk earlier this morning. I scarf it down as I exit the building into the parking garage, and I'm sucking in the last bit of it when a gust of wind blows through the garage. I'm reveling in sweet, cream-cheesy goodness when I realize I've caught a hair with my last bite. I grab it with my fingers and pull it free of the pastry mash in my mouth, and it comes out covered with half-chewed pastry. I try to flick it away, but it sticks to my fingers. So I walk over to the concrete column next to my car and scrape the hair off onto it. And then I stand there staring at it. My mind starts whirling, thinking, sorting, and I feel a trill of excitement.

I get in my car, start it, and pull out onto the street. I drive a couple of blocks away—just enough to be out of sight of the reporters and make sure I'm not being followed—and then I pull over to the curb. I take out my phone and dial Jonas's number. He answers after the first ring.

"Kriedeman."

"Hey, Jonas, it's Mattie. I have a question about the motel case. There was a hair we found in Craig Knowlton's car, a blond hair that we collected as evidence."

"Yeah, I remember it. What about it?"

"Were we able to get any DNA from it?"

"I sent it to Arnie," he says. "I don't think he tried. There was no root attached, so there was no point. Besides, all it would prove if we had a match was that the person it belonged to had ridden in Knowlton's car at some point."

"Okay, thanks. I need you or Laura to look into something else for me." I tell him what it is, and then I disconnect the call. Next, I look up something on my phone and place another call. When that's done, I dial Hurley's number.

"What are you up to?" I ask him when he answers.

"Just got back to the station. I went out and had a chat with Mrs. Andruss."

"Andruss? Who's that?"

"It's a long story," Hurley says cryptically.

"Well, you can tell me all about it when I pick you up in a minute. I have some interesting information for you, too. And we need to go buy Emily a car."

"Right now?"

"Yes, right now."

"Mattie, I thought we discussed this. I want her to earn the car herself."

"And she has, Hurley. Remember, when she has a car, she still has to pay for things like insurance and gas. She's worked hard to save up her money, and she's done it without complaining. And it would help us with our schedules if we didn't have to drive her everywhere all the time."

"She has the bike," he reminds me.

"It has a flat tire."

"I can fix that."

"Sure, but what if it happens again? Plus, I have an ulterior motive." I sense he's going to object again, so I tell him what I have in mind.

"Of course," Hurley says with a *doh* tone. "I'll meet you out back in a minute."

I drive to the police station, and true to his word, Hurley is waiting for me in the parking lot. As soon as he gets into the hearse, I say, "Tell me about your chat with Mrs. Andruss."

"She called me earlier today and invited me out to her house," Hurley says. "She saw the news items about our alien bones and said she thought she could clarify things for us. She's Ted Jenkins's granddaughter."

Ted Jenkins is the elderly farmer we bought our land from. "What did she have to say?" I ask.

"It seems Mr. Jenkins is suffering from dementia. That's why there was a power of attorney who signed the paperwork when we bought the land. Mrs. Andruss says they put the old man in a home last week, and she's been going through his stuff at the house, clearing it out, because they're going to sell it to help pay for his care. And while going through some old albums and papers she found in the attic, she came across these."

Hurley pulls out some photos and shows them to me. I gape at them and nearly drive off the road.

"Whoa!" Hurley says, pulling the photos back. "Pull over."

I do so, pulling to the curb and shifting the car into park. Then I take the photos from Hurley and look at them again. There are five of them, each one showing a little boy who looks to be somewhere around the age of five. The boy has a large, bulbous head, a small jaw, close-set eyes, a narrow, cylindrical chest, and spindly arms and legs. I look at his hands and see that he has only three fingers on each one, a thumb and two other fat digits that look like fingers that have fused together.

"That's Oskar," Hurley says. "Those pictures were taken in the fifties, and they span about five years."

"Who is he?" I ask.

"He was the son of Mr. Jenkins's wife's sister, Anna," Hurley explains. "Anna was about eight years younger than her sister, and lived down south somewhere with her parents. She got pregnant out of wedlock and gave birth to Oskar. As you can see, Oskar had some serious birth defects. Anna's parents wanted to put him in an institution, but Anna refused. The problem was, she couldn't take care of the kid on her own because she was essentially a kid herself. She was only sixteen. And her very strict and religious parents were determined to hide the shameful results of her sins."

"So in 1951, when Oskar was about a year old, Anna ran away from home and came here to Wisconsin to live with her sister and brother-in-law. She kept it a secret from the rest of the family, afraid her parents would come and try to take her back and lock Oskar away somewhere. Despite his physical deformities, Oskar was fairly bright mentally, so his mother and his aunt homeschooled him and kept him out here on the farm. They kept him secluded and hidden, fearful that if someone in town saw him, word would get out and spread.

And then he would be subject to bullying kids, teasing, rude stares, curiosity seekers, and the like. Plus, word might make it back to Anna's parents. He grew up on the farm until the age of ten. He had something of a fixation with Flash Gordon, Buck Rogers, and space travel, so his aunt made him his own space uniform."

Hurley hands me another picture. In this one, Oskar is wearing a costume that is basically a one-piece suit with a round emblem sewn onto the chest. The emblem has a lightning bolt shape on it. Oskar has a huge, joyful smile on his face, and he's holding a carved wooden item in his hand that looks like a ray gun.

"The poor kid," I say. "He looks so happy here, but that body . . ." I look over at Hurley, tears in my eyes. "What was wrong with him? Did they try to get it fixed?"

"Mrs. Andruss found some medical records that she showed me. It looks like Oskar saw some sort of specialist in Milwaukee who told his mother that he had a rare form of that elephant man disease."

"Neurofibromatosis," I say, nodding. "It makes sense with the hydrocephalus and the other musculoskeletal deformities." I look at the picture again. "What happened to him? How did he die?"

"Apparently his uncle built him a spaceship, cobbling together pieces from some old farm equipment, a sled, and whatever else they had lying around. Oskar would haul that spaceship out through the fields to the bluff where we're building our house, sit in it, and look out over the valley, pretending he was flying. One day he went out there and never came back. When they went to look for him, they found him at the bottom of the bluff, with his spaceship smashed all around him. It had rained a lot in the days right before that, so the top of the bluff was covered with a lot of mud. They found a track in it that looked like the spaceship had slid downhill and over the edge. They figured either Oskar couldn't stop it when it started to slide, or perhaps he slid on purpose, hoping he could fly."

"The fact that he lacked sinuses would have made him prone to dizziness and loss of balance," I say.

Hurley shrugs. "Whatever happened, there were no other footprints in the area on top of the bluff, so they didn't suspect any foul play. And because no one knew of Oskar's existence, they decided to bury him out there on the farm, at the top of the bluff he loved so much. Before she got locked away, Anna kept a diary. That's where Mrs. Andruss got her information, though she said she'd heard hints of the story over the years."

"Oh my God," I say, fighting back tears for that poor little boy and his family. "How awful that must have been for Anna."

"Apparently, it was too awful," Hurley says. "Mrs. Andruss also had documents showing that Anna was placed in a home for the mentally ill in October of 1960, and she stayed there until she died from pneumonia four years later. Also in the trunk was a blanket embroidered with Oskar's name and the dates of his birth and death. He died in May of 1960."

"What a horrible tragedy," I say, shaking my head. I hand Oskar's pictures back to Hurley.

"It is a sad story," Hurley agrees. "But knowing it is good news for us. It means we can clear our land and go ahead with the construction."

I look at him, eyes wide. "Oh . . . right! That is good news." I break into a big smile but immediately feel guilty for doing so. On the heels of the heartbreaking story I've just been told, my happiness seems inappropriate.

"And it also means we can get those damned reporters to go away," Hurley says. "I swear, they're like bloodhounds, calling the station ten times a day, trying to catch us going in and out. The dispatchers said they've been driving them crazy."

"Well, maybe this story will be an even better one for them," I say. "It will make a sweet human-interest piece." I shift the car back into drive, pulling out onto the road. And as I'm thinking about those reporters and their drive to get a story, I get the beginnings of an idea.

CHAPTER 30

We arrive at our destination five minutes later. As often happens, the sight of the hearse pulling into the parking lot garners some odd stares. We are at a car dealership, and you'd think the hearse would create less of a stir here than it might elsewhere, but that doesn't seem to be the case. Faces are lined up inside the showroom windows, staring at us and pointing.

I park, and Hurley and I get out and head for the showroom. We are immediately descended upon by two salesmen. They come at us from opposite sides, one of them saying, "What kind of vehicle would you like to test-drive today?" and the other one saying, "Have you seen the hands-free capabilities in our new Jeep Grand Cherokee?"

When the two men realize they've hit on us at the same time, they stand there and glare at one another for a few seconds. I'd love to watch and see which one of them backs down first, but Hurley destroys both of their hopes by saying, "We're here to see Chip Cook."

Both men immediately drop their happy, expectant expressions and turn away, leaving us standing there. The one who had come at us from the right seems to realize their faux pas a few seconds later, and he turns back. "His office is through that door and up the stairs on the right."

He then skulks back into the office he came from. Left to our own devices, we follow his directions upstairs and find a large glassed-in office with the name CHIP COOK stenciled on the door. The door is open, and we can see a man who looks to be somewhere in his forties seated behind a desk, a phone to his ear. He is leaning back in his chair, facing to the right, holding the phone with his left hand and shooting tiny foam balls at a mini basket mounted on the wall across from him. His aim isn't very good, and I see there are a half dozen foam balls scattered about on the office floor.

Hurley walks up and knocks on the door. Cook sees us and immediately straightens up, sets the ball he was holding on his desk, and tells whoever is on the phone that he has to go but will call back later. He hangs up the phone and stands, waving us in, and then coming around the desk to shake our hands.

"I take it you're the lady who called?" he says, looking at me.

"I am. My name is Mattie Winston, and as I said on the phone, I'm looking into a case that I think you can help us with. This is Steve Hurley, the primary detective on the case."

I see Hurley frown ever so briefly and wonder if it's because I've taken the lead, which isn't usually the case, or because I've introduced myself as Mattie Winston. That last name thing is going to be an ongoing problem for us, I think.

Cook shakes our hands, introducing himself to Hurley as he grabs his. He then gestures toward a couch and a couple of chairs in the corner. "Please, have a seat," he says. Hurley and I settle in to the chairs. "Can I get you a drink of some sort?" Cook asks.

"No thanks," I say. Hurley shakes his head, and then Cook settles in on the couch.

Hurley fires off the first question. "Mr. Cook, you're the ex-husband of Penny Cook, is that right?"

Cook takes on a wary expression. "What the hell has she done now?" he says. "Are you going to serve me with something?"

"No, sir," Hurley says. "We're interested in whatever information you can give us regarding Penny and her relationship with her sister, Pamela. I don't know if you heard the news or not, but Pamela's husband died a few days ago."

Cook nods, a sober look on his face. "I heard. Apparently, it was some sort of murder-suicide thing involving a woman he was having an affair with?"

"At first blush, it appeared that way, yes," I say. "But now we're not so sure."

"Really?" Cook looks surprised by this. "I have to say, the whole scenario seemed a bit off to me. Craig and Pamela have always had such a strong, solid relationship. Those two seemed genuinely in love. The idea of him having an affair never occurred to me, much less doing something as drastic as killing the other woman and himself."

"Are you privy to any of the financial assets Pamela and Craig have?" Hurley asks.

"Not specifics," Cook says. "But I know their business has been doing quite well. And, of course, Pamela still has her trust fund."

"Trust fund?" Hurley and I both say at the same time.

"Oh, yeah. Pam and Penny's parents were financial planners, and their wills specified that their assets be equally divided and set up in trust funds for the two girls. Penny went through her fund paying to keep herself and her sister going. Penny essentially raised Pam, and Pam couldn't access her money until she turned eighteen. When Pam came of age, she was able to obtain a scholarship for college, and she also worked while attending school. As such, she was able to not only leave most of her fund untouched, but she invested it very smartly and made herself a nice little bundle."

"That must have been hard for Penny," I say. "Did Pamela offer to reimburse her sister for any of the expenses incurred in raising her?"

"Oh, yeah," Cook says, his eyes growing big momentarily. "Pam has always been supportive of her sister. Too much so, if you ask me."

"What do you mean?" Hurley asks.

Cook sighs, leaning back on the couch and folding his hands over his stomach. "My wife . . . my ex-wife has a bit of a gambling habit. When I married her, she was already hooked, but I didn't know it. It took me many years and the loss of my entire retirement account before I caught on to what was happening."

"Are you saying Penny gambled away your money as well as hers?" I ask. I feel my face flush as I ask the question. I had a bit of a gambling habit myself for a while, right around the time I got pregnant with Matthew. If I were to set foot inside a casino again, I suspect I'd be sucked in just as hard. I think about it a lot, and it's only because I won't let myself go any-where near a casino that I've been able to keep things reined in. Even so, I play two sets of lottery numbers every week. Every time I think about stopping, I imagine my numbers coming up the first week after I stop and me losing out on the jackpot I've been paying into week after week. Some part of my mind recognizes the illogic of it, but another part of my mind simply doesn't care.

"Penny not only gambled away all of our money; her sister bailed her out numerous times, and she gambled that money away, too." Cook pauses and shakes his head. "I tried to get her to go to Gamblers Anonymous meetings, but she insists she doesn't have a problem, that she's in control."

"Your divorce didn't wake her up to the realities?" Hurley asks.

"No, but when she lost custody of the kids, I think it gave her pause. Not enough, though."

"You have custody of the kids?" I ask. I find it interesting that Penny left this information out when she was filling me in on her life's story that day at Pamela's house.

"I do," Cook says. "I petitioned for full custody when I filed for the divorce. Given Penny's history with the gambling and all the money she had burned through, it was an easy decision. She has visitation, and we split the holidays, but the kids are with me the bulk of the time."

"And what does Pamela think about it all?" I ask.

"Those two are very close," Cook says. "It's understandable, I suppose, given what they went through together. It doesn't help that Pamela keeps bailing Penny out, but the dynamic between the two of them is an odd one. I think Penny is a little jealous of her sister's success, but she won't admit to it. I've heard her talk several times about how she wishes she could go back to the way it was in the old days, just the two of them, with no kids, no husbands, no hassles. And I think Pamela harbors some guilt about Penny using all of her money supporting the two of them, although I think Penny might have been gambling even then. Pam feels like she owes something to Penny, that she's indebted to her. Penny is clearly the one in charge whenever they're together, and Pamela defers to Penny on a lot of decisions. I suppose it's understandable, given both the age difference and the fact that Penny raised Pamela for a number of years."

"Was it the gambling problem that destroyed your marriage?" I ask.

"For the most part," Cook says. He takes on a sheepish look. "Penny always cared more about Pam and the kids than she did me. I think she was jealous of Craig because he took up so much of Pam's time and affections. Things between Penny and me weren't great even before I learned about the money situation, and I started looking outside our marriage. I had an affair, and that was the nail in the coffin."

"Where does your wife live?" I ask. "Is she in the family home?"

"Family home?" Cook scoffs. "No, we lost that, too, thanks to her gambling. We were forced to sell it. Took a loss on it, too. I just bought a place last year over on the other side of town, but Penny is renting a duplex apartment near here. I think that's all she can afford."

"She has a car," I say, recalling the nondescript sedan I saw in Pamela's driveway on the day we were at the house.

Cook chuckles. "Yeah, I'm not a total bastard, despite what Penny says about me. I own several dealerships, so I'm able to provide her with wheels. I give her the beat-up trade-ins that I likely wouldn't be able to sell anyway. I have my mechanics tune them up so they run decent." He pauses and shrugs. "I just gave her a new one the other day, in fact."

I perk up. "What day, exactly? And why did you give her a new one?"

Cook thinks a moment, pulling at his chin. "I'm pretty sure it was on Thursday. She said the one she had was back-firing and not starting for her all the time." He shrugs again. "I had one of my mechanics take a look at it, and it seemed to be running fine, but sometimes cars can be temperamental, just like women." He glances over at Hurley and winks. "Right?"

"Indeed," Hurley says, wearing a smile.

"Mr. Cook," I say, eager to break up the bromance, "we are here for more than just our investigation. We're also in the market for a car for our daughter."

"Really? That's great!" He pops up from the couch and heads for his office door. "What sort of vehicle did you have in mind? Used or new? Sedan or SUV? You probably want to consider four-wheel drive, given the winters we have here.

That's much safer for your daughter. To be honest, if you want the safest vehicle, you should probably buy new. They've got so many great safety features now with the side airbags and hands-free Bluetooth phone and messaging capabilities."

He pauses in the doorway, realizing that we haven't popped up from our chairs and followed him. He arches his eyebrows expectantly, smiling at us.

Hurley and I get up from our seats and head for the door. "I think we'd like to start by looking at the car your wife traded in the other day," I say.

Cook frowns at this and shakes his head. "You wouldn't want that for . . ." He trails off then, realization dawning on his face. "You're not interested in buying that particular car, are you?" he says, tapping the side of his head. "You want to look at it for your investigation. You never did answer my question about Penny. What the hell has she gone and done now?"

We still don't answer his question, but he doesn't seem bothered by this fact. Cook leads us downstairs and out onto his lot, heading for a back section where there is a collection of used cars. He takes us to a 1995 Ford Escort that looks like the car I saw the other day. I'm surprised at its age because it has a surprisingly good-looking exterior for a Wisconsin car. The salt and sand on our roads in the winter tend to be hard on car finishes. Cook unlocks the door and opens it. The front seats are cloth-covered, and the inside of the car has a funky smell.

Cook sees me sniffing and wrinkling my nose. "Yeah, I think Penny might have spilled something in here, or maybe something crawled into the ventilation system and died. It smells funny, and it didn't when I gave it to her. I suspect that's the real reason she traded it in."

I pull my head out and look at Hurley. "It's stale urine. Sadly, I'd know that smell anywhere." I then point to the passenger seat. "It looks like there's a stain on that seat. And there's also a big wrinkle in the cloth material. Remind you of anything?"

Hurley looks at the seat, then at me. "A line that might leave a mark on someone's legs," he says.

I nod. "And if that someone was . . ." I hesitate, glancing at Cook. "If that someone was not fully in control of their bodily functions . . ."

Hurley nods. He gets my drift. Both Craig and Meredith had leaked urine onto their clothes and the bed in the motel, a common thing that happens when people die. Their sphincters relax and things are released. Since we know Craig Knowlton was dead before he got to the motel, odds are pretty good that he had leaked some urine before getting there, too.

"Gotcha," I say to Hurley with a smile.

He smiles back at me and then turns to Cook. "I need to seize this car as evidence in a homicide," he says. "I need you to lock it back up and give me the key. I'll call and arrange to have a tow truck come and get it and take it to our evidence garage."

"Homicide?" Cook says, his eyes big. Then he narrows them. "Wait, are you guys for real? You never showed me any kind of badges. Are you trying to scam me? Did Penny put you up to this?"

Hurley takes out his badge and assures Cook that he is legit. "I'll give you a receipt for the car," he says. "And whenever we're done with it, you can have it back." This seems to placate Cook, who may not realize that if he ever does get the car back, the interior will likely have been dismantled.

To distract him, I ask him a personal question. "When you had your affair, Mr. Cook, where did you typically go for your rendezvous?"

"That motel out on Morals Road, the one with the bear. I thought it would be far enough away to be safe, but Penny was more suspicious than I realized. She followed me out there once and caught me with Rita. We had a bit of a . . . confrontation. That was what precipitated the divorce."

Hurley and I share a look, and when he and Cook head inside to make the necessary arrangements, I meander through the lot and do some browsing. One of the salesmen who accosted us when we first entered the showroom pops outside and comes running up to me again.

"Hello, Ms. . . . ?" He words it as a question, waiting for me to fill in the blank. When I don't, he continues on, barely missing a beat, and apparently not remembering that he already tried to pick me up for a sale inside the showroom. "I'm Pete. What can I interest you in today? We have some really nice Jeep Grand Cherokees that we just got in. They're fully loaded."

Since *fully loaded* to me is generally a reference to my order of potato skins or nachos, I'm not sure what it means in car speak. "I'm looking for something for our teenage daughter, hopefully something safe, with hands-free technology."

"Are you looking to buy used or new?"

"Depends on the price and how old and used a used car might be," I say.

"May I ask what you're currently driving?" Pete asks. "You might consider getting yourself a new car and letting your daughter have yours."

I shake my head. "We've ruled that out already." This is true, but the decision didn't come easily. I ruled it out because I've come to love the hearse and all the quirkiness that goes with it. Hurley, on the other hand, liked the idea of Emily inheriting the hearse. This is mainly because he had the thing pimped out like the Popemobile two years ago when I was pregnant and being stalked by a crazed killer. He added steel reinforcements to the door panels, run-flat tires, and bulletproof glass, so he thinks of it as the ultimate safe vehicle. But it doesn't have side airbags, or Bluetooth anything, or four-wheel drive. And to me, all of those things are more important, particularly for a cell-phone-crazy teenager. Hurley has finally come to see my side of things in the matter.

"Are you sure?" Pete says. "Let me make you an offer on your current vehicle. I think you'll be pleasantly surprised."

I'm about to say no again, but Pete's determined look changes my mind. I suspect he won't give up on this matter unless I can find a way to convince him.

"Okay, Pete, it's that car over there, the midnight blue one parked by the cherry red F-150. It's got very low mileage."

Pete stares where I'm pointing, looking like the cat that just ate the canary. Two seconds later, his expression falters, and he gives me a sidelong glance. "You're not talking about the hearse, are you?"

"I most certainly am," I say with great enthusiasm. "It's quite roomy with seating for six. Seven if you count the coffin space. And like I said, it's got relatively low mileage. I won't say it's been driven by a little old lady its entire life, although it has hauled a lot of little old ladies. But it has been driven gently for the most part. And it has some fun add-ons you might be interested in."

Pete's shoulders sag, and he gives me an irritated look. "You've just been messing with me this whole time?"

"No. I really do want to buy a car for my daughter. But I don't want to be upsold, I don't want to be pressured, I do know my numbers, and I'm a close acquaintance of your boss, Mr. Cook. So can we keep all that in mind while we're looking?"

Pete looks appropriately kowtowed. "Got it," he says, his lips pinched. "Why don't you tell me what price range we're looking at?"

"Now we're talking, Pete," I say. "Here's what I'm thinking."

CHAPTER 31

By the time Hurley and I leave the car lot, we are running late for my sister's party. Hurley agrees to go by the house and pick Emily up while I run out to a store to buy a birthday card and try to find a gift. My sister isn't an easy person to buy gifts for, and trying to do so at the last minute isn't helping the situation any.

Kitchen gadgets are a safe bet because Desi loves to cook, and in a somewhat selfish move that I hope will steer her future cooking efforts in a certain direction, I settle on a pasta-making machine, along with a nifty little rubber tube made for peeling garlic cloves with a simple roll of your hand. I wait while the store wraps the items for me, pacing as I watch time slipping by.

By the time I arrive at my sister's house, I am more than an hour late. The inside is decorated with balloons, banners, and a festive table complete with confetti, a birthday cake Desi probably made and decorated herself, ribbons, a punchbowl filled with some sort of pink drink, and several wrapped gifts. I wonder if Desi did all of the prep and decorating herself, or if her kids helped. I can't imagine her husband, Lucien, assisting since I've never seen him lift a hand to do stuff around the house, and Ethan is a loner whose only talent and interest lies in his bug collection. If anyone helped Desi, it was Erika.

Desi looks happy and totally in her element. Her smile is broad and warm as she walks around, greeting and chatting with her guests. Not surprisingly, given my late arrival, there are a number of people at the party already. In addition to Desi and Lucien, there are a handful of Desi's neighbors, Hurley, Emily, some acquaintances from about town whom Desi and I both know from growing up here in Sorenson, Izzy, Dom, Sylvie, and my mother's live-in boyfriend, William (or William-not-Bill, as those of us in the family call him, thanks to his constant reminders of this fact).

My mother is noticeably absent, and I doubt she'll come. She's become the geriatric sector's version of the Bubble Boy, rarely leaving her immaculate, air-filtered house for the dreaded outdoors, doing so only when she absolutely has to and then with a mask and sometimes other protective gear in place. My mother has been a hypochondriac and has had OCD for as long as I've known her. I got used to her quirks growing up, though I spent most of my formative years alternating between trying to decide which friends Desi and I would go to live with when my mother died (which she declared she was doing on a regular basis) and weaving a fantasy existence a la *The Chronicles of Narnia* wherein Desi and I went to live in a foster home that had a magic portal hidden in a closet.

My mother's OCD, specifically her germaphobia, has worsened over the years. Now that I know the truth about my father's disappearance thirty-plus years ago, I wonder if those events had something to do with the start of her disorder. I'm fairly certain all the failed marriages she's had since then helped to nurture it. Her relationship with William has also nurtured it because he's a germaphobe, too, making them a perfect pair and their house the cleanest one in town, maybe in the whole state of Wisconsin.

I gravitate toward William first, wanting to ask him how my mother is doing. Ever since the return of my father and our discovery of my mother's past secrets, she has been on a cleaning frenzy unlike any I've seen before. William said she scrubbed the floors so vigorously that she wore holes through her gloves and scraped her knuckles raw. The raw knuckles triggered an episode of hypochondria in which my mother was convinced she had leukemia and was on the verge of becoming septic. When the knuckles healed just fine on their own, my mother went back to her maniacal scrubbing and developed some muscle aches in her back and shoulders, as well as fatigue, all of which she immediately assumed was caused by the spread of the leukemia she didn't really have.

After nearly two weeks of scrubbing, she donned one of her many elaborate nightdresses and took to her bed, informing William yet again of where her will was, where her funeral plan was, and what type of service and burial she wanted. These reminders were unnecessary since she gave him this information regularly, every time she came down with an imaginary illness. But William, bless him, has been infinitely patient with my mother's quirks. In fact, I think he loves her all the more for them.

"Hey, William," I say, giving him a hug. I have a genuine affection for the man, part of which stems from the fact that I met him on a blind date, a disastrous event that led to me fixing him up with my mother. "How is Mom doing?"

"She's still terminal," he says in a blasé tone. "Although she has started talking about the need to dust the valances in the living room, and move the stove and fridge out so we can kill the dust bunnies living under there."

"As if any self-respecting dust bunny would dare try to survive in my mother's house," I scoff. William smiles. "The cleaning fixation is always a good sign," I tell him, though I suspect he's managed to figure this out on his own over the past three years. "It means she's ready to give up on her current terminal illness and prepare herself for the next one."

William nods, still smiling. But then the smile fades, and he gives me a concerned look.

"What?" I say. "What's wrong?"

William sighs and chews his lower lip. "Your father came by last week."

My eyebrows shoot up. "Really? Did Mom talk to him?"

He shakes his head. "She claimed she was too ill, dying any minute, and she didn't want to waste her last seconds on earth on a cheating, lying con artist."

"Ouch," I say, wincing. "How did my father take it?"

William shrugs. "Okay, I suppose. I invited him in, and we chatted for a bit."

"Really? What about?"

"Mostly about you, and Desi, and how much he regretted not being a bigger part of your lives when you were growing up." William frowns and looks down at his feet. "He also talked about how much he cared for your mom back then."

"That must have been difficult for you," I say, silently cursing my father for his lack of tact.

"It wasn't that bad," William says. "Despite what he said, I could tell that that part of his life was behind him. In fact, I think he's angry with your mother, not only for refusing to come with him all those years ago when he entered witness protection, but for not telling him she was pregnant with their second child and then lying about Desi's paternity."

"It *was* rather thoughtless of her to do that," I say, "although I can kind of understand why she did it, given the circumstances."

"I suppose," William says in a doubtful tone. "Whatever the history, this current state of affairs seems to have triggered a whole new level of intensity in her behaviors. I'm a little worried about her."

"Anything I can do to help?"

He shakes his head. "No, but thanks for the offer."

I give his arm a squeeze and then leave him to go talk to my sister. She is playing the perfect hostess, replenishing the drinks of her guests from the punch bowl. I sidle up to her and wait for her to finish charming Nathan, the elderly man who lives next door.

Once Nathan has been topped off and has wandered away, I nudge Desi with my elbow. "What is that?" I ask, nodding toward the punch bowl.

She grabs a glass—plastic champagne glasses with HAPPY BIRTHDAY written on them—and ladles me a drink. "Try it," she says, handing me the glass. "It's a raspberry lemonade mix with club soda and a hint of rosemary in it."

I sip the drink, which has a sparkling, fruity flavor. "Very good," I say, meaning it. I take another, bigger taste. "Did you do all this yourself?" I ask her after I've swallowed.

"I did," she says, her eyes sparkling nearly as much as my drink. "Does it look okay?"

"It looks fantastic," I say. "But you shouldn't have had to do it all yourself."

She gives me a dismissive wave of her hand. "Oh, I don't mind. I was in the mood for a party, so why not?"

I look around and see that we are relatively alone for the moment. "So tell me about your visit with Dad," I say in a low voice.

"It was interesting," she says. "He's really pissed at Mom for hiding me from him, and I have to admit I'm a little annoyed about the whole thing myself. I confronted my father—well, the man I always thought was my father—right after you told me. He admitted that he knew the truth, but loved Mom and wanted to make sure she was safe. So he went along with her plan. He apologized for duping me, and said he genuinely cares for me and considers me his daughter." She scoffs. "Of course, there are the three kids he has in his new family, too." Desi gives me a sad look and shakes her head. "What a web of lies."

"I know. It's a big mess. And I don't know what to think about Dad. I spent all those years thinking he was a selfish, conniving, thieving con artist, when in reality he left us because he wanted us to be safe. Of course, he was—and probably still is—a con man, and if not for that none of this would have been necessary."

"I know," Desi says, nodding. "My feelings are mixed, too."

"It's certainly more understandable in your case, given that you only just found out the truth. Does Lucien know? The kids?"

Desi nods. "They all know. In fact, they all met him when he came by."

"How did that go?"

"Lucien was a bit cold, and Erika kind of followed his lead. Ethan, however, hit it off with him right away. In fact, it's the most socially animated I've ever seen Ethan."

"Did he say if he was staying somewhere close by?" I ask.

"We didn't discuss that, but . . ." Desi winces and gives me a forced smile.

"What?" I say, eyeing her warily. "What aren't you telling me?"

"I told you I invited him here to the party," she says, with a smile that's half grimace. "He said he was definitely coming."

"Yeah, well he says a lot of things that never happen," I grumble. "I wouldn't hold your breath."

"We'll see," Desi says with a sly smile. "I should go and mingle with my other guests."

I'm fairly certain she simply wants to escape my scrutiny, but I let her go. It is her birthday, after all. As she heads for a group of people I don't know, I make my way over to Izzy, who is standing next to his mother. Sylvie is seated in a chair, drink in hand, looking out over the crowd with a reverent smile as if it was her birthday.

"How's it going?" I say to Izzy.

"So far so good," he says. "But check in with me again after they cut the cake. I don't think I can pass that one up."

"You can have a small bite," Sylvie says. "A life without little pleasures isn't really a life at all, now is it?" She reaches up and pats an imaginary stray hair on her head into place. Her hair is so thin I can see her scalp.

"How are you doing, Sylvie?" I ask. Even as I pose the question, the nurse in me is doing a quick assessment, checking her overall color, scanning her ankles for edema, studying her chest to see if she's breathing faster than normal.

"I'm fine," she says. "But I would be better if I had my granddaughter here with me."

"Where are the kids?" I ask Izzy.

"Erika has them in her room," Izzy says.

I would like to get Izzy off to himself so I can fill him in on what Hurley and I learned earlier this evening, but I know he will be reluctant to leave his mother's side. Not because he's a devoted son—although he is—but more because if he leaves her alone, Sylvie will have a conniption. She will clutch at her chest, cut loose with a string of *oy veys*, and declare in a voice that will be surprisingly loud and robust coming from such a frail-looking old woman that the world must be coming to an end. So I decide to try something different.

"Sylvie, I want to go and check on Matthew. I haven't seen him all day. Would you like to come with me and see Juliana?"

Her face lights up. "Yes," she says, and then she starts the tedious process of getting out of her chair. Izzy and I both stand by and watch, knowing from past experience that trying to assist her will result in getting our hands slapped and our efforts chastised. Eventually, Sylvie makes it up and takes her walker in hand. Slowly, the two of us navigate through the room and the guests, making our way toward Erika's bedroom. It's a slow go, but eventually we get there. And when I open the door to Erika's room, I am greeted with an unexpected surprise.

Erika is on the floor with Juliana on a blanket beside her. Matthew is not on the floor, however; he is being held by the man standing in the room.

"Hello, Mattie," says my father. "Good to see you again."

CHAPTER 32

"Please put my son down," I tell him.

"I'm not allowed to have a little time with my grandson?" my father says.

Sylvie, who is clueless as to the animosity and history between me and my father, says, "Oh, yes. It is important to spend time with the wee grands, yes?"

"Why, yes, it is," my father says. He smiles at Sylvie, who is walkering her way toward a chair near Juliana.

I stride over to my father and extend my arms out to Matthew, who comes to me without hesitation. Not that he looked uncomfortable in my father's arms. Quite the contrary.

"How's my boy doing?" I say, kissing him on his head. "Did you have a good day today?"

"Goo day," Matthew says.

I look at my father, who is watching us, still smiling. "What are you doing here?" I ask him.

"I came to celebrate my daughter's birthday," he says in a Captain Obvious tone. "And to see my grandchildren. I have a lot of lost time to make up for."

Erika looks at me, then away, focusing instead on Juliana.

"I gave my gift for Desi to Erika," my father says. "She can give it to her later. I don't want to cause any disruptions at the party."

"No, you just want to cause disruptions in our lives," I say. He doesn't deny this. Instead, he looks down at his feet.

Sylvie gives me a *tsk*, followed by an *oomph* as she drops into the chair she has finally reached. "One should be more respectful to one's elders," she says. Then she smiles up at my father and adds, "Particularly one as handsome as this."

Great. Now Sylvie is flirting with my father. Can my life get any weirder? Turns out it can.

"Mattie, I wonder if I could have a word with you in private," my father says. "Perhaps we could step out back for a moment?"

"Whatever you have to say to me, you can say here," I say. I'm angry, but I'm trying to keep my tone neutral so as not to upset the kids.

"I don't think this topic is for general ears," he says. He narrows his eyes at me, and I sense he's trying to send me a mental message. I wonder if this is part of his con repertoire, this eye fixation combined with certain word combos. I saw something like it on a TV show once. "It's regarding royalty," he adds, his eyebrows arching suggestively.

I have no idea what he's talking about, and I know I should just leave, or ask him to, or both. But my damned curiosity is getting the better of me. I set my son down on the floor and kiss him again. "Mommy needs to go do something, but I'll be back in a minute. Can you stay here and play with Erika?"

"Look, Matthew," Erika says, "I've got a Thomas the Tank puzzle." She shows him the wooden puzzle, which has seven large pieces in it. Since my son loves trains and puzzles—a trait he was bound to have given that both his parents are puzzle fanatics—it's an easy sway.

I back out of the room as my son drops to the floor, grabs

the puzzle, and dumps its pieces out. My father follows me, and once we're in the hallway, we make our way to the kitchen and the back door. I step outside onto the covered patio, having a momentary flashback to my wedding, which was held here in my sister's backyard.

"Your wedding was lovely," my father says.

I shoot him a surprised look. "How would you know?"

He gives me an enigmatic smile, one I suspect he put to good use back in his swindling days. "I was here," he says.

"No, you weren't."

"Oh, but I was. You may not have seen me, but I was here. I wasn't about to miss my daughter's wedding."

I stare at him, wondering if I can believe him. Was this just another one of his cons, his way of trying to win me over?

"You were wearing a lovely dress in a blue shade that matched your eyes. Your son had a mini-meltdown halfway down the aisle. And just as the ceremony ended, Ethan's giant cockroach put in an appearance and created quite a panic."

"You could have learned all that from talking to Desi, or looking at pictures," I say.

"I suppose I could have, but I didn't. You can ask her. The topic of your wedding never came up."

"Whatever," I say, tired of trying to determine if he's being honest or not. "What is this royalty you want to talk about?"

"Mr. Prince," he says.

He has my full attention now. "What about him?"

"He was a hired gun, right? And I'm betting he did his job because his family had been threatened. And when he turned himself in to your husband, they had him killed."

I try to figure out how he could have learned this. Jeremy Prince's name had appeared in the news, and he was identified as the killer of Hal, Tina, and Carolyn Abernathy. But the reason for the killings that appeared in all the media sources was that Prince suffered from a severe case of PTSD brought on by his time in the military, and that he went off the deep end and embarked on a killing spree. The deaths were determined to be random and unrelated.

The media also reported that Prince's family was missing and presumed dead as well, even though their bodies hadn't been found. The "official" explanation of how Prince died was that he attempted to take the gun of the police detective who had arrested him, and a struggle and shootout ensued, one that unfortunately also claimed the life of reporter and photographer Alison Miller.

This was far from the truth, of course. But in order to protect ourselves and our case, this was the official line that came out of the police department. So how did my father know the truth behind the public story?

"I'm right, aren't I?" my father says.

"I'm not at liberty to discuss this with you," I tell him.

"These people are very dangerous," he says. "Their reach is enormous. You need to be careful."

"Yeah, thanks to you. If you hadn't carried out that con thirty years ago, none of this would have happened, and all these people wouldn't be dead."

He at least has the grace to look ashamed. "You're never going to let this go, are you?" he says.

"How can I?"

He shakes his head woefully, shifting from one foot to the other. Then he reaches into the pocket of his pants and pulls out an envelope. "Here," he says, handing it to me. "I don't know if it will help at this point, but it's the best I have to offer. But I caution you to think carefully, Mattie. This thing is much bigger than you realize. You are biting off way more than you can chew. Please don't pursue this on your own."

What he does next startles me. He steps forward, grabs me by the shoulders, and kisses me on my forehead. "I love you, Mattie," he says. And then he turns and walks away, heading through my sister's backyard and into the neighbor's. I watch him until he disappears.

A tornado of emotions whirls through me: anger, surprise, frustration, curiosity, and something that feels frighteningly close to worry. Not for myself, but for him. I care for him, I realize. I don't want to, but I do. And I'm afraid for his safety as well as ours.

I look at the envelope he gave me. It is sealed closed, a plain white envelope like hundreds of others you could find in any store or home. I'm tempted to leave it unopened, guessing that it's probably some sort of letter, a plea for forgiveness, or a request to be a part of my life. Either of these things are possible down the road, I realize. But for the moment, I'm too confused, too overwhelmed to deal with it.

"It's probably one more con," I say aloud, though there is no one to hear me. I turn to head back into the house, determined to stash the envelope somewhere and deal with it later. But as I grab the knob on the back door, I hesitate.

My damned curiosity is nagging at me, and I know from past experience that it won't stop until I open the envelope.

I slide my finger under the flap and rip the envelope open. Inside are several sheets of folded paper. They appear old: wrinkled, yellowed, and stained in spots. I unfold them and read the first one, then read it again, unwilling to believe what my eyes are seeing. My heart skips a beat. I look up and gaze around the yard, which suddenly seems immense and threatening. The trees look menacing, the bushes intimidating, the shadows hostile.

I refold the pages and stuff them back into the envelope. Then I head inside in search of Hurley. Life is about to get a whole lot more interesting.

CHAPTER 33

I make a quick excuse to my sister, apologizing for leaving early and telling her that something urgent has come up at work. I gather up Matthew, Emily, and Hurley, telling them we need to go home. Hurley starts to question me, but when he sees the look on my face, he acquiesces. Emily doesn't seem bothered by the fact that we're leaving. All she wants to know is whether or not she can call Johnny and do something with him for what's left of the evening. When I tell her no, that I need her to be home to watch Matthew, she is clearly unhappy. Her displeasure is quickly mitigated, however, when I tell her that I'll pay quadruple time for tonight's services.

She and Hurley drive home in his car; I take Matthew in mine. When we get to the house, I tell Emily to order in something for dinner, and then I leave her and Matthew downstairs while Hurley and I head upstairs to the privacy of our bedroom.

"What's going on?" Hurley asks me as soon as we are behind closed doors.

I take the envelope out of my pants pocket and hand it to

him. "My father was at Desi's party tonight," I tell him as he peers into the envelope. "We had a little chat in the backyard, and he gave me this right before he disappeared."

Hurley looks intrigued as he takes the papers out of the envelope. He unfolds them the same way I did and starts to read. After a moment, he looks at me, his eyes wide, and then he looks back at the papers. "Are these—"

"The original Miller-Weiss memos? Yes, I believe they are."

"Well, I'll be damned."

I let out a mirthless chuckle. "Yes, that is what my father seems to believe, that we are both damned. He warned me that this thing was too big for us and that we need to be careful."

"We already know that," Hurley says a bit irritably.

"I think he may have a point," I say. "The little guy bringing down the big one, the whole David and Goliath thing, that plays well in books and movies. But I'm not so sure it works in real life."

Hurley gives me a questioning look. "What are you saying?"

"I'm saying that I think we need to let it go." Hurley gapes at me in disbelief. "Not give up," I clarify. "But rather hand it off."

"To whom?" Hurley asks, clearly perturbed. "I already tried to get the FBI involved, but we don't have enough evidence yet."

"Now we have those," I say, pointing toward the papers that were in the envelope.

"Thirty-year-old memos from a company that no longer exists? Involving company employees who likely no longer exist either?"

"But we have some names that we can start with, names that might lead to other names. And we have the evidence that Laura dug up."

Hurley shakes his head, his lips pinched. "That's not evidence," Hurley says. "It's speculation."

"What about the stuff I found on the computer at the clinic? They tried to cover up the death of that patient David had, but if we investigate it more thoroughly, maybe we can prove that. They had those receipts for liquor purchases, and the bottles they found at the man's house, but all of that had to have been staged. Maybe there are family members we can talk to who would testify to the fact that the man wasn't really a drinker. There has to be a trail somewhere. We just need to find it."

"First of all, you know that we can't use any of the clinic information because you obtained it illegally. And even if we do try to use it, it's going to implicate your ex big-time. Are you going to be okay with that?"

Given what I learned about David, that he's already running around and cheating on his new wife—his *pregnant* new wife, no less—I'm tempted to say yes. And yet there is some vestige of protectiveness holding me back, some lingering bit of concern for the man who I, at one time, thought was the love of my life.

"We have so many pieces," I say. "There has to be a way to put it all together."

"It would take an army of people to put it all together, and we don't have that kind of manpower," Hurley says. "I'm sorry, Mattie. It's great that your dad finally came through and gave us these memos, but they're useless. There's no chain of evidence, and any halfway decent lawyer could get them dismissed. We need something bigger. A smoking gun."

I frown, irritated that these people have been getting away with these cover-ups for over thirty years. But I realize Hurley's right: We need a smoking gun. Or a whistleblower, and the odds of that happening are minuscule given that everyone with any knowledge of what went on is either dead or threatened into silent submission. And as much as I hate to admit it, my father is also right. Anything we do to pursue this case puts us and our family in danger.

An idea buds in my head, growing off a thought I'd had earlier. I seize on it, watering it, fertilizing it, letting it grow. A few minutes later, it goes into full bloom.

"Hurley, I have an idea. Tell me what you think." I run my thought process past him, waiting for him to shoot it down, stomp my flower of an idea into a mash of petals. But he doesn't. He listens, and when I'm done he sits on the bed, quiet, lost in thought. I give him some time to think it through.

Finally, he looks over at me, and I see a hint of a smile on his face. "It just might work," he says.

I burst into a big smile, excited.

"Or it might not," he cautions me. "We can't be sure how it's all going to pan out, but it's the best idea I've heard yet." He bends toward me, sandwiches my face in his hands, and gives me a nice, long kiss on the mouth. "You are bloody brilliant," he says when he's done.

"Thanks," I say, feeling a warm glow inside that I'm certain isn't just from my self-congratulatory moment. "I'm also a bit horny at the moment."

Hurley's eyes darken. "Is the bedroom door locked?"

I hop up off the bed and hurry to the door, throwing the lock. "It is now," I say in a sultry voice. I saunter my way back to the bed and put one knee on it. Hurley reaches for me, pulling me down toward him.

And then we share fifteen minutes of utter bliss.

"Wow," I say as I lay on my back in the bed, staring at the ceiling. "That was certainly nice. Definitely the highlight of my day."

Hurley reaches over and laces his fingers with mine. "Mine, too. Want to go again?"

I look over at him, tempted. But I know if we do, I'll be

too exhausted to do what I need to do next. I roll over, kiss him on the cheek, and say, "Rain check?"

He lets out an exaggerated sigh of relief. "Thank goodness. I'm not sure I have the stamina to follow up on that invitation." He winks at me, and then we both roll over and get out of bed on our respective sides.

Five minutes later, we are dressed and sorted out, ready to present ourselves to the world. I grab my cell phone, which has somehow ended up halfway under the bed, where there is also a cat lurking, and dial a number. After a brief conversation, I hang up and look over at Hurley.

"It's a go. I'll call you when I'm done to let you know if we can proceed with phase two."

"Are you sure you want to do this alone?"

I nod. "I think I have to. Wish me luck."

I leave the bedroom and go downstairs, where I kiss both of my kids on the head. "I need to run out for a while," I tell Emily. "And your father is leaving, too. Quadruple pay, okay?"

She gives me a Grinch-like grimace of a smile and rubs her hands together. I kiss her again and head out.

Five minutes later, I drive the hearse into the underground garage of my office, lock it, and head upstairs. The place is dark, with only the night security lights on. Some people might find that creepy, given that we have dead bodies in the refrigerator, but it's never bothered me. I suspect it might bother my anticipated guest, however, so I turn on some lights. I've just finished lighting up the library when my phone dings with a text message. I check it and head back downstairs to the garage, where I exit the building and head for the gate at the entrance. No sooner do I arrive there than a car pulls up. I use my badge to make the gate arm elevate, and the car pulls in.

I walk up to the car as its occupant opens the door and

climbs out. "Hello, David," I say. "Please follow me." I then lead the way back into the building and upstairs to the library. David follows me silently, and when I gesture toward a chair at the library table, he takes it. I settle in across from him.

"What is so urgent that we have to have this clandestine meeting?" David says.

"There are some things I need to tell you about, things that might impact you directly. So I want you to just listen to me for a few minutes." Though he looks impatient and fidgety, he nods. So I start talking. Over the next ten minutes, I explain to him every detail of the Jeremy Prince case, beginning with my father's involvement thirty years ago, who we suspect the key players are, how it led to the deaths of Carolyn Abernathy as well as my coworker, Hal, and his fiancée, Tina. He listens with interest and some concern until I end with my use of his badge to access confidential files and medical records.

"What the hell?" he says, clearly angry. "Why would you do that? I could have you fired from your job, have your nursing license taken away . . . hell, I could probably have you arrested for doing that."

"Yes, you probably could," I say. "If you could prove any of it. I've admitted it to you here, but I'll deny it to my dying breath if anyone else asks."

"Why are you telling me all of this?" he asks, his anger ramping down a notch.

"Because you're a part of this whole thing, David. You have reaped the benefits of these pharmaceutical companies' illegal doings. And I believe one of your patients died as a result." I then explain to him what I know about his Leptosoma patient who died, and about what happened to Hal's sister. "They're killing people, David. They know that a successful weight-loss drug has a huge potential for turning big profits, so they're trying to cover up the problems it has in any way they can. And this isn't the first time. This has been going on for more than thirty years."

I take out the Miller-Weiss memos and show them to him. He reads them, his brow furrowing, his teeth raking over his lip. When he's done reading, he looks at me.

"They're going to take you down with all the rest of them," I tell him. "Unless we can find a way to take them down first. That's where you come into the picture."

"Why should I get involved?" he says. "I didn't know what was going on, and I doubt anyone can prove I did."

"You took their money, David, money you knew was exorbitant for the speaking fee, as they called it. You said as much to me ten years ago when we went on that trip to Miami."

"Well, then you're involved, too," he says petulantly.

"Potentially," I say, "but as the wife who merely went along with the practice, thinking there was nothing wrong with it, I'd wager I'd get off with nothing more than a slap on the hand. And I have that Italy trip to show that I'd become uncomfortable with such perks and no longer wanted to be involved."

"You missed that trip because you were sick," David says, his voice laced with disgust.

"Yeah, but they won't know that."

"You're crazy," David says. He starts to get up from the table, but what I say next makes him sit back down.

"How much will Patty take you for when she files for divorce?"

David stares at me, saying nothing.

"Can you afford another division of your assets?"

"Patty and I aren't divorcing," he says.

"I suspect you will be when she learns about your latest infidelity. Honestly David, can't you just keep it in your pants?"

David's face darkens as he scowls at me. "You wouldn't tell her about that," he sneers.

"Oh, I most certainly would," I say. "For God's sake, David, she's pregnant with your child. Of course, that may play in her favor because it will entitle her to even more of your assets than what I got."

We engage in a stare-down for a full minute, maybe more. Finally, David says, "What, exactly, do you want from me?"

"I knew you'd come around to my way of thinking," I say. "Here's how it's going to work."

CHAPTER 34

I leave David in the library to stew and go to Izzy's office to make my next phone call. It takes me a couple of tries to reach the person I want, but once I do, he is more than eager to come and meet with us. As soon as that call is finished, I call Hurley, who is two blocks away at the police station.

It's late enough at night that the reporters who have been hanging out by the station and our office have disappeared for the night, so I let both Hurley and Cletus in through the front door. The four of us convene in the library, and over the next two hours, we outline the plan. At the end of that time, David leaves and goes home.

Cletus, who arrived wearing baggy shorts, another Hawaiian shirt, and a repeat of the socks and sandals he had on the other day, looks young and eager. But I worry that he's also overwhelmed and in a bit over his head.

"Are you comfortable moving forward with this, Cletus?" I ask him.

"I am. I just don't know how much credibility I'll have when I take this to one of the bigger papers. I'm pretty new to this stuff, you know."

Like we couldn't have guessed that on our own.

"It's true that you don't have much experience," I say, "but Detective Hurley and I have an idea about how we can increase your exposure as well as your credibility."

Cletus looks from me to Hurley and back again, his eyes narrowed in suspicion. "I'm listening," he says.

"First off, you need to consult a stylist. If you keep walking around dressed like you are now, no one is going to believe a thing you say. They won't hear you because they'll be laughing so hard."

Cletus looks hurt.

"Dude, she's right," Hurley says.

"Don't worry. I have some people in mind who will get you fixed up in no time," I tell him. "The second thing you need to do is prove your ability to be a decent investigative reporter. That means letting go of this ridiculous alien bones story and instead getting the scoop on the real story behind that skeleton. Trust me, it's one that's much more heart-warming and newsworthy. And when you add that to the scoop you're going to get tomorrow morning, well . . ."

"What scoop? What's happening tomorrow morning?"

"We're going to reveal the truth behind the Grizzly Motel deaths, which, by the way, wasn't a murder-suicide at all. Both of those victims were murdered. And you are invited to the showdown tomorrow morning that will reveal who is behind it and why."

"Seriously?" he says, trying not to smile. His facial muscles are twitching so hard and fast that he looks like he's having a seizure. "Why are you doing this for me? You guys hardly know me."

I look at Hurley, who looks at me, then at the floor. "Let's just say we feel like we owe a debt to journalists," I say. "One in particular, but she's dead, so we don't have a way to pay her back. We've decided to give a leg up to someone else instead. Sort of an *in memoriam* kind of thing."

"You're talking about my predecessor?" Cletus says.

"I am. Alison Miller was a huge pain in my ass," I tell him with a little laugh. "But she was one hell of a journalist with a nose for news and a fearless, can-do attitude. And she was also my friend, so I feel like I need to do something in her memory. My one caveat with regard to the larger story, the one involving my ex, is that Alison needs to get credit for turning the case around. Her name needs to be mentioned. Maybe that way her death won't be totally in vain."

Cletus nods slowly, looking somber and serious.

"And along those same lines, our names need to be totally left out of it."

Cletus frowns at me. "If I do that, how do I explain all this information I was able to find?" he asks, nodding toward the small pile of papers in front of him.

"Dr. Winston will be your whistleblower," I explain. "It was his ID that accessed the medical records, and his e-mails that got you on the right path. As for the information we got from the thumb drive, I don't care where you claim you got it from, and to be honest, if you do your homework, I suspect you won't need to use it. The evidence is out there to be found. Tap into some of your journalist buddies who have access to databases of things like phone records and addresses. Let them and their cohorts help you. Do you know anyone in the Chicago area?"

"Of course," Cletus says with a shrug. "That's where I went to school. Several of my classmates work in that area."

"Then use them," I tell him. "Work at it, Cletus. But remember that this thing goes very high up in the justice hierarchy, so you can't go to anyone in a DA's office or a police station unless you have vetted them thoroughly." I pause and lean back in my seat. "I don't want to sugarcoat things," I say, looking very serious. "This is the kind of story that can launch a career, maybe several careers, but it could be a very dangerous assignment for you, Cletus. You and anyone who helps you. Are you up to the task? Because if you're not, we'll take it to someone who is."

Cletus straightens in his seat and even puffs his chest out a little. "I can handle it," he says.

"Good," I say with a smile, "because we're counting on you. We expect big things from you, Cletus."

"I won't let you down," he says, full of bravado.

"Okay then," I say. "Let's go get 'em."

Cletus gathers up his papers and stands.

"But first," I say, holding up a hand, "we have some work to do. "Come with me."

Three hours later, Cletus is standing in front of a mirror in my sister's house. He looks at his reflection with an expression of awe. Standing behind him, taking in that same reflection, are me—as much in awe as Cletus is—my sister, Desi, and Barbara, my personal hair and makeup stylist.

The Cletus standing before us is hardly recognizable as the one I was speaking to just hours ago. His hair is neatly trimmed, with subtle highlights on top, his acne is well hidden behind a mask of makeup, and he is wearing a pair of fashionable glasses. He is dressed in black slacks, a royal blue, button-down shirt, and a tie with black, blue, and gold stripes. On his feet are a pair of loafers, sans socks—something he grumbled about, reminding me of my son and his peculiar pickiness with clothes.

"Wow," I say. "You guys are good."

"It helps that Cletus is the same size as Lucien," Desi says.

"That new airbrush makeup system you used is perfect for something like this," I say to Barbara. I haven't yet told Cletus that Barbara works in a funeral home doing makeup and hair for the dead most of the time, and I have no intention of doing so.

Barbara nods and says, "It works well on my, um, regular

clients. Next time you come in, I'll use it on you. It's amazing how well it covers."

I figured we'd given Cletus enough to worry about already, so I had coached Barbara ahead of time on keeping her regular occupation mum for now. I could tell that the fact that she made him lie down while she worked on him was something he was curious about but wisely accepted without question.

Barbara hands Cletus a bag of stuff. "If you use these products religiously every day and night, I promise you those zits will be gone in no time. For tomorrow, I'll meet you at Mattie's office at eight and redo this for you."

"Thanks," Cletus says. "This is really impressive."

"You can keep those clothes," Desi says. "Lucien has no idea what's in his wardrobe because I buy all his stuff. And frankly, he doesn't take very good care of most of it. He's constantly coming home with food stains, tears, you name it. These were a couple of the only pieces I could find that were still in decent shape."

"Thanks," Cletus says again.

"Those clothes will work for tomorrow morning," I tell him. "But you need to buy some new clothes. Or at the least, learn how to better use the ones you already have. And under no circumstances is it okay to wear socks with sandals, particularly those mid-calf black socks. Got it?"

He nods.

"Okay then. I think we're done for tonight," I say. "Cletus and Barbara, I'll see you in my office in the morning. And Desi, thanks so much for giving up part of your birthday to my little project."

"It was my pleasure," she says. "This is the most fun I've had on a birthday in a long time."

With that, we bid one another good night. I see Cletus and Barbara off before getting into my hearse and driving home. The house is mostly dark, just some under-cabinet lights and one lamp in the living room glowing on the first floor. The kids are both in their rooms asleep, and after checking on each of them, I head for my bedroom. I find Hurley in bed but awake, reading through a file.

"How did it go?" he asks.

"Amazingly well," I say, stripping out of my clothes. "You won't recognize Cletus in the morning."

"Do you think he'll be able to pull this thing off?"

I grab a nightgown from a drawer and pull it on over my head. Then I crawl into bed next to Hurley, snuggling up to his side. "I hope so," I tell him. "I don't think I can bear it if I find out I've sent someone else to their death."

CHAPTER 35

Barbara and Cletus are on time the next morning, and while Barbara repeats her magic ministrations, Hurley and I get ready. At a little before nine, we say good-bye to Barbara, once again thanking her for her help, and then Cletus and I climb into Cletus's van, while Hurley gets into his own car.

We caravan over to Pamela Knowlton's house, park at the curb, and get out, heading for the front door. Hurley rings the bell, and I hoist my video camera and turn it on.

A moment later, Pamela opens the door. "Detective," she says, her expression not particularly welcoming. "Are you here to arrest me?"

"No," Hurley says. "We've uncovered some more information regarding your husband's death. May we come in and talk?"

"I think I need to call my lawyer," Pamela says.

Hurley shrugs. "You can do that if you want. But I think you're going to want to hear us out first. You don't have to say anything, and you don't have to allow us to look at anything. We just want to talk. We're filming this in order to provide you with a level of comfort. I'm telling you now that you are not under arrest at this time."

For a moment, I think Pamela is going to say no and make us go back to the drawing board, or wait for some legal eagle in a suit to show up. But in the end, she relents, opens the door, and waves us in. Hurley walks to the breakfast bar, and I bite back a smile. I'm guessing he chose this particular spot because he's hoping Pamela will once again grace him—and hopefully Cletus and me as well—with one of the beverages from her stellar coffee machine.

"May I offer you something to drink?" Pamela says. "I have some bottled water, or if you prefer I can make you a latte or a cappuccino."

Hurley arches one brow and smiles at her. "I would love another one of those coffee drinks you fixed for me the other day," he says.

"If it's not too much trouble," I say, lowering the camera for the moment, "I'd like one too. Hurley hasn't stopped talking about it since you made him that first one."

Pamela looks pleased at this. She gives Cletus a questioning look, and he nods and shrugs. "Sure," he says. "Whatever they're having."

Pamela sets about making the drinks, and as she does so, Hurley brings her up to date on the status of the case.

"Mrs. Knowlton," he begins, "as we mentioned before, it appears your husband didn't commit suicide after all. Nor did he kill Mrs. Lansing."

Pamela turns and looks at him over her shoulder, a puzzled expression on her face. "Then how did he die?"

"He was murdered," Hurley says. "They both were."

Pamela sets down the coffee mug she is holding. "By whom? Do you even know?"

"Yes, we do. I'll explain," Hurley says. And over the next twenty minutes, he does. Fortunately for us, Pamela is the type of person who likes to stay busy when she's dealing with stress, and so our drinks get made. She even makes one for herself, and when she's done with all of them she stands across the bar from us, holding her own mug close to her chest, staring at Hurley with a bewildered expression on her face. I have set the camera down on the bar—still filming—in a spot that takes in most of our setting.

"I don't believe you," Pamela says when Hurley is done.

"I understand this must be difficult for you to accept," Hurley says. "I think I have a way to convince you." He then explains what we have in mind.

Pamela listens, sipping her drink periodically, but I'm not sure she's buying it. When Hurley's done, he gives her a questioning look.

"I don't think so," Pamela says. She shakes her head and sets her mug down near the sink.

"What have you got to lose by trying?" Hurley says. "If we're wrong, we'll go away, and life can continue as before."

Pamela weighs this, her back to us as she stares out the window over her kitchen sink. I watch her body language, looking for clues, and when I see her shoulders sag in resignation, I know we've convinced her. She turns around then, looks Hurley in the eye, and says, "I guess I have a phone call to make."

We listen as Pamela makes her phone call, and when she's done, she goes into her living room and sits by herself. While we're waiting, Hurley goes out to his car to fetch the printer we brought with us—still with its evidence tag—and brings it in to the kitchen, setting it on the breakfast bar.

Fifteen minutes later, the doorbell rings, and the front door opens. Penny comes flying into the house, her face appropriately panicked-looking.

"You people," she says in a chastising tone as she looks at the three of us sitting at the breakfast bar. "Where is Pammy?"

"I'm right here," Pamela says from behind her. She has left her chair in the living room and come to join us.

Hurley takes out his handcuffs and walks over to Pamela. "Pamela Knowlton, you are under arrest for the murders of your husband, Craig, as well as Meredith Lansing. You have the right to remain silent."

"Hold on a second!" Penny says as Hurley slaps a handcuff on one of Pamela's wrists. "You can't arrest her. What evidence do you have?"

"I told you on the phone, Penny," Pamela says. "Apparently, the note they found in the motel room was printed from a computer. And there was some sort of flaw in the printing that they say is identifiable to a specific printer." She nods toward the printer on the counter. "They've printed something on my home printer, and apparently that flaw is there. It's a match."

"Of course it is," Penny says dismissively. "Craig used the same printer."

"There's more," Pamela says. "They found the gun near Craig's right hand. And the shot that killed him was fired from the right-hand side."

"So?" Penny says, shaking her head in confusion.

"Craig was left-handed," Pamela says quietly.

We watch the cacophony of emotions that crosses Penny's face. I see hints of shock, fear, paranoia, and then resignation. "You killed Craig?" she says finally, staring at her sister.

"No!" Pamela says. "How can you even think I would do such a thing?"

Penny gives Pamela a sad, but solicitous look. "Don't worry, Pammy. I'll help you. We'll get you a good attorney. You can afford the best."

"I doubt that," I say to Penny. "I'm afraid all of Mrs. Knowlton's monies will be seized and held. Given the nature of her work, that money will be available to cover the lawsuits filed by her clients. And I'm sure there will be plenty of them."

"What?" Penny says. "No." She looks over at Hurley. "That's not true."

"I'm afraid it is," Hurley says. "It's a special set of rules that apply when someone who has a fiduciary duty to others perpetrates felony fraud. And this certain qualifies."

"You can't do that," Penny says.

"Oh, but we can," Hurley says. "We can take it all, including her car and her house."

Penny looks stunned. "Pamela, you need to call a lawyer right away. Or tell me what number to call and I'll do it."

Pamela tilts her head, giving her sister a sad look. "I already called him," she says. "What they've just told you is the absolute truth."

"No," Penny says, shaking her head. She starts to pace. "No, no, no, no, no. This can't be."

Pamela starts to sob softly, and it distracts Penny, who gives her a withering look. "Oh, for God's sake," she says. "Don't start blubbering."

"It's true, isn't it," Pamela says, looking at her sister with the saddest expression I've ever seen. "What they said about you is true. You killed Craig."

Penny scowls at her sister. "What sort of nonsense are you spewing?"

"They say they have evidence, Penny. They confiscated the car you just turned in, and there were traces of urine on one of the seats. They say they're testing it for DNA and that it will turn out to be Craig's."

Penny pauses her pacing, her brows drawn together in thought. Then her face relaxes. "So Craig peed in my car once. That doesn't prove anything."

"We also found your tire tracks out on County Road P by the woods behind the Grizzly," Hurley says.

"The what?" Penny says very fast. It's clear we're starting to rattle her.

"The Grizzly Motel?" I say. "You know, the place where you stalked your ex-husband and his fling, the woman he had an affair with?"

Penny glares at me, but her expression quickly morphs

into that of a trapped animal. She looks around the room wildly. "You're all crazy," she says. "It was Craig who had an affair with that lab woman," she says. "You have the proof with those cell phones."

I look at Hurley and see his face curl into a satisfied smile. "What cell phones?" he asks Penny.

Too late she realizes her mistake. The information about the extra burner phones hasn't yet been released or shared.

Hurley slips off the handcuff he had placed on Pamela's wrist. He lets the cuffs hang from his hand as he approaches Penny. "Here's what happened," he says. "You tell me if I'm wrong at any point. You found yourself broke and abandoned by your husband and kids, and you needed a way to get back on your feet, to get your hands on some cash. Your sister here has done quite well for herself and has plenty of cash. You know that because she's bailed you out several times in the past. Not to mention the nice house and cars she and Craig own. And she owes you, right? I mean, you spent all those years raising her, spending your own money."

Penny stares at him and says nothing.

"Somewhere along the way, you met John Lansing," Hurley continues. "I haven't quite figured that part out yet, but I'm guessing it was at a casino. My guys are canvassing them now with his picture and yours, and I'm certain we'll not only get a match eventually, but we'll find evidence of the two of you commiserating. You shared your common woes regarding your lack of funds, the bad turn of luck you had both experienced, and your dissatisfaction with your marriages and spouses. And between the two of you, you cooked up a plan to get rid of Meredith and Craig so that you could collect on the life insurance policies."

"That's absurd," Penny says. "I wouldn't collect on anyone's life insurance."

"You would collect Craig's eventually," Hurley says, "along with all the rest of his and Pamela's money once you moved back in with Pamela and took control over her life again. Just like it was back in the day, right? Or better yet, if your sister is arrested and convicted for Craig's murder, the money is all yours."

Penny says nothing, so Hurley continues.

"John Lansing was willing to settle for the insurance and retirement money his wife had, or perhaps you offered him a share of your funds. So you cooked up a scheme wherein you faked an affair between Craig and Meredith. You bought two burner phones, and you and John each kept one of them. You sent regular text messages back and forth, and called one another at times to check in. You changed the passwords on all of the victims' computers to make it look like they were trying to hide something. I have to admit that your patience in planning all of it was quite remarkable. You spent over a month plotting out that nonexistent affair."

Penny is frozen in place, still staring silently at Hurley. But with this last compliment, one eyebrow arches almost imperceptibly.

"And when the time came, you carried out the rest of your plan," Hurley continues. "You ordered two Italian dinners of some sort from the same place so it would appear that Craig and Meredith had shared a meal, and you bought two of the same bottles of wine. Then you each spiked the food with crushed up sleeping pills from Meredith Lansing's prescription. Before the sleeping pills kicked in too hard, you got your victims into cars and drove them out to the Grizzly Motel. I'm guessing John drove Meredith in her car first, booked the room, carried her inside, and then returned to town and parked the car in the hospital lot. John looked enough like Craig for it to work, especially if the plan was to shoot Craig in the head, thereby distorting his appearance some. But the owner of the motel already identified John as the person who actually checked in when we showed her his picture."

"You shot Craig in the head?" Pamela says, looking at her sister in horror.

"I didn't shoot Craig," Penny snaps. "I didn't shoot anyone."

"I suspect that's true," I tell Pamela. "She killed Craig, but I think she had John do the actual shooting. She picked him up at the hospital parking lot with Craig already doped up in her car. They drove out to the motel together, and I'm sure it took the two of them to get Craig's body into the motel room." I pause and look at Penny. "Did you know that Craig was already dead at that point? Did the two of you carry him into the room like he was drunk?"

Penny's eyes narrow at me, and one of her hands starts opening and closing, opening and closing.

"That's my guess, anyway," I say with a shrug, continuing. "Then you left John in the motel room and drove your car around to the adjacent county road and parked where that path emerges from the woods behind the motel. John's job was to shoot both Meredith and Craig, drop the gun by Craig's hand, and then bolt from the room, disappearing down that path in the woods. By the time anyone looked out to see what was going on, he was already gone."

"Ridiculous," Penny mutters, her arms folded over her chest as she glares at me.

"Actually, it's ingenious," Hurley says. "You are clearly a very smart and clever person to have pulled off something this complicated."

Penny can't help herself. She actually preens beneath Hurley's praise. "I am smart," she says. "I may not have book smarts or math skills like Pamela, but I'm smarter than she is in my own way."

Pamela, who has stopped crying at this point, closes her eyes and walks over to the breakfast bar, settling on a stool, and cradling her head in one hand

"If you're so smart," I say, "why did you screw up so much of your plan?"

"I didn't screw up!" Penny yells.

"But you did," I say. "You missed the very significant fact that Craig was left-handed, a rookie mistake. You didn't realize that your car would leave tracks on the muddy shoulder of the road. You had a backup plan all along to pin this on John Lansing if we figured out the motel scene was staged, didn't you? You even managed to get him to handle a bullet so there would be a partial print on it. But if we arrested him, you knew he would spill the beans, so when we ramped up our investigation to the point where you thought we'd figured it out, you eliminated him. But you messed that up as well. And you miscalculated how much of the drug Craig could handle, killing him before the scene could be staged. Not much of a nurse, are you?" I taunt.

Penny's mouth tightens, and she stares me down like I'm a toreador and she's a bull. I can practically see steam coming from her nose.

"And I'm guessing you also messed up with the phones when you texted John Lansing to meet you under the double arches the day of the murders," I add. "That was your practice run, right? Except you used the burner phones to communicate the meeting place by mistake instead of your regular phones."

Penny closes her eyes and sighs heavily. "This is all speculation," she says. "You have no actual proof."

Hurley says, "Oh, but we do. The gun that was used was stolen from a man named Philip Conroy last year, and we've discovered you once took care of him at the nursing home where you worked at the time. And we confiscated the car you traded in the day of the murders. When we get the results of the DNA test on Craig's urine, it will be a done deal."

Penny stands frozen for a moment, then she opens her eyes and turns to her sister. "I did this for you, for us, Pammy," she says.

Pamela shivers. "The hell you did. You did it for yourself. I loved my husband."

"But he wasn't good for you," Penny says. "You were wasting all that money on trying to have a kid, and I could see the kind of stress it was creating for you. In fact, that's how I got Craig to meet me for dinner that night. I told him that I knew of a new fertility treatment you and he could try, one that would almost guarantee success."

"My God," Pamela says, shaking her head. "How low can you go?"

"I'd do anything for you, Pammy," Penny says, giving her sister a pleading look. "It's always been you and me together, just the two of us. That's how it's supposed to be. People just don't understand the bond we share. Even Mom and Dad didn't understand. They were going to send me away from you, you know. When they found out that I'd accessed their bank accounts so I could have a little fun at the casino, they threatened to have me jailed. I begged them not to turn me in, and they finally said they would let it go if I went to a rehab facility for a six-month program." Penny chuffs her disgust at this idea. "Rehab," she spits out. "Can you imagine that? Six months away from you? I couldn't let that happen."

"Oh my God," I say. "You killed your parents, didn't you? You blew the house up."

Penny sighs impatiently. "It's not like they gave me any choice," she says with irritation. "They wanted to send me away. And they were cutting me off financially. I had to do something. So I blew out the pilot lights on the stove and turned all the burners on right before Pammy and I left that morning. Then I lit a candle in the dining room."

I hear a sound like a low rumble that quickly grows in intensity and pitch until I realize what it is. Pamela lets out a blood-curdling scream and hops off her stool, lunging at Penny. She starts hitting her sister with her fists, screaming the entire time. Hurley and I both jump in. I manage to contain Pamela's flailing arms, dragging her back. Hurley grabs Penny by the arm and pulls her in the opposite direction.

Once they are separated, the two sisters engage in a stare-off. Pamela, her chest heaving, her rage-infused face red, says nothing at first.

Penny, her hair wild where Pamela grabbed at it, stands beside Hurley looking at her sister with an almost pitiable sadness. "I did it for us, Pammy," she says. "Someday you'll come to see that."

"Get . . . her . . . out . . . of . . . here," Pamela says through gritted teeth. Her next words come out shrill and screaming. *"Get her out!"*

Hurley snaps his handcuffs on Penny and informs her she is under arrest. He recites the Miranda warning to her. As they are walking toward the front door, I hear Penny say, "That stuff about Pamela's money being confiscated, was that true?"

"Nope," Hurley says.

My last image of Penny is of a woman with her arms cuffed behind her back, crazy hair sticking out all over her head, emitting an insane, maniacal laugh.

I release my grip on Pamela and ask her if she's okay.

She looks at me with a blotchy, tear-stained face. "I don't think I'll be okay for a long time, if ever. But I'm not going to kill myself or anyone else, if that's what you're asking."

I study her and decide she's telling me the truth. "Okay then," I say. "I'm really sorry for the way things turned out."

"Yeah, me too," she says with deep sarcasm. "Would you mind showing yourselves out?" She doesn't wait for us to give her an answer. She shambles off, heading down the hall-way toward her bedroom.

I turn and look at Cletus. "Did we get it all?" I ask him.

He picks up the camera from the counter and pushes a couple of buttons. "Looks good," he says. "Will you e-mail me my copy today?"

"I will," I tell him. "So what do you think of this new career plan so far?"

"I'm liking it," he says. "I have a scoop on a great human-interest story, and a front-row seat to the capture of a serial killer."

"All in a day's work," I say with a wink. "Now you need to go out there and catch a bunch more."

CHAPTER 36

Six months later

I roll over in bed and feel a warm body beneath my arm. A gentle squeeze tells me that it's too small a body to be Hurley. I open an eye and look. My son's big blue eyes are staring back at me. His face cracks into a big smile.

"Morning, momma," he says.

"Good morning, Matthew," I say.

"Maffew loves momma."

"And momma loves you," I say, kissing him on the forehead. "Where's daddy?"

"He's making breakfast. He's making on-a-lets."

"Omelets," I enunciate carefully.

"I said that," Matthew says with a big pout.

"Okay. Let's go have some omelets."

"On-a-lets! On-a-lets!" He scrambles down to the bottom of the bed and jumps down. Then he goes running down the hallway, still yelling. "On-a-lets! On-a-lets!"

"Don't run on the stairs, Matthew," I yell.

"I be careful," he says, and I pray he means it. We taught him how to go down the stairs safely months ago, when we were still in the old house and realized he had figured out how to undo the lock on the gate we put up. My son has a mind of his own, and most of the time, it's even odds whether or not telling him not to do something will work. So simply telling him not to go downstairs alone wasn't much of an option.

I listen, holding my breath and counting footfalls as I hear his little feet clump down the stairs. Two feet for each stair. When I get to twenty-four, I breathe again.

I roll over and look at the clock. It's six-thirty and a workday, so I need to get moving. I toss back the covers and grab my robe. It's early February, and Old Man Winter is clinging to life with a vengeance. The temperature outside is a frigid 4 degrees, and there is a wind howling past my brand-new, double-paned, thermal windows that promises some chapped lips and cheeks.

I shuffle into the bathroom, which is as big as the living room I had in the cottage. I turn on the shower with its multiple jets and overhead rain shower, and brush my teeth while I wait for the water to heat up.

Fifteen luxurious minutes later, I step out of the shower and dry off. Then I head into the large walk-in closet off the bathroom, pick out some heavy slacks and a blue wool sweater, and dress for work.

By the time I make it downstairs to our state-of-the-art kitchen with its six-burner stove, a refrigerator almost as big as our shower, and beautiful stone countertops, Hurley and Matthew are seated at the table in our breakfast nook, having a man-to-man discussion about the importance of eating vegetables. I grab a cup of coffee—just plain old coffee for now, although we do have one of those fancy coffee machines that can give Starbucks a run for its money—and join them.

"Morning, Squatch," Hurley says. He half stands so he

can lean across the table and kiss me. "Should I make you an omelet?"

"No, thanks. I'm not very hungry at the moment. And today is the day that Christopher and I overlap, so he's going to be in the library with me all day. It's hard to deal with that on a full stomach."

Despite his physical ailment, which has been mitigated somewhat by Izzy finding a product called Shreddies—underwear with an activated charcoal lining—Christopher has turned out to be an excellent employee. He is smart, reliable, eager to work, and has a good sense of humor, even about his gas problem. The Shreddies aren't bulletproof, which is why I'm passing on breakfast for now, but they have definitely helped.

"Are they calling for more snow?" I ask Hurley.

"Not today. But there's a storm coming in tomorrow that will probably drop half a foot or so."

"Buying that plow was a brilliant idea," I tell him. In truth, it was a necessity. Negotiating our driveway when there's a significant amount of snow and ice on the ground is a daunting challenge.

"Personally, I think the truck that goes with it was an even better idea," Hurley says.

Our car shopping turned into quite the escapade back when we met with Penny Cook's ex-husband. He was so delighted to learn that we had taken Penny off his hands for good that he gave us an unbelievable deal on a new four-wheel drive truck (in a shade of blue that matches Hurley's eyes) in addition to the cherry-red Jeep Cherokee we bought for Emily. Hurley was hesitant at first, worried about the costs, but Cook made us such a good offer both on price and the trade-in on Hurley's car, it was impossible to refuse. And once Hurley got behind the wheel of that truck, he was sold.

We presented Emily with the car at the end of August so

she would have it when she started school. She had been shopping for used cars for several weeks and bemoaning what she could get for the money she had saved up. We let her whine for a while and got what babysitting services out of her that we could before surprising her with the car. Her reaction was priceless. She laughed, she cried, she yelped, she danced, and in the end, she hugged both of us so tight we could barely breathe.

Of course, Hurley mitigated the joy shortly thereafter by giving her a stern lecture on safe, defensive driving, and then making her drive him around in it and show him how she planned to make use of the Bluetooth capabilities. The fact that the car could provide hands-free phone and messaging capabilities gave us a semblance of comfort. The heated seat and steering wheel would give Emily a lot of comfort on days like this.

I'm glad we sprang for four-wheel drive on both vehicles. It has proven invaluable this winter. I still have the hearse, and while it doesn't have four-wheel drive, it handles nicely in the snow because of its wide wheel base and heaviness. The thing drives like a tank.

As I sit at the table in my brand-new, spacious kitchen, sipping my coffee and watching my husband and son eat their breakfast and banter with one another, I feel a rush of contentment. Life is good right now. Hurley and I are both getting plenty of sleep, we are all happy and healthy, and Matthew is finally pooping and peeing in the potty with regularity. For the first time since Matthew's birth, I start to think that maybe Hurley is right. We should have another kid.

Before I can let that thought get too far into my head, I get up and carry my cup to the sink, rinse it out, and put it in the dishwasher. "I'm going to head into the office," I tell Hurley. "When you drop Matthew off with Dom, ask him when opening night is for his new play. I think it's coming up soon."

"Will do," Hurley says. I walk toward the foyer and the coat closet, glancing out the huge wall of windows in the living room that look over the bluff. I stop when I see a car chugging up the drive, a small, black SUV that I don't recognize.

"Hurley, someone is here," I holler.

Hurley is at my side seconds later. The two of us watch as the car pulls into the circle out front and stops, and then Hurley goes to the coat closet, punches in the number code for the gun safe on the top shelf, and removes his service weapon.

Matthew appears at my side and looks out the window with me. "Who dat?" he asks, pointing at the car.

Just then, the driver-side door to the car opens, and a young man steps out. I breathe a sigh of relief and hear Hurley do the same in the foyer. I hear the sound of his gun going back into the safe, and the safe door shutting and whining as the lock resets. Then I hear Hurley punching in the numbers for the front-door alarm. He opens the door before our visitor has a chance to knock or ring the bell.

"Cletus!" I say once he's inside. "I hardly recognized you." Cletus clearly took our advice to heart and has totally cleaned up his act. The skin on his face is almost completely clear, his hair is still looking great even when he pulls off the knit cap he's wearing, and beneath his long, wool coat he is wearing khakis and a button-down shirt. "What brings you out this way?" I ask him.

"I have some news for you," he says, taking off his stylish glasses because they have fogged up. "Is there somewhere we can talk?" He shoots a sidelong glance at Matthew.

"Um, sure," I say. "Just give me a minute." I take Matthew by the hand and walk him into the living room, sitting him down in front of the TV. "Want to watch some cartoons?" I say.

"PongeBob," he yells. I turn the TV on and then hand him

the remote. I don't know if SpongeBob is on any of the channels, but I figure hunting for him will keep Matthew occupied for a while.

Hurley, Cletus, and I move into the kitchen and huddle around the end of the breakfast bar, far enough away from Matthew to talk without him hearing us, but still within line of sight of him. Cletus is carrying a briefcase, and he sets it on the counter and opens it.

"I don't know if you have seen this yet or not, but this is today's copy of the *Tribune*." He sets the newspaper on the bar with the front-page headline showing. I read it, and then I read it again, wanting to believe it but afraid to:

INDICTMENTS ISSUED IN BIG PHARMA SCANDAL

I look at Cletus. "You did it?" I say.

"I did it," he says with a big grin. "Of course, I had a little help. Actually, I had a lot of help," he adds with a sheepish grin.

I start scanning the article, and my eyes zero in on several words and names: Leptosoma, Drake Industries, Algernon Medical, Desmond and Marilyn Townsend, Wesley, Jason, and Randall Kupper. There are several other big, recognizable names in the article, including a couple of political bigwigs, a district attorney in Milwaukee, doctors, and several lawyers. I note that the law firm hired to represent Tomas Wyzinski is mentioned, but I don't see Joan Mackey's name anywhere. Maybe she wasn't in on it. Either way, Tomas should be able to get a second trial, if nothing else, though I'm hoping we can simply get him exonerated and freed. With the help of Marshal Washington, we had his brother, Lech, hidden away in the Witness Protection Program six months ago, a fact I communicated to Tomas when I paid him a second visit—this time without Mackey—and told him to sit tight.

"Holy cow, Cletus. You really did it!" I say.

"And it's not done yet. There are more names coming. You were right. This thing is huge."

I open the paper to continue reading the article on another page, still scanning for names.

"Once we cracked this nut a little, a whole lot of stuff spilled out," Cletus says. "We have people who are now willing to come forward. That ME who disappeared down in Brazil was offered immunity and protection, and he's now willing to testify. And I heard a rumor that Tomas Wyzinski might finally talk."

I've finished scanning the article, and one name didn't show up anywhere. I look at Cletus. "David?"

"He's cooperated fully and been guaranteed immunity by the DA's office. We made sure we had a DA we could trust before moving ahead with it. I don't think he'll see any repercussions from this, and his real name was never used anywhere in any of the documents. So I think we're good."

This is good news. I saw Patty just the other day, and she looked like an overinflated balloon ready to burst. She's due to drop that kid any day now, and as far as I can tell from what's circulating on the rumor mill, she and David seem to be doing just fine. And since David now has a new office nurse, I'm hoping that just maybe he's finally seen the error of his ways. But I wouldn't bet money on it.

Thoughts of betting money make me think of Penny Cook, and as if Cletus has read my mind, he says, "I spoke to Pamela Knowlton yesterday. She sounds like she's doing well. She really likes it down in Arizona, and she said she has plenty of clients, thanks to all the retirees down there."

"That's good to hear," I say. "She was smart to relocate. And Arizona is sounding mighty good right about now."

"No kidding," Cletus says.

Hurley has remained quiet throughout our discussion, and he's now reading the article on the front page. I offer Cletus a cup of coffee—or a latte, if he prefers. He opts for the plain coffee, and while I'm pouring him a cup, he asks me how his replacement at the local paper is doing. Cletus quit his job here several months back and headed out of town. We didn't contact him or ask any questions at the time because we didn't want to rouse anyone's curiosity.

"It's some goofy guy named Irwin Cleese who's tall, thin, has huge feet, and is clumsier than I am," I tell him. "I swear, that man must have rubber for bones, because he's fallen more times than I can remember, but he never seems to hurt himself. So far, he's been easy enough to work with other than that. He cooperates with us."

"That's good," Cletus says.

"And what are you doing these days?" I ask him. "Are you with the *Trib*?"

"I am," he says with a smile. "Thanks to you."

I am about to hand Cletus his cup of coffee when Hurley comes up behind him, grabs him by the shoulders, and spins him around. He holds him at arm's length and says, "Man, you did one hell of a job with this. Mattie saw something in you that made her think you could pull this thing off, but I'll be honest, I was skeptical. I figured you'd end up dead."

Cletus coughs, and lets out a nervous laugh. "Um, thanks, I think?"

Hurley lets go of Cletus's shoulders and extends a hand. Cletus takes it, and the two men shake. "Thank you, Cletus," Hurley says. "We owe you one. If you ever need help with anything, don't hesitate to ask."

"Thanks, man," he says. "You guys have done enough for me already, but I appreciate the offer."

"Hey," I say. "Never turn down an offer like that. You never know when you might need our help down the road."

Cletus nods and smiles. "Okay." He glances at his watch and says, "On second thought, I think I'll have to pass on that coffee. I have a lot of ground to cover today, and I should get going."

"That's an easy fix," I tell him. I take the mug of coffee I've prepared and pour it into one of the dozen or so to-go mugs we have. "Take it with you," I say, handing it to him. "And keep the mug. We have a ton of them."

"Thanks," Cletus says, accepting the mug.

"I'm heading out myself," I say. "Give me a second to get my coat on, and I'll go out with you." I hurry into the living room, give my son, whose attention is riveted on the TV, a kiss on the head, and then grab my coat, scarf, gloves, and boots from the foyer closet.

"Ready when you are," I announce to Cletus. Hurley has him again, one arm draped over his shoulder, telling him how impressed he is with what he's done. Cletus is smiling, but it looks forced, and I suspect his decision to leave is because Hurley's attention is making him uncomfortable.

Hurley finally releases him, and the two of us make a quick exit. "Hold on a second, Cletus," I say as I shut the door behind us. "I want to show you something." I lead him off the porch and over to the side of the house near one edge of the bluff. A few feet from the edge is a large boulder some three feet across and two feet high. It was the very last piece of landscaping we had installed, and getting it up here was a bit of a nightmare.

"Check it out," I say, pointing to a flat area on top of the rock. "We put him back where we found him."

Cletus looks and then nods as he reads what's etched into the stone:

IN MEMORY OF OSKAR

1950–1960

NOW FLYING FREE

Annelise Ryan also writes as Allyson K. Abbott.
In August don't miss Allyson's next book
LAST CALL
from her critically acclaimed series:
A Mack's Bar Mystery!

Turn the page for a sneak peek of
LAST CALL

CHAPTER 1

It is the beginning of a new year, and for many, it feels like a fresh start, an artificial marker that gives the day some imagined significance over its predecessor. For some, it signifies hope for the future; for others, it may mean establishing new motivations for personal growth. Sometimes it simply offers a fresh outlook on life. For me, it means better than average business, and in the case of this particular coming year, a fresh—or at least different—outlook on death.

My name is Mackenzie Dalton, though everyone calls me Mack, and I own a bar located in downtown Milwaukee. The post-holiday season is a busy one for the bar. Some people come in hoping to extend their holiday spirit by lifting a few holiday spirits with their friends, family, or coworkers. Others come in to celebrate the end of the hectic mad rush that always seems to be a hallmark of the holiday season. Still others come in simply because it's part of their regular routine to visit the neighborhood bar, exercise their elbows, and share their holiday tales with other regulars they see throughout the year. And more than a few come in simply to escape the bone-chilling cold that is part and parcel of a Milwaukee winter. Cozying up to a drink with some friends is a great way to warm both the body and the soul.

My bar has a lot of regulars, the most notable of whom are an assemblage of bar stool detectives who call themselves the Capone Club. This group is an eclectic collection of folks from many walks of life who share a common interest in crime solving. The Club got its start through some tragic events that happened over the past year, not the least of which was the murder of my father, Mack, exactly a year ago today. My father opened Mack's Bar thirty-five years ago, naming it after himself and then giving me a name that would allow me to eponymously inherit. It was a huge assumption on his part that I would want to do this, but he guessed right. For me, the decision was a no-brainer.

My mother died shortly after giving birth to me, so it was always just me and Dad, running the bar day in and day out. We lived in a three-bedroom apartment above it, and this made for a strange and memorable childhood. I knew how to mix a host of cocktails before I knew my ABCs, my extended family consisted of some of the bar's regular customers, and I was the envy of many of my high school friends, who coveted my constant exposure to free alcohol. Despite my unusual childhood, I'd have to say it was a happy and simple one. My life up until a year ago was uncomplicated and enjoyable for the most part.

Of course, there were a few rough spots. One in particular that marked me as different from the other kids and nearly got me declared insane, is a neurological disorder I have that is called synesthesia. It's an odd cross-wiring of the senses that results in its victims experiencing the world around them in ways that others don't. According to the doctors who evaluated me over the years, my synesthesia is a particularly severe case. The most commonly ascribed-to theory about how I acquired this disorder is that it resulted from the unusual circumstances surrounding my birth. My mother ended up in a coma due to injuries from a car accident that happened while she was pregnant with me. She sustained severe brain damage that left her essentially dead, but her heart—and mine—kept going. So she was hooked up to machines, and her body was kept alive until it was safe for me to be born. Then the machines were removed, and she was allowed to die. Whenever I asked about my mother's death, my father always told me it was peaceful—he believed my mother's soul had slipped away the night of the accident—but there was a haunted look in his eyes whenever he spoke of it that let me know he had his doubts.

The doctors speculated that the conditions surrounding my gestation and birth contributed to an abnormal development of my neurological system. The end result is that I experience each of my senses—sight, sound, smell, taste, and touch—in at least two ways. For instance, I taste certain sounds; this typically is the case with men's voices. Other sounds, such as music, are accompanied by visual manifestations, like floating geometric shapes or colorful designs. Most of my tastes are accompanied by sounds. The taste of champagne makes me hear violin music, whereas beer makes me hear the deep bass notes of a cello. But there are some tastes that trigger a physical or emotional sensation instead. For instance, I confess to being something of a coffee snob, and when I drink coffee that's brewed just right, it makes me feel happy inside, almost giddy. Bad coffee makes me feel irritable and angry. I'm something of a coffee addict, and no coffee for a length of time makes me feel almost homicidal, though I suspect this is more of a caffeine addiction issue as opposed to a manifestation of my synesthesia.

In addition to the five basic senses, I also have synesthetic reactions to my emotions, either a visual manifestation or a physical sensation. My emotions were put through the wringer at times when I was growing up. I would say things like, "This song is too red and wavy" or "This sandwich tastes like a tuba." It didn't help me fit in with the other kids, and my teachers grew concerned when they realized I was seeing things that weren't there . . . or at least things that weren't there for most people. The visual manifestations I had were very real to me, and they still are. But the lack of understanding regarding my condition left many people fearful and confused. I quickly learned to keep most of my experiences to myself rather than share them. After spending time observing other people's reactions to things, and hearing their comments and descriptions regarding their own sensual experiences, I gradually learned which of my responses were considered "normal" and which ones were my own peculiarity.

When the hormonal surge of adolescence hit me, my synesthesia became even more pronounced. Had it not been for one particularly patient and insightful doctor, I would've ended up committed to a psychiatric institution. Instead, my father and I learned how to control my disorder and hide it from the outside world. However, in private, he and I played with my abilities from time to time. My synesthesia is not only more severe than most, my senses are greatly heightened. I can smell, see, and feel things that others can't. I can often tell when something has been recently moved because I can feel changes in the air pressure or see a difference in the air surrounding the spot where the item used to be.

The aspect of my synesthesia that has turned out to be the most significant of late is that I'm something of a human lie detector. In the vast majority of people, the voice changes ever so slightly when they're lying—a subconscious thing. This results in a variation in whatever manifestation I experience when listening to their voice. Once I've learned what someone's voice normally tastes or looks like, I can tell when they're lying because that taste or visual manifestation will suddenly change.

Because of my experiences as a child, I spent most of my life trying to hide my synesthesia from the world. It was an embarrassment to me, a handicap, a disability, something to be scorned and laughed at, something that made me stand out from the rest of the world . . . and not in a good way. That all changed this past year, however. It began with the murder of my father in the alley behind our bar, though I had no way of knowing at the time how that one event would drastically alter the route my life was taking. Eight months later, Ginny Rifkin, the woman who was my father's girlfriend when he died, was also murdered, her body left in the same alley. Her death led to Duncan Albright entering my life and my life becoming focused on death.

Duncan was a relatively new detective with the police force in our district, and he was the detective in charge of investigating Ginny's murder. When he determined that the culprit was likely someone near and dear to me, he decided to do some undercover work at my bar, pretending he was a new hire so he could gain the confidence of my staff and customers, and dig for information and clues. In the process, he discovered how my synesthesia helped when it came to interpreting crime scenes, analyzing clues, or talking to witnesses and suspects. With the help of some of my customers, who formed the basis for what would become the Capone Club, we solved the murders of both Ginny and my father.

Intrigued by my ability, Duncan invited me along to some other crime scenes, where I was able to pick up on subtle clues that led to solving the cases. Duncan started calling me his secret weapon, and I relished the fact that my synesthesia was finally making itself useful. Instead of feeling like it was a shameful secret I needed to hide, I began to think of it as my superpower. We made a great team. I enjoyed helping Duncan, and he reaped the benefits of my abilities. Unfortunately, not everyone saw it the way we did, and things got messy fast.

The press caught on to me, and sensationalistic news stories started cropping up about how the police were using magic, witchcraft, and voodoo to solve their crimes. Then I got a little careless on one case and ended up nearly getting shot. Endangering a layperson in this manner didn't sit well with Duncan's bosses, and as a result, he was suspended for a few weeks and ordered not to associate with me.

This might not have been a huge issue but for two things. One, I had invited Duncan into my bed as well as into my life by then, and we were in the process of exploring the potential behind our relationship. Letting go of that wasn't easy. And two, I'd discovered I liked this crime-solving stuff and putting my synesthesia to good use. The intrinsic high it gave me was strangely intoxicating, and I didn't want to let it go. My synesthesia had been an albatross around my neck most of my life, almost literally so, because whenever I grew nervous about exposing it or revealing it to someone for the first-time, it triggered an uncomfortable strangling sensation around my throat.

As if Duncan's suspension and the edict to avoid me weren't big enough nails in the coffin of our relationship, things got even more complicated when I attracted the attention of a deadly stalker, someone who wrote letters that demanded I solve a series of complicated puzzles by a prescribed deadline, and do so using only my "special talent" without the assistance of Duncan or the police. The consequence of failing to do so was the death of someone close to me. The letter writer proved this wasn't an idle threat by killing one of my customers—someone who was also part of the Capone Club—and using the first letter I received to tell me where the body was. Then, a week or so later, my bouncer, Gary Gunderson, was murdered in cold blood when I failed to correctly interpret clues in one of the letters by the set deadline.

After several harrowing and frightening weeks of skulking around so I could still see Duncan with no one being the wiser, the stalker was finally exposed and caught. Sadly, it turned out my stalker wasn't a lone wolf. One of the trusted members of the Capone Club was working with the culprit, and the whole thing left everyone involved reeling and feeling unsettled. We were all struggling at this point to regain some semblance of normalcy.

For me, the definition of normalcy remained unclear. In our hunt for the stalker, I was approached at one point by the police chief and the DA, both of whom had decided that a philosophy of *if you can't beat them, join them* was their best recourse at this point. In a period of a few days, I went from being persona non grata with the police department to being invited to work with them on a consulting basis. While I suspect the motives of the chief and the DA were primarily political in nature, given an upcoming election, their offer benefited me in enough ways that I accepted their invitation. It not only allowed me to use my synesthesia in a way that was intrinsically rewarding, it provided me with a new stream of income and freed me to openly pursue my relationship with Duncan.

So after a year of incredible loss, emotional pain, tumult, and confusion, I found myself starting the new year with a renewed sense of hope for the future. Ironically, it resulted in me standing in a home and staring at a dead man on the anniversary of my father's murder. I couldn't decide if this was a good omen or not.